RAMAGE AND THE SARACENS

Lord Nicholas Ramage, eldest son of the Tenth Earl of Blazey, Admiral of the White, was born in 1775 at Blazey Hall, St Kew, Cornwall. He entered the Royal Navy as a midshipman in 1788, at the age of thirteen. He has served with distinction in the Mediterranean, the Caribbean, and home waters during the war against France, participating in several major sea battles and numerous minor engagements. Despite political difficulties, his rise through the ranks has been rapid.

In *Ramage and the Saracens*, his seventeenth recorded adventure, Captain Ramage is caught up in a series of naval engagements as he sets forth to rid the seas around Sicily of a troublesome band of ruthless pirates.

DUDLEY POPE, who comes from an old Cornish family and whose great-great-grandfather was a Plymouth shipowner in Nelson's time, is well known both as the creator of Lord Ramage and as a distinguished and entertaining naval historian, the author of eleven scholarly works.

Actively encouraged by the late C. S. Forester, he has now written seventeen 'Ramage' novels about life at sea in Nelson's day. They are based on his own wartime experiences in the navy and peacetime exploits as a yachtsman as well as immense research into the naval history of the eighteenth century.

Available in Fontana by the same author

DUDLEY POPE

Ramage and
the Saracens

FONTANA/Collins

First published in England by
The Alison Press/Martin Secker & Warburg Limited 1988
First issued in Fontana Paperbacks 1990
Second impression May 1990

Copyright © 1988 by Dudley Pope

Printed and bound in Great Britain by
William Collins Sons & Co. Ltd, Glasgow

For Kay Again
with Love

AUTHOR'S NOTE

With the exception of Sidi Rezegh, all the places mentioned in this narrative actually exist and are described as they would have been in 1806.

DUDLEY POPE
St Martin
French West Indies

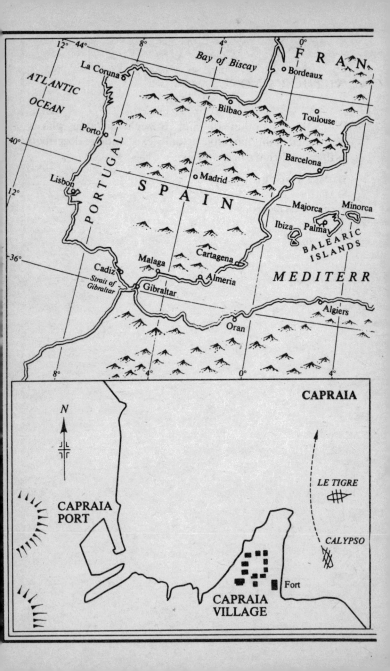

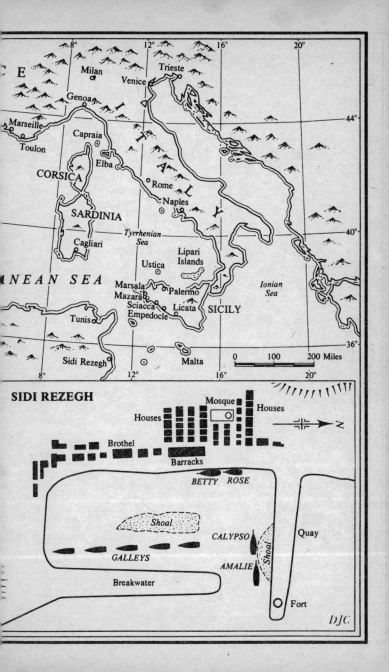

SIDI REZEGH

Milan
Trieste
Venice
Genoa
Marseille
Toulon
Capraia
CORSICA
Elba
Rome
SARDINIA
Naples
Cagliari
Tyrrhenian Sea
Lipari Islands
Ustica
MEDITERRANEAN SEA
Marsala
Palermo
Mazara
Sciacca
Licata
Empedocle
SICILY
Ionian Sea
Tunis
Sidi Rezegh
Malta

ITALY

0   100   200 Miles

Houses
Mosque
Houses
Brothel
Barracks
BETTY ROSE
N
Shoal
CALYPSO
Quay
Shoal
GALLEYS
AMALIE
Breakwater
Fort

DJC

Chapter One

Southwick counted the pieces of salt beef as the cook's mate lifted them out of the cask, banging each piece before he removed it to shake off the encrusted salt. Each piece of meat was as dark as old varnish and the salt was stained like muddy sand.

It would take many hours of soaking in fresh water in the steep tub to dissolve that hardened salt, the master thought to himself, and a lot of boiling afterwards before the men could get their teeth into the meat.

This cask was full of old meat: from the look of it many months had passed – even a year or more – since the carcase had been cut up in the contractor's slaughterhouse and salted down in the cask. Still, it was not as bad as some he had seen in the old days, before the Great Mutiny had led to an improvement. Then it was not unusual to find meat so hard it could be carved, looking rather like mahogany.

He continued marking the slate and looked at the side of the cask on which was stencilled the legend "54 pieces". Well, it might contain fifty-four pieces; it was not entirely unknown for the number of pieces to match what the contractor had painted on the outside, but it was rare, and the discrepancy was always on the side of the contractor.

Southwick, like every other master in the King's service doing this particular job, had to note the difference in his log, and as the cook's mate finally lifted out the last piece and Southwick looked at the tally on the slate, he could see they were fortunate: the log entry would simply say: "Opened cask of beef, marked 54 pieces, contained 52."

In theory the Navy Board claimed back from the contractor the value of the difference, but Southwick wondered if they ever did.

1

The seamen were cheated by the dishonest contractors, not the Navy Board: the clerks at the Navy Board had their dinner whether or not a cask was missing several pieces of meat. It was only the seamen who went without: a ship was issued with so many casks of salt beef and salt pork for a commission or voyage, and that was that: the men just had to make it last.

With the last piece taken from the cask, Southwick said: "Very well, get all this into the steep tub," gesturing at the pile of meat, most of which seemed to him to be fat or bone, and he turned to go below to make the entry in his log.

Captain Ramage, standing at the forward end of the quarter-deck, asked: "Short again?"

"Only two pieces, sir," Southwick said, adding gloomily: "The Navy Board seems to have been getting rid of some old stock: looked more like off-cuts of mahogany from the carpenter's shop than salt beef."

Ramage nodded and noted that they were lucky: it was usual for there to be half a dozen pieces missing, or even more, and much of the meat comprised chunks of fat which, when the meat was put in the coppers to cook, would float on top of the boiling water, to be skimmed off by the cook's mate and sold illicitly to the men as "slush", providing something to spread on their hard biscuits and giving the cook's mate the nickname of "Slushy". Did the cook demand his share of the proceeds?

Ramage shrugged his shoulders and found he did not care: it was a fine day with a brisk wind, just enough to raise a few white horses and the Mediterranean was unbelievably blue, as though welcoming back the *Calypso* after the spell in the Atlantic.

How many times had he passed through the Strait of Gibraltar up to now? A score of times? Anyway, Europa Point was a familiar enough landmark, and now the men would be commenting on being "Black Strapped", their description of being in the Mediterranean and deriving either from Black Strap Bay, on the eastern side of Gibraltar, or from the coarse Spanish red wine which would soon take the place of their rum issue, and which was not very popular.

The *Calypso* stretched along under all working sail, pitching slightly in the head sea, as though curtsying. Each pitch brought a slight groan from masts and yards, as though they were protesting;

every now and again the sails slatted as an unusual wave made the ship pitch more than usual, spilling the wind momentarily and then letting the sails fill again with a bang.

A sudden shout of "Deck there!" from the foremasthead sent the red-headed second lieutenant, Kenton, lunging for the speaking trumpet and shouting up an acknowledgement.

"Sail two points on the larboard bow, sir!" shouted down the lookout.

Kenton turned to Ramage, to make sure he had heard.

Ramage nodded. "How far off?"

Kenton's hail brought the answer of eight or ten miles.

Without bothering about a cast of the log, Ramage estimated the *Calypso* was making about seven knots. He took out his watch. It would soon be noon. "Pass the word to Mr Aitken not to secure the guns," he said. For the past hour the men had been busy at gunnery practice: without actually firing, they had been loading, running out and pretending to fire the guns, the sharp cries and the rumbling of the trucks punctuating the lazy noise of the *Calypso*'s progress.

A sail in sight: in this position and at this time it was routine: probably another frigate bound for Gibraltar from Malta or Naples, or even an Algerine: they sneaked out of the Barbary coast ports to see what they could pick up – just pirates. The chance of the sail being French was slight: they were still licking their wounds after Trafalgar. He corrected himself: at Trafalgar they had lost many ships of the line, not frigates, so in theory the sail in sight ahead could be a French frigate, but it was not likely. The defeat of the French at Trafalgar had been a blow to their confidence as much as to the total number of ships they had: it would probably be many months before they ventured to sea again.

"Deck there, foretopmast here: there are two sail!"

Kenton answered the hail and Ramage thought: two sail meant even less chance of them being French. But soon the men would be sent to quarters, because in wartime every sail had to be treated as potentially an enemy, to be met with guns run out and a hoist of flags challenging her to reveal her identity.

Ramage realized that he could not remember the secret signal for the day and went below to his cabin, unlocking a drawer in his desk to look it up.

3

The secret signal comprised a table lasting three months which set out the challenge and the correct reply for each day. The table was issued by the commander-in-chief and applied only to the area he commanded. It was without doubt the most secret thing on board the ship: the penalty for allowing it to fall into enemy hands was a court martial to begin with, and no captain of a ship could expect any mercy from the court: that was made more than clear in the preamble to the signals.

The secret signal and the ship's number in the List of the Navy – they were the flags to be hoisted as soon as a strange ship was close enough to distinguish them. Unless one recognized the other ship it was always a slightly tense moment: from the very first day when one went to sea as a midshipman, one was brought up to consider every strange sail as potentially an enemy. And for most of the years since then at least half the time it usually was. He put the signals away and went back on deck.

Southwick came up the quarterdeck ladder. "A couple of sail, eh? Getting like Spithead round here!"

"Probably a couple of frigates bound for Gibraltar," Ramage said. "Or even a couple of our merchantmen with olive oil and wine."

"Could be," Southwick agreed. "It's safe enough now for them to risk sailing without a convoy."

No convoys, no escorts, Southwick thought. Escorting convoys was the dreariest job that could be given to a frigate, and it was a sign of the times that the *Calypso* had been sent out to the Mediterranean alone: until quite recently, almost any frigate bound for the Mediterranean from England would have to escort merchant ships; there were usually enough of them waiting to sail to make up a convoy, even if only comprising half a dozen ships. Yet, Southwick reflected, it did not matter whether there were half a dozen or the hundred more usual to or from the West Indies, there was always at least one ship that was a veritable mule, always reducing sail at night and falling behind, no matter what threats were made.

Ramage picked up his telescope and looked at the two tiny specks now coming into sight over the curvature of the earth. He calculated they were not on an opposing course, which was strange: they should be steering the reciprocal of the *Calypso*'s

4

course if they were bound for Gibraltar, since she had left there not long since. No, the two ships were steering more to the north-west: that much was clear from the line of their masts. Perhaps they had a different slant of wind over there, though that would not account for the course they were steering, only the trim of their sails.

Their course, he thought idly, seemed too far to the north-west for any ship not bound for Toulon! But there could be several explanations – they could be British frigates investigating a strange sail out of sight from the *Calypso*. But even as he watched, both ships began to alter course, coming round to larboard so that they would meet the *Calypso*.

"Pass the word for Orsini," Ramage told Kenton, "and then send him aloft with a bring-'em-near: I'm beginning to doubt if those two are frigates."

Ships of the line usually meant problems: either one of them carried an admiral who wanted to give fresh orders, or the senior of the two captains had some task to be carried out. Well, Ramage thought grimly, he was sailing under Admiralty orders, which should make him proof against being humbugged about by any passing senior officers.

He watched Orsini arrive on the quarterdeck, collect a telescope and jump up into the ratlines in a smooth scramble aloft. If Gianna could see her nephew now, he mused. That was a big "if", since it was by no means certain that she was still alive.

How the years passed. In many ways it seemed no time ago that he had rescued the young and vulnerable Marchesa di Volterra from the beaches of Tuscany, snatching her (with the help of the seaman Jackson) from under the feet of Napoleon's cavalry. It seemed no time at all that he had fallen in love with her (*thought* he had fallen in love with her, he corrected himself) and back in England the refugee Marchesa had gone to live with his parents. And then later her nephew had escaped from Volterra, a lively lad who had wanted to join the Navy and, at Gianna's request, Paolo Orsini had come to the *Calypso* as a midshipman and quickly learned seamanship and become a popular young officer.

And then . . . and then had come the peace following the Treaty of Amiens, and Gianna had decided that she must return to her kingdom of Volterra. His father and he had argued with her, warning her that she would be at risk from Napoleon's assassins,

5

and that the peace would not last. But she would not listen and she had left London for Paris, on her way to Italy. They had heard nothing more of her, and in the meantime Ramage had met and married Sarah, now his wife. Gianna was an ever-fading memory, jogged into existence again whenever he looked at Paolo and remembered. As he had just done. But memories of Gianna were fading, of that there was no doubt; he had difficulty in recalling the details of her face; all that remained was a picture of her personality: lively, at times imperious, warm yet hot-tempered, but for all that very much the ruler of the kingdom of Volterra which, small on the map, yet loomed large in the life of the young girl who – until Napoleon's Army of Italy drove her out – was its sole ruler.

He put the telescope back to his eye. What a long string of memories had been called up by watching Paolo climbing the rigging. How different was Sarah, the wife he had left in England.

It was strange how the *Calypso*'s ship's company knew both women so well. Gianna because many of them had helped rescue her and been on board the ship that took her back to England, and Sarah for a similar reason, only this time the rescue had been from an island off the coast of Brazil.

Yes, those two sail had hauled their wind to meet him, and he was sure they were not frigates: more like ships of the line. A couple of ships making their way from Naples to Gibraltar – or through the Gut on their way to England – would be nothing out of the ordinary; in fact it would be a commonplace, a one-line entry in his journal, merely noting the date, time and names of the ships.

Orsini hailed from the masthead and Kenton snatched up the speaking trumpet to reply. The two sail, Paolo reported, were ships of the line and they had come round on to opposing courses. Their hulls were still below the horizon so it was impossible to identify them.

"Tell him to keep a sharp lookout," Ramage said without thinking.

Paolo of all people would keep a sharp lookout. His hatred of the French would make sure of that. Ever since the end of the brief peace following the Treaty of Amiens, when his aunt had vanished and it seemed only logical to suppose that she had either been murdered by Napoleon's men or imprisoned, he had added bitterness to his hatred. No Frenchman, Ramage suspected, should ever ask Paolo for quarter.

Down at one of the forward guns on the starboard side a group of seamen gossiped, having completed the morning's exercises and expecting any minute to get the order to run the gun in and secure it. They had heard the lookout's hail and Midshipman Orsini's report; they knew that now they would have to wait until the two ships were close enough to answer the challenge.

"We seem to spend 'arf our life waitin'," growled Stafford, a Cockney seaman. "Ships of the line – must be ours: stands to reason, after Trafalgar."

"It'll take more than Trafalgar to change the rules," said Jackson. "We didn't sink every French ship of the line, you know."

"The way Staff tells the story, we did!" said Rossi, the Italian from Genoa. "Not one escaped!"

"We didn't do too badly," Stafford said complacently. "A few frigates got away, but they'll be too scared to come out for months."

He spoke without considering that the other four of the gun's crew were French, royalists who had signed on in the Royal Navy after helping Ramage and his wife Sarah escape from France when war had broken out again.

"Don't underestimate Napoleon," said one of the men.

"Boney wasn't at Trafalgar, Louis," Stafford said contemptuously. "Pity 'e wasn't; we'd have taken him prisoner and led 'im up Ludgate 'ill with a chain round 'is neck and 'anded 'im over to the Lord Mayor."

"He's cunning," Louis persisted. "See how he has gone off to attack Russia . . ."

"Well, he don't need a navy to attack them, I must say," Stafford admitted.

"And it means he has time to rebuild his navy," Louis insisted.

"He ain't got much time," Stafford said emphatically. "Yer can't build a ship of the line in six months, 'specially if you ain't got no wood to speak of, and we know 'e ain't."

"He's got enough wood to repair those ships we knocked about," Jackson said. "Patch 'em up and send 'em to sea to interfere with our shipping – that would soon have us hopping about.''

"I don't see why," Stafford said stubbornly.

"Use your head," Jackson said sharply. "A ship of the line at sea on the loose means at least one of our ships of the line finding her. And it means a dozen or more looking for her. Don't think it'd be a question of sending out a frigate or two . . .''

"All right, all right, I get your point," Stafford conceded. "But I presume their Lordships will be keepin' a blockade on places like Brest, Lorient, Cadiz and Toulon.''

"And Ferrol, and Cartagena . . . You forget the Dons have more ports than the French – as many, anyway. And to prevent one ship slipping out on a dark night it has to be a tight blockade.''

"Frigates," Louis said unexpectedly. "Supposing the French turned loose all their frigates to raid convoys. Don't forget we rarely have more than a couple of frigates escorting the big West Indian convoys – just imagine three French frigates attacking . . .''

"The way you all tell it, we won Trafalgar and lost the war," Stafford grumbled.

"No, nothing like that," Jackson said placatingly. "We're only saying don't expect we won't see another French sail at sea.''

"You'll be saying next that these two up ahead are French and steering down to sink us," Stafford retorted.

"No, they're probably Russian," Louis said drily. "With snow on their decks!''

"Wild men, these Russians," Stafford said. "I remember seeing a Russian ship in Malta some years ago. Their seamanship was 'orrible. Good job they 'ad strong ships, the way they came alongside the jetty. 'Bang, crash, sling a rope' – that's 'ow they did it.''

Ramage put the telescope to his eye again and then said to Southwick: "I don't like the cut of their sails. Their hulls will be coming up over the horizon any moment now, and we'll hear from Orsini, but in the meantime those sails have a strange cut.''

"Could be a couple of Algerines," Southwick commented. "They've got a few big ships.''

Ramage shook his head. "I don't think so," he said. "They could be, but why would there be two of them?''

8

Southwick shrugged his shoulders. "No telling with Algerines."

Several more minutes passed before Orsini hailed, and there was no mistaking the excitement in his voice. "Deck there! I can make out their hulls now. They look French!"

Ramage glanced across at Southwick. "Could be like us – captured and put into service."

"Aye," Southwick said. "Maybe even taken at Trafalgar. Could have been bought in at Gibraltar and commissioned there."

Ramage nodded again. "The battle was four months ago, so there's been enough time."

And that, he thought to himself, settles that: it was an uncomfortable thought that two French line of battle ships could be bearing down on them. There could be no escape; the *Calypso* would be pounded into firewood unless she could get far enough away to escape in the dark of night.

Ramage knew that now he had two options: first, to turn away this minute, and make a bolt for it. This could get him the reputation of the captain who fled at the sight of two of his own ships. Or, second, carry on and meet them, making or answering the challenge, assuming they were the King's ships, captured from the French.

It was not the first time he had had to make the choice, and looking at it another way, since the *Calypso* had been captured from the French and bought into the Royal Navy, she too could be mistaken for French by any other ships and in fact more than once he had passed her off to fool the French.

"The man who ran away" – no, he did not want that reputation, and with two ships involved it would be one to spread quickly. Not that anyone would really blame him: a frigate being engaged by two ships of the line would be as brief an episode as a kitten being savaged by two bulldogs.

Five minutes later, when Ramage put the telescope to his eye again, there was no mistaking the correctness of Orsini's hail: the two ships were French; that much was clear from the sweep of their sheers and the cut of their sails. But there was no reason to suppose that since they were French built they were not King's ships. The more he thought about it, the more likely it seemed that they had been taken at Trafalgar.

Ramage noted that both ships were staying close together: they were sailing within a couple of ship's lengths of each other. If they were French and planning mischief, they would spread out to cut off the *Calypso*'s escape. But in fact they were behaving just like two British ships of the line after sighting a friendly frigate . . .

"Beat to quarters, Mr Kenton. Have the challenge and our pendant numbers bent on, and the reply, in case they challenge first."

The thudding of the drum as a Marine drummer hammered away with his drumsticks suddenly brought the *Calypso*'s decks to life, as though an anthill had been disturbed with a stick.

The gunner and his mate hurried below to the magazine, unrolling felt curtains as they went, to prevent any flash from the guns penetrating to the powder stowed in scores of cartridges and in casks in the powder room.

Men rigged the washdeck pumps and began sluicing water across the decks as others scattered sand: water would soak any spilled gunpowder and the sand would prevent feet slipping. The second captains of all the guns hurried down to the magazine to collect the locks from the gunner which would provide the spark to fire the guns. They collected priming wires and lanyards for the locks as well as horns of priming powder and boxes of quills, which were already filled with priming powder.

Ship's boys, known as powder monkeys, waited in the long corridor leading to the magazine, ready with their cylindrical wooden boxes to receive the cartridges for the guns.

The guns themselves, thanks to the exercises just completed, were all ready for loading: each had its crew round it, with the officers at their divisions, with the exception that the first lieutenant, Aitken, who would normally be on the quarterdeck at general quarters, was taking Kenton's place while he was on watch.

All the implements for loading the guns were ready; the rammer on its long handle was ready to ram home first the cartridge, then a wad, and then a roundshot. The sponge which, soaked with water, would be used to sponge out the burning residue in the bore of the gun so that it would not prematurely ignite the cartridge or any loose powder, was lying ready along with the wormer, which looked like a giant corkscrew on a long handle and was used to ream out any remaining piece of burning cartridge left behind after the gun had been fired.

10

Small tubs beside each gun were filled with water for the sponges (and for the men to dip their heads in to cool themselves off in action) and between each gun another, smaller tub was partly filled with water and short lengths of slowmatch – in effect fuses – were fitted into notches cut into the rim. The slowmatches were fitted so that the burning ends hung over the water – a further precaution against stray grains of powder being ignited.

As soon as he received the word from the quarterdeck, Lieutenant George Hill, the third lieutenant and commanding the division of guns that included Jackson's, gave the order to load.

By now Stafford had returned from the magazine with the lock and had bolted it on to the gun, threading the lanyard through the trigger and coiling it neatly on the breech. He now stood with the horn of priming powder round his neck like a hunting horn with the pricker ready in his left hand.

Jackson, as gun captain, stood to the rear while Rossi, Louis and the other two Frenchmen were ready to take the cartridge from the powder monkey waiting behind Jackson and ram it home, followed by a roundshot after the wad, a thick circular piece of felt. Wads were now lying in piles beside each gun in what were called cheeses.

At the order to load and as soon as powder and shot had been rammed home Jackson took the lanyard, which was three feet longer than the distance the gun recoiled, and stood behind the gun, ready to give aiming orders. Squatting with his left leg flung out sideways so he could sight along the barrel, he would when the order to fire was shouted, give a sharp pull on the lanyard after Stafford had cocked the lock and jumped clear of the recoil.

Every movement had been practised so many times that the men could carry out their tasks blindfolded. And after a few rounds had been fired and the deck filled with smoke from the guns, they were as good as blindfolded, as well as being stunned and deafened by the detonation of all the guns, so that most of what they did was instinctive.

Up on the quarterdeck Ramage listened as first one division of guns and then another reported itself ready. Aitken had come up to the quarterdeck to take over the watch from Kenton, who had gone below to his own division.

Aitken had looked at the approaching ships and in his broad

Scottish accent agreed that they were French built and, without any prompting from Ramage, reckoned they were former prizes taken at Trafalgar and now bought into the King's service.

"If they sail anything like this one," he commented, "they'll be useful additions to the Fleet."

How many hundreds of times have we stood here like this, Ramage thought, all the guns loaded, ready to greet a friend or attack an enemy, quizzing the other ships – usually just a single ship – with a telescope? Usually, he had to admit, someone recognized the other ship: usually there was a man who had served in her, or recognized her from a previous voyage. Most ships had some peculiarity of build or rig, like a person's walk.

Ramage looked over the bow at the approaching ships, noting yet again that, with the wind astern of them, it was impossible to see their colours and that it would be equally difficult to read their reply, except that by the time they had hoisted it they would be several hundred yards closer.

"Hoist the challenge," he told Aitken.

"I thought they'd have beaten us to it, sir," the Scot said, after passing the order.

Both ships were now a mile away, and Aitken's remark reminded Ramage that he had expected to be challenged: it was a habit rather than a tradition, that the larger ship challenged the smaller.

He heard the slatting as the flag hoist was hauled up on its halyard, and he repeated to himself the answer, picturing the colours on the flags. With the wind in this direction, the best chance of identifying them would be as they were hoisted, when they would be flickering in random eddies of wind blowing off the sails.

The two ships sailed on, dipping and rising in the following sea, a flurry of foam at their stems. Their masts were almost in line and Ramage watched, along with Aitken and Southwick, for hoists of flags to snake up on their halyards.

The *Calypso*'s challenge had been hoisted for a couple of minutes before Ramage felt a cold hand clutching at his stomach. He tried to will one or other of the two ships to hoist the reply, but there was nothing.

"They're French," he finally said to no one in particular, his voice hollow. One tiny frigate against two ships of the line which had the weather gauge. Two 74s against a 32-gun frigate. Before the *Calypso* could wear round and begin to escape one or both of the ships would bear up to loose a broadside into her: 32-pounder shot would crash through her hull . . .

What to do? He shook off the momentary paralysis brought on by the lack of reply to the challenge and found he was angry: angry with himself for taking it for granted that the two ships were British, and angry with them for being French. He wanted to smash them – just as they were about to smash the *Calypso*. But how?

There was only one way: he would ram one of them: crash the *Calypso* right across her bow, tearing away the jibboom and bowsprit and, with luck, tearing away enough of her rigging to bring down the foremast, disabling her.

Which ship? The *Calypso* was on the starboard tack, so it would save time to steer for the ship to leeward, the one on the larboard side. But whatever he did, there was no time to waste: the *Calypso* and the ships were approaching each other at a combined speed of more than fourteen knots, the Frenchmen wallowing along in a following sea, the *Calypso* butting herself to windward.

"We'll ram the larboard one," he snapped at Aitken and Southwick. "Warn the starboard side batteries to open fire if their guns bear."

Southwick picked up the speaking trumpet and bellowed forward. From aloft Ramage was aware of a plaintive hail from Orsini asking permission to come down. Aitken was shouting to seamen to man the sheets and braces.

Ramage did a quick sum in his head, calculating the forward movement of the French ship and the *Calypso*, working out the point at which they would collide.

He saw at once that on the present course the frigate would pass twenty or thirty yards ahead of the Frenchman unless he luffed up at the last moment, and that would mean that the Frenchman would merely collide with the *Calypso*, whereas it was vital that the *Calypso* was moving fast when she aimed herself at the enemy, so that her bow hit the Frenchman's bow at the exact spot to create the most damage.

"A point to starboard, Mr Aitken: haul in those sheets as though your life depended on it."

13

He had an absurd urge to laugh at the order: Aitken, like the rest of them, was done for whatever happened.

The *Calypso* turned a few degrees, heading for a point many yards ahead of the Frenchman so that they would collide in – about three minutes.

He heard a sound like ripping calico and instinctively looked aloft: the other Frenchman was opening fire with her bowchase guns, and the first shot had gone overhead, apparently without damaging masts, rigging or sails. A difficult feat at this range, Ramage thought.

In a second he saw exactly what would happen: the French ship would come ploughing on and the *Calypso*, slicing across her course, would just clip her bow, taking away, as he planned, jibboom and bowsprit and perhaps the foremast. If she was lucky, the *Calypso* would emerge beyond the Frenchman with her own masts still standing, but more likely – there were only a few feet in it – the Frenchman would in fact ram the *Calypso* and, while probably not rolling her over, smash a great hole in her starboard side and pin her while the boarders swarmed on board.

What was the second ship going to do? If she bore away for a couple of minutes she could bring her entire starboard broadside to bear. The only thing was she had no idea what the *Calypso* intended doing.

Should he pass the word to stand by to repel boarders? No, it meant taking men from the guns, and they would probably do more good there: if they could keep firing the starboard side guns while the two ships were locked together they might do some damage.

He looked over the starboard bow at the enemy. She was painted black with red and green trim; the paintwork was faded and the black forward was now greyish with salt drying out from the spray. Sails patched – more patches than original cloth, in fact. And now he just caught sight of the Tricolour flapping aft. All her guns run out; stubby black fingers protruding from her hull.

And she seemed to be getting bigger every moment: her great jibboom and bowsprit stuck out from the bow like a fisherman's rod, the lower end a complex web of stays, the most vulnerable part of the ship. The yards were massive, the sails hanging from

14

them like bulging curtains. And men: he could see men now standing on the fo'c'sle, staring at the approaching frigate.

The French officers on the quarterdeck would not be able to see the frigate's hull now: it would be hidden beyond the bow. They would see only the masts and yards. What were their thoughts? That the English frigate captain had at last panicked, and was trying – very clumsily – to turn away to attempt to make a completely futile run for it?

Ramage glanced at Southwick. The old master's face was impassive: he was just leaning against the quarterdeck rail looking at the Frenchman without any visible emotion. In two minutes the old man could be dead but he gave no sign of knowing it. Ramage could not think how many times Southwick had been in action but one thing was certain: death was no stranger to him: he had stared it in the face scores of times.

Nor did Aitken betray any emotion: the Scotsman had also gone into action many times with Ramage. At no time, though, with less chance of surviving. As he caught sight of Orsini swinging down from the shrouds and dropping on to the deck, Ramage thought fleetingly that it mattered not at all whether or not Gianna was alive: Paolo, too, was unlikely to survive the next few minutes to see her again. And, he reflected bitterly, it was all his fault: he had approached these two ships of the line as though they were fishing boats: he had not considered for a moment that they might be French. Oh yes, he had noted that they were French built, but he had let the great victory at Trafalgar drive out any thought that they might be flying Tricolours. He had, quite simply, been careless and overconfident, and now he was going to pay for it with his own life and the lives of all the men in the *Calypso* who had for years trusted him. Well, it was the first time he had let them down – and, he reflected, it would be the last.

He continued the line of the *Calypso*'s course to where it intercepted the Frenchman. A couple of hundred yards. Even now the Frenchman obviously had no idea what he intended. Not two hundred yards – more likely a hundred and fifty and the distance shortening rapidly.

"Steer fine, blast you," Aitken said conversationally to the men at the wheel, and then commenting calmly to Ramage: "Just about right, don't you think, sir?"

"Yes, we should catch his jibboom in our foreshrouds. Her stem should ram us amidships."

Southwick gave one of his famous sniffs, only this time it was an approving sniff: clearly the old man agreed with both Aitken and Ramage.

At his gun on the starboard side, Jackson finally walked to the gunport and joined Stafford looking through it.

The Cockney was staring at the approaching French ship and he muttered to the American seaman: "What d'you reckon the Old Man is trying to do?"

"Ram the bastard," Jackson said succinctly. "It's the only thing left. No good firing our pop guns at her."

"Ram?" Stafford repeated, awe in his voice. "We'll just bounce off her!"

"Not if we clip off her jibboom and bowsprit. Probably bring down her foremast as well."

"Then she'll ram *us* and capsize us!"

"Maybe," Jackson said. "That's the price you pay for thinking every ship at sea is one of ours."

"Bit o' an 'igh price!"

Jackson shrugged his shoulders. "You've got to pay it when you mistake a Frenchman for one of ours."

"Our number's up, ain't it, Jacko?" Stafford commented, his voice flat and unemotional.

"I reckon so," Jackson said, turning back to the gun.

Rossi had overheard the conversation. "Is not Mr Ramage's fault," he said defensively. "Is hard to see the colours of a ship coming directly like that."

"Quite right, Rosey," Jackson said calmly. "Just 'cos we beat 'em at Trafalgar, we thought we'd driven them from the sea. Where these two came from I don't know. Egypt, I suppose."

"We ram, you think?"

"Her jibboom and bowsprit are where she's vulnerable," Jackson said, "and it looks as though that's where Mr Ramage is heading. Our only chance of disabling her."

"What about the other ship?" Louis asked.

"She'll have to tow this one all the way to Toulon, unless they can manage a jury rig."

16

Louis shook his head regretfully. "Pity we can't disable both of them."

"No miracles in the Mediterranean," Jackson said. "You chaps haven't been saying your prayers." He walked quickly to the gunport again and peered forward. "You have about a minute to say them now," he said, "then there's going to be an almighty bang."

Chapter
Two

Ramage narrowed his eyes in concentration. Yes, the *Calypso* would hit the French ship exactly where – no, damnation, she would pass too far ahead. He blinked and then blinked again. Much too far ahead. What on earth was happening? The men at the wheel had not moved it a spoke and a quick glance at the luffs of the sails showed the wind had not changed. But nevertheless the *Calypso* was now going to pass too far ahead of the Frenchman.

Suddenly he realized that the gap between the French ship's masts was widening. Damn, damn, she was altering course: she was turning to larboard: her captain must have guessed what Ramage intended doing, and he was turning violently to avoid a collision. And there was no way Ramage could get the *Calypso* two – no, three – points to windward. Nor was there time to tack across the Frenchman's bow. Instead he would receive her full starboard broadside in a matter of moments. Just then the first of the *Calypso*'s guns fired as the Frenchman began to swing past the starboard side.

But the Frenchman did not fire back. Why? Ramage realized that she would have been manning her larboard side guns: the sudden swing round was made before guns' crews could run across the ship to the other side.

He turned to keep her in view and out of the corner of his eye he saw the second ship, much closer than he expected. She was staying on the same course as before but the first ship was heading straight for her.

Had the first ship's captain not realized the danger? They were trimming her yards as if she was the only ship at sea, and as she came round on to a broad reach, all her sails bulging under the

18

weight of the wind, she increased speed: this was her fastest point of sailing.

She was now on almost an opposite course to the *Calypso* and heading straight for her consort. Ramage gave a gasp: a collision was inevitable, and he gripped the capping on the rail at the forward end of the quarterdeck.

As he watched, the first ship's sails began to flutter as men let fly the sheets and braces in what was obviously a desperate last-minute attempt to get the way off the ship but by now, as the sound of the slatting canvas carried across to the frigate, the two ships were only twenty yards apart.

Already, Ramage could see that the jibboom and bowsprit that he had been aiming for was now pointing at the mainshrouds of the second ship and in a few moments would catch them as though the ship was a lancer lunging at a passing bush.

Southwick's exclamation of "Ye gods!" was overlaid with Aitken's awe-struck "Will ye no look at that!"

Then the ship crashed into her consort: jibboom and bowsprit smashed through the mainshrouds and brought the mainmast toppling down, the topmast and topgallant tumbling as though hinged. The foremast of the first ship tumbled forward as though the effort of staying upright was too much for it and crashed down on to the deck of the second ship.

The impact brought the two ships alongside each other and their remaining yards locked. For a moment or two the first ship's mainmast swayed and then, with no stays supporting it forward and with her consort's yards tugging on the larboard side, it toppled slowly and gracefully, leaving the ship, now bereft of two masts, looking strangely naked.

Ramage, hardly able to believe what he had seen, fought down an urge to giggle; expecting any moment to be killed and then seeing the anticipated killer suddenly reduced to helplessness was a new experience which left him weak with relief.

"I'll trouble you to bear away a point, Mr Aitken," he said in a voice which sounded oddly strangled.

"Aye aye, sir," Aitken said, his Scots accent thicker than Ramage had ever heard before. He watched the first lieutenant bring the speaking trumpet to his lips after snapping an order to the men at the wheel.

At that moment Southwick turned to Ramage, gave a prodigious sniff and commented: "They're a lubberly lot, these Frogs."

"And we should be suitably thankful," Ramage said.

"Look!" Orsini said excitedly, "there goes the other ship's foremast!"

They all watched as the mast fell forward, moving very slowly at first, and then crashing in a welter of wood splinters and dust, spreading the sails like a shroud over the fo'c'sle.

"Well, that evens 'em up; two masts each," Southwick grunted.

"We'll tack across their sterns, Mr Aitken: we need to get their names," Ramage said, thinking of the report he had to write. Describing the way that two French ships of the line had been dismasted and left wallowing helplessly alongside each other was going to be difficult enough, and it was straining credulity not to have their names.

The *Calypso*'s sails slatted and banged as she tacked; sheets and braces were hauled home and she settled down on her new course which would take her diagonally across the sterns of the two crippled ships.

Ramage looked round the horizon. It was empty. What he needed now was a British ship of the line to heave in sight. Preferably two. Then they could take possession of the French ships and tow them into port, with the *Calypso* hovering round like a distracted moth . . . But the horizon was empty; the two ships were going to have to be left.

"Pity we can't take possession," Southwick growled.

"They might be dismasted but they still have their broadsides," Ramage said shortly. "One broadside could leave us like them!"

"True enough," Southwick agreed. "It's just that having two ships of the line lying there like that . . ."

Ramage nodded but said: "I thought it would have been us."

He picked up his telescope as the two transoms came into sight. Slowly he spelled out the first name and Orsini wrote *Artois* on the slate. Then he saw the second name and spelled it out, *L'Aigle*. Neither ship – as far as he could remember – had been at Trafalgar. Which meant that almost certainly they were on their way back to Toulon after a visit to Egypt. Ramage shrugged his shoulders: it mattered little where they were coming from or going to: both had a lot of work to do before they could do anything but drift with wind and current.

Stafford, standing to one side of the breech of the gun and with a better view through the gunport, had seen the collision and had given an excited commentary. Until he had time to dash to the ship's side and look for himself, Jackson had not believed the Cockney, thinking he was indulging in some complicated joke.

What he saw left him speechless. When he found his tongue again he said: "And not a broadside fired! What do we do now – offer them a tow?"

"Yus," exclaimed Stafford. "Tow 'em to Toulon and get a reward from Boney!"

"Are we just going to leave them like that?" asked Louis, after looking through the port.

"I don't reckon we've much choice," Jackson said. "They may have lost their masts, but their batteries are still in place. Every gun loaded, too."

"I know how you feel, Louis," Rossi said sympathetically. "I'd like to go across and set fire to them."

Stafford laughed quietly to himself. "What a story we've got to tell. Two line of battle ships an' we didn't fire a single broadside."

"Bluff, that's what it was," Jackson said. "And carelessness on the part of the French captain. He tried to sidestep us when he saw we were after his bowsprit – and stepped right into his mate!"

"Very careless," Stafford said. "Look what a mess it's got him into."

"Got them both into," Louis said. "Neither would do as dancing masters!"

Two hours later, with the *Calypso* back on her original course, the two disabled ships were just tiny blobs far astern, their hulls slowly dipping below the horizon. In the frigate the men had stood down from general quarters; the guns had been unloaded, run in and secured. The deck had been washed down and the sand brushed out of the scuppers. The match tubs had been emptied and the slowmatches extinguished, rolled up in coils like light line and returned to the magazine along with all the flintlocks, prickers and cartridges.

21

Now the men were waiting to be piped to dinner; they were still gossiping excitedly among themselves about the collision and speculating on their fate if the French captain of the ship of the line had not lost his nerve at the last moment to avoid the *Calypso*.

On the quarterdeck, Ramage was thinking of the report he had to write about the episode. It was a bizarre affair, and it was going to sound even more bizarre when reduced to the bare wording of a stylized letter to the Admiralty, beginning with the usual: "Sir, be pleased to inform their Lordships . . ."

The report had to go to the Admiralty because he was sailing under Admiralty orders; otherwise it would be to a commander-in-chief, and he would probably be seeing the admiral personally at the time he handed in the letter containing the report.

The watch changed and the third lieutenant, George Hill, took over the deck from Kenton. Hill was an unusual man: debonair, tall and thin, he was bilingual, thanks to a French mother who had married his father, a banker, and then found herself almost completely unable to learn English.

He had a dry sense of humour which Ramage found amusing; he was a very competent officer, and the men liked him. Almost more important, he could make Southwick laugh.

"Have you ever heard of a collision like that one, sir?" he asked Ramage.

"No, never. But they were unusual circumstances."

"Perhaps we were lucky in coming across a Frenchman so sensitive about his jibboom and bowsprit."

Ramage laughed and then said: "If I'd been him I'd have been just as sensitive. If you're a Frenchman this is no place to lose a foremast."

"You'd already worked that out, sir?"

Ramage shook his head. "No," he said frankly, "at the time it seemed the only way of escaping from at least one of the Frenchmen. Not escaping really, of course, since we'd have been pinned by him, maybe even holed. But that would have been better than being trapped between them and pounded to pieces: we'd have lost most of the ship's company."

"Well, we've learned a new trick!"

Ramage held up a cautionary finger. "It's not one we're likely to be able to use again."

Hill grinned and said: "No, sir, true enough; I'm thankful we were able to use it once!"

Both men glanced aloft as the lookout at the foremasthead hailed.

"Land ho! One point on the starboard bow!"

Chapter Three

Both Ramage and Hill picked up telescopes. Ramage could just make out a faint blur, a blue-grey hump with a dark cloud just above it. "It's probably the island of Capraia," he said shortly.

Was it a coincidence that the two French ships of the line had passed so close to the island? It was a barren sort of place, admittedly. It might be a good idea to pass close and have a good look: he would look a fool if the French had put a couple of battalions on shore there, though he could not think of a good reason why they should.

"We'll harden sheets so that we can lay the island, Mr Hill."

The third lieutenant gave an order to the men at the wheel and then picked up the speaking trumpet. The men on watch hauled on sheets and braces and the ship steered a couple of points to starboard, heading for an invisible place to windward of the island.

Capraia. From memory, there was just a small fishing port once protected by an old fortress called San Giorgio. And six years ago there was the tragedy of the *Queen Charlotte*.

"Capraia, sir? Why does the name stick in my memory?" Hill asked.

"Pirates and the *Queen Charlotte*, I expect."

"Ah yes, she blew up, didn't she?"

Ramage nodded. "It's a barren sort of place but pirates love it. As far as I remember, the people living there appealed to Lord Nelson – who was in Leghorn at the time – to send them a ship to get rid of the pirates. His Lordship sent the *Queen Charlotte*, but while she was on passage and passing Gorgona at the north end of this group of islands she caught fire and blew up, killing more than six hundred men."

"So Capraia never did get rid of her pirates?"

Ramage shrugged his shoulders. "Probably not. We might find some there . . ."

"Where do they come from, sir?"

"Most of them from the Barbary coast, I think. The local people just call them *Saraceni*. At one time nearly all pirates in the Mediterranean were Saracens, but now I suspect that quite a few of them are Algerines."

"There must be a good harbour there."

"No, it's just a small fishing harbour. The pirates only come there during the summer. That's why we aren't very likely to find any now – too early in the year: they don't want to get caught in a storm with no port to leeward."

By now Hill, who did not know the Mediterranean at all well, was intrigued at the idea of meeting pirates, and looked at the distant island once again with his telescope.

"What do these pirates do, sir?"

"Mostly raid towns and villages. Seize a few fishing boats, but mainly they're interested in targets on shore. They are not seamen; just Arab bandits with boats to get to the various islands. They even raid places on the mainland of Italy, looting, kidnapping men for their galleys and women for the brothels."

"I don't think I want to live around here," Hill said.

Half an hour later the lookout reported a small sail ahead, following up with a hail saying it was a fishing boat which had just altered course to cross ahead of the *Calypso*.

Ramage pinched his nose. Altering course to cross ahead? That was unusual: normally, local fishing boats kept away from ships of war; they could be visited by pressgangs on the lookout for ablebodied men. It was not unknown for a party from a frigate to confiscate their entire catch.

"Send Jackson aloft with a glass," Ramage told Hill.

Jackson, rated one of the sharpest-eyed men in the ship, was soon shouting down to the deck that the fishermen were waving cloths, trying to attract the *Calypso*'s attention.

What had the fishermen got to say? Surely they were not trying to sell their catch. Ramage shrugged: there was only one way of finding out.

"We'll heave to just to leeward of them," he told Hill. "Pass the word to Mr Rennick to have a dozen marines standing by at the entryport."

Rennick, the red-faced Marine lieutenant, would be only too glad of the opportunity to parade some of his men: he had about the most monotonous job in the ship. No, perhaps the surgeon did, since it was rare for any of the frigate's men to report sick.

At that moment Southwick came up on to the quarterdeck.

"Trouble, sir? I heard the lookout hailing."

Ramage shook his head. "No, just a fisherman up ahead who is trying to attract our attention."

"Probably wants to sell us some fish," Southwick said gloomily.

Ramage nodded. "That's what I thought. Still, some fresh fish would be welcome: our men don't seem to be having any luck with the lines we're towing astern!"

Southwick rubbed his hands together. "Yes, a nice tuna steak would not come amiss."

Ramage could see the fishing boat quite clearly now through the glass. It was quite large; he could make out eight or nine men on her deck, several of them waving cloths, probably their shirts.

Their little ship was flying no colours, but that was not surprising. They were almost certainly from Capraia, the island ahead.

Hill gave an order to the quartermaster, who passed it to the men at the wheel. The *Calypso* bore away a few degrees to larboard, so that the fishing boat was now ahead and under half a mile away.

She had once been painted red and blue, but now her sides were saltcaked and the nail sickness, the streaks of rust from the nails used in her planking, looking like dark tear stains. Her sails were so patched that there were more patches than original cloths, and as she pitched Ramage could see baskets on her foredeck, waiting for fish. Or maybe they held the catch they wanted to sell.

Ten minutes later the *Calypso*, her foretopsail backed, was lying stopped to leeward of the fishing boat and Ramage, the speaking trumpet reversed so that the mouthpiece was against his ear, was trying to understand what the fishermen, who seemed excited, were trying to shout to him.

Finally he put down the speaking trumpet. "It's no good, I can't make out a word," he told Hill. "Hoist out a boat and bring the captain over."

Southwick sniffed disapprovingly. "We're going to a lot of

26

trouble for a pack of fishermen," he muttered. "Why not let 'em use the boat they're towing astern?"

"It'll be quicker using one of our own boats. And," Ramage said, "they're not trying to sell fish."

"You heard that much, then?"

"No, but all their baskets are empty – I can see them from here. So they're not selling fish. They may be reporting seeing some ships. Perhaps they saw the two French ships of the line and want to tell us about them!"

It took several minutes to hoist out a boat and then Jackson clambered down into it with a crew. The boat was rowed over to the fishing boat which, sails now lowered, rolled heavily.

The fishing boat's captain, when he came on board, was a tall man so thin his face was gaunt. He had several blackened teeth and very large hands on the end of extraordinarily long arms.

He saluted Ramage awkwardly and started off a long explanation in Italian which had a heavy local accent.

Ramage listened carefully, nodding from time to time, but otherwise standing with his head inclined forward while the Italian gesticulated frequently, holding up a finger to emphasize a particular point.

Finally the Italian finished his story, with Southwick, Aitken – who had come on deck as the *Calypso* hove-to – and Hill watching him impatiently, not having understood a word. They saw Ramage hold out a hand and the Italian shake it vigorously.

As the Italian went to the entryport to climb back down into the boat, Southwick looked at Ramage questioningly. Ramage looked puzzled and shook his head, as if to clear his thoughts. "It seems there are a lot of Frenchmen around these parts. He was reporting the two ships of the line but what really worries him is that there's a French frigate at anchor just outside the harbour at Capraia."

"Have they landed any troops?" Aitken asked.

"No, they marched some seamen through the streets – probably just to impress the local people – but that was all."

"And the frigate, she's still there, sir?"

"She was still there when that fellow sailed last night."

"So they're not interfering with the fishermen?"

"No, the fishermen are free to come and go. He couldn't think of any reason why the Frenchman is there."

"Just waiting for us to come and do him in," Southwick growled. "Two ships of the line and a frigate will make a good score."

Ramage nodded and rubbed a scar on his forehead. It was a gesture Southwick recognized at once, and knew there was no need for any more talk.

As soon as Jackson returned with the boat it was hoisted in. They watched the fisherman hoisting its lateen sail and draw clear, and then Ramage said: 'Very well, Mr Hill: let's get under way again. Steer direct for the island – you can just about lay it with this wind."

Hill bellowed a string of orders through the speaking trumpet and the watch on deck hauled on the brace which swung round the foretopmast yard while other men hauled on the sheet, so that the sail filled and then curved into shape as wind filled it. From being dead in the water, stopped by the backed foretopsail's weight pressing against the thrust of the other sails, the *Calypso* slowly got way on: the water began chuckling under her stem, the men at the wheel had to brace themselves against the rudder's kick, and the ship came alive.

The frigate began to pitch as she beat up towards the island and Southwick spread a chart across the top of the binnacle and began to comment on what he saw.

"It's a mountainous island, steep-to on this western side and sloping down on the eastern side. A chain of mountains runs roughly north and south the length of the island, with a very high peak at the north end and at the south end. Nothing on the west side of the island except cliffs and rocks; the only place is Porto Vecchio, which is simply a wide bight, with the small harbour of Capraia in the south-west corner. A couple of old forts . . . that's all there is. I can't see anything to interest the Frenchman."

Ramage thought for a moment. Why assume the French frigate had called at the island for any reason concerning the island? Clearly Capraia had nothing to offer except shelter – and olives, fish and goat meat if you were hungry.

"Perhaps the Frenchman is doing some repairs," Ramage said. "Repairs that need a quiet anchorage for a few hours . . ."

Southwick slapped his knee and said enthusiastically: "That's it! Sprung his bowsprit, most likely. Or shifting yards. Probably sailing in company with those two 74s, and then bore up for the lee of Capraia when something went wrong. Not that Capraia gives

28

much of a lee with this wind, but it looks as though it'll haul round to the west, and the French captain may think the same."

The old master seemed relieved. "It was worrying me," he admitted. "I couldn't for the life of me see why a French frigate would call there. But to do some repairs – yes, that's a good enough reason."

Through his telescope Ramage could make out the largest peaks on the island: there were four, one at the northern end of the island and another at the southern, as if to balance it, with two in between. It was so mountainous – on the western side anyway – that the inhabitants must live a hard life. Southwick had said that it sloped down on the eastern side, but it would give little land suitable for crops since the whole island could not be five miles long.

He considered a nagging thought. Those two French 74s. Should he have made more of an effort to destroy them? He took off his hat, wiped the inside of the band and jammed it back on his head, perplexed. The only thing he could have done was sail back and forth across their sterns, raking them. They would have brought up a couple of sternchase guns each, so four would have been firing at him as the *Calypso* raked them with sixteen 12-pounders. It would have done as much good as a mouse gnawing at a thick oak door. He knew that; but would their Lordships take the same view, or the admiral at Naples when he reported to him?

He shrugged his shoulders: it was all over now; there was no question of going back. Now he had to concentrate his attention on this frigate anchored off Capraia. The frigate presented the same problem – how to achieve surprise. He had done it against the two 74s by unexpectedly steering straight for the *Artois*'s bow, obviously intending to carry away her jibboom and bowsprit, and as a result the captain of the *Artois* had panicked and collided with the other 74. Now to surprise the frigate. At least the Frenchman could not see him coming: even at this moment he would be lying at anchor off the little harbour, unaware that the *Calypso* was approaching from the other side of the island – unless he had posted lookouts at the top of one of the mountains, which would be very unlikely.

He looked at his watch and then told Hill: "Send the men to dinner; we may not get another opportunity for several hours."

Men fought better with full stomachs, even though for some it might be their last meal. A sobering thought, he reflected; but it was a foolish optimist that thought an enemy frigate could be captured or destroyed without casualties.

Seven men sat round the table at mess number eight, eating salt beef from wooden plates.

"Give the bread barge a fair wind," Stafford said to Rossi, who was sitting at the inboard end of the table. The Italian pushed across the wooden box, known as a "barge" and which contained hard biscuit, which went by the name of "bread". This bread had reached the stage where it was beginning to soften; no matter what anyone did, weevils would start to inhabit it and the wise seaman would give the biscuit a brisk tap on the table before starting to chew. The tap was intended to stun the weevils; it stopped them wriggling in the mouth, reminding a hungry man of their presence.

"What did that fellow really tell the captain, Jacko?" Rossi asked as he helped himself to biscuit, one of the few things that were not rationed.

"I didn't hear; I was in the boat," the American said. "All I heard was them talking to each other, the Italian skipper and his mate."

"Well, what were they saying?"

"They had such thick accents it was hard to understand them," said Jackson, who had learned his Italian in Tuscany, where the accent was comparatively pure. Although Capraia was one of the islands which made up the Tuscan Archipelago, each island had its own accent which bore little relation to what was generally known as "the Tuscan accent". "But they were talking about a French frigate, and I think that's what they wanted to talk to us about."

"Where were they from?"

"This island ahead of us, I think."

"Aha," Stafford said delightedly. "Stands to reason, they were warning us that there's a French frigate there!"

Jackson shrugged his shoulders. "They might have been reporting that they saw a French frigate three days ago – they haven't much idea about time."

" 'Ere, this beef died of old age," Stafford grumbled. "Just look at the colour of it. Boiled mahogany, that's what it is, and it's as tough as wood.

30

"Needs to spend another day boiling in the coppers. Another week," he amended, "not another day."

"So if there is a French frigate at this island," said the Frenchman, Gilbert, whose English was almost fluent, "what do you think we are going to do?"

Jackson waited until he had finished chewing a piece of the beef. "We were piped to dinner half an hour early, and knowing Mr Ramage that was to make sure we had eaten by the time we go into action. So if you ask me, he reckons we'll find this Frenchman in the next hour or two."

"And then what do we do?" asked another Frenchman, Auguste.

"We capture it," Jackson said simply.

"Just like that, eh?" said Gilbert, gesturing towards the bread barge, which Stafford pushed towards him.

"Why not?" asked Jackson.

"What's a French frigate doing at this island, then?" asked Stafford.

"Damned if I know," Jackson said. "I've never even heard of the place before. Either the Frenchies are capturing the place, in which case half their ship's company will be on shore, or else they're repairing damage, in which case they might not be able to get under way."

Rossi soaked a biscuit in the juice left on his plate. "After this morning, we deserve something easy. I thought we would be deaded."

"Killed," Jackson corrected. "So did I. It's nice to feel alive."

"To tell the truth, I'm surprised there are so many Frenchies at sea. I thought we got most of 'em at Trafalgar." Stafford sat back as though he had spoken his share of wisdom for the day.

"I did, too," Jackson admitted. "But when you come to think of it, there must have been ships at sea in other places, and now I suppose they are making for home."

"They're a bit late," Stafford said.

"Takes time for the French to get out orders to all the ships: they were probably short of frigates in Toulon to pass the word."

"I don't know about French frigates," Rossi said crossly, "but that beef is the worst we've had for a year or two."

31

"Yus, I reckon the contractor or the Navy Board are getting rid of some old stock. Just our luck to get it."

"Having fresh meat every three days while we were in Plymouth has spoiled you," Jackson said unsympathetically.

"Well, that was one good thing that came out of the Great Mutiny," Stafford said defensively. "Getting fresh meat from the shore every two or three days made me feel I was living like a lord."

"Lords get fresh meat *every* day," Jackson said drily. "That's one of the advantages of being a lord."

"Mr Ramage is a lord but he don't get fresh meat every day."

"Don't be daft, how could he?"

"Beats me," Stafford said with something approaching a sigh, "why someone like Mr Ramage, the son of an earl and a title of his own, should join the Navy in the first place. T'isn't as though he was pressed."

"Runs in the family," Jackson said. "You know as well as I do his father's an admiral. If Mr Ramage has a son, I expect he'll go into the Navy as well. It's a sort of tradition."

"Yus," Stafford said sagely, "it's time he had a family. He made a good choice marrying Lady Sarah. Never could see him marrying the Marcheeza."

"Marchesa," Jackson corrected without thinking. "No, well, she was a bit wild, on account of her being Italian. And she could never settle down in England on account of her being the ruler of Volterra. She got pulled two ways."

"You think she's still alive?" Rossi asked.

Jackson shook his head. "I can't see Boney letting her go back to Volterra: she'd rouse up the people to throw out the French within a week of unpacking her bags."

"You reckon Mr Ramage thinks that?"

Jackson nodded. "From what I understood, he and his father did all they could to persuade her not to leave England when the peace was signed because they knew it would not last."

"And Mr Orsini? After all, she's his aunt."

"He must know by now. He's not a kid any more. Just think of him when he first joined the ship. Just a young boy then. Now he's a young man. Almost, anyway, and as good a seaman as anyone in the ship, except Mr Ramage and Mr Southwick."

"This Marchesa," Gilbert asked. "Was she beautiful?"

Jackson nodded. "Yes. She was tiny – about five feet tall. Black hair. Very Italian, if you know what I mean. Very fiery. You could see she was used to ruling."

"And Mr Ramage, he fell in love with her?"

"We thought so: after we rescued her in Italy, she went to live with Mr Ramage's parents, and we thought they'd get married."

"But Mr Ramage went off and married Lady Sarah," Gilbert said, "and she is very English!"

"Very," Jackson said. "A real lady. Just about the opposite to the Marchesa in every way. Don't get me wrong," Jackson added hastily, "the Marchesa was a real lady too, but she – well, a lot of the time, she seemed to be in a passion about something or other. Lady Sarah always seems so calm – as you know, since you saw her in France."

"Ah, what calm," Gilbert said, and Auguste, Louis and Albert nodded their heads in agreement. "Calm without being cold. A very passionate lady under that calm, and so brave."

"It must be sad for Mr Ramage not knowing for sure about the Marchesa," Rossi said. "If he knew for certain she was dead, well, that would be that. And if he knew she was alive, then there is nothing to worry about. But never being sure . . . that must be hard, for him and his family, let alone Mr Orsini."

"Well, worrying about it ain't going to sink that frigate," Stafford said, beginning to collect up the plates. "Since I'm the mess cook this week, let me get on with washing up these mess traps. Gawd, you're a messy eater, Rosey," he said, using the side of his palm to sweep crumbs from the hard biscuit on to a plate.

Chapter
Four

Ramage leaned with his elbows on the top of the binnacle box, looking at the chart spread out by Southwick and held down by paperweights. There was the island of Capraia on the chart, and there it was in fact almost dead ahead.

On this course and with this wind the *Calypso* should just pass the southern end of the island. If the wind backed a point or two, she would have to tack, which he wanted to avoid.

"You can lay the southern end of the island comfortably?" he asked the quartermaster.

"Aye, sir, with a point in hand," the man answered.

The mountains and cliffs were sharp now: the island seemed to grow taller as they approached. I would not like to hit this coast on a dark night with a *libeccio* blowing, he thought to himself: nor, for that matter, would he want to have to land a boat on a calm day: there seemed to be no beaches: only rocks and cliffs.

How far was the southern end of the island? Perhaps two miles, and the *Calypso* was making about five knots against a head wind. Well, there was no need to leave everything to the last minute.

"Beat to quarters, Mr Hill," he said. "I want the guns loaded with grape."

The look of surprise on Hill's face reminded Ramage of the chance he was taking. It was not much of a chance if his guess was correct, but there was no avoiding the fact that a guess was a guess. He was, quite simply, guessing that either a proportion of the French frigate's crew would be on shore, or that they would be working on deck or aloft on some repairs.

In either case they would not be at quarters: grapeshot should cut them down, without doing a lot of damage to the ship. Surprise should be fairly easy: the *Calypso*, being French built, would be taken as a French-owned ship at first glance, and the rules of war allowed you to fly enemy colours, as long as you hauled them down and hoisted your own before opening fire. Surprise should be complete.

"Haul down our colours and hoist a Tricolour," he said. "Use a separate halyard for the Tricolour and leave our colours bent on, so that we can switch them quickly."

"Very well, sir," Hill said with a grin: he immediately saw what Ramage intended doing. It was hardly a new trick, but given the *Calypso*'s French sheer it was likely to succeed.

Ramage looked up again from the chart as the drum began thudding its urgent summons to quarters; a thudding reinforced by the shrilling of bosun's calls and the harsh and urgent cries of the bosun's mates.

Once again the whole process began: decks wetted and sanded; the magazine unlocked by the gunner and the second captains of each gun collecting locks, lanyards and prickers; boys hurrying down with their wooden cases to collect cartridges; the guns run in ready to be loaded; rammers, sponges and wormers put ready; slowmatches lit and hung over the edges of the tubs of water.

How many times have I given that order? Ramage reflected. Hundreds of times. How many times had it ended with action? He had lost count. Most times, of course, it was routine: every day the ship greeted the dawn at general quarters, when a sail could come out of the vanishing darkness and, in wartime, any sail could be the enemy. And in daylight, whenever a strange sail was sighted – unless it was obviously a fisherman or some other harmless vessel – the ship went to quarters. A minimum of three times a day; more likely ten or a dozen times. On top of gunnery exercises, which he ordered almost daily, there was plenty going on to keep that wretched gunner busy: he was always complaining that he never had an opportunity to black the guns, because the blacking took several hours to dry.

Looking forward over the quarterdeck rail he could see the men running to their stations. To an ignorant eye the men seemed to be running in all directions, like a disturbed anthill; to a trained eye the men were running with a purpose, the direction the result of months of training and experience.

Aitken came up the quarterdeck ladder to take over the conn

from Hill, who had to go down to his division of guns, and now Southwick came up the ladder, adjusting the strap of the scabbard in which was housed a great double-bladed sword which he delighted to swing like a flail whenever he could get into action.

Soon Aitken was reporting to Ramage as each division of guns shouted that it was loaded and ready to be run out. If he was going to surprise the French, running out the guns would be one of the last orders he gave before opening fire.

Until he saw where the French frigate was lying, he would not know which broadside he would be using; but each stand of grapeshot comprised ten shot, each larger than a hen's egg and weighing a pound. So one broadside, not including the carronades, would see 160 grapeshot being hurled at the Frenchman by sixteen guns.

The idea, he thought grimly, is to kill Frenchmen without damaging the ship too much: he did not want to end up capturing a hulk which he would have to tow to Naples: he wanted a ship that a prize crew could sail in the *Calypso*'s wake, British colours flying over the French. Of course, he thought, wryly, everything could go wrong and the Frenchman would end up towing the *Calypso* into Toulon, French colours over the British . . .

"I'm just going below for a moment," he told Aitken, and went down to his cabin. He sat down at his desk and unlocked the top drawer. First he took out a canvas pouch which was rolled up and pushed to the back. The mouth of the pouch had brass eyelets through which a drawstring ran, and the pouch itself was heavy because there was a strip of lead in the bottom. From the drawer he took out the signal book, the little booklet containing the secret challenges and replies, and his journal. He stuffed them into the bag and pulled the drawstring tight. He put the bag back in the drawer, which he left unlocked so that in an emergency the canvas bag could be grabbed and then thrown over the side where it would sink rapidly, taking its secrets with it.

With the canvas bag taken care of he walked over to the forward bulkhead and took down his sword from its rack. He slipped the strap of the scabbard over his shoulder, adjusting the sword down his left side. Secret papers and sword: that was all he had to do. He went back up the companionway, acknowledging the salute of the sentry at his door.

36

Standing on the fore side of the quarterdeck again, looking over the bow, the island now seemed much nearer: he could make out the folds and fissures in the cliffs and see the waves breaking as a lacy fringe against the rocks lining the coast.

He looked across at Southwick, who grinned cheerfully and said: "Another mile and we'll be able to see round the corner. We'll probably find that the frigate's not there: she left last night north-about round the island bound for Toulon."

"I hope not: you haven't been in action for several weeks, and I don't want you to get out of the habit."

"If she's there, let's lay alongside and board her," Southwick said, slapping the scabbard of his sword. "Let me lead one of the boarding parties: that'll save m'sword from getting rusty."

Boarding parties! The ship's company was already organized into boarding parties in the quarters bill, which every man knew by heart. But it was necessary to give specific orders to the Marines.

"Pass the word for Mr Rennick," he told Aitken.

The Marine lieutenant arrived, smart in his uniform, face redder than usual because of the tightness of his collar, and with his sword swinging by his side.

"Ah, Rennick. If we get the chance of boarding this fellow round the corner – and we don't even know yet if he's still there – I want you and your Marines to board aft and secure the quarterdeck, particularly the wheel. It'll be up to you, in other words, to seize control of the ship."

"I understand perfectly, sir," Rennick said cheerfully. "Do you want us to cut the wheelropes?"

"No, certainly not," Ramage said hastily. "I want to get her under way again with the least delay."

"Very well, sir," Rennick said, saluting smartly and hurrying down the ladder, to where his men were drawn up in two files, the drummer boy on the right and Sergeant Ferris standing in front of them. Ferris had previously inspected every man. He had found fault with the pipeclay on four crossbelts and the straps of three muskets. Two men's hair was not tidy enough and the polish on four pairs of boots did not measure up to his exacting standards. The names of all the offending men had been taken; after the action they would be called to account.

Rennick stood in front of the men while Ferris called them to attention. Briefly Rennick gave them their orders. Without saying so in as many words, Rennick managed to convey the idea that the Marines had been singled out to secure the quarterdeck; that it was a task that could not be left to the sailors. Rennick was a firm believer in healthy competition; in his imagination he could already see himself reporting to Mr Ramage that the Frenchman's quarterdeck had been secured. Most of the time the Marines had to do all the humdrum tasks in the ship – sentries at the watercask, the captain's cabin door, the magazine and so on. Very occasionally – all too rarely – they had the chance to shine.

Ramage felt surprisingly cheerful. It was probably the reaction from earlier in the day, but frigate against frigate was a much more cheerful proposition than a frigate against two ships of the line was. In fact, he admitted, the prospect of a frigate against two ships of the line was very depressing, and it was no credit to him that they had survived the encounter. It was a point that would not be lost on their Lordships, that it was a mistake on the part of the French captain which had caused the collision, not a brilliant stroke by Captain Ramage. The most that he could claim, Ramage thought, was that he had given the Frenchman a hint. Not a hint that had caused the collision, but a hint that set him moving in the right direction.

Meanwhile the southern tip of the island was a great deal nearer and now fine on the larboard bow. Ramage took up his telescope and examined the headland.

"There looks to be deep water close in," he told Aitken. "We'll pass round it a cable off."

Two hundred yards should keep them clear of any stray rocks without making them pass round the headland so far off that the Frenchman would spot them sooner than he need. Round the corner the cliffs would drop away, likely as not, giving way to flatter land. The vital thing was the first sight of the frigate. On it would depend the way the *Calypso* attacked her: which broadside would be fired first, whether it was going to be a matter of slamming alongside her as she lay at anchor and boarding her in the smoke, or whether it would turn into a battle of broadsides, the Frenchman cutting her anchor cable and getting under way so that she could manoeuvre.

If she got under way, Ramage realized, he would have lost

his greatest advantage, surprise: if only he could get round the headland and on to the anchored ship – presupposing she was there and at anchor – he would gain several minutes because the *Calypso* looked like a French ship and was flying French colours, but it would be a matter of minutes before the Frenchman challenged and then became suspicious of the way the *Calypso* was manoeuvring.

Suddenly the *Calypso* was round the headland. Spreading out on the larboard side the coast went straight for a mile or two, then came eastward and seaward to form a small peninsula with an old fort perched in the middle of it, and then beyond the land curved round in a great bight, with a small harbour – obviously Capraia itself – in the corner. And the frigate was at anchor just off the end of the peninsula, her main and foreyards down on deck, obviously being worked on by the French carpenters. She could not get under way: that much was certain.

Rake her or board? Ramage thought quickly. Raking her meant sailing to and fro across her stern, firing broadsides into her unprotected transom to hurl the shot the length of the ship. Boarding meant pitting the *Calypso*'s boarding parties against the entire French crew, with only a certain amount of surprise on their side. Practically none, in fact. It would take them time to load guns and run them out to fire broadsides: it would take only a minute to snatch up sword or pike to repel boarders.

So rake her: there was room enough to pass between the end of the headland and her stern as she lay head to wind. Much would depend on that first raking broadside.

Quickly he gave instructions to Aitken. "Clew up the courses and the t'gallants," he said. "We'll manoeuvre under topsails, and that'll fool the French a bit longer because it'll look as though we're going to anchor.

"Then we'll cut close across their stern, firing the starboard broadside. Then we'll get clear, turn and come back to give 'em the larboard broadside. After we've done that a few times we might see them strike their colours."

"Aye aye, sir," Aitken said cheerfully, obviously delighted at the thought of going into action. He picked up the speaking trumpet to give the first of the sail orders.

Ramage gave fresh orders to the quartermaster and the *Calypso* bore away a point, sailing closer to the coast and now almost on a broad reach. There was a slatting of canvas as the men started clewing up the huge courses, and the *Calypso* slowed down. Ramage watched as the corners of the great sails were hauled in diagonally, and then the centre was drawn up vertically, as though folding a napkin. In the meantime men were scrambling aloft, taking the shrouds at the run, clambering up the ratlines like monkeys, and then working their way outward along the topgallant yards, stepping along the footropes.

From the deck the men seemed tiny, but these topmen were the most agile and well-trained in the ship, and they hauled the topgallants on to the yard and passed the gaskets that secured them.

Ramage nodded approvingly. "Quite a harbour stow," he said to Aitken. "I hope the French appreciate it."

Now he could make out the Tricolour flapping from the French frigate's stern in what was a little less than a strong breeze. A breeze that would mean the frigate was lying steady to her anchor cable and not yawing about. A breeze that meant raking her should be comparatively easy.

Ramage hitched his sword round so that it hung more comfortably at his side. If they were going to board, he would get a brace of Sea Service pistols loaded. The thought of pistols had obviously crossed Southwick's mind because he handed two, butt first, to Ramage. "You might be needing these, sir," he said. "I had a couple of brace loaded while you were collecting your sword."

Ramage noticed that the master had a pistol tucked into each side of his belt. What with the pistols and that great meat cleaver of a sword, obviously it would break the old man's heart if they did not board. Ramage shrugged to himself: they might end up boarding yet; a sea fight was more unpredictable than the weather.

Reduced now to her topsails, the *Calypso* was making less than five knots, with her bow wave making little more than a chuckling sound under her stem.

Then Orsini hurried up the quarterdeck ladder, saluted Ramage and reported: "Starboard side guns all ready to fire sir. But they are loaded with grape," he added anxiously.

"I know," Ramage said, and then, conscious that it was the only way that Orsini would ever learn, said: "We are going to rake her. Grape will cause more casualties."

Ramage noted that Aitken had sent the young midshipman round to the guns, instead of relying on a bellow through the speaking trumpet.

He looked across at the French frigate and at that moment Orsini snatched up a telescope: "She has just hoisted two flags, sir!" he said. "Probably the challenge for the day."

"Well, we don't have the answer so we'll ignore it. Make sure we have a couple of men ready to lower the French colours and hoist ours."

"I have a couple of men waiting at the halyards, sir," Orsini said.

Ramage nodded. Paolo was turning into a good young officer: if only Gianna could see him. He shook his head: this was no time to be thinking about her fate. Worrying about it, rather.

"Courses are clewed and t'gallants furled, sir," Aitken reported.

The anchor! Ramage realized that the Frenchmen would be watching the *Calypso* through telescopes, and sharp eyes would notice that although she was reducing sail, her anchors were still catted.

"Send half a dozen men to the starboard bower," he snapped. "Tell them to look as though we're preparing to anchor."

Southwick swore and Aitken looked crestfallen as he shouted the order. He put down the speaking trumpet and admitted: "I didn't think of that."

"Neither did I," Ramage said. "I hope the French haven't either."

The French frigate was now five hundred yards away on the starboard bow, with the short peninsula to larboard and the gap between them about six hundred yards wide: the French captain had anchored to give himself plenty of swinging room.

Just enough room, Ramage noted ironically, for an enemy frigate to wear back and forth across her stern. And if she cut her cable the wind would blow her straight on to the rocks at the foot of the peninsula. Her captain could not be blamed for that because with this wind the whole coast was a lee shore, and with her yards struck down on deck she could not move, although if the weather turned bad they could get the yards up again and under way in a few hours.

41

The wind was freshening: seaward there were the occasional whitecaps and the boulders at the foot of the cliffs were growing white collars of spray. Occasionally one of the topsails slatted, caught by an odd eddy of wind and enough to make the quarter-master glance aloft anxiously.

Now the *Calypso* was heading for the gap between the frigate's stern and the peninsula. Ramage guessed that the crews would be waiting for the guns to be run out. The second captain of every gun on the starboard side, after a quick glance through the port, was now preparing to cock the flintlock and then stand well back. The gun captains would be getting ready to take up the strain on their long lanyards, crouching behind the guns, left leg flung out to one side and sighting along the barrel, waiting for the target to appear.

Should he then switch to roundshot? He decided not; he wanted to kill men without damaging the ship: he had already decided that, so he would continue with grapeshot. It would be easy enough to change later on, when he could see the effect of the fall of shot.

He gave a helm order to Aitken, who passed it on to the quartermaster, and then another, a half point this time. Then, a couple of minutes later a quarter point. Now the *Calypso* was lined up precisely to go through the gap, passing the French frigate's stern about twenty yards off.

Now for the waiting. One could wait an hour for a postchaise to arrive at the next post inn; one could wait half an hour for one's wife to finish primping her hair and generally getting ready to go to a reception; but the last minute or two before going into action were as much as a man could bear: not because of nervousness but simply because of the tension mounting before the first gun fired.

She was *Le Tigre*: he could now read the name on her transom as she swung in the wind. Red lettering on yellow, a vivid slash of colour on an otherwise black hull. Guns not run out; fore and main yards down on deck. Through the glass he could see a group of officers watching the *Calypso* from *Le Tigre*'s quarterdeck: no doubt waiting for the challenge to be answered and the *Calypso* to run up her numbers in the French Navy List.

They seemed to be in no hurry; there were three officers and a couple of seamen on the quarterdeck, and Ramage could see the sun glinting on a couple of telescopes, but there seemed no sense of urgency in the Frenchmen's stance; no indication that they regarded themselves as in any danger.

They were fooled by the *Calypso*'s build and the fact that she was flying a Tricolour, a perfectly legitimate *ruse de guerre*, providing you lowered and hoisted your proper colours before opening fire.

Now he could distinguish the salt dried along *Le Tigre*'s waterline; her quarterboats were lowered it and secured to the boat boom amidships; there was a line of laundry rigged forward and displaying a couple of dozen shirts in different bright colours.

Ramage noticed that the hammocks were not stowed in the nettings on top of the bulwarks: presumably they had been left slung below, in contrast to the Royal Navy's strict practice of having them stowed first thing every morning. Apart from clearing out the lowerdeck, it provided a thick canvas barricade against small arms fire.

Through the glass he could see a dozen men working on the mainyard and another dozen grouped round the foreyard. Obviously *Le Tigre* had sprung both yards; it looked as though a sudden change of wind (or a mistake by the men at the wheel) had resulted in the ship being caught aback, the wind on the foreside of the sails pressing the yards back against the masts. It was easy enough to do; and if that was what had happened, then *Le Tigre* was lucky to escape with only a couple of sprung yards; ships had been dismasted by being caught aback.

And that has passed another minute, Ramage realized, beginning now to feel excited rather than just tense: in another minute he would give the order to run the guns out; then number one gun on the starboard side would fire, and then the rest would follow in sequence.

There was one task remaining. He turned to Orsini and said sharply: "Lower the French colours and hoist our own!"

He turned to Aitken: "Run out the guns!"

He lifted the telescope to his eye again, watching the group of French officers. He saw one of them gesticulating and was conscious that behind him the *Calypso*'s Tricolour had been hauled down. But it was too late for the French now; in a few moments the British colours would be hoisted and a few moments after that the first round of grapeshot would be smashing into her stern – he could hear the rumbling of the guns being run out.

He glanced aft, saw the British colours hoisted home, and looked forward again. Almost at once a gun gave a throaty cough and smoke streamed out of the *Calypso*'s side; then there was a ripple of noise as the rest of the guns fired in succession.

The French frigate's stern seemed to pass quite leisurely along the *Calypso*'s starboard side, giving the gunners plenty of time to aim, Ramage noted. And, as he watched, *Le Tigre*'s transom appeared to dissolve in a cloud of dust, the stern lights of the captain's cabin beaten in as the grapeshot smashed their way through and went on the length of the ship, killing or maiming anyone in their path and flinging up lethal splinters.

Finally the last gun in the broadside had fired and Ramage was beginning to cough as the smoke billowed aft, curling along in oily coils to cover the quarterdeck. He turned to Aitken: "Ready to wear round? Now we'll give them the other broadside!"

A shouted order to the quartermaster set the men spinning the wheel, and Aitken's bellows through the speaking trumpet brought the *Calypso* round to larboard, her sails slatting as the wind passed across her stern. Seamen hauled at braces to swing the yards round and then others hardened in the sheets to trim the sails. Then Aitken shouted down to the gunners to prepare to fire the larboard broadside.

The *Calypso* did not have enough men to fire both broadsides at once and crews from the starboard guns ran across the deck to the other side. Gun captains hurriedly snatched up the lanyards and uncoiled them: second captains checked the quills in the vents and the priming powder before cocking the locks and standing back.

As Jackson and his crew ran across the deck Stafford exclaimed: "Did you see what we did, Jacko? Just about bashed his sternlights in!"

As Jackson reached for the lanyard coiled on the breech he grinned: "Yes, we've spoiled that French captain's furniture!"

By now the *Calypso* had swung round and was steering an opposite course across the frigate's stern. There were no last-minute aiming instructions: when they had loaded the gun they had left the barrel elevated just enough to hit the French frigate's stern; the wedge-shaped quoin adjusting the elevation of the barrel was pushed in more than three-quarters of its length, so that the barrel was horizontal.

Suddenly to Jackson's right the first gun of the broadside fired and was followed by the second, and by the time the French frigate's stern was passing the port in front of Jackson the deck was a swirling cloud of smoke.

Jackson waited until the battered sternlights were in his sights and then gave the lanyard a brisk tug. The gun barked and spewed smoke and flame before crashing back in recoil, and as soon as it was thrust hard up against the breeching, Rossi and the Frenchmen went into action: a water-soaked sponge was thrust down the bore, a powder monkey ran forward with a cartridge which Gilbert snatched up and cradled into the bore, Auguste pressed it in with the rammer and, as he felt it come hard up in the chamber of the breech, gave the rammer a sharp jab.

Albert slid in a wad which Auguste rammed home while Rossi stood by with the stand of grapeshot. He swung it up and into the muzzle helped by Louis and once again Auguste thrust with his rammer, helped by Rossi because of the weight of the grapeshot. Albert was ready with another wad, and as soon as it was rammed home he lifted his hand and the men ran to the tackles to run the gun out again. As soon as it had rumbled into position, Stafford thrust the pricker into the vent hole and wriggled it about to make sure the point had penetrated the cartridge case and made a passage for the powder. Then he slid in a quill and sprinkled priming powder on top. Now the gun was loaded and ready for the next broadside when the *Calypso* had worn again.

Jackson had coiled the lanyard ready and put it on the breech, and as soon as he saw that Stafford had finished he shouted and the crew ran back to their gun on the starboard side. By now the last gun of the larboard broadside had fired and yet again the *Calypso*'s sails were slatting as she wore round clear of the rocky tip of the peninsula.

By now the *Calypso* was streaming smoke through all her gunports as she turned, drifting aft to the quarterdeck, where the smoke from the carronades already had Ramage, Aitken and Southwick coughing and wiping their eyes.

Ramage could see that with *Le Tigre's* transom now smashed in the grapeshot must be sweeping through the length of the ship below deck, and there could be few men left alive below.

"Orsini!" he shouted, "run round and tell all the officers at their

45

quarters that I want their guns sweeping the Frenchman's decks now!"

Paolo ran off down the quarterdeck ladder, glad to have something to do in a battle in which up to now he had been only a spectator. He quickly found Hill and passed on the order, which the third lieutenant at once bellowed to his excited gun captains. Paolo ran on along the length of guns passing the word to the red-haired Kenton and finally the fourth lieutenant, William Martin.

At once the gun captains shouted orders to their crews, who snatched up handspikes, long iron-tipped levers, which were slid under the breeches of the guns and took the weight while the quoins were pulled further out to raise the elevation of the barrels.

The *Calypso* was now ready for her third run across the French frigate's stern and Ramage found himself wishing the wind would freshen to clear the smoke from the deck. The thought had hardly formed in his mind before the first gun in the starboard broadside was firing, followed in turn by the bronchitic coughing of the rest of the guns.

Ramage watched the grapeshot sweep the French ship's deck, seeing men fling up their arms as they were cut down.

Then the *Calypso* wore round again and the guns' crews ran across to the other side, snatched up handspikes and adjusted their aim. With quoins newly positioned and the captains sighting along the barrels to make sure the elevation was correct, in a matter of moments the first gun was firing, followed in sequence by the rest of the guns.

Ramage could see the grapeshot slamming into the yards as they lay across the deck. The mainyard slewed slightly as all the grapeshot from one gun smashed into the end.

At Aitken shouted out the orders to bring the *Calypso* round again, Southwick gave a bellow of delight and snatched at Ramage's arm. He was pointing aloft at the French frigate, and a few moments later Ramage realized what the master had seen: the French ship's colours were being lowered. She was surrendering. Honourably so, Ramage thought: with those two big yards down on deck and unable to manoeuvre, it was only a matter of time before the *Calypso*, wearing relentlessly across her stern, pounded her to pieces.

Ramage was just about to tell Aitken to order the guns to stop firing when he realized that a breathless sailor was standing in front of him. "Mainmast lookout, sir, I can't make you hear," he gasped. "There's a French frigate coming down from the north, close in with the coast."

Chapter
Five

Another frigate! This part of the Mediterranean seemed to have become a French sea! Ramage hurriedly passed the lookout's report to Aitken and Southwick and tried to think clearly with the thunder of gunfire still numbing his brain.

Le Tigre had surrendered but there was no time to take possession of her: that probably meant that she would wait until she saw if her compatriot defeated the *Calypso* and then hoist her colours again. But what of the second frigate?

There was no choice: that made the decision a lot easier, he thought grimly: no time for second thoughts or misgivings – or, for that matter, doubts. He called Orsini, told him of the second frigate, and ordered him to warn the officers at their quarters, and make sure that all the guns were loaded with round-shot.

There was no chance of any tricks to gain surprise: the approaching frigate would have seen the gunsmoke, even if at this distance she could not distinguish the British colours. There were probably a few moments of doubt as they saw a French hull attacking a French hull, but the smoke would have been enough to send their men to general quarters: by now all her guns would be loaded and run out, ready to engage whichever of the two ships proved to be the enemy.

"Get the boats hoisted out and towing astern," he said to Aitken. That would reduce the risk from splinters.

"It'll make a change," grunted Southwick. "Just a ship-to-ship action, with no nonsense."

With his "no nonsense" Southwick dismissed actions against ships of the line and disabled frigates: the forthcoming action, he clearly considered, would be fought on equal terms, frigate against frigate. All else, his four words implied, was heresy; not to be considered by honest men.

How to tackle this frigate? A battle of broadsides or try to board? Ramage picked up the telescope and looked at the distant ship. Yes, like *Le Tigre*, she was a 32-gun frigate, the same as the *Calypso*; gun for gun they would be evenly matched. How many men would she have on board? Like the British, the French were always short of trained seamen; but unlike the British they frequently drafted soldiers on board. It was not unusual to find a ship with half a battery of artillerymen serving the guns. With luck, Ramage reflected, if there was anything of a sea running, the artillerymen had to fight seasickness as well as the enemy, so their rate of fire was slow and erratic.

But the sea was not rough; the brisk breeze was scudding clouds across the sun and knocking up white horses, but not enough to make a frigate roll or interfere with queasy gunners.

He turned to Aitken: "Steer straight for her, and warn that the guns on the larboard side will probably be firing first."

And that, he thought, covers the tactics: stay up to windward of the enemy, so that the smoke of the guns blows clear, and then it would be a straightforward battle of broadsides, hoping that the enemy would make a mistake.

Through the telescope he could see that the approaching frigate was painted black and her sails had enough patches to indicate that she had probably been at sea some time. Was she part of a squadron which had included the two ships of the line? Was it a coincidence that she was coming along the coast of Capraia when *Le Tigre* was at anchor doing repairs? Ramage shrugged: the answers to the questions hardly mattered: she was approaching from ahead, and that was the only thing that concerned him for the moment.

The Sea Service pistols stuck in his belt were bruising his ribs; they grated every time he took a breath. He pushed them further round after deciding not to put them down: there was always a chance that the *Calypso* would end up boarding the frigate, and he did not want to waste time looking round for a brace of pistols.

He found he was becoming pleasantly excited: the prospect of an evenly matched fight against another frigate was sufficiently unusual to be welcome.

He gave an order to the quartermaster and told Aitken to harden in the sheets: he wanted to get to windward just another point, so there would be no question about the *Calypso* keeping up to windward of the enemy. Of course, the French frigate could always tack to the north-east – she could even turn on her heels and make a bolt for it. But Ramage was sure that she would come down to help *Le Tigre*. The French captain would not want to face a double charge – of cowardice, and deserting a comrade.

The frigate was a mile away now, sailing fast along the coast. Ramage glanced at the chart: there were no outlying rocks: they could manoeuvre without risk, except that if either of them was dismasted they would be blown on to the rocks, since this was a lee shore.

Could the Frenchman try any tricks? Ramage thought carefully and decided there was nothing he could not counter in time.

Three quarters of a mile, and her bow wave was curling away like a white moustache, with her sails bellying with the wind. All her guns were run out; they jutted from her side like stubby black fingers. As usual, the first broadside would be the most important because it would be fired carefully by men not coughing from gunsmoke, stunned by the noise of the guns firing, or wildly excited by the ritual of loading and firing.

Half a mile. "Orsini," he called, "run round the larboard side guns and warn them that they'll be firing in a matter of minutes."

The Italian youth ran off down the quarterdeck ladder and Ramage was thankful he could trust the youngster: he not only understood the orders but what was more important he understood the significance of them. He had been in action dozens of times now and one of his proudest moments, Ramage knew, was that he had taken part in the Battle of Trafalgar. It was becoming clear now that that battle was going to be the new yardstick by which actions were measured. Previously a man could say, "I was at Copenhagen", or "I was at the Nile", or Camperdown, the Saintes, the Glorious First of June, and other men could measure him. But Trafalgar had changed all that: it had been a victory the like of which had never before been seen. It was a new Agincourt. Ramage thought, and it would be sufficient for a man to say quietly: "Yes, I was at Trafalgar."

But what mattered for the moment was that the *Calypso* was off the east coast of Capraia steering north for a French frigate. Compared with Trafalgar there was little honour in that; but an unlucky shot or splinter could make you just as dead. That was the ironic thing about death; you were still dead whether you died in a great victory like Trafalgar or from falling down a hatchway on a dark night and breaking your neck. Death worked indiscriminately.

A quarter of a mile. Ramage could imagine the second captains cocking the locks and jumping back out of harm's way, and the gun captains would be taking up the tension on their lanyards . . .

He had a momentary picture of Jackson, poised at his gun. The sandy-haired American would be grinning; not because he was amused but because he always grinned at times of stress. Along with half a dozen others still in the *Calypso*, Jackson had served with Ramage since before he had been given his first command, here in the Mediterranean; he had been one of the men – the most important man – helping in the rescue of Gianna from that beach at Capalbio. Gianna had come to regard him as a favourite retainer. And Jackson? Ramage had the feeling that he thought of her as a wayward niece.

Now the gun captains would be waiting for that black blur to pass twenty yards off a gunport; a black blur which gave them the signal to tug the lanyard to send the gun coughing back in recoil.

No, the Frenchman had not altered course. He was just about hard on the wind, thanks to a bend in the coast, and could do nothing to prevent the *Calypso* keeping up to windward.

As the *Calypso*'s first gun roared out Ramage saw a spurt of smoke come from the muzzle of the first French gun. A moment later, as Southwick and Aitken gripped the rail at the fore end of the quarterdeck, there was a confused roar made up of the coughing of the *Calypso*'s broadside and the lighter thudding of the French broadside. The sound of ripping calico warned of French roundshot passing overhead.

As though a flash of lightning on a dark night had lit up the scene for a moment, Ramage had a medley of impressions: the French frigate's black hull was stained with salt; the luff of the flying jib was wrinkled; there were at least two rusty holes amidships showing where roundshot had penetrated, and there were several more further aft, showing that several of the *Calypso*'s gunners had taken a few moments to react to the rapidly passing target. The Tricolour was streaming out; the sails were even more patched than he thought from his view through the telescope. The small group of officers on the quarterdeck had crouched down as the *Calypso* passed.

And then he was yelling at Aitken while watching the passing enemy: "Come about! Don't let him get away!"

The last gun of the *Calypso*'s broadside had hardly fired before topsails were slatting as the frigate tacked. Ramage realized that the enemy had the advantage in speed because she had all plain sail set; but she would be more difficult to handle with all that canvas. As the *Calypso* swung round to starboard, Ramage looked over the quarter at the enemy just in time to see her beginning to clew up her courses. So she was going to fight under t'gallants and topsails. Ramage was sure the French would soon furl the t'gallants; they were not handy sails for fighting – but furling them took topmen away from the guns . . .

The *Calypso* quickly turned and Ramage saw an opportunity. "Steer across his stern," he ordered Aitken. "We'll give him a raking broadside, even though at long range."

The *Calypso* seems to be spending most of the day raking French frigates, Ramage thought, although this time it would be at a range of a couple of hundred yards, instead of twenty.

As soon as the ship came round on to the other tack and Aitken had braces and sheets trimmed, Ramage watched the departing enemy frigate closely and gave helm orders which would make the *Calypso* pass across the enemy frigate's stern at an oblique angle, so that she had plenty of room to wear again to avoid running aground.

Now the Frenchman had his courses clewed up – and yes, he was furling his t'gallants: at least he was getting down to topsails, the usual rig for fighting. And it meant that he was slowing down, reducing the range for the *Calypso*'s raking broadside.

By now the first of the *Calypso*'s larboard broadside was firing again, the gunners hastily adjusting the quoin for the increased range. Ramage found himself counting with the slower rate of fire. He took up his telescope and trained it on the Frenchman's stern, and was just in time to see a spark as a roundshot hit a piece of metalwork, probably a fitting on the rudderhead. As his count

52

reached sixteen Ramage realized that the French frigate – he had just read the name on the transom as *Le Jason* – was bearing away and was going to cross ahead of the *Calypso*.

"She's going to rake *us*," growled Southwick.

"And there's nothing we can do to stop her," Ramage said quietly.

Nor was there. The *Calypso* was committed to wearing to get away from the shore, which was fast approaching, and the Frenchman would pass across her bow firing a raking broadside into her. Ramage thought of the ship of the line they had encountered earlier in the day: please, no damage to the jibboom and bowsprit!

The quicker the *Calypso* wore, the less time her vulnerable bow would be exposed to the Frenchman's broadside. Ramage listened to the slamming of the sails and hoped the gunners were hard at work reloading.

And then *Le Jason* was crossing the *Calypso*'s bow, wreathed in smoke, her whole side a line of winking red eyes as her guns fired. Ramage heard a crash aloft and glanced up to see a wild shot had smashed six feet off the end of the foretopgallant yard. The calico ripping noise of a dozen more roundshot passing overhead showed him the French gunners had not yet settled down.

There were four or five shotholes in the topsails: nothing that needed repairing. And the jibboom and bowsprit were still standing, with no damage apparent from where Ramage stood.

"We've been lucky," he commented to Aitken, and a moment later saw he could turn the tables on the Frenchman.

"Luff up and we can rake his stern as he goes past."

He looked round for Orsini. "Warn the gunners that they'll be able to rake the Frenchman on the starboard side!"

By now the Frenchman was heading north-west, steering for the shore and obviously about to tack or wear. The *Calypso* bore up slightly and *Le Jason*'s stern came round on to her starboard beam. Sounding like a huge drum being beaten irregularly, the *Calypso*'s guns started firing, and once again Ramage saw sparks as round-shot glanced off metal. And the sternlights were now an irregular shape: instead of being rectangles enclosing the glass, they were ragged shapes, chewed at by roundshot.

Would it work? "Wear round," he shouted to Aitken, "we'll rake him again!"

The Frenchman seemed to be manoeuvring very slowly; after raking the *Calypso*, Ramage expected *Le Jason* to tack or wear to get offshore again, but she was staying on the same course, north-west, as though careless of the risk of going up the beach.

Then Ramage stared hard through his telescope. *Le Jason* was leaving no wake: she was stopped in the water! And he noticed that her rudder was hard over.

"She's aground, by God!" exclaimed Southwick just as Ramage was about to speak.

"We must have damaged her rudder with that raking broadside," Ramage said.

"How close in can we go?" Southwick growled, reaching for the chart.

"Close enough to rake her again,' Ramage said grimly. "And again and again. It probably won't take them long to repair that rudder."

Aitken gave orders to the quartermaster and the *Calypso* came round a few degrees. Ramage looked round for Orsini and sent him off to warn the gunners to expect to rake the enemy with the starboard broadside.

Ramage saw a red winking at the transom and realized that *Le Jason* had got a sternchase gun in action. Almost immediately there was a crash aloft and the *Calypso*'s foretopgallant mast crashed down, hanging by rigging, the yard swinging like a pendulum.

"Go and sort that out," Ramage ordered Aitken. "I'll take over the conn."

Of all the damnable luck: at least, damnable for the *Calypso* and almost beyond belief for *Le Jason*. That a single shot from a sternchase gun should bring down the *Calypso*'s foretopgallant mast was an almost unbelievable piece of good fortune for the French.

But it did not make the *Calypso* unmanageable. By now she had worn round and Ramage was giving the quartermaster careful orders which would bring the frigate into a good firing position.

Another red wink and puff of smoke at *Le Jason*'s stern showed the French had managed to get a second sternchase gun into action, and Ramage found himself admiring their coolness; they were in a lot of trouble, but they still had the will to fight back.

Ramage heard nothing of the shot and assumed it must have missed. At that moment Orsini appeared in front of him. "A message from Mr Bowen, sir."

What had the surgeon to say at a time like this? "Well?"

"He said six men dead and five wounded, two seriously, from two roundshot and splinters, sir."

Ramage was dumbfounded: he had not heard or felt shot hitting the ship and knew nothing of casualties.

"Very well. Does Mr Bowen need help?"

"No, sir, I asked him. He has a couple of loblolly men and three seamen to help him, and that's enough."

Six men dead . . . And he had not realized that the ship had been hit. Yet when he thought about it, it was obvious that some shot from *Le Jason*'s broadsides would have struck home. Fighting at these ranges meant casualties. He wondered how many Frenchmen had been killed.

Two points to starboard and trim the yards and sheets. That should bring them across *Le Jason*'s transom. How was the Frenchman going to get off? He had run ashore at an oblique angle; there was just a chance that if he ran all his guns over to the larboard side, hardened in the sheets on the starboard tack and prayed for a strong gust of wind, then he might just come clear. But Ramage realized that would not help: the Frenchman probably had no rudder, or at least not one that functioned, and without that the wind would just blow him harder aground. Was he actually aground on the beach, or an offlying shoal? It was hard to tell from this angle.

Ramage decided that a hundred yards was as close as he was going to approach; there might be a spit of land or a spur of the shoal stretching well out, and having the *Calypso* going aground on the same bit of shoal would be a piece of irony he could do without.

"Do you need me here, sir?" Southwick asked. "Otherwise I'll go and give a hand clearing up that mast."

"No, I can manage," Ramage said. "The sooner we get that wreckage down on deck the better. It'll be ripping the topsail any minute."

The two pieces of the mast, along with the yard, were swinging like pendulums on pieces of rigging and halyards, and each time the ship rolled or there was a stronger than usual puff of wind, they slammed into the side of the topsail. Ramage could not understand why the splintered ends of the broken mast had not yet torn the canvas. Yes, he could order the topmen to furl the topsail, but the *Calypso* would be hard to handle with only the maintopsail, and anyway Aitken needed the topmen to secure the wreckage.

Two hundred yards to go. Two hundred yards to sail and he had to make sure the *Calypso* passed about a hundred yards off the Frenchman's stern. The square on the hypotenuse – no, that did not apply because the hypotenuse was on the other side. Well, there was some mathematical formula to cover the situation, but he was damned if he knew it.

"You're sure Mr Bowen didn't need help?" he asked Orsini.

"No sir," Paolo said firmly. "There are only five wounded and he has them bandaged up. It was a shot from the first broadside," he added, to show Ramage that Bowen had plenty of time.

Once again Ramage stared over the starboard bow. They were approaching *Le Jason* fast now and Ramage imagined the French gunners hurriedly reloading the sternchasers. They would be under no illusion: they would know that within a matter of minutes they would get up the full raking broadside from the *Calypso* and the quarterdeck would be swept with shot. But – there, again a red wink and spurt of smoke as they opened fire at what must be the extreme traverse of the gun. Again Ramage did not hear the shot: perhaps it hit the hull well forward.

Five hundred yards . . . four hundred . . . three hundred . . . The *Calypso*'s gunners would sight her out of the corner of the ports. Two hundred yards, and a hundred: gun captains would be taking up the strain on the lanyards and the second captains would have cocked the locks and jumped clear. Fifty yards and he could see the lettering on *Le Jason*'s transom. The other sternchase fired and Ramage felt rather than heard a thud as its shot hit the *Calypso*'s hull.

The leading gun in the *Calypso*'s starboard broadside coughed and Ramage saw a spurt of smoke. Then the second gun, and the third. He picked up the telescope and trained it on *Le Jason*'s stern. Yes, there was a cloud of dust, so at least one shot had ploughed through the planking on the transom. Yes, another puff of dust as another shot smashed through. Suddenly he saw a black shape rear into the air above the taffrail and realized that a roundshot had dismounted one of the sternchase guns.

One by one the *Calypso*'s guns fired. A shot sent up a spurt of water twenty yards short of the French frigate: one of the gun captains had fired on the downward roll so that his shot fell short. It was an easy mistake to make: a matter of a second late in tugging the lanyard.

And that was the last gun. Ramage saw the spurt of dust it caused as it hit the corner of one of the sternlights. Now the guns crews would be hard at work sponging and ramming – worming too, by now, in case a piece of burning cartridge was left in the bore and likely to explode the next cartridge prematurely.

Suddenly Orsini was gesticulating at the French frigate and Ramage glanced across in time to see her courses being let fall. He snatched up the telescope and saw the yards being braced round and the sheets trimmed so that as soon as the huge sails tumbled down they filled and bellied out. A moment later the fore and main topgallants were let fall and as soon as the halyards had hoisted them the yards were braced and the sails trimmed.

What on earth was going on? As far as a puzzled Ramage could see, setting the sails would only drive *Le Jason* further up the beach. But the French captain must have a very good reason. And a moment later he saw what it was.

The frigate began to move slowly, and as soon as she had way on her yards were braced sharp up and she began to claw offshore.

At that moment Southwick hurried up the ladder, red-faced and breathless. "You've seen, sir? The dam' fellow wasn't ashore after all!"

Ramage shook his head. "No, he must have been caught on a spur of rock, And his rudder wasn't damaged after all: they must have had it hard over to try and get off."

"I hope the rock stove in a plank or two," Southwick growled.

Ramage realized he had a chance to rake the Frenchman's bow as he clawed off the shore and gave new orders to the quarter-master. It meant altering course only a point or two and the *Calypso* would pass fifty yards or so ahead of *Le Jason* before her captain had got his ship squared away properly for the beat to windward that would get him clear of the coast.

He shouted orders through the speaking trumpet to get yards

braced and sheets trimmed, and then he bellowed down to the gunners to get ready for a target to larboard.

So an easy time passing up and down raking a stranded French frigate was turning back to be a battle of broadsides: Ramage thought of the six men killed already. What would be the butcher's bill before the sun went down? In all the actions he had fought up to now, in the Mediterranean and the West Indies, he had never suffered heavy casualties. Was his luck going to run out today? He had already had one lucky escape: if that ship of the line had pinned the *Calypso* across her bows, she would have sent across a boarding party which would have slaughtered most of the ship's company. Was this damned frigate going to do a lot of damage through lucky shots, like the one that had brought down the mast?

Ramage snapped out another order to the quartermaster and then asked Southwick: "What about that damage forward?"

"They'll have the wreckage lowered in a few minutes, sir; there's no chance of damage to the topsail now."

"I hope it won't take too long; I want those men back at the guns."

"Mr Aitken has it under control, sir," Southwick said soothingly. "I say, are we going to rake that fellow again?"

"We're getting into the habit," Ramage said lightly. "Not that it seems to be doing him much harm."

"We've smashed in his sternlights!" Southwick said.

"Yes, but it's his jibboom and bowsprit we want to smash. Right at the moment we're doing as much damage as a crowd of mice."

By now *Le Jason* was plunging her way seaward, the waves from the shallower water slapping into her bow and sending up small sheets of spray which darkened the foot of her forecourse. She was beginning to pitch slightly and her Tricolour streamed out aft like a board.

As the *Calypso* sailed northwards to pass across *Le Jason*'s bow with fifty yards to spare, she too began to knock up the spray, her starboard bow shouldering into the waves, sending the sea drifting aft over the deck like heavy rain. Ramage could taste the saltiness on his lips and noted that the wind was increasing, though the sky apart from a few scurrying clouds was clear and the usual bright blue that was special to this corner of the Tuscan coast.

Raking broadsides: he doubted if he had fired as many in his whole life as he had fired against *Le Tigre* and *Le Jason*. But as far as *Le Jason*'s fighting ability was concerned – apart from the dismounted sternchase gun – he might as well be bombarding her with snowballs.

Well, in a couple of minutes he would have his next chance: with a bit of luck this broadside would really damage her bow. Even bring the foremast toppling down? He shrugged: one could only hope.

A gust of wind caught the *Calypso* and she surged forward, her bow wave hissing down her sides. The masts and yards creaked, acknowledging the gust rather than protesting at it.

"Orsini – whip round and tell the gunners they've two minutes!"

Ramage was sure that giving the gunners a warning when he could was increasing their accuracy: he had noticed that the broadsides had been fired with a comforting regularity, rather than three guns going off at once. The regular fire meant that the gun captains were firing when the enemy was precisely in their sights, rather than jerking the lanyards hopefully.

He looked across the larboard bow at the French frigate. One minute to go – and Orsini should have got to all the gunners by now. Half a minute – and he could begin to make out details of the Frenchman's rigging and patched sails. She had a figurehead but they had not bothered to paint it; the old paint was faded and peeling. Was that as a result of the Revolution, that seamen no longer bothered about things like figureheads? In the King's ships they were prized and regularly painted, and many of them were covered with canvas in rough weather to protect them.

Then the *Calypso*'s first gun fired with a satisfying cough. The smoke would bother Aitken's working party, but they would have to cough and bear it: the faster they cleared away the wreckage the sooner they would be out of the smoke. They would not, of course, because most of them belonged to the guns, and as soon as they finished they would return to the guns – and the smoke.

The guns settled down to firing regularly and once again the smoke streamed aft up to the quarterdeck. Ramage watched the French frigate's bow with the telescope but could not spot any hits. Two shots fell short, sending up tall spouts of water, but there seemed to be no damage to the jibboom or bowsprit.

Southwick, also watching with a glass, gave a disgusted sniff. "Don't know what's happened to our gunners," he said disgustedly. "If they can knock us about with a sternchaser, we ought to do better with a raking broadside."

By now the *Calypso* had passed across *Le Jason*'s bow and Ramage gave orders for her to go about, so that on the starboard tack she would range up alongside the French ship, exchanging broadside for broadside.

As the *Calypso* swung round on to a parallel course and while the gun crews prepared the starboard broadside, Ramage wondered whether to let fall the maintopgallant.

As if the French captain read his thoughts, he saw *Le Jason* begin to clew up her courses and, a minute or two later, start furling her topgallants, so that – now she was afloat again – she was back in a fighting trim of topsails only, matching the *Calypso*.

Once again Orsini was sent round the gundeck with the orders that they should fire as soon as their guns bore, and Orsini had not returned to the quarterdeck before the first gun fired.

The range was about a hundred yards and Ramage decided to halve it, giving an order to the quartermaster to ease over to starboard half a point. The last few guns of the broadside had just finished firing when *Le Jason* opened fire, the usual red winking eyes passing down her side. Ramage heard an occasional thud as one of the French ship's roundshot landed but there were no screams of wounded men and no reports of damage.

Aitken came up to the quarterdeck to report that the wreckage of the foretopgallant mast had been cleared away, along with the remains of the yard.

"We have a spare mast, and a topgallant yard, and the carpenter says that anyway he can fish the damaged yard, sir," he said. "The sail has only one tear in it, about eight feet long, so it won't take long to patch that."

Ramage nodded. They had been lucky: if the shot had landed a few feet lower, it might have been the foretopmast, bringing down the topsail.

For the next ten minutes the two frigates sailed almost alongside each other, exchanging broadsides, but without either ship showing much damage. Five more of the *Calypso*'s men were killed by roundshot or cut down by splinters and number nine gun was dismounted by a random shot which came through the port and smashed into the carriage without hurting any of the men.

With the glass Ramage could see that the *Calypso*'s gunners were firing reasonably accurately: the French frigate's side was now pockmarked with rusty marks showing where roundshot had punched their way through the hull. But she still kept up a regular rate of fire, replying broadside for broadside, aiming for the *Calypso*'s hull, instead of following the usual French habit of firing at the rigging in the hope of dismasting the enemy.

They had been sailing alongside each other at a range of forty or fifty yards when Ramage commented to Aitken: "We seem to be drawing ahead of her."

"I had that impression, too, sir. Yet she has the same sails set and they are properly trimmed."

Ramage examined the frigate through the glass. Yes, there were a few more shot holes but she was still firing as fast, with smoke streaming out of her ports. Then he noticed a thin stream of water pouring over her side.

"She's got her pump going," he commented. "An odd time to be pumping the bilges."

Then he could see with the naked eye that the stream of water was getting larger: the pump must be working harder.

The water was clear, not stained, so it was not just a question of pumping the bilges to get the last few tons of water out of the ship to increase her speed. Had a lucky shot stove in some butts of fresh water? No, there was more water being pumped out than could be accounted for by that.

Again and again the *Calypso*'s broadsides coughed out. Ramage thought of crashing alongside the ship and boarding her, an idea he later dismissed when he thought of the casualties.

Then Paolo Orsini said respectfully: "Sir, she seems to be a little deeper in the water."

And she was: as soon as Ramage inspected the French ship carefully, he could distinguish that she was throwing up a bigger bow wave and the pump dale was emptying as much water over the side as the pump could handle.

"She's got a bad leak," Southwick said happily. "But it's not from one of our shotholes, I'll be bound. She's not been rolling enough for any hits 'twixt' wind and water to cause her much trouble."

Ramage saw movement up in the bow and looked with his telescope, startled to see a group of men round the anchors. Suddenly an anchor dropped from the cathead and was then cut adrift so that it fell into the sea.

"Look at that!" Southwick bellowed, pointing astern, where a boat was bobbing half submerged in *Le Jason*'s wake. "And there's another!" he exclaimed. "My oath, they're cutting their boats adrift."

"And their anchors," Ramage said. "They're trying to save weight!"

At that moment he caught Aitken's eye and both men nodded.

"She stove in a plank or two when she went aground: probably stranded on a rock and strained herself when they sailed her off," Ramage said.

Southwick groaned and Ramage stared at him.

"I was thinking of rescuing all those Frenchmen," the master explained. "They'll probably outnumber us!"

"And all the men in the other frigate," Aitken said. "We'll have five hundred prisoners!"

"Steady on," Ramage said. "We haven't captured either ship yet and this fellow is showing no sign of surrendering."

"Well, we don't want to board her unless we want wet feet," Southwick growled.

"No, we'll just hold off as we are and watch her sink."

And a few thousand pounds in prize money will vanish before our eyes, Ramage thought. There will be head money for the prisoners – but what a risk, to saddle the ship with so many survivors. But there was no question of leaving them to drown: the captain was cutting away the boats and anchors, and presumably the spare yards, masts and booms would be next to go.

Obviously he would have started all the fresh water, stoving in the casks so that the water ran into the bilge and could be pumped out. That would save him – well, if he was halfway through his cruise, about twenty-five tons.

"We haven't finished with her yet," Ramage reminded the two men. "As far as I can see, every one of her guns on this side is still firing . . ."

Ramage tried to put himself in the place of the French captain. A bad leak, every spare man at the pump, cranking the handles round as fast as possible to keep a steady stream of water pouring into the pump dale and over the side. But men could only pump for a certain amount of time before becoming exhausted, and it was obvious since the ship was becoming lower in the water and the captain was getting rid of all the extra weight he could, that the leak was gaining on him: more water was leaking in than the pump could deal with. So it reduced itself to an interesting problem of time: just when would the captain decide that the battle with the leak was irretrievably lost, and surrender his ship? Or perhaps he was one of those fanatical captains who would fight on, letting the ship sink under him. Or he might have the sense to turn the frigate round and run her ashore properly, stranding her so that he could save his crew but knowing the British could never refloat his ship. Strand her and set her on fire after the ship's company had scrambled to safety.

Well, the way *Le Jason* was ploughing on eastward, keeping up a high rate of fire from her broadside guns, obviously her captain was not going to give in easily.

He beckoned to Orsini. "Go down and see Mr Bowen: ask how many casualties we have up to now."

"We're taking quite a few hits," Southwick said.

"At least they're not doing their usual dismantling shot trick," Aitken commented.

Coincidentally, at that moment the carpenter came up to report to Ramage: "Just sounded the well again, sir," he said. "We're not making any water."

Ramage nodded. "Very well; carry on, sound every ten minutes and report to me."

"We're rolling just enough to get an unlucky one 'twixt wind and water," Southwick said. "So's he," he added, pointing at the French frigate, "but he's getting sluggish: not rolling nearly as much now."

"Makes her a steadier platform for the gunners." Aitken commented.

"Aye, but wait until the water floods her hanging magazine," Southwick said. "No one's yet found a way of making wet cartridges fire roundshot!"

The *Calypso*'s broadside sounded ragged now, not because the gunners were failing to do their jobs properly but every gun was reloaded at a slightly different speed, and now they had their target broad on the beam the guns' crews were loading as fast as they could, and as soon as the second captain cocked the lock and jumped clear the gun captain was tugging his lanyard.

Jackson, his face becoming blackened with smoke, was grinning with pleasure and urging his crew on to load faster. Rossi was bellowing out a string of Italian oaths but apparently because of happiness at being in action. The four Frenchmen were hurrying about their tasks, sponging, ramming and worming as though they had never done anything else. Stafford crouched over the lock every now and again to make sure that the flint still had a sharp edge and was delivering a good strong spark.

"You're not hitting her, Jacko!" he bawled amid the thunder of the other guns firing to the left and right.

"I dam' well am," Jackson shouted back. "She just won't sink!"

"Her pump's going," Rossi called. "Maybe you had a lucky shot!"

One more thump with the rammer and they sprang to the tackle and ran the gun out. Stafford stabbed down with his pricker and then pushed a fresh quill into the vent, shaking a small amount of priming powder into the pan. Then he snapped back the cock of the flintlock, and lifting his hand up as a signal to Jackson, jumped clear.

Jackson sighted along the barrel and waited as the *Calypso* rolled slightly. He tugged the lanyard on a downward roll a fraction of a second before the French frigate appeared in the crude sight and once again the gun sprang back with a bronchitic cough and a spurt of flame and smoke at the muzzle.

At once the crew again sprang into action. The soaking sponge was thrust down the bore and a powder monkey ran forward with a cartridge which Gilbert snatched up and slid into the muzzle. With the rammer poised Auguste lunged forward and thrust the cartridge down the muzzle and gave an extra hard thrust before withdrawing it and standing aside for a moment to let Albert put in the wad, which he thrust home and then stood back with the rammer as Louis came up, cradling a roundshot, which he rammed home, followed by another wad which Albert had ready.

Dropping the rammer, Auguste helped run the gun out and Stafford went into action again with his pricker. As Jackson prepared to sight along the barrel he saw the black shape of the French frigate through the port. Yes, her pump was going, and the wind was whipping away the water as it sluiced over the side from the pump dale.

Back on the quarterdeck Orsini came hurrying up the ladder. He saluted Ramage and reported: "Mr Bowen's compliments sir: ten dead and eleven wounded, three very seriously. He says there may be more dead that he doesn't know about."

"Yes," Ramage said, talking to himself, "they'll just drag bodies clear and leave them in the scuppers . . ."

Twenty-one dead and wounded, and the damned Frenchman seemed to be unscathed by the *Calypso*'s guns. Admittedly they were firing into her hull and it was impossible to see what damage they were doing: they might be cutting men down in swathes, for all he knew, but it was not affecting the French ship's rate of fire, even though she was apparently slowly – very slowly, curse it – sinking under them.

A lucky dismasting shot might let the Frenchman escape yet.

He looked at the Frenchman again with his telescope. Still the same group of officers on her quarterdeck. He swung the glass forward and trained it on the pump dale. Yes, it was still pouring out water, and the wind was whipping it away. He looked at the frigate's waterline. Yes! It was definitely a little lower. He waited a minute to make sure it was not the rolling, but then he was sure: he could no longer see the copper sheathing. That had been carried a good foot above the waterline, and now he could not see it despite the roll. So *Le Jason* was at least two and probably three feet lower in the water. What did that mean in terms of tons of water sloshing around below? Without knowing her tons per inch immersion – the number of tons needed to immerse her hull one inch – it was hard to tell, and he knew his own weakness in doing mental arithmetic. But it was scores of tons. The water was coming in faster than the pump could get rid of it, and that was all that mattered. Nearly all, anyway. If only he knew how much faster . . .

Options: he must consider them carefully. Yes, the Frenchman could turn back and make a run for the shore, planning to beach the frigate before she sank. Or he could carry on firing until the ship sank under him – it would take a brave man to do that after having cut all his boats adrift, and it would mean throwing his ship's company on the mercy of the British. And, Ramage thought, what were his own choices? Well, he could carry on as he was now and wait for the Frenchman either to turn for the shore or sink. Or he could haul off out of range and wait for the Frenchman to sink, even if he did not bolt for the shore. That way he would save his men.

But supposing the Frenchman managed to stop the leak? Supposing he managed to stop the water entering and pump out what was already in? Then, setting courses and topgallants (and royals too) she could make a bolt for it. If she escaped, he would look foolish. And he would get his knuckles rapped by the Admiralty.

No, there was no question of standing off, and unless the Frenchman turned for the shore, then this present battle of broadsides would have to go on, while the French pumped their way to windward.

While Ramage was watching the water pouring over the side from the pump dale he noticed a dozen seamen swarming up the forward shrouds. As he looked they worked their way out along the footropes of the topsail and within moments had started to furl it.

Furl the topsail? Leave only the maintopsail set? That would just above halve the Frenchman's speed. Why? There could be only one explanation – by slowing down the ship the French captain was hoping to cut down the rush of water through the leak. That must mean he had no hope of overtaking it with the pump without drastic measures.

Ramage told Aitken to furl the *Calypso*'s foretopsail, so that they could conform with the Frenchman's speed. The alternative would be to weave across *Le Jason*'s stern and fire raking broadsides. Was it worth it? The damned ship would sink anyway, and soon her rate of fire would begin to slacken as men were taken away from the guns to replace those exhausted at the pumps.

"Hard pounding," Southwick commented.

"Yes, but we don't have much choice. If we haul off and she stops the leak and gets away . . ."

"Aye," said Southwick. "But she must be leaking badly if they have to slow down."

"She must have been making seven or eight knots when she went aground. If it was a sharp rock it could have stove in several planks, or started some butts."

Ramage watched *Le Jason*'s side as another of the *Calypso*'s broadsides coughed out, and saw several rusty marks appear on her hull. Well, his gunners were shooting accurately and with luck some of the shots were hitting 'twixt wind and water, increasing the flooding.

Ramage found himself almost sympathetic with the French captain; he had cut the quarterboats adrift and hoisted out the boom boats and dropped them over the side, so there were no boats for survivors: they would be left clinging to wreckage.

Taking some 250 survivors on board: one Frenchman for each member of the *Calypso*'s crew. It was a daunting prospect: if the French were well led – and there was no reason to doubt that they were – they might try to take the ship.

"If we have to pick up survivors," Ramage told Aitken and Southwick, "we put them below and then clap the gratings across the fore and maindeck hatch. Have them guarded by all the Marines and covered with a couple of guns loaded with caseshot, and then we'll land them on Capraia as soon as possible: I'm not risking having that number of the enemy on board a moment longer than necessary."

"It's a big enough risk that we'd be justified in leaving them to drown," Southwick said. "Ducking them in sea water isn't going to turn them into lambs."

"If it was us, we'd feel a bit hard done by if the French left us to drown," Ramage said.

"But we'd try to take their ship," Southwick pointed out.

Ramage shrugged his shoulders. "A hundred muskets and pistols aimed at them, and a couple of guns loaded with case, might put them off their stroke."

"Well, we'll need to bring them on board a few at a time, and make sure that we never have more than a couple of dozen on deck at a time," Southwick said grudgingly.

"Of course," Ramage said. "Don't forget they'll be a bit shaken up by the time we fish them out."

"The frigate hasn't sunk yet," Aitken pointed out. "Here comes another broadside," he added, gesturing to the rippling spurts of flame and smoke along *Le Jason*'s side.

Aitken stared at the frigate. "She's definitely lower in the water now," he said. "She's gone down several inches since they furled the topsail."

Ramage examined the hull with the telescope. Yes, Aitken was right: the distance between the lower edge of the gunports and the waterline was less. And yes, the ship was beginning to wallow now. Ramage could imagine the great quantity of water surging round below, weight which transferred from one side to the other, and from forward to aft, with terrifying speed. Like swirling water in the bottom of a bucket. It would be a tremendous surge of water to one side which would eventually capsize her.

The problem of guarding survivors stepped several paces closer.

Five minutes and several broadsides later, Ramage happened to be watching *Le Jason* when he realized that she was now regularly rolling with a slow, almost inexorable movement: her masts were like upside-down pendulums and her gunners were slowing down their broadsides because they had to wait longer until their guns would bear.

Southwick, too, noticed the roll. "The leak is beating the pump," he commented.

"It's been doing that for some time," Aitken said. "Every man except those in the guns' crews must be working the pump."

Ramage pictured exhausted men hauling round the cranked handle of the pump. There was enough water floating around now to pick up things and block the pump, so that men would be constantly freeing the strainer. Round and round would go the crank, but the pump would never suck dry. The noise of the bilge pump sucking dry was, Ramage reflected, one of the most satisfying heard in a ship. It was one the French were doomed never to hear again – in that ship, anyway.

Yes, the rolling was getting wilder; it was lasting longer as the ship heeled first to larboard and then slowly came over to starboard as tons of water swirled from one side of the ship to the other. The rush of water would, he realized, be enough to knock men off their feet; it would hinder men as they ran out or ran in guns. Soon the water must flood the hanging magazine. Even now, he guessed, the French were getting out cartridges and stowing them high enough to be out of danger from the surging water. But having so many cartridges out of the magazine always risked a flash from one of the guns, or an unlucky shot from the British. Then there would be a tremendous explosion, and the French would no longer be worrying about a leak . . .

Ramage was looking round the horizon with his telescope when Aitken said laconically: "Their pump has stopped."

Ramage swung round with his telescope. There was no more water streaming out of the pump dale and pouring over the side. The pump must have blocked, or the cranked handle jammed.

For a moment Ramage imagined himself in the French captain's position: now would be the time of black despair. Water would still be pouring in through the leak, and now he could only get the men bailing with buckets – a hopeless job if the pump was being overwhelmed.

The rolling was getting worse: or, Ramage corrected himself, getting better. The French rate of fire was being badly affected: for longer and longer periods the guns were either pointing too high or too low to be fired. Even better, from the British point of view, the heavy roll was exposing the underwater hull so that roundshot could smash through copper sheathing and make more holes in the hull to increase the leaks.

"Ah – there goes the pump again!" Aitken called as he caught sight of a small stream of water starting to run over the side again. "Not the full flow. Must be a blockage – or maybe it's been damaged by one of our shot."

Ramage watched as *Le Jason* slowly rolled to larboard again, checked and then slowly began to roll back to starboard. Then he saw men gathering at the foot of the main shrouds.

"They're going to furl the maintopsail," he said to Aitken. "They want to try to reduce the rolling. Stand by to heave-to."

At that moment the *Calypso* fired another broadside, and the group of men scattered, many of them vanishing below the bulwarks as roundshot cut them down.

But the French frigate continued her rolling: the movement was getting massive and wild now; her masts were slicing great arcs through the sky and, Ramage realized, it would be only a matter of time before the gunports dipped into the water.

Prisoners – or survivors, call them what you will: more than two hundred of them. No, he was not going to risk having them on board all the way to Naples: in fact with the island of Capraia just astern that was as far as he would take them. They would be prisoners on the island – unless they set to and made rafts – and they would be no danger to anyone, though they would run the local people short of food.

The French captain seemed to have given up trying to lighten the ship – he could still cut yards adrift, and he had not thrown all the booms and gratings over the side yet – but Ramage knew he must have given up: a hole in the hull which let in a leak which overcame the pump was the ultimate; apart from fire, it was the end.

With the freshening wind driving the frigate ahead, the rolling caused by the leak was giving her a curious corkscrew motion through the water, as though she was reluctant to move. Ramage watched as she rolled heavily towards him, paused for several agonizing seconds well heeled over, and then slowly rolled back again, to pause before returning.

"She hasn't got much more time," Southwick commented.

"Neither have we," Ramage said. "I've changed my mind: we'll put the survivors up on the fo'c'sle. I want a couple of the aftermost guns on each side trained round on to the fo'c'sle and loaded with case. And pass the word for Rennick."

The master trotted off down the ladder, his long white hair flowing in the breeze, to arrange to have the guns slewed round and their tackles made up again. A couple of minutes later Rennick was standing in front of him, waiting for orders.

"The survivors, when we pick them up," Ramage said.

Rennick made a face. "There'll be plenty of them, sir."

"I know," Ramage said. "They might even outnumber us. But I'm going to put them on the fo'c'sle with four guns trained on them, and I want all your Marines covering them but keeping out of the way of the guns. They'll escort them from wherever they're brought on board up to the fo'c'sle. Any nonsense, they're to shoot to kill."

"After they've swum around a bit, the French might have any wrong ideas washed out of them, sir," Rennick said with a grin.

"I'm hoping so. But the point of keeping them up on the fo'c'sle is that I'm going to take them back to Capraia and dump them

70

there. They'll only be on the fo'c'sle a couple of hours, and if they give any trouble a few whiffs of caseshot should quieten them down."

"Very well, sir," Rennick said and saluted before hurrying down the quarterdeck ladder.

Le Jason was lurching rather than rolling now: as Ramage watched the stricken ship he could imagine the hundreds of tons of water sloshing from one side and then to the other, each time the weight heeling the ship and throwing men off their feet.

"Her rate of fire is slowing down, sir," Aitken said. "The water has probably flooded her magazine, apart from the difficulty of laying the guns."

"She hasn't much time left."

"I wonder why the Frenchman hasn't hauled down his colours."

"It doesn't make much difference whether he surrenders or not," Ramage said sourly. "He's going to sink whether or not he's hauled down his colours. Anyway, he's fought well. It was his navigation that put him on that rock: but for that I think we'd have had an even tougher fight."

The more he thought about it, the more Ramage was convinced that his gunners were only wasting powder: they could not damage the enemy more effectively than she was already, and it was time for the guns' crews to get muskets and pikes, pistols and tomahawks ready for the influx of French survivors.

He gave the order to Aitken which would silence the guns for the first time since they had opened fire on the first frigate, and which would send the men to get the weapons allocated to them in the quarters bill. Most of the men had a note against their name indicating what weapons they were to have, and whether they were boarders if the *Calypso* should board another ship.

A sudden hush fell over the *Calypso* as the guns stopped firing and all that Ramage could hear was the rush of the sea against the hull and the occasional slatting of a sail. He realized that he was deafened by the broadsides and he held his nose and blew hard, but it made no difference.

Southwick hurried back to the quarterdeck. "Those guns are trained round, sir," he said. "We can't get the tackles hooked on to anything substantial, so there's no telling how they'll recoil. Still, only have to fire them once, I expect," he said complacently.

71

"Probably not even once," Ramage said. "We'll point them out to the French officers: that should do the trick."

Even as he spoke he watched the French frigate heel right over until her deck on the larboard side was in the water. She seemed to stay there for an age, and then, as though tired of the struggle, she very slowly capsized: the masts came down below horizontal, the yards slewing round, and the trucks of the masts dipped into the sea and then began to sink as the ship continued turning.

She turned very slowly, great bubbles of air bursting out through the hatchways and ports. Ramage saw the Tricolour dip into the water and then there were splashes as guns broke loose and dropped through the ship's side.

"Furl the maintopsail," Ramage snapped at Aitken, and to Southwick he said: "Get the boats hauled round ready."

From a distance of fifty yards Ramage found the sight of the frigate sinking both sad and, in another sense, a relief. It was sad because the sinking of any handsome ship – and *Le Jason* was a handsome ship – was always distressing, and yet a relief because her guns could not kill or wound any more men of the *Calypso*.

While the boats were being hauled round alongside, Southwick was shouting orders for the boats' crews to stand by, and while the men left the guns and ran to their stations, Ramage watched *Le Jason*. She had turned over completely and was lying in the water like a great turtle. Her copper sheathing was green except near the waterline, where it was pitted, restored to its normal colour by shots which had torn into it 'twixt wind and water.

Great gouts of air escaped as the capsized hull rolled; then it gave a gigantic convulsion as though shaking itself free of something, and Ramage guessed that the masts had come adrift. A minute or two later he saw first one and then another mast break water close beside the hull, a tangle of spars and rigging, and now freed of their weight the hull began to slide below the surface, water erupting in little volcanoes, propelled by random air pockets.

The surface of the sea was scattered with floating wreckage. Here and there he could see men, random black figures, clinging to spars.

Now all that was left was a great circle of smooth water, punctuated every now and again by a bubble of air coming up from the sinking ship. More pieces of wreckage, spars and other pieces of wood breaking loose came up to the surface, shooting out of the water like lances with the force of their buoyancy.

By now Aitken had the *Calypso* lying-to, and Ramage told him: "Get the boats away and start picking up survivors. Two Marines in every boat as guards."

Within five minutes the *Calypso*'s four boats were rowing round, through the wreckage, dragging men out of the water and, with little ceremony, tossing them into the bottom of the boats.

The first boat came back to the *Calypso* with more than twenty survivors. The two Marine guards looked almost sheepish because the rescued Frenchmen were coughing or vomiting; there was no fight left in even one of them.

Rennick was waiting with Ramage by the entryport and as soon as the survivors arrived on deck they were escorted, five at a time, on to the fo'c'sle.

"We've nothing to worry about from those fellows for an hour or so," Rennick remarked.

"No, it's the old story of only a few of them being able to swim."

"I don't think many have escaped from the ship, sir," Rennick said.

Ramage shook his head. "No. I did a very rough count and saw about a hundred. Looks as though more than half of them went down with the ship."

"Yes, even though she was rolling heavily, she went very suddenly in the end."

When the third boat came alongside the cox'n shouted up: "We've got a couple of officers here, sir!"

When the two men were helped up the ship's side, clothes torn and hair soaking, Ramage walked over to them and said in French: "Perhaps you would introduce yourselves."

The elder of the two bowed, coughing at the same time: "Jean-Louis Peyrafitte, *lieutenant de vaisseau*, and captain of *Le Jason*, frigate. This," he indicated the other man, "is the second lieutenant. He was with me on the quarterdeck."

"M. Peyrafitte," Ramage said, "I am afraid you have lost at least half your ship's company."

"I know. It was my fault. I did not realize she was so near capsizing. I should have cleared the decks."

73

Ramage shrugged his shoulders. "It was easier to see from over here," he said quietly. "You fought until the last moment."

The Frenchman looked up for the first time. "You think so?"

Ramage nodded. "You were rolling so much that I don't know how your men aimed their guns."

Now it was the turn of the Frenchman to shrug. He gestured round the *Calypso*'s decks and then up at the masts. "They were not very successful," he said sadly.

"They were earlier," Ramage said grimly. "I lost some good men."

He turned to Rennick. "Put a Marine guard on these two and then take them down to my cabin: they can dry off there."

Rennick was about to protest that the wardroom would be more suitable when he realized that Ramage was paying a small tribute to the French captain's bravery. "Very well, sir," he said.

Ramage saw Orsini and told him: "Go down and tell my steward to give these two men towels and dry clothes."

For more than three quarters of an hour the boats combed the wreckage for survivors, but when they were finally recalled they had found only one hundred and sixty-three men. The only officers to survive were still the two found by the third boat, the captain and second lieutenant. Most of the others, Ramage guessed, had stayed with their divisions of guns.

Finally, the four boats were hoisted on board, the foretopsail and maintopsail were hoisted, and Ramage gave orders for the *Calypso* to wear round and set a course for Capraia.

"I wonder what we'll find with the other frigate," Southwick said.

Ramage laughed. "You want two frigates in one day, eh?"

"I don't see why not," the master said.

"Pass the word for Bowen – providing he's not in the middle of operating. I want to know what the butcher's bill comes to."

Bowen came up on deck, his clothes still bloodstained, and reported to Ramage.

"Twelve dead from gunshot wounds and splinters, five badly wounded from splinters, and seven slightly wounded, gunshot and splinters, plus one man completely dazed when the gun was dismounted. It's only the second time I've seen such a case, but he is speechless and although he's not deaf, he doesn't understand what is said to him."

"We've been lucky," Ramage said grimly. "If *Le Jason* had not had that leak, we could have lost half a hundred men."

Bowen looked up at the ragged group of men up on the fo'c'sle. "At least. Are those the French survivors?"

"A hundred and sixty-three, and two officers."

"How many men did she have on board?"

"I haven't asked the captain yet, but probably about two hundred and fifty."

Chapter Six

The trip back to Capraia was a run of less than two hours, and Ramage steered for a position on the coast about three miles north of the little port. He took the *Calypso* in to three quarters of a mile from the beach and then, wary of the kind of outlying rocks that had holed *Le Jason*, brought the frigate head to wind and anchored.

"Hoist out the boats, Mr Aitken," he said after Southwick assured him the anchor was well dug in. "Let's get rid of our passengers."

During the run back to the island he had a long talk with Peyrafitte. *Le Jason* had had a complement of two hundred and seventy-seven when she began the action, so that one hundred and twelve men had been lost, either from the *Calypso*'s gunfire or by drowning.

The French captain confirmed that the ship had hit a rock off Capraia and the impact had started several planks. At first the pump had kept up with the leak but after that *Le Jason*'s speed through the water while engaging the *Calypso* had made it worse, and towards the end he was having to take men away from the guns to replace those exhausted at the pump.

Peyrafitte, a stocky and black-haired man with deep brown eyes, said ruefully: "But for the leak, we may have taken *you!*"

"You had fifty more men and we had the same number of guns," Ramage said. "We should both have lost a great number of men."

"I did anyway," Peyrafitte commented.

Ramage shrugged his shoulders. "There could have been more. Considering everything, you are fortunate that you have more than half your men up on the fo'c'sle."

76

"I know," the Frenchman said, "but I will have to account to my admiral for my navigation."

"Your navigation?" asked a puzzled Ramage.

"That rock," Peyrafitte explained. "It was shown on my chart. I thought we were farther offshore."

"Your chart is better than mine: I had no indication that there were any rocks there."

It was the Frenchman's turn to shrug. "Your chart showed no rock and mine did. You didn't hit it and I did. My admiral will want to know why. He will order a court of inquiry . . ."

"But a court of inquiry is routine anyway," Ramage protested.

"Yes," the Frenchman agreed, "but what can I answer when they ask me that question? They won't even know that your chart did not show a rock: it will be enough that mine did and I hit it."

Ramage wanted to console the man: he had fought bravely and he had been beaten by a leak. But from what Ramage had heard the French Navy dealt harshly with anyone who made mistakes, even if they involved misjudging the position of a rock by a few score yards in the midst of an action.

It took an hour to ferry the prisoners ashore. The two hours spent up on the fo'c'sle had done much to revive their spirits; so much so that Ramage told Rennick to put four Marines in each boat, just in case a wild spirit decided to try to rouse his comrades into making an attempt to get control.

The first frigate, *Le Tigre*, was out of sight round the bend in the coast, and after the boats had returned and men had weighed anchor, Ramage ordered the ship to general quarters.

"She probably won't be there," he said sourly to Aitken.

"They've certainly had time to send up the yards, but we damaged the mainyard."

"She could have got under way with topsails," Ramage said. "She could have gone southabout round the island and we would not have seen her."

"Well, we gave her a battering," Aitken said. "For sure the captain won't be able to use his cabin without dockyard repairs!"

Ramage recalled the raking broadsides they had poured into *Le Tigre*'s stern. How many of those broadsides had swept the length of the ship, dismounting guns and slaughtering men? Perhaps not

77

enough to prevent her escaping while the *Calypso* pursued *Le Jason*.

Jackson sat on the deck surrounded by his gun's crew. Stafford said firmly:

"She won't be there. She's had plenty of time to bolt. You fink she's going ter 'ang about after *Le Jason* came down to rescue 'er?"

"Didn't do *Le Jason* much good," Rossi observed.

"Nah, but what's ter stop *Le Tigre* escaping?"

"We left them in a mess," said Jackson. "Could they have got the yards up?"

"They'd 'ave escaped with what they got up already," Stafford said scornfully. "Topsails, t'gallants – enough to get under way."

"True enough," Jackson agreed, "providing our raking broadsides didn't do any damage. When we swept the deck I saw a lot of damage. Must have cut a lot of cordage, apart from putting paid to that mainyard."

"We shall know in a few minutes," Gilbert said, getting up and going over to the port. "No, we're not far enough round to see yet."

"Who is making a bet?" Auguste asked. "I bet a tot that she is still there. Any takers?"

"Done!" exclaimed Stafford. "I say she's gone."

"Who'll bet that if she's gone we don't start chasing her?" Jackson asked.

"Cor, you'd 'ave to be mad to take that bet," Stafford said scornfully. "If she's gone she could only have gone round to the westward, and Mr Ramage'll be after her like lightning."

"We'd never catch her," Rossi said. "She'd have a two-hour start on us."

"But she'd be under reduced canvas," Jackson pointed out. "She won't have her main course up. She'll be just jilling along under topsails and topgallants."

"Two hours is two hours," Rossi said doggedly. "Why, she'll probably be out of sight – there's plenty of haze about."

"Let's wait and see," advised Jackson. "We'll know in a few minutes whether or not Staff's won his tot."

78

Up on the quarterdeck Ramage waited as impatiently as Stafford as he watched the coastline with his telescope.

"It's nice seeing our fo'c'sle clear of prisoners," he commented to Southwick.

"Aye, but they'd had all the fight washed out of 'em!"

"Maybe," Ramage agreed, "but it only needed one hothead to rouse them up."

"It would have taken more than one hothead," Southwick said. "Most of them had swallowed a lot of the Mediterranean, and all they wanted to do was sick it up."

Ramage gestured ahead. "I thought that dam' frigate was anchored in this next bay, but it's not the right shape."

"No, it's another mile or so yet. And the bay cuts in so you won't see anything until you pass the first headland."

Aitken said: "I expect the ship's company are making bets whether or not she's still there."

"What odds are you offering?" Southwick asked jocularly.

"If I was a betting man – which I'm not – I'd give twenty to one that she's gone," Aitken said. "She'll be halfway to Toulon by now."

"We'll see," Southwick said calmly. "If she's gone we'll have a hard time finding her in this haze – it seems to be getting worse."

"She's still there," Ramage said calmly. "I can see the trucks of her masts over the headland."

"Twenty to one, eh?" Southwick said to Aitken. "Don't start taking bets – you'd be bankrupt in short order. Horses are more unpredictable than Frenchmen!"

Ramage tapped one hand with the telescope. "If they've hoisted their colours again – and are still anchored as before – we'll rake 'em a few times: they'll probably take the hint and haul down their colours again."

"I wish we could rake her across the bow," Southwick said. "There can't be much aft for us to smash up."

"I want to sail her out of here," Ramage said sharply. "So we don't want to risk any damage to her jibboom or bowsprit."

"Oh, I realize that, sir," Southwick said. "It was just getting rather boring raking her stern!"

"Just bear with us a little longer," Ramage said sarcastically.

"Anyway, they may haul down their colours again as soon as they sight us."

"They couldn't have seen us coming back, sir?" Aitken asked.

"I thought of that – in fact I was trying to spot them," Ramage said, "but the bay they are in cuts up to the north-west, so they can't see out to the east or north-east."

"So, we'll surprise them," Aitken said cheerfully. "We've been surprising Frenchmen a lot today."

"As long as they don't start surprising us," Ramage said. "Let's not get too confident."

He gave Aitken a helm order to start rounding the headland and looked for Orsini. The young Italian was standing five yards away, pretending he could not hear the conversation.

"Go round all the guns on the larboard side and warn them that they will probably be raking the Frenchman in about five minutes," he said. "And tell the officers that the Frenchman is here."

His telescope showed the stunted, gnarled olive trees growing along the headland, their leaves glinting silver as the wind caught them. There were dark green patches where cactus grew in sprouting clusters. The ground was rocky: there was little soil on this eastern side of the island and what little grass there was had been ripped up by goats, whose tracks made spiders' web trails.

Le Tigre must be lying in the same position, head to wind and her bows to the east, her stern pointing at the far headland and leaving little room for manoeuvre. At least, that much he could make out from the position of her masts.

And then suddenly the *Calypso* had rounded the first headland and there, fine on her larboard bow, was *Le Tigre*, looking much the same as when Ramage had first seen her. The mainyard was still down on deck but her stern was still out of sight. The Tricolour had been hoisted again; it streamed aft in the breeze in what seemed to Ramage a pointless act of defiance. Not so pointless, he corrected himself: *Le Tigre* thought she had been rescued by *Le Jason*; she was not to know about that rock further up the coast.

"It'll be like a wasp's nest on her quarterdeck," observed Southwick. "They never expected to see us again."

"There were times when I didn't expect to see her," Ramage said sourly.

He turned to Aitken. "We'll rake her astern with our larboard broadside, if you please; pass thirty yards off her transom."

Roundshot this time at a range of thirty yards. And if they approached carefully, at right angles to the French ship, only a few of the enemy's guns would be able to fire at them.

The *Calypso*'s first broadside smashed even more of the French ship's transom into dust: it always surprised Ramage just how much dust was created. Dust you could see, clouds of it; splinters, many six feet long, you could not see: they were flung up faster than the eye could detect, and they scythed along to kill more men than the roundshot.

The smoke of the guns was just sweeping across the quarterdeck, setting the three officers coughing, when Ramage gave the order to wear round and cross *Le Tigre*'s stern on the other tack.

Slowly, with sails slatting and men hauling at the braces, the *Calypso* wore round and, after reloading their guns, the crews ran across to the starboard side to be ready for the next broadside. As Aitken shouted orders for trimming the sails the *Calypso* steadied on her new course and increased speed.

Southwick, staring grimly at *Le Tigre*'s stern, growled: "She won't be able to take many more broadsides like that!"

As he spoke, the Tricolour fluttered down, something first seen by an excited Orsini. Ramage at once seized the speaking trumpet and shouted to the guns to cease fire, but five had already fired before the order was understood through the ship.

"Serves 'em right," Southwick commented unsympathetically. "They should have hauled down their colours the minute we hove in sight."

Two frigates in one day: as Ramage thought back to how the day had begun – with the prospect of destruction by those two ships of the line – he was hard put to believe what he saw. But the Tricolour had been lowered at the run and he had to admit that, with the prospect of another raking broadside, he could not blame the French captain. Blame him, yes, for not getting the yards across and preparing to get under way, instead of assuming that the other frigate would drive off the Englishman. But that was a piece of unjustifiable optimism since he knew that both ships were evenly matched.

"Back the foretopsail, Mr Aitken," Ramage said, wanting to

heave-to outside the arcs of fire of *Le Tigre*'s broadside: there was no need to start trusting the Frenchman just because he had hauled down his colours.

But he was back with the same problem: what to do with prisoners. Only this time he would have almost a whole ship's complement, less those killed by the *Calypso*'s broadsides . . . Well, it was the same problem, and there was the same answer: put the prisoners ashore while *Le Tigre* was repaired and got ready to be sailed away by a prize crew from the *Calypso*. But the prisoners from *Le Tigre* would not be half-drowned men unlikely to put up a fight. "We'll anchor, Mr Aitken. And then I want a boat gun fitted in the cutter."

And that was the only safe way of putting the Frenchmen ashore: loading the cutter with a boat gun and a dozen Marines with muskets, and using it to escort the other boats ashore with the prisoners. But first he had to go over to *Le Tigre* and take her surrender. Was the captain still alive?

The French captain was dead; he had been killed when Ramage had ordered the *Calypso*'s guns to sweep *Le Tigre*'s decks. Ramage saw that the ship's first lieutenant had been so shocked by the attack and the death of his captain that instead of getting the ship ready for sea he had spent the time having the men clear up the ship and prepare the bodies for burial. More than thirty bodies were lined up on deck, neatly sewn into their hammocks, and waiting for the funeral service to be read.

The lieutenant, Christian La Croix, had met Ramage at the entryport and immediately offered his sword, as though scared that if he did not do it immediately Ramage would open fire again.

La Croix told Ramage that *Le Tigre* had originally been part of a force which had included the two line of battleships, but she had sprung her mainyard and foreyard and had been ordered into the lee – as it then was – of Capraia. The wind had changed, making the island a lee shore, but the captain had not considered the wind strong enough to be a threat.

The captain had never expected to see a British ship, and he had been caught completely unawares when the *Calypso* had suddenly appeared round the headland. The first raking broadsides had swept through the ship, cutting men down in swathes. Since they could not manoeuvre and thus could not bring any guns to bear, and when the captain was killed, the lieutenant had decided the only thing he could do to stop the slaughter was to surrender, and hardly had he hauled down his colours than he saw *Le Jason* (also part of the original force but detached to inspect a distant sail) returning. The *Calypso* and *Le Jason* had engaged each other immediately, and when the *Calypso* had not returned two hours later he assumed she had been taken. A wrong assumption, he admitted ruefully.

Then, he said quite openly, the *Calypso* had suddenly re-appeared, round the northern headland this time, and once again caught him unprepared. He had not seen the masts of the British frigate approaching; the first he knew was when a lookout saw the ship rounding the headland with her guns run out.

Ramage had been told all this story while they stood on deck by the entryport. He was quite ready to take La Croix's word for it that the dead captain's cabin no longer existed.

After returning the lieutenant's sword – much to La Croix's surprise, since he thought that by surrendering he had brought dishonour on himself twice in one day – Ramage told him that he intended putting all *Le Tigre*'s ship's company ashore, except for the wounded, who would be taken to the *Calypso* for treatment. Those too badly wounded to be moved would be treated on board *Le Tigre*. The ship's surgeon, Ramage said, would have to remain on board as a prisoner. In the meantime one of the officers could read the funeral service over the dead.

Back on board the *Calypso*, Ramage revised his orders. The prisoners would be ferried ashore in the two cutters, and the jolly-boat would be armed with a boat gun and would carry a dozen Marines. The two cutters would be rowed to the shore keeping either side of the jolly-boat. If the French prisoners tried to take control of one or other of the cutters, Ramage instructed, the men at the oars should jump over the side, leaving the way open for the boat gun in the jolly-boat to open fire.

Orsini was put in command of the jolly-boat with Jackson and his boat crew, with Marines to handle the gun, which fitted on the forward thwart and fired two pounds of musket balls.

To take the first boatload of prisoners ashore, the jolly-boat was rowed over to *Le Tigre* and she stayed close to the entryport while the cutters went alongside. Two Marines searched each man as he came down the ship's side to make sure that he was not concealing a pistol or a knife.

The wind was kicking up a chop as the two cutters and jolly-boat set off on their first trip to the shore. Orsini, proud and excited at commanding a little flotilla of three boats, kept a sharp lookout and steered for a forty-yard-long stretch of beach between rocks. There was a slight swell breaking on the sand but each boat had a grapnel ready to drop as it went in and which would prevent its stern from swinging round so that the boat broached.

Ramage had left Hill and a dozen seamen on board the French ship to supervise the transfer of prisoners and had taken Lieutenant La Croix over to the *Calypso*: he would remain a prisoner of war on board. La Croix had been taken below under guard and Ramage was idly watching the two cutters return empty, escorted by the jolly-boat. Suddenly he saw the cutters as they approached *Le Tigre* quickly swerve away and wait about thirty yards from the entryport. The jolly-boat went up to the entryport, paused for three or four minutes, and then turned and headed for the *Calypso*.

A puzzled Ramage called Aitken and Southwick and went to wait at the entryport. As soon as the jolly-boat came alongside and hooked on, Orsini hurried on board and saluted Ramage.

"The French prisoners have seized Mr Hill and the Marines," he reported angrily. "They warned me and the cutters to keep off . . ."

"What are their demands?" Ramage enquired.

"They made none, sir. I think they just seized our people without any plan."

"Do they have a spokesman?"

"There's a big fat seaman who shouted down at me. He looks like the ringleader."

Ramage thought for a moment. If he made a single mistake now there would be an inglorious stalemate: a stalemate which he had caused by not putting a strong guard on board *Le Tigre*. He had assumed, since she had surrendered and could not get under way, that all her men were helpless. Clearly they were not.

"Go back to *Le Tigre*," he told Orsini. "Tell the ringleader that we shall start raking his ship as soon as we get under way again, and will go on raking her until they hoist a white flag showing they surrender."

"But Mr Hill . . . ?" asked Orsini.

"Mr Hill and the rest of them will have to take their chance," Ramage said abruptly.

As Orsini scrambled down to the jolly-boat, Ramage gave his orders. Southwick was told to get the ship under way again – which meant letting the foretopsail draw – while Aitken was ordered to make sure the guns on both broadsides were loaded, and the crews were distributed as evenly as possible, since many men were away in the two cutters and jolly-boat.

"Supposing the French put Hill and the rest of our men right aft, sir?" Southwick asked.

"I'm assuming they will," Ramage said bitterly, "in which case they'll be killed – if we have to open fire."

Southwick nodded reluctantly, because he liked Hill. "I suppose we have no choice."

"None that I can think of," Ramage said.

By now the foretopsail was drawing and she began to wear round to pass across *Le Tigre*'s stern.

"Pass the word to the guns that they are not to fire the first time we cross *Le Tigre*'s stern," Ramage told Aitken. "But we shall tack and pass back, if necessary, and they will open fire with the starboard broadside."

"Pass just close enough to keep our yards clear," Ramage said to Southwick.

As the *Calypso* turned, Ramage watched the group of Frenchmen by the entryport. The jolly-boat had been up to the ship and, now that Orsini had delivered his warning, was rowing clear, followed by the cutters. Ramage could imagine the debate among the French: they could now see the English frigate, with guns run out, manoeuvring to deliver another of her raking broadsides which had already killed so many Frenchmen. Would the fat spokesman (ringleader, most likely) now realize that he had just signed the death warrants for another score or so of his shipmates?

The *Calypso* slowly turned as though to bring her larboard broadside to bear as she passed across *Le Tigre*'s stern, and Ramage watched the French ship closely. He had decided to make one false run to give the French time to find a white flag: they would have to make one up from an old sheet, or even hoist up a square of canvas, though the colour would be far from white.

Then, as Ramage's telescope swept *Le Tigre*'s stern, he saw running men waving shirts. Then the Tricolour was hoisted a few feet and then hauled down again. There was no mistaking the movement.

"They're surrendering again," Southwick said with a contemptuous sniff. "They can't find a white flag!"

"Keep going," Ramage said. "It won't do 'em any harm to think they're going to be raked again."

The *Calypso* passed close under *Le Tigre*'s stern without firing and then wore round to pass back again and returned to her original position, where she hove-to.

Almost immediately Orsini was alongside with the jolly-boat and coming on board for orders.

"Bring that spokesman over here, and then carry on with the cutters taking men ashore," Ramage said. "But I want to talk to the fat man."

Orsini said: "I thought you were going to rake her, sir: it looked very frightening from the jolly-boat."

"It had to look frightening for the bluff to work," Ramage said.

"You mean you would not have fired, sir?" Orsini asked.

"That fat man thought so, and that's all that matters," Ramage said.

"I thought you would, too," Orsini said with a shiver. "I thought I'd seen the last of Mr Hill."

"I expect Mr Hill thought he had seen the last of us, too," Ramage said grimly.

Orsini went back to the jolly-boat and ferried the fat man before resuming escorting the cutters. Ramage could see the crowd of Frenchmen assembled on the beach growing larger and larger.

The fat man was made to stand at the gangway with two Marines behind him. He was, Ramage thought, one of the most repulsive men he had ever seen. The fat on his stomach made him look like an inflated bladder; the fat on his face hung down like the jowls of a bloodhound. The man was greasy and unshaven. But even as he stood in front of the two Marines he was wringing his hands, like an apologetic innkeeper. He said nothing but his hands kept on moving. Clearly, Ramage realized, the man expected to be shot and thrown over the side. Well, there was no reason to let him think differently – for a while, anyway.

"Well," Ramage said coldly in French, "your commanding officer had surrendered the ship, hadn't he?"

"Yes, *M'sieur*."

"And that included you?"

"Yes, *M'sieur*."

"Then why did you make my men hostages and tell the boat to keep off?"

"I don't know, *M'sieur*," the man said miserably.

"Don't be stupid: you persuaded the rest of your ship's company to follow you."

"Oh no!" the man exclaimed. "No, they didn't. At least, a few did but the rest said it was suicide. Why – they ran aft and surrendered the ship again just as you were going to open fire!"

"Oh, so it wasn't you surrendering?"

"No, sir," the man said, perspiring freely and wiping his forehead with his hand. "No, not me."

"Why not? Didn't you agree with them surrendering?"

"I was too scared," the man admitted. "I thought you were going to rake us again – and I was afraid of being killed."

Well, Ramage thought, at least you are an honest man. He turned and told Aitken in English to pass the word to Rennick to have a file of half a dozen Marines line up on the gangway facing the fat man.

It took several minutes and during that time Ramage did not speak a word. The fat man, eyes bulging, watched every move round him. Finally the file of Marines were ready and Sergeant Ferris saluted Ramage smartly. "The men you requested all fallen in and ready, sir."

"Very well, sergeant," Ramage said formally, returning the salute.

By now there was almost complete silence on deck: seamen had stopped and were watching the fat man; Aitken and Southwick stood to one side of Ramage and Sergeant Ferris stood beside the Marines.

Ramage turned again to the Frenchman, who was perspiring so heavily he looked as though he was melting.

"What you were doing," Ramage said deliberately, "was

fomenting a mutiny. Your captain – the lieutenant who had taken over command – had surrendered. In other words he had given you orders to cease fighting. But later you – whoever you are – gave new orders to the men: you told them to drive off the English, to whom your new captain had surrendered.

"Death!" Ramage suddenly thundered at the man, who immediately fainted in an untidy heap.

The two Marines behind him put their muskets down on the deck and dragged him to his feet, letting go of him as soon as he could stand unaided.

Ramage said: "Death! That is what I could order, and there –" he pointed to the Marines, "– are the men of a firing squad. Yes, death is what I could order for you. And I may yet. For the time being you will be taken below and put in irons."

As soon as the man had been taken away, Southwick said: "I thought you meant it! It would have been the first firing squad you've ever assembled."

"The fat man thought I meant it, too," Ramage said. "I've never seen anyone faint like that before!"

Ramage waited until the two cutters had finished ferrying the prisoners ashore and as soon as they turned back towards the *Calypso* with the jolly-boat he said: "Pass the word for the carpenter, Mr Southwick: we'll go over and inspect *Le Tigre*. I want to see what repairs have to be done to make her seaworthy."

The three men went across in the jolly-boat to find Hill ready to greet them.

"I expect I gave you a few minutes of worry," Ramage said to Hill. The third lieutenant grinned.

"You did, sir: I had a feeling that you were serious."

"I was," Ramage admitted, "but I thought the Frenchman's nerve would fail first."

Ramage led the way below. Aft the captain's day cabin, dining cabin and bed place were no longer recognizable: the bulkheads had been smashed in along with the sternlights: there was no sign that windows had ever been fitted in the transom. The grapeshot, after smashing in the cabins, had swept forward to pepper the mizenmast and rip at the carriages of the aftermost guns.

On deck the mainyard had been hit by three shot which had, fortunately, not split the spar. The original damage which had caused the French to lower the spar down on to the deck comprised a long shake, or split, in the middle which the French had already begun to fish by fixing battens round it, like long splints.

The carpenter inspected the spar with Southwick, and then reported to Ramage: "A day's work to repair it and the foreyard and sway them up again, sir."

"Very well," Ramage said. "Have as many men as you want. What about the damage below?"

The carpenter shrugged his shoulders. "We can't do anything about the damage from our broadsides, sir: that's a dockyard job. I'll just check the steering and the foot of the mizenmast, and sound the well. But that's all I can do."

"A day, eh? So we can get the ship under way in two days."

"Unless I find the steering damaged, sir, or something unexpected."

"Good. All I want is to get her under way; she need not be in fighting trim, but she must sail."

He then sent for Hill, and talking to him from amid the wreckage of the captain's cabin he said: "You are going to be the prizemaster, with Orsini as your second-in-command. From now on you will live on board and start getting the ship ready for sea. I'll send you twenty-five men, and as soon as you can you'll have the rigging fitted and the mainyard and foreyard crossed."

"Aye aye, and thank you, sir," Hill said. "Where do I make for?"

"Naples. You'll sail in company with the *Calypso*, but get what charts you might need from Southwick and copy them: we might be separated by bad weather."

Having given his orders, Ramage took the carpenter back to the *Calypso* to collect the tools he needed and the carpenter's mates. Ramage told Aitken to choose twenty-five men to go across and put themselves under Hill's command. "There should be plenty of provisions and water," he said, "but pass the word to Hill to check them."

Fishing the two yards and plugging the worst shot holes took the full day that the carpenter had estimated, but in the meantime Hill's men had lowered the topgallant and foresails and overhauled them, before sending them up again. Hill had the maincourse spread out over the deck and overhauled, several patches being stitched in where there was chafe. Finally, the two yards were hoisted up and fitted in place.

Later that afternoon Jackson and Stafford were standing on the *Calypso*'s fo'c'sle with Rossi and Gilbert. The sun was still high, there was little more than a gentle breeze from the south-west – giving the two ships a lee from Capraia at last – and the clouds were rounded into fantastic shapes, reminding Jackson of Trade wind clouds and making him nostalgic for the West Indies.

"Yer know," Stafford said, "I can't see 'ow all those prisoners from the two frigates are going to survive on that island. There can't be much more food than the local people need . . ."

"I can guess who is going to go without," Jackson commented.

"Yus, so can I, but it don't seem fair."

Jackson shrugged his shoulders. "It wouldn't be fair to have 350 French prisoners on board us, either. They'd outnumber us by a hundred or so, and with a few chaps like that fat man they'd soon try to take the ship. Probably succeed, too: sheer weight of numbers."

"All right, all right. I'm persuaded Jacko," Stafford said. "But what d'you think, Gilbert?"

"I think Mr Ramage was right. It wouldn't matter to me if Capraia was a desert island with no water: I wouldn't keep those men on board as prisoners. They'd turn on us and cut our throats."

"What's Mr Ramage going to do with the fat man?" Stafford asked Jackson.

"How should I know? If it was up to me I'd throw him over the side, but I suppose he'll be brought to trial, or something."

"I thought I'd fall down laughing when he fainted," Stafford said. "I quite believed Mr Ramage when he said 'Death!' – it's about the only French word I understand. I expected the Marines to shoot him there and then."

"So did I," Gilbert admitted, "and it's a pity they didn't. That man is evil."

"Well, he's down below in irons now," Jackson said.

"Yus, that's all very well, but he could have been the death of Mr Hill and the Marines. Mr Ramage was all ready to rake 'em again!"

"I wonder," Jackson said. "He wanted the fat man to think so,

90

and the only way to do that was to sail across his stern. But don't you reckon he was bluffing?''

"There's no way of telling," Rossi said. "If he was bluffing, well, it worked, and that's all that matters.''

"Gave Mr Hill a bad five minutes, though.''

"Gave everyone a bad five minutes," Jackson said, "including Mr Ramage. If his bluff hadn't worked, he'd have had to open fire, and can you imagine how he'd have felt, firing on his own men?''

"Not half as bad as the men," Stafford said ironically. "But you're probably right, Jacko; he was bluffing, and he guessed right that the fat man's nerve wouldn't hold out.''

"It wasn't Mr Ramage's first bit of bluff today," Gilbert pointed out. "That was bluff when he steered across the bow of that ship of the line.''

Jackson shook his head.

"I don't agree with you there, Gilbert. No one knew the Frenchman would turn away, and I'm damned sure Mr Ramage wasn't going to. It's just that the French captain lost his nerve.''

"Exactly!" exclaimed Gilbert, showing excitement for the first time that Jackson could remember. "The French captain's nerve broke before Mr Ramage's, just as the fat man's did. That's where Mr Ramage is so clever, he knows the French so well. He knows exactly when they will break.''

Jackson shook his head again, only this time it was because of near incredulity. "I believe you are right, Gilbert. I never thought of it like that but, as you say, it's the second time today.''

Gilbert nodded contentedly. "Yes, to understand Mr Ramage's mind, you have to think like a Frenchman.''

"He's right, Jacko," Rossi said. "He understands the French mind. The Italian, too: you remember all the tricks he played when we've been in Italy.''

"Well, he speaks Italian and French: they're very much alike, and perhaps speaking the language gives you an insight into the way they think.''

"Try and think of another explanation," Stafford said. "There isn't one. Not unless you want to believe in magic and voodoo.''

"I tell you someone else like Mr Ramage," Gilbert said, "and that's Mr Orsini.''

"You're right!" Jackson exclaimed. "He would have stayed

almost alongside that frigate this morning if I hadn't steered us away without orders. I thought then he was just excited and forgot to get us out of range, but I think you're right; he knew Mr Ramage was bluffing."

"He's a bright young lad, that's for sure," Stafford said. "It's a pity the Marcheeza can't see him."

"Marchesa," said Jackson. "She's dead by now," he added lugubriously. "Boney's men will have murdered her."

"I don't see why," Stafford said.

"Don't be stupid!" Rossi said explosively. "You don't think Bonaparte would let her go back to Volterra, do you? Why, if she suddenly arrived just about everyone would rally to her and revolt against the French."

"Yus, but he can put her in prison in Paris."

"That's not Bonaparte's way. He'd be afraid she would escape. No, he'd kill her. Then there's no risk of her escaping and no risk of her marrying and having children, which would mean heirs."

"She was a wonderful woman," Stafford said. "What times we had with her on board. I always reckoned Mr Ramage would marry her."

"Religion," Jackson said laconically. "She was Catholic, he's a Protestant. Anyway, she was very hot-tempered, you know; I don't reckon she would have suited Mr Ramage over the long haul. I reckon Lady Sarah suits him in every way. A fine woman, Lady Sarah."

"I'm not saying she isn't," Stafford said hastily. "I was just thinking about the Marcheeza. It's horrible to think of her murdered. She was so young – and so, well, alive."

"Well, you'd better get used to the idea that she's dead," Jackson said quietly. "I'm sure both Mr Ramage and Mr Orsini think she's dead. Not that they have any way of knowing one way or another."

"It's a damned shame," Stafford said. "Such a beautiful lady she was."

Chapter Seven

Rear-Admiral Charles Rudd was extremely angry. "Damnation, Ramage, you let a couple of ships of the line slip through our fingers while you went chasing after a couple of frigates!"

"But sir, I could never have got here in time for you to send a force to take those ships."

"How do you know? You've no idea how long it took them to get seaworthy again. I'd been looking everywhere for those two. It was your duty to get here as fast as you could and warn me."

Ramage repressed a sigh. He had already described to the Rear-Admiral in both words and a written report the circumstances of the collision, and how he had considered and finally turned down the idea of making a dash for Naples to raise the alarm, knowing there was no time, but the Rear-Admiral could not get out of his mind the picture of two ships of the line locked together and helpless, just waiting to be captured.

It was hot in the cabin of the flagship; the *Defender* was lying at anchor in an airless Naples Bay, a 100-gun ship with two 74s nearby. Rudd, a thin-faced, morose man with a high-pitched voice, had greeted the *Calypso*'s arrival with *Le Tigre* without enthusiasm. Almost his first words when Ramage had reported on board the flagship had been: "Let me have your written report." It was only after he had read the report and discovered about the collision between the two French ships that he had become enraged, vowing that his two 74s could have got to the French before they could have made themselves seaworthy.

The sinking of one frigate and the capture of another, even though the circumstances were fully described in the report, were dismissed as being of slight importance. Finally Ramage thought of a way to change the subject slightly.

"The prisoners I put ashore on the island of Capraia, sir: I doubt if there is nearly enough food on the island for them and the local people."

"I should think not," Rudd growled. "I don't know why the devil you landed all the prisoners there."

The remark was so stupid and unfair, in Ramage's view, that he made no comment: one could not argue with flag officers, at least not with this one, who seemed to be a singularly obtuse man.

Rudd's day cabin in the *Defender*, extending the width of the ship, was sparsely furnished. Either Rudd liked to live a Spartan existence or he was a poor man, unlucky where prize money was concerned. There were half a dozen chairs, a small table that showed he did not do much entertaining on board, a battered mahogany wine cooler which most flag officers would have scorned, regarding it as only suitable for the wardroom, and the curtains drawn back on either side of the sternlights were of heavy red velvet, well faded by sunlight.

The furnishings of the cabin, Ramage thought, were a clue to Rudd's attitude: he was a disappointed man.

Rudd tapped Ramage's report, which he was still holding in his hand. "I shall forward this to their Lordships, and I can tell you they won't like it. No, they won't like it a bit. They will consider – as I do – that you have not backed up your flag officer: instead, you have chased after prize money. Well, I warn you now, I may not buy in *Le Tigre*; she needs a great deal of repair, judging from your report, and I have next to no facilities here. So let that be a lesson to you: do your duty instead of chasing after prize money."

The remark was so obviously that of an embittered man that before Ramage could stop himself he said: "I don't need the money, sir."

"Ha, that's an old excuse! Where do you think your present command came from?"

"I captured it in the West Indies," Ramage said quietly, and Rudd gave a dismissive wave of his hand.

"Well, Ramage, you arrive here with a frigate and another one which is badly damaged, and a tale of four hundred prisoners abandoned on the island of Capraia. What am I supposed to do?"

Ramage realized that whatever he said would be wrong: the

Rear-Admiral was still dazzled by the prospect of two French ships of the line locked together, just waiting for him to come along and capture them and pocket the prize money – and buy some new curtains, Ramage thought.

And why, Ramage thought angrily, if I can sink one and capture another French frigate in a morning, are Rudd's frigates and 74s spending their time at anchor in Naples Bay? Yet he knew that a junior post-captain expecting to be treated fairly by a new flag officer was whistling in the dark. Or, rather, singing to the moon.

"I suppose I have to collect those prisoners," Rudd continued. Then apparently not realizing the contradiction, said: "I'll need to send both my 74s if there are four hundred of them."

So, Ramage thought bitterly, two 74s are going to be sent to carry out a task that a few minutes ago you expected to be done by one frigate's ship's company . . .

"You'll forfeit the head money," Rudd said. "I'm not paying out for prisoners I have to collect myself."

"I don't know the statutes concerning head money, sir," Ramage said bitterly, "but I thought it was paid to the ship that captured the prisoners, not to the ship that simply transported them."

"Absolutely rubbish," Rudd said. "All you did was put them ashore on the island."

"I captured – indeed rescued from the sea – the men in *Le Jason* and certainly captured those in *Le Tigre*. The fact I put them ashore on Capraia doesn't alter the fact I captured them in the first place, sir."

"Don't argue with me," Rudd said brusquely, "there's no head money for you."

So the captains of the two 74s (presumably Rudd's favourites) would get the head money. Yes, it was unfair, Ramage thought; but this sort of thing happened when you had flag officers like Rudd. They would play favourites all the time. Favoured frigate captains could be sent to cruise in areas where they would be most likely to find prizes; frigate captains out of favour – or simply not well known to the flag officer – would be sent off escorting convoys, the most tedious and profitless task in the Navy.

Well, there was nothing he could do about it; Rudd was a rear-admiral and flag officer on the station; Ramage was, he realized, probably the most junior post-captain and certainly the latest arrival on the station. All it needed now, he thought grimly, was orders to escort a convoy to somewhere like Malta, or Gibraltar.

But Rear-Admiral Rudd was clearly considering something: his narrow and lined face was contorted with thought; he was gripping one thin hand in another, as though trying to twist off the fingers. Finally he said: "I'll send you with the 74s because you know where you landed the two groups of Frenchmen, and I don't want the 74s to have to comb the island for them. You won't take off any of the prisoners, so it won't affect the head money; you'll just act as a pilot."

Ramage said nothing; in due course he would be getting written orders and that would be that. He would pilot the two 74s to their head money, and no one would say thank you.

"I've heard about you," Rudd said unexpectedly. "You have quite a reputation in the Navy. Among other things, for not being very strict in obeying orders. I want to make it clear that while you serve on this station you obey both the spirit and the letter of my orders. I hope I make myself quite clear, Ramage."

"Indeed you do, sir," Ramage said politely. "Abundantly clear."

So now we get that too, Ramage thought: a flag officer jealous of a junior officer who had many of his despatches published as *Gazette* letters. The flag officers never considered that one had to do something in the first place, and publishing a despatch in the *Gazette* was up to their Lordships at the Admiralty: they were the people who decided which despatches were printed.

It was ironic, he thought, that famous admirals like Lord St Vincent and the late Lord Nelson were delighted when one had a letter published in the *Gazette*; it was only little men like Rudd, who had probably reached the summit of his career and knew it, who were resentful.

"Very well," Rudd said, "you'll be getting written orders in due course; in the meantime, I presume you have your weekly accounts and returns ready for me?"

"Yes," Rossi agreed, "the Bay of Naples is very beautiful, but stay in the Bay – don't go on shore!"

"What's wrong with the shore?" demanded Stafford.

"The shore is full of Neapolitans, and they are to Italy what the Cockneys are to England."

"'Ere," demanded Stafford, "wotcher mean by that?"

"In two minutes they have all your money; in three they have your shirt; in four they've stuck a knife in your back and left you for dead!"

"Oh, so that's what happens among the Cockneys, too?" asked an offended Stafford. "Well, I might remind you that when you came to stay at my 'ome when we was given leave from Chatham, you didn't lose a penny piece nor an 'air off your 'ead!"

"Excuse me, I exaggerated," Rossi said placatingly. "What I mean to say is all Neapolitans are *lazzaroni*: pickpockets and murderers. So be careful if you go on shore."

"What about where you come from?" Stafford persisted. "Is it any better in Genoa?"

"The worst you ever hear about Genova is that the *Genovesi* are, how do you say, tight-fisted; a bit careful with their money."

"Mean," Stafford said. "Mean like the Scots."

Rossi shrugged. "Call it what you like, but I think it is only sensible to keep your hand on your money when standing in a crowd of pickpockets, and to count your change when dealing with cheats."

Gilbert laughed softly. "Between Neapolitans, *Genovesi* and Cockneys, how is a poor Frenchman to survive?"

"Don't ever go on shore," Jackson advised. "Pass the bread barge."

Louis slid it along the table towards him. Then Jackson continued: "On shore all is wickedness. Why, London was so wicked that it shocked poor old Staff into joining the King's service and coming to sea. Genoa was so wicked even Rosey could not stand the competition and came to sea. And I wonder about you four –" he gestured at Gilbert, Louis, Auguste and Albert, "– what made you leave Brest?"

Gilbert laughed. "Well, we are the only ones with a good excuse because we escaped with Mr Ramage and Lady Sarah. The only thing wrong with Brest is Bonaparte's men; they are all murderers."

Stafford gave a melodramatic sigh. "Well, it seems the *Calypso* is a home for us poor refugees!"

97

"Refugees be damned," Jackson said. "I volunteered."

"I should think so," said Stafford. "Revolting, that's what you Americans are! You didn't know when you were well off."

"I jumped out of the frying pan into the fire when I took the King's shilling," Jackson said mildly.

"But I bet you took the precaution of getting that Protection first," Stafford said. "With an American Protection in your pocket you can get out whenever you want."

"Aye, I have a Protection," Jackson admitted, "but I don't think getting out 'whenever I want' is so easy. I have to apply to an American consul, and there aren't many of them about. That's where Americans get stuck: they can't get leave to go on shore, so they can't get to a consul."

"Then they shouldn't have joined in the first place," Stafford said unsympathetically.

"A lot of them don't join, as you well know," Jackson said stiffly. "They get pressed into service from some British or neutral ship even though they have Protections just because the officer in charge of the pressgang reckons they're British."

"They usually are," said Stafford. "They just got a Protection at the Customs House – or an American consul – when they managed to get on shore. I've met dozens of British seamen with Protections. After all, what does a Protection prove? Nothing. It just says the man appeared before the Customs officer or consul and said he was an American subject born in such and such a place. He doesn't have to *prove* it. Then it goes on to say he appears to be a certain age, has a certain colour hair, and so on. Half the Navy have dark brown hair, light complexion and 'stand about five feet eight inches'."

"You're just bitter because you don't have a Protection," Jackson said teasingly.

"Oh yes, I do!" exclaimed Stafford. "I bought it off a chap five years ago. It says my name is Matthew Fletcher and I was born in Wilmington, Delaware. It is signed by the Customs collector there, and it describes me perfectly."

"Why don't you use it, then?" Jackson asked.

"For the same reason you don't use yours," Stafford said. "I'm quite happy where I am."

"I'll remind you of that when you have one of your fits of

grousing," Jackson said. "There are times when you sound like the most miserable man on earth."

"Wot a lie," Stafford exclaimed. "Why, 'appy Will Stafford from Bridewell Lane – everybody knows me!"

"Don't lose that Protection," Jackson advised. "You might need it some time to save yourself from us."

Ramage wriggled in the chair, which was too small for a grown man, and he wondered how it had got into the captain's day cabin of the 74-gun ship. Yet the chair was no more uncomfortable than the manner of the captain, Edward Arbuthnot, commanding the *Intrepid*.

Arbuthnot was just the opposite of his admiral: where Rudd was thin and tall, Arbuthnot was stocky and plump. The only similarity, Ramage reflected, was that both men had a shifty manner; neither inspired confidence; they were not the men to find it easy to get credit at a gaming table. They were men, Ramage decided, with whom all transactions would have to be in cash.

"Well, Ramage," Arbuthnot said, "since you know where you landed these dam' Frenchmen on Capraia, the Admiral tells me you will act as our pilot."

Ramage shrugged his shoulders and said politely: "I don't know what good I will be able to do. The French will have moved since then. I put one group ashore north of the port and the other south. By now they'll probably have joined up at the port – it's the only village on the island."

"It'll be up to you to find them," Arbuthnot said shortly. "You landed them, you find them."

Ramage saw the trap: Arbuthnot was preparing the way for his own men failing, and was making sure he had a scapegoat ready. "The Admiral's orders to me do not say that," Ramage said carefully.

"Perhaps not, but I do, and I'm the senior officer on this operation," Arbuthnot said sharply.

"You and the *Phoenix* will be carrying five hundred troops, as well as your usual ship's company," Ramage pointed out. "I'll just have my ship's company."

"You seem to have plenty of excuses even before you start," Arbuthnot sneered.

"No, but it shouldn't be too difficult to round up the Frenchmen with all the troops you have at your disposal."

Clearly Arbuthnot did not want to be reminded of that. "Rounding them up will not be difficult," he said. "But first they must be found."

"Indeed," Ramage agreed. "I can't see them staying in the village after two British 74s and a frigate come and anchor in the bay. If they have any sense they'll take to the hills, and there are plenty of them on Capraia."

"Well, you find them and tell us where they are, and the troops will come and capture them."

And that, thought Ramage, is just too blatant.

"If you'll excuse me," he said, standing up, "I must go and see Admiral Rudd and get my orders clarified. My orders from him state that I pilot you to where in Capraia I landed the French. You now say you expect me to find the French and lead the troops to them. I am not a soldier, nor do I command any of the troops. I think I need Admiral Rudd's views on the point."

As Ramage turned to leave the cabin he saw that he had taken the wind out of Arbuthnot's sails. Immediately he too stood up, stretching out a hand placatingly.

"Do sit down again, Ramage; there is no need to bother the Admiral over a small point like this!"

"That's why I want to speak to him: to me it is not a small point; in fact it concerns the whole aim of the operation."

"Now, now, Ramage," said Arbuthnot, "tell me what is bothering you. Do you want some troops to command?"

"The troops are your concern," Ramage said, determined not to fall into that trap. "I am just saying that my orders are to show you where I landed the French. I can't be expectecd – nor am I ordered – to comb the island looking for the French: that is why you are carrying five hundred troops, quite apart from your Marines."

Clearly Arbuthnot did not want the question referred to Rear-Admiral Rudd: obviously his own orders from the Admiral were more in line with how Ramage saw the situation.

"Very well, Ramage, you point out the landing areas and the troops will be landed to round up these fellows," he said. "Mind you, I shall expect you to co-operate as best you can."

"I assure you I will," Ramage said. "It's simply that I can't search an island the size of Capraia, with all those mountains, with a handful of Marines and a score of seamen."

"No, indeed not," Arbuthnot said. "You just carry out your orders from the Admiral and co-operate with me and Captain Slade – he commands the *Phoenix*."

Back in his day cabin on board the *Calypso* Ramage described the meeting with Arbuthnot to Aitken and Southwick. Aitken, by virtue of being the first lieutenant, was the second-in-command of the frigate and entitled to know what was going on if only because he would take over command if anything happened to Ramage. Southwick, on the other hand, was only a warrant, not a commission officer: he held his rank by warrant, not a commission, and officially he ranked below the fourth lieutenant, the most junior of the commission officers.

Southwick's strength – why he was brought into many discussions to which his rank did not entitle him – was that he had been master of the little *Kathleen* cutter when Ramage was given her as his first command. Over the following years – when Ramage had been promoted from commanding a cutter to a brig, and then from a brig to a frigate – Southwick had always gone with him as master. Ramage had pulled many strings to arrange it, but to him having Southwick with him was almost as important as the promotion itself.

With his mop of white hair and benign manner of a country parson, Southwick combined common sense and the courage to express it (particularly when his views might not be popular). If Ramage had been asked to describe Southwick's role, he would probably have said he was a benevolent grandfather who, given the chance to board a French ship wielding his great two-handed sword, was given to bouts of violence.

Now, Southwick was comfortably seated in the armchair while Aitken sprawled on the sofa, and Ramage said: "It seems to me that in the end Arbuthnot is going to expect us to find these damned Frenchmen."

"What's he going to do with all those soldiers?" Southwick asked. "We can muster a couple of dozen Marines and a score of sailors: doesn't seem much compared with five hundred soldiers, as

101

well as the Marines from two 74s and a couple of hundred or so seamen."

Aitken said: "I don't think Captain Arbuthnot has any faith in the soldiers."

"That would explain it," Ramage agreed. "He doesn't want to risk his reputation on five hundred men from the 38th Regiment of Foot."

"I can't say I blame him," Southwick admitted. "Those men have been parading round Naples and getting soft. Suddenly they are going to have to scramble over those hills and mountains of Capraia in the heat and the dust. These French seamen will probably be the first enemy they've ever seen."

"At least they're not Neapolitan troops," Ramage said jokingly. "If they were, I could understand Arbuthnot's nervousness."

"Aye," Southwick said with a contemptuous sniff. "I wouldn't match five hundred Neapolitans against fifty French seamen. Fifty *unarmed* French seamen."

"That's quite a point," Ramage said. "These seamen will be unarmed, unless they've been able to find some old blunderbusses and fowling pieces in the port."

"Did this Captain Arbuthnot strike you as a bit of an old woman, sir?" asked Southwick.

Ramage nodded. "Yes, and querulous too. I'm inclined to think he's suffering from nervousness at the prospect of handling soldiers."

"It'd be a joke," Aitken said, "if we arrive and find out all the Frenchmen had billeted themselves on houses in the village. It's quite likely because they'll all want a roof over their heads, and the only roofs will be in the village."

Ramage laughed and said: "There'll be a few donkey shelters up in the hills. Flea-infested and smelly, but they'd keep the rain out."

"So what do we do, sir?" enquired Aitken.

"If we have to, we'll send out Rennick with one party of Marines and Sergeant Ferris with another, and Martin and Kenton can take a dozen seamen each – the exercise will do them good. Oh yes, and we'll send off Orsini with a dozen men, too. That'll use up some of his surplus energy."

"Two parties of Marines and three of seamen," Aitken said. "Five search parties. They ought to turn up something."

"Orsini should be useful: he speaks Italian and French, so he'll be able to question local people if necessary."

"And bully them, too," Southwick added. "They might want encouraging to talk, even though it's for their own good. Very stubborn, these Italian islanders. They hate everyone not born on their island."

"Very true," Ramage agreed. "They probably put the British in the same category as the French: *stranieri*, and not to be trusted."

"What with the islanders, the French and Captain Arbuthnot, it seems to me we're in for a busy few hours. And we don't get a penn'orth of head money, either," Southwick grumbled.

"That's the Admiral looking after his favourites," Ramage said bitterly. "It's not the first time something like this has happened and it won't be the last, but it's hard on our chaps."

"It's certainly hard on our chaps," Southwick said, "though thanks to Mr Ramage and prizes, I don't need the money."

"Yes, when are you going to retire?" Ramage asked teasingly, "and live the life of a wealthy country squire?"

"Ah, a few years yet. Live in the country and you get rheumaticks, and I don't want to have to listen to the same parson preaching the same sermon. Gets monotonous, I should reckon. One thing about this life, it doesn't often get monotonous."

"Don't you reckon slogging to windward for a month against a Levanter is monotonous?" asked Aitken sarcastically.

"Oh yes, but then I never did like going to windward," Southwick said. "Going to windward is for fools and those without an option."

"Well spoken," Ramage said. "I'll try and make sure you're never bothered by anything more strenuous than a reach or a run."

"Thank 'ee," Southwick said. "Tell the Admiral, as well!"

Chapter Eight

Ramage led the way into the bay and turned the *Calypso* into the wind before anchoring as close as he could to the beach where he had landed the *Le Tigre*'s ship's company. The *Intrepid* followed, rounded up and dropped an anchor a cable to the northward while the *Phoenix* came in and anchored the same distance to the south.

Ramage had been watching the shore with his telescope. There was no sign of anyone on the beach or walking about the land at the back of it. There was no sign that a single man had ever landed.

"You were right," Southwick said. "They didn't stay here. Why Captain Arbuthnot insisted we search here first I don't know; it was obvious they would move on to the village."

"Well, we'll put a cutter ashore with a dozen Marines, just to be able to reassure Arbuthnot. Mr Aitken, hoist out one of the cutters if you please."

Within fifteen minutes the cutter was pulling for the shore carrying a dozen Marines and Lieutenant Rennick, with Kenton in command of the boat. Ramage's orders to Rennick were brief: he was to follow any tracks from the beach, and when he was absolutely sure of the direction in which the French had gone, he was to return to the ship and report.

It took less than two hours for Rennick to return and report that the French had gone off towards the village: Rennick had followed their tracks until he had stood on a hill a mile from the village and looking down on it.

"I didn't feel justified in going after so many Frenchmen with only a dozen Marines," he said matter-of-factly, "but they made for the village all right: they skirted the side of a mountain on their left and they kept to the right, following the flatter land along the edge of the sea."

Ramage said: "Go over to the *Intrepid* and report to Captain Arbuthnot, and tell him that I propose going up to the village now."

Rennick was back from the *Intrepid* within half an hour with instructions for Ramage: he was to proceed north to the village and land and investigate.

Rennick's manner showed that he had not enjoyed his meeting with Arbuthnot. "He asked so many questions I began to doubt whether or not I had been ashore," he told Ramage. "What sort of tracks, how could I be sure they were made by the French – he even suggested they might be goat tracks!"

Southwick went to the fo'c'sle and soon the men were singing as they turned the capstan and brought the anchor cable home. Then the reports came quickly: the cable was at long stay, short stay, up and down – when the cable led vertically into the sea from the stem – and finally aweigh, when the anchor was off the bottom.

Then, at a signal from Southwick, Aitken gave the orders to let fall the fore and maintopsails and the topmen swarmed out along the yards to cast off the gaskets. The sails dropped like huge curtains and as soon as the men were back in the top others hauled on the halyards to hoist the yards so that the sails could be trimmed.

Both the *Intrepid* and the *Phoenix* were also weighing, and Ramage took the *Calypso* out from between them to head north. It took less than half an hour to reach the village. Once again the *Calypso* anchored and this time Ramage ordered all the boom boats to be hoisted out and the quarter boats lowered.

"I hope you have your Marines standing by," he said to Rennick, and to Aitken he said: "Your three parties of seamen are ready?"

"Fallen in on the gangway with Kenton, Martin and Orsini, sir."

"Right, get them into the boats as soon as possible."

Within ten minutes the two cutters, named and painted the red and the green to distinguish them, the gig and the jolly-boat were rowing for the port: the two parties of Marines and one of seamen under Kenton were divided up in the two cutters, Martin was in the gig with his seamen, and Orsini was in the jolly-boat with his dozen men.

105

In the meantime Ramage and Aitken had been examining the port with their telescope. Finally Ramage snapped his shut and said crossly: "There seem to be fewer people about than one would expect on a normal day."

"Can't blame them, sir," Aitken said. "They saw two 74s and a frigate approaching, and they know it can only mean trouble for them."

"Damn this waiting," Ramage grumbled. "It's all I seem to be doing today."

"Better than traipsing across dusty hills being stung by insects," Southwick said cheerfully. "And in that village it'll be the stink of rotting cabbage, sewage and pigs."

"Even that would be a change from the smell of our bilgewater," Ramage said sourly. "One day I'll invent a way of getting the pump to suck out those last few inches of water."

"The ship wouldn't be the same without that stink," Aitken commented. "Makes it seem like home!"

"It doesn't say much for the way you live in Scotland!" Ramage commented.

He pulled out the tube of his telescope and adjusted it to the mark for the right focus. Then he looked at the boats as they made their way to the shore. The *Intrepid* and *Phoenix* were just coming into the bay, Ramage was pleased to see: Arbuthnot could not complain that he had been kept waiting.

Waiting – he was the one who was having to wait. Ramage cursed that he had not gone with one of the boats, but leading a search party was not the job for a post-captain commanding a frigate: let junior lieutenants get blistered heels!

He began pacing up and down the quarterdeck, impatience fighting with the knowledge that he should not show it. This was the part of command that he hated: it emphasized just how alone he had to be; he could talk with his officers, but ultimately he had to stay remote, never indulging in the sort of small talk which passed the hours at a time like this.

He looked again with the telescope. The boats were now lying at the quay, and he could just catch sight of the Marines' jackets as they moved about the streets. Well, they were not being attacked by an angry crowd of Frenchmen armed with sticks and staves. Where the devil had the French gone? Further north? That seemed unlikely because there were no more villages. Well, he would have to wait for one of the boats to return.

Ten paces aft, turn and ten paces forward again. The sun was bright but compared with what he was used to in the West Indies, there was no heat in it: there was no need for an awning, and the pitch in the deck seams was not soft. The wind was a little more than a gentle breeze, and there were few clouds. It was, Ramage thought, a typical spring day in the Mediterranean, although one always had to bear in mind that the weather could be treacherous; that a vicious gale could spring up in less than twelve hours, or a *scirocco* could set in and blow hard for three days, bringing a depressing effect which seemed uncomfortably humid but which seared the leaves of shrubs and bushes.

So, he thought to himself as he turned again, make the best of today. Finally he stopped by the quarterdeck rail and took up his telescope for yet another search of the shore.

He was startled to see the jolly-boat being rowed out fast. There were only the men at the oars in the boat. In fact they looked as though they were racing another boat, and he could see Paolo standing up in the sternsheets, apparently urging the men on.

What on earth was happening? Bad news? But what bad news could there be, and what urgency? An emergency? But what emergency? – there was no sign of shooting round the quay; in fact he could clearly see boat-minders sitting in the cutters. He shrugged: once again the answer was to wait and see.

Finally the jolly-boat came alongside and Orsini scrambled up the ship's side. By then Ramage was waiting for him at the entryport and Paolo, after a hasty salute, said breathlessly: "They've gone, sir!"

"Gone? Gone where?"

"Gone completely, sir: they've escaped from the island. The local people tell me that a French frigate arrived two days ago – the day after we landed the prisoners – and took them all off."

Ramage swore. Three frigates in the area within such a short time.

"In which direction did the frigate go?"

"To the north, sir."

"Hmm, going northabout to Toulon, I suppose."

107

"With all those men on board, she'd want to get into a French port fairly quickly."

Paolo was right about that: she would have many more than double her normal complement and may well have run short of water and provisions. Ramage suddenly wanted to laugh: the errant French frigate had done Arbuthnot and Slade out of their head money!

"Who did you speak to ashore?"

"At first fishermen on the quay, but when I heard what they had to say, I made them take me to the mayor. He confirmed it. He's a fisherman too and his boat was commandeered to help take out the French, so he saw the name of the frigate: the *Marie*."

"There's no doubt that all the French were taken off?"

"None at all, sir: the mayor had counted them up from the number of boats that were used. His figure is within a dozen or so of ours."

Ramage thought for a moment or two. Martin, Kenton and Rennick could wait: right now he had to go over and report to Arbuthnot.

"Wait here: I want you to take me over to the *Intrepid*."

Ramage hurried down to his cabin to collect his sword and straighten up his stock. He came back on deck and sent for Aitken, telling him where he was going and why.

Then he climbed down the ship's side after Orsini and settled down in the sternsheets. He felt very cheerful at the news he was going to give Arbuthnot, not because he gave a damn whether the French were still on the island or not but because he felt a spiteful delight that there was no head money. He found that Admiral Rudd's decision over the head money was what really rankled; it was a petty piece of twisting the *King's Regulations and Admiralty Instructions* so that the *Calypso*'s men were cheated after a particularly hard-fought battle against *Le Jason*.

Ten minutes later Ramage was sitting opposite Arbuthnot in his cabin. The senior captain had pedantically stopped Ramage making his report on the quarterdeck; instead he had insisted that Ramage follow him down to his cabin, where he had carefully seated himself at a desk, waving Ramage to a chair opposite.

"Well, Ramage, what have you to report?" Arbuthnot fiddled

with his stock, as though it had suddenly tightened. "I see that all but one of your boats are still at the quay."

"The French have gone," Ramage said bluntly. "All of them. They have left the island."

"Don't be absurd!" Arbuthnot said angrily. "You are just trying to dodge having to search."

Ramage shook his head wearily: it was disheartening when someone behaved exactly as expected, and so far Arbuthnot was conforming to the patterns with depressing precision.

"No, sir: they were taken off two days ago by a French frigate, the *Marie*. They were counted by the mayor of Capraia and his total came to within a dozen of ours."

"But that's three French frigates!" Arbuthnot protested feebly.

"And two ships of the line," Ramage reminded him, trying to keep the malice out of his voice.

"But how did this *Marie* know about the prisoners?"

"I'm sure she didn't sir. She may have had a rendezvous with one or both of the other two frigates, and when she didn't find them here she may have sent a boat on shore to get news and found the two crews there."

Clearly Arbuthnot was now puzzled what to do next: should he give chase or return to Naples? That was obviously a question to which for the moment he had no answer.

"When did you say this frigate arrived?"

"Two days ago. The day after I landed the prisoners."

"And which way did she go?"

"To the north. The wind would have been from the south-west."

"To the north, eh? Then she could have rounded Capraia and made for Toulon."

"She could have done," Ramage agreed. "Especially if she was short of water or provisions."

"Two days on her way to Toulon . . . no, we'd never stand a chance of catching her."

Ramage said nothing: it was Arbuthnot's decision, and with this kind of man if he was blamed by the Admiral he would mention that Ramage had agreed with him, even if all Ramage had done was rub his nose. No, Ramage decided, if Arbuthnot wanted any second opinion, let him get it from Slade, in the *Phoenix*: Slade was second-in-command of the little squadron, and was a devil of a sight higher up the Post List than Ramage.

"You can return to your ship," Arbuthnot said. "I will talk to you later."

Yes, Ramage thought, you'll give me orders after you have had time to talk it over with Slade. You are scared of Admiral Rudd: responsibility does not sit easily on your shoulders.

As soon as Ramage was back on board the *Calypso* he sent Orsini on shore with instructions for Kenton, Martin and Rennick: they were to return with their men at once.

The signal for Ramage to return to the *Intrepid* was not made for two hours, during which time Orsini reported that Captain Slade had visited the *Intrepid* and returned to the *Phoenix*. Arbuthnot, Ramage thought to himself, has got his second opinion. It was ironic that a man who dodged responsibility would get promotion to admiral – providing he lived long enough – simply because of seniority. Ramage did not know Arbuthnot's number on the Post List, but (like Ramage himself) he was advancing up it as those captains above him died off or were killed and new ones appeared below him, to help push him up the List.

That was the fault of promotion in the Navy: once one had made the final step – through influence or merit, because they were the only two things that could do it – of being made post (which was a complicated way of saying that you had been given command of a ship that had to be commanded by a post-captain) then becoming an admiral was simply a matter of staying alive and accumulating seniority: promotion to rear-admiral, the first rung on the nine steps of admiral, came when you reached the top of the list of post-captains and one of the rear-admirals died. Then you survived as a rear-admiral until you reached the top of the list and you became a vice-admiral when one of them died and made a vacancy. And having got thus far, you hoped to stay alive so that you became full admiral by the same process. Nor did one have to be serving at sea because promotion was automatic: an admiral, be he rear, vice or full admiral, could be retired and drawing a pension for longer than he had served at sea. Indeed, there was one notorious case of an admiral ninety-nine years old who had been retired for forty-nine years after serving at sea only forty years, when his highest rank had been post-captain. Forty-nine years an admiral and never commanded a fleet; indeed, had never commanded more than a 74.

Arbuthnot would like that, Ramage thought sourly; he would not mind that the only people that called him admiral were the domestics and the people in whichever village he chose for retirement. He wondered for a minute what sort of man Captain Slade was: did he like being a second opinion? Perhaps he liked the responsibility. Perhaps he did not.

Again Arbuthnot went through the ritual of taking Ramage down to his cabin and seating him in the chair opposite the desk.

Arbuthnot clasped his hands together and composed his face into what he clearly thought was a stern and confident look.

"I have given the situation my attention," he told Ramage, "and I have come to the conclusion that it would be a pointless waste of time and quite beyond the scope of my orders to search for this frigate. By now it is probably halfway to Toulon."

Ramage was clearly expected to make some sort of comment.

"Very well, sir," he said.

"I could of course send you in chase," Arbuthnot said. "What do you think about that?"

Ramage decided that two could play at this game. "If you think there is any chance of me catching her, sir, I would be happy to try."

It was obvious that it was an idea that Arbuthnot had already discussed with Slade, and it was equally obvious what their conclusion had been.

"You think you might have a chance?" Arbuthnot asked, obviously startled by Ramage's reply. Ramage shrugged his shoulders. "One can but try, sir."

Arbuthnot seemed to decide that this sort of sparring could go on all afternoon; that he was not going to trap Ramage into saying something that he could relate to Admiral Rudd as confirming whatever decision he had made.

"You agree with me that a two-day start is an advantage we could never hope to overcome."

Again Ramage shrugged. "It's impossible to say, sir, because we don't know for sure that she is making direct for Toulon. She might have a rendezvous with another ship somewhere so that she could unload some of the survivors on board. She may be becalmed. Who knows?"

Now it was Arbuthnot's turn to shrug his shoulders. "I consider that most unlikely, and so does Captain Slade."

"In that case, sir," Ramage said, "what are my orders?"

Arbuthnot again composed his face. "I intend taking the squadron back to Naples and reporting to Admiral Rudd," he said. "He will not be very pleased at the idea of losing so many prisoners."

And you and Slade are annoyed at losing so much head money, Ramage thought; how blatant can you be?

Down in the wardroom Martin was playing his flute and the red-haired Kenton was sitting in the doorway of his tiny cabin listening to him. Although they were physically very different types, both had family links with the Navy. Martin, known to the other lieutenants as "Blower" because of his flute playing, was the son of the master shipwright at Chatham Dockyard while Kenton, heavily freckled and with his face continually peeling from sunburn, was the son of a half-pay captain.

When Martin paused, Kenton said: "You know, Blower, we were damned unlucky that French frigate just happened to come along and rescue those survivors."

"I don't know, I wasn't looking forward to climbing over the island looking for them."

"No, but we lost a lot of head money."

"No, we didn't," Martin contradicted. "I heard the captain telling Southwick that the Admiral said all the head money would go to the *Phoenix* and the *Intrepid* because technically they would have captured the men."

"Why, that's monstrous!" Kenton exclaimed.

"All admirals are monstrous," Martin said lazily. "With the exception of Lord Nelson, and that was why he was killed. He was the only man who wasn't a monster ever to be made an admiral."

At that moment Hill came into the wardroom. "Come on Blower, start playing that thing."

"I've been playing for an hour. I was just telling our friend here that we didn't lose any head money over the prisoners."

"No," said Hill, "we had already been cheated out of it by the Admiral, judging from what I heard Mr Ramage tell old Southwick. So our French friends have helped spread a little justice round: we get cheated out of head money, and then the *Intrepid* and the *Phoenix* get cheated out of it by the French frigate. No head money for anyone."

"Well, we earned it," Kenton grumbled.

"We certainly did, but unless we had carried all of the prisoners back for the Admiral to count, we ran the risk of losing it. You must get out of the habit of thinking there is any justice in this world."

Kenton acknowledged Hill's remark with a dismissive gesture that implied he was annoyed at being thought so naïve. "We don't need the money, at least I don't," he said airily. "Thanks to prize money I shan't be reduced to shining boots when I'm retired on half-pay. Nor will Martin. You joined too late, George. Still, if you fall on hard times in the future I'll employ you as my valet. Would you make a good valet, George?"

"That depends on the state of your wardrobe. If you expect me for ever to be stitching stocks and darning stockings, then the answer is no. I shall only valet for the gentry – the *rich* gentry."

"By the way," asked Martin, putting his flute back in its case, "has anyone heard if we are going back to Naples?"

Hill shook his head. "I should think so, but I haven't heard anyone mention it. Why? Do you fancy a Neapolitan romance?"

"Orsini tells me the Neapolitan women are very beautiful," Martin said seriously, "but there's some difficulty with what I think Orsini said were *cicisbeos*."

"You mean husbands?" asked Hill.

"No, as far as I can make out, a *cicisbeo* is a lady's recognized follower: the husband knows all about it and agrees: the *cicisbeo* acts as a combined escort and chaperone."

"If I was the husband I wouldn't agree to that," Kenton said.

"No, he escorts the lady to the opera or takes her for rides in a carriage: it is all very honourable."

"It wouldn't be if I was a *cicisbeo*," Kenton said firmly. "The husband would be a cuckold within the hour."

Hill said: "There's probably an old Neapolitan tradition among husbands that *cicisbeos* who overstep the mark get their throats cut within the hour, too!"

Martin snapped the catch of the flute case and said: "It all sounds too easy, so there's bound to be a snag. I can't see Neapolitan husbands, of all men on earth, making their wives freely available. On the contrary, I would say that of all places on earth Naples is where the wife's honour – or perhaps I mean the husband's honour – is the most closely guarded."

"I'll bear that in mind when I go on shore," Hill said lightly. "No married women!"

"The unmarried women will be guarded by mothers who can make a wild tiger look tame, you can be sure of that," Kenton said.

"You two aren't making Naples sound a very attractive place," Hill grumbled. "I must say that from seaward Naples Bay looks very romantic."

"Obviously we are going to have to question Orsini more closely," Martin said. "He just mentioned it in passing. I don't think he knows Naples very well – Volterra, where he and his aunt come from, is about a hundred miles north of Rome."

"Do they have *cicisbeos* in Rome and other places?" Kenton wondered.

"From the way Orsini spoke," Martin said, "they are peculiar to Naples. Don't forget that Naples is so far south that it is a very different city from Rome or those places in the north."

"Well," declared Hill, "we're going to have to wait and see. But thanks for the warning: it seems the innocent young English naval officer is in great danger from both the *cicisbeo* and the husband, and he has to beware the mother if the girl is a spinster."

114

Chapter Nine

The *Calypso* had been at anchor in Naples Bay for three days before the flagship hoisted her pendant number and the signal for captain. Both cutters were swinging at the boat boom, and as soon as he had changed to a fresh stock and buckled on his sword, Ramage set off.

From the time the *Intrepid* and *Phoenix* had arrived in Naples Bay with the *Calypso* in company, Ramage had heard nothing from Arbuthnot. Orsini had reported seeing Arbuthnot being rowed over to the flagship soon after they had anchored, and the Admiral had sent for him once. Otherwise, until now, Ramage had been left to himself.

Now what was the matter? He thought it seemed a long time had passed for the Admiral to want to rake over the Capraia affair. But it was hard to be sure: Admiral Rudd had not given him the impression of being a very stable sort of man: the more Ramage thought about it, the more likely it seemed that the Admiral could have spent three days brooding, working himself up into a temper, and now he was going to unleash it.

What could have caused it, though? The loss of head money, the fact that the French frigate had appeared on the scene, that the *Calypso* had not gone off in chase? No, the question of the *Calypso* going off in chase was Arbuthnot's decision; he had been the senior officer and Ramage could not have gone off without Arbuthnot's permission even if he had wanted to. So what was bothering the Admiral? Ramage shrugged his shoulders: it was impossible to guess, and anyway there was very little point in trying: he would know for sure in ten minutes' time.

Jackson brought the cutter alongside the flagship, hooked on and waited for Ramage to board. He was met at the entryport by the flagship's first lieutenant who, Ramage had to admit, ran a smart ship: there had been sideboys holding out handropes, and the handropes were well scrubbed. The deck was almost white from vigorous holystoning, and the brasswork's shine showed that many men had been busy polishing with brickdust.

"The Admiral will see you in his cabin, sir," the first lieutenant said with the superciliousness that first lieutenants of flagships inevitably adopted to post-captains at the lower end of the Post List. However, Ramage had met this too often to be intimidated.

"If you lead the way down," he said, at once putting the first lieutenant in the position which could have been occupied by a midshipman, and leaving him with no chance of a direct refusal.

Ramage found Rear-Admiral Rudd seated at his desk, and he acknowledged the Admiral's gesture to sit in the chair in front of him.

"So now we have got over the farce of Capraia," the Admiral observed sourly. "You might have anticipated that a French frigate would pick up those survivors."

The comment was so absurd, Ramage found it easy not to answer: any admiral who tried to blame a subordinate in such a crude way deserved sympathy: he must be very unsure of himself.

Admiral Rudd shifted in his chair and said suddenly: "You know about the Algerines?"

Ramage nodded. "I captured one of their ships once," he said.

"They're still present; in fact they are increasing. We've just had an official complaint from the King of the Two Sicilies, and we have to do something about it. They've suddenly started swarming over the ports along the coast of southern Sicily – kidnapping for their galleys and looting and raping. They are also taking fishing boats and apparently adding them to their own fleet."

"Do we know roughly what ships they have?" Ramage asked.

"All small stuff. Nothing like a frigate. Galleys, fishing boats crowded with men, that sort of thing. As far as I can make out a dozen or so of them attack a particular port one day – they don't bother to wait for nightfall to do their work – and then vanish for a few days, then they attack somewhere else."

Ramage thought for a minute and then asked: "Is there any pattern to these attacks, sir, or are they random?"

"No, they're not random: I was just going to tell you. Appar-

116

ently they work their way along the coast, attacking one port and then, a few days later, they arrive off the next. They've nothing to fear from the Sicilians so they needn't bother about surprise."

"What about the Sicilian Army?"

"What do you expect?" Rudd asked sourly. "They are doing nothing and His Majesty has a dozen reasons for their inactivity. He says the ports are often separated by cliffs, and it is almost impossible for troops to move along the coast. That's why he has come to us."

"It seems reasonable enough," Ramage admitted. "But catching two dozen fishing boats is like trying to catch a shoal of herrings with a single hook."

"I don't see why," Rudd said uncompromisingly. "Anyway, I can't spare any of my brigs or sloops: you're the only person I can send."

"Very well, sir: I'll do my best."

Rudd held up a small packet. "Here are your orders. And don't forget the King of the Two Sicilies and the British government are involved in all this. The British Minister is particularly concerned that we root out the scoundrels."

Ramage took the packet. "Will that be all, sir?"

"Yes, but make sure you understand that this isn't just a jaunt chasing pirates: with the King involved this becomes a major operation. If I had anyone else to send," Rudd said bluntly, "I would. I am not very satisfied with your behaviour so far under my command. You seem far too light-hearted."

"I'm sorry, sir: I do assure you I take my duties very seriously," Ramage said, wishing he could make a comment about his opinion of the attitude of the flag officer under whom he was serving. After a polite farewell he left the cabin and went back to the cutter.

Seated at his desk back on board the *Calypso* Ramage broke the seal on his orders and unfolded the single sheet of paper. After the usual formalities they told him that the Algerine pirates had so far raided Marsala and Mazara at the western end of the island of Sicily, and appeared to be making their way eastward. In view of representations from the Court of the King of the Two Sicilies, Ramage was requested and required to take the ship under his command and destroy the pirates.

And that was it. One thing about Rear-Admiral Rudd, Ramage thought ruefully, he does not waste any words. Even more surprising, the orders were straightforward and unambiguous; there were no hidden threats concerning the penalty for failure.

Before calling his clerk to have the orders copied into the orders book, Ramage sent for Aitken and Southwick: it was his habit to discuss orders with them, not because he had any doubts but because he had long since accepted that he was mortal, and if he was killed then it would be up to Aitken as first lieutenant, and therefore second-in-command, and Southwick, as the ship's wise old man, to complete his orders. They would have more chance of doing that successfully if they knew how he had been thinking.

Southwick settled himself in the armchair as Aitken first read the orders and then handed them over to the master. Southwick read them and gave a contented sniff. "It isn't often one reads orders that don't have a lot of concealed threats in 'em," he said. "But it isn't often that one of the King's ships is sent off chasing pirates. What have they got – an old frigate or some such?"

"No, it's not going to be that easy," Ramage said. "The Admiral told me that they have a couple of dozen fishing boats – either local Sicilian craft they've captured with lateen sails and carrying twenty or thirty men, or vessels they've come over in from the Barbary coast."

"Chasing two dozen vessels with one frigate isn't going to be easy," grumbled Aitken. "Those damned things are fast and they go to windward like a ferret out of the bag. They're shallow draft, too, so they can run up on a beach. Half the time they'll be out of gunshot of us if we have to cruise round in deep enough water."

"Come now," Ramage said chidingly, "you're letting the thought of a couple of dozen Algerines beat you before we've set sail!"

"Maybe so," Southwick said gloomily, "but you mark my words: it'll be like trying to catch eels with slippery hands."

"How shall we start finding out where they're operating, sir?" Aitken asked.

Ramage thought for a minute or two. "Well, we can either go round the north coast and catch them up, or we can go round the south coast and meet them as they work their way eastward."

118

"Northabout," Southwick said firmly. "It'll be easier following them – we shall know where they are. If we go southabout we'll never know when we are going to run into them – or maybe run past them."

Ramage nodded: Southwick had put into words his own thoughts. He took the orders and folded the paper along the original creases. A single sheet of paper, but it brought a shipload of problems.

Marsala – he had only been there once: a town which looked as though it should be in Africa. And, of course, the home of the strong, sweet wine. And the port's name as far as the Algerines were concerned was the Port of God, Marsah el Allah. Saracen, Algerine, Barbary – they were all pirates and had been for centuries, whether they came from the Levant in the east or Algiers in the west. A pity they had sacked Marsala – had they set fire to the place? From what little he knew of the Algerines, they tended to kidnap, rob and rape; they rarely burned down a town, for the simple reason that they planned to return a year or two later and repeat their raid.

And curiously enough, they were as anxious to capture human beings as anything: men to man their galleys – slaves chained to the oars did not live long – and women to put in their brothels. The trade in human beings was what made Algerine raids so sickening. The Italians called them *Saraceni*, Saracens, and there were few towns along the coast of the Tyrrhenian Sea which had not been raided half a dozen times in the last hundred years or so. The forts which dotted the coast were used mostly to keep a watch for the *Saraceni*. There were few Tuscan coastal towns that he knew of which did not have some legend about the *Saraceni*.

There was the story of *La Bella Marsiliana*. Marsilia was a little town just north of Monte Argentario and according to legend the Saracens raided the town. Among the women they carried off was one of great beauty and charm, and when she was brought back to the Saracen headquarters, a prince fell in love with her and married her, and they lived happily ever after.

But the story of *La Bella Marsiliana* must be a rare one as far as the women were concerned; most of them probably spent the rest of their active lives in brothels, killed off when they were too old to be useful.

119

No, the Saracens, or Algerines, call them what you will, were barbarians who regarded everyone else as infidels, unbelievers to be enslaved or put to the sword. They were not the sort of people, Ramage thought, to be taken prisoner.

British warships would be welcome at Marsala, Ramage reflected: once the Spanish ports had been closed years earlier so that British ships could not call in for wine for the men's daily ration, one of the favourite replacements had been the wine of Marsala.

The *Calypso* passed Trapani, with its high striated cliffs, and the great grey castle, centuries old, peered down from the summit of Monte San Giuliano, where it sat four-square in the village of Eryx almost surrounded by pine forests.

Over to starboard were the Aegadean Islands of Levanzo, Favignana and Marettimo, sitting a few miles offshore like giant teeth set in the sea. Ramage thought about calling at the islands to see if they had been raided, but they were almost uninhabited, the haunt of tunny fishermen.

The lookouts had reported a few tartanes, probably carrying salt from the salt ponds round to Trapani itself. Then, beyond the point, the frigate headed south to round Punto Scario and then turn in to Marsala. Ramage had an old history of Sicily in his cabin and he had looked up Marsala. Like most places in Sicily it was ancient, originally Phoenician, and when Rome was busy with Carthage, it became a busy port. The most extraordinary thing that he read was how often the port had been blocked by rocks being rolled into the entrance. The Romans had done it once; then the Venetians had shut it off at the time of the Battle of Lepanto, to make sure that the *Saraceni* – this time Turks – should not use it. But, according to the book, Marsala had begun to thrive thirty years ago when a couple of Englishmen started to export the local wine to England. The sweet wine, like a heavy sherry, immediately became popular. It was curious how the Royal Navy's demands influenced the fortunes of places: in the West Indies, rum was king because the Navy wanted it to issue to the men, and for ships serving this side of the Atlantic, Spain had supplied much of the wine that replaced the rum, until Spain threw in her lot with France, when Italian wines – and particularly Marsala – came into favour.

So that was how prosperity came to a little port on the south-west corner of Sicily – because its grapes produced a particular wine. At least, not just Marsala itself produced the grapes, the countryside around shared the harvest.

And why, Ramage wondered, was the cathedral of Marsala dedicated to St Thomas à Becket, whose glory surely was to be found at Canterbury?

Southwick walked across to him and said: "At Marsala we have to watch out for Il Marrobbio."

"Do we indeed, and what is that?"

"Well, it has three names, depending on which part of Sicily you happen to be in: Marrobbio, Carrobbio and Marrubio. It's a series of waves which can spring up at any time, usually when the weather is calm. The waves are two or three feet high, and they come in surges at intervals ranging from ten minutes to half an hour.

"You get them along the western, southern and eastern coasts of the island but they are most prevalent in the south-western corner – at Marsala, in fact. So we must watch out. We need an extra two or three feet under our keel, and the boat crews need warning to be on the lookout; it's enough to capsize 'em."

"Any other cheerful warnings?" Ramage asked sarcastically.

"No, sir, only that the Marrobbio can churn up a nasty current inside the port."

"What a pity it doesn't catch some of these *Saraceni*!"

Marsala was a sullen, frightened town: when Ramage landed by cutter he was told by the mayor that the Saracens had taken an estimated three hundred men and at least fifty women. The cathedral had been looted along with the town hall and most of the big houses near the quay. In many warehouses big casks of Marsala had been stove in, apparently just deliberate vandalism since none of the wine had been stolen.

"But the boats," one of the men lamented. "They took all our big fishing boats. We've nothing left to fish with or to fetch wood to build new ones."

And that, thought Ramage, covers another of Sicily's tragedies: it is always short of wood. It was said the Phoenicians first cut down all the trees, having learned that was a quick way of reducing the rainfall and turning a place into a desert, and thus making Sicily –

which cut the Mediterranean in half – uninhabitable and therefore not a threat. Since Phoenician times trees had had a hard time trying to survive in Sicily, and in recent years even bushes were cut down to satisfy the charcoal burners. Without charcoal the people could not cook their food; without wood they could not build the boats to catch the fish to feed on. It was a miracle that people could survive in Sicily, and it was significant that the Saracens came mainly to capture men and women.

When Ramage had himself rowed back to the *Calypso* he was depressed. First, it seemed tragic that people with so little to lose should be raided by the Saracens and second that the only other thing they had to lose, their very lives, should have been taken to be worn out in the galleys and brothels.

Soon the *Calypso*'s capstan was turning as the men weighed the anchor, and half an hour later the frigate was stretching along in a northerly breeze heading for a next port along the coast to the eastward, Mazara del Vallo. Quite apart from the distance the *Calypso* had run, it would not have been hard to identify Mazara because of the many belfries and cupolas. The cathedral had a high cupola with a greyish-red belfry next to it. Another church (Ramage found out later it was called Santa Veneranda) had twin belfries, and the belfry of the church of San Francisco was alone in the north-west part of the port, square and surmounted by a pyramid.

The harbour, such as it was – it was badly silted – stood at the mouth of the Torrente Mazara, and when the *Calypso* anchored in six fathoms off the entrance, Southwick reported a bottom of rock and weed. Once again the cutter, which had been towing astern, was hauled alongside and Ramage climbed down following Rennick and a dozen Marines.

The story he heard was much the same as at Marsala: men and women had been taken, along with the four biggest tartanes which had been anchored in the harbour. But the surviving people in Mazara were pleased over one thing – the *Saraceni* had not damaged the statue of St Vitus, the town's patron saint, nor had they discovered a silver statue of him. This was particularly precious and every year it was carried round the town in a colourful procession.

But apart from that, Mazara was a town of weeping women and

men walking round as though they had been stunned. There was not much damage to the town and that, Ramage thought to himself, was about all that could be said in favour of the *Saraceni*.

Ramage had a long talk with the mayor: he had managed to escape being taken prisoner by hiding in the belfry of one of the churches. The *Saraceni* had raided the town in broad daylight, taking about a hundred men and fifty women, and had left to the eastward. When Ramage compared the dates, he found that Mazara had been raided twelve days after Marsala. Why the long delay, since the voyage between the two took only a few hours?

The answer, when he finally thought of it, was very obvious: the Saracens had only small boats – fishermen, tartanes and the like – which could not hold many people, so after each raid they had to return to their base to unload the prisoners, and then come back to the Sicilian coast for more.

Ramage almost breathed a sigh of relief: he was – probably – not as far behind the *Saraceni* as he thought: there were only five more ports along the south coast that the pirates were likely to raid. Would they then work their way round the east coast? Or would they start along the northern coast?

The *Calypso* spent the night anchored off the port and next day weighed to sail eastward to the next little port, Sciacca, an old town perched on the side of a steep hill overlooking the harbour.

As the *Calypso* anchored off Sciacca – the harbour was too shallow to allow the frigate in – Ramage saw that the port was surrounded by a wall, with the ruins of a castle at the eastern end. At the other end was a church with a green cupola. He had no trouble finding Punta Pertuso, marked on the chart – it had bright yellow cliffs and had a hole through it.

There were only a few boats lying alongside down in the harbour and Ramage, accompanied by Rennick and a couple of Marines, had to walk up to the town, which was obviously originally Aragonese. The square in the middle of the town was pleasantly cool, and when Ramage asked the way to the mayor's house he was directed to a small house two streets behind the square.

The mayor was home, a stocky little man with a large flowing black moustache which contrasted with his grey hair. The man was obviously intrigued at this visit from a British naval officer and his escort and Ramage, already hot from the walk up the hill, was thankful to be invited into the house, out of the sun.

Ramage explained the reason for the *Calypso*'s arrival off the port and the mayor admitted that at first when he had seen the ship he had been alarmed.

"We are defenceless," he said. "A few fowling pieces and scythes. Not enough, you understand, to drive off six *Saraceni*, let alone a hundred."

"So they've been here. How many prisoners did they take?"

"About a hundred men and twenty women. And they took most of our fishing boats: all those of a good size. You saw the ones they left down in the port."

"When were you last raided?" Ramage asked.

"When I was a boy. Thirty years ago, perhaps more. Marsala, yes, they raided there only about five years ago, but not here: they left us in peace until now. So we have lost our best young men. What can we do?"

"We can't do anything about the men already taken," Ramage said. "They are probably already in Algiers or Tunis or some such place. But I am here at the King's order –" Ramage thought the exaggeration was in order, " – to try to destroy these pirates, to stop them raiding more towns."

The mayor shrugged his shoulders hopelessly. "Marsala, Mazara, here – why, if Selinunte had been inhabited they would have raided there."

Selinunte was the ruin of a large Greek city ten miles or so west of Sciacca: Ramage had seen the huge stone columns as the *Calypso* had sailed past, and his book told him that there were great blocks of stone and many sculptures left there after the Carthaginians sacked the city five hundred years before Christ.

"At least the *Saraceni* did not burn your town," Ramage said gently. "At least your survivors still have somewhere to live."

"Some life," the mayor said bitterly. "I have lost a son and three nephews, and a niece. And the people call me lucky: many of them lost more."

The man was about to cry, and Ramage knew of no way of comforting him: there was no way of disguising the fate of the men and women he had lost, and at the moment there was no guarantee that another such raid would not happen.

124

Ramage said his farewell, and with Rennick and the Marines he walked back down the hill again.

As they walked, Ramage told Rennick what the mayor had said. Finally Rennick said: "I wonder if I would have been so controlled if I had lost so much."

"I don't know if he is controlled or stunned. I think it is too soon after it happened. It'll be another week or two before he realizes exactly what he's lost. Or what has happened to them. Yes, he knows they've been captured; but he hasn't yet thought about the galleys and the brothels. That is what will break him up."

Back on board the *Calypso*, he called Aitken and Southwick to his cabin and repeated to them the mayor's story. Their reaction was the same as Rennick's.

"There's no chance of rescuing any of them, that's the terrible thing about it," Southwick said.

"It's obvious that the Algerines have hundreds of slaves," Ramage said. "And no one dares guess how many women go into the brothels."

"It's a pity we can't do something about it."

"That's what the British government has been saying for a hundred years," Ramage said. "But first you have to capture Algiers. Then half a dozen other places. And by the time you have captured them, most of the slaves will have been put to death. There's no man alive more ruthless than a Saracen."

"Where now?" Southwick asked.

"We'll just carry on eastward along the coast. Porto Empedocle is the next place, and I have a feeling we shall arrive there too late."

The mayor of Porto Empedocle told a similar story to that of the mayor of Sciacca: the *Saraceni* had arrived three days earlier, turned out all the men and women and lined them up in the street, and then taken their pick. The mayor had lost four nephews but as the good lord had not seen fit to give his wife any children, he had not lost any sons. The *Saraceni* had gone off with their prisoners, seventy men and thirty women, many of whom were crowded into fishing boats stolen from the harbour.

"We shall never recover," the mayor said. "We have lost our best young men and our boats. What is there left?"

And Ramage knew he was right: there was nothing left. On the ridge above Empedocle stood the temples of Agrigento: a vast Greek city whose now ruined walls enclosed a couple of square miles. At the height of its power, it was estimated, the population had been a million people. Even before then the Cretans had tried to capture the city for five years. And what did it all mean now for the mayor of Empedocle, grieving at the *Saraceni* raid? Nothing, Ramage decided; it simply emphasized how, in the sweep of history, none of it mattered.

As Ramage returned to the *Calypso* in the cutter he considered the three days. If he was correct, the Empedocle prisoners were still on their way to Algiers or Tunis, or wherever the Saracens were based.

Back in his cabin, relating to Aitken and Southwick what the mayor of Empedocle had told him, Ramage repeated the information about the three days, and Aitken immediately said: "We should find that the next port, Licata, hasn't been attacked yet."

"Not only that," Ramage said, "but we have eight or nine days to get ready for the next attack."

Aitken shook his head: he was puzzled and dispirited. "From what all the mayors have been saying, the Saracens have picked up another twenty or so boats. If they started off with twenty – and I doubt if they had fewer than that – they now have forty. How can we deal with forty boats even though they won't be carrying guns – at least half of them won't, anyway. It'll be like trying to snatch sprats out of a barrel: those tartanes and galleys will be just as slippery."

It was a point which had been worrying Ramage since he first arrived off the coast: how could a lumbering frigate sink the fast and agile Saracens? Because it was a question of destroying them, not just driving them off. Drive them off today and they'll be back next week, or the week after, warier but just as determined.

Southwick gave an enormous sniff, and Ramage recognized it as the warning that he had an important pronouncement to make.

"We can't do it," he said. "There's no way. I don't usually say something is impossible, but there is no way we can stop forty boats – or even twenty – and destroy them, even if they are drawn up in a regular line of battle, which of course they won't be, being Saracens."

"I've been thinking the same thing for days," Ramage admitted.

126

"But so far I can see no alternative but to wade right into the middle of them and sink as many as we can."

"I don't think we'll sink many," Southwick said. "They're all fast and weatherly craft. Tartanes can eat their way to windward and those damned galleys can turn on a penny piece."

"Makes me think we shouldn't be at sea," Ramage said enigmatically.

The little port of Licata, some thirty miles along the coast, was the next place to visit. Nor was it difficult to find: it stood at the mouth of the *Fiume* Salso and a big castle, Castel San Angelo, was built on Monte Ecnomo on the western side of the town with the church of San Angelo, which had a very prominent cupola, on the eastern side.

The *Calypso* anchored off and Ramage went in with the cutter. He was surprised how small was Licata, and it seemed too unimportant for the *Saraceni* to raid. Nor had it been attacked. The mayor was a sturdy, grey-haired man who regarded Ramage as a saviour.

"When we heard every port had been attacked between here and Marsala," he said, "we gave ourselves up for lost. But then at the last minute you arrive with your great ship, *Commandante*. Our prayers have been answered just in time."

Ramage held up his hand to stop the man. "We can't do much against so many of their vessels," Ramage said. "We think they'll have about forty or more, and how can just one ship destroy them?"

The mayor looked crestfallen. "But you have such a big ship, and all they have will be tartanes and galleys."

"Yes, I know," Ramage said patiently, "but they are very agile. It would be like a man in a large boat with a trident trying to spear little fishes. You spear one but there are many more . . ."

"Then send your men on shore and help us fight the *Saraceni* in the streets," the mayor said, and immediately Ramage knew his idea was a practical one, and he wished he had discussed it with Aitken and Southwick.

"How many people are there in Licata?" Ramage asked.

The mayor shrugged his shoulders. "Who knows? Perhaps four thousand, but maybe only three."

"How many men have you who can fight?"

"Fight? It will be mostly with swords and cudgels: I doubt if there are fifty fowling pieces in the whole town, and the powder for them is probably damp."

"Very well, how many with swords and cudgels?"

"Young men who can fight, perhaps two hundred. Most of our men are now old and decrepit; not fit for much more than sitting in the sun and puffing a pipe."

"And what about water?"

"Plenty – we have two good wells. Why?"

"If I land a hundred men they can bring provisions but they'll need water. Not just for a day or two but every day until the *Saraceni* arrive. If they arrive, that is."

"They'll come," the mayor said grimly. "They're picking off the ports like ripe oranges. We're the next to last one along this south coast. They'll come all right."

He is right, Ramage told himself, and nodded. "Yes, I think they'll come – in six or seven days."

The mayor looked puzzled. "What makes you so sure? Why not tomorrow, or the next day?"

Ramage explained the timetable for the previous raids, and how it seemed that the *Saraceni* needed twelve days or so to take the prisoners back to their base and return to the coast of Sicily. Empedocle had been raided three days before the *Calypso* arrived, and the frigate had taken a day to get here because of light winds, making four days in all since the raid on Empedocle.

The mayor was now getting excited: he had been living with the thought of a Saracen raid for so long that he had given up hope; now Ramage's arrival had changed everything.

Ramage interrupted his spate of excited speculation with a harsh remark. "We must destroy these men, every one of them. There is no point in driving them off. Drive them off and they'll be back again in days or weeks."

"Yes, yes, we must trap them," the mayor exclaimed.

Ramage nodded. "I am going back to my ship to make plans," he said. "Be patient; I shall return."

Chapter Ten

Ramage's cabin was crowded: as usual Southwick sat in the armchair, Aitken, Kenton and Martin were crowded together on the settee and Hill and Rennick stood either side of the door, their heads canted because of the low headroom.

Ramage looked up from his desk and said without any preliminaries: "There's little doubt that Licata will be the next target for the Saracens, probably in about eight days' time."

With the exception of the first lieutenant and master, the rest of the officers looked startled; as though their captain had started fortune telling. Ramage immediately noticed and went on to explain how he had reached that conclusion.

As Ramage finished with his estimate of the number of vessels that the Saracens would have, Hill said: "How are we going to tackle that number, sir?"

"We aren't," Ramage said shortly. "There's no way we can. In other words we can't deal with them at sea."

He stopped with that remark and it was left to Hill to echo, questioningly, the phrase: "At sea?"

"Yes," Ramage said briskly. "We've got to destroy these damned pirates, and the only way we can do it is trap them on shore. They might outnumber us – probably will – but we'll have to make up for that with surprise.

"I intend landing every Marine and seaman that can be spared, and every carronade and boat gun we have. We will mount the guns where they will do the most harm – in houses covering quays, places like that – and the men will be billeted in the houses, armed with muskets and pistols, along with pikes and cutlasses.

"The *Calypso* will then disappear over the horizon: we don't want her presence to frighten off the Saracens. She will return every few days and look for a signal flying from the Castel San Angelo – that's the big castle you can see on the hill overlooking the town – but unless the signal is flying, to show that it's all over, she will go out to sea again and disappear over the horizon."

He put his hands flat on the desk. "I have had a difficult time selecting officers because some of you are bound to be disappointed. But we must remember that our primary concern is the safety of the ship; the operation against the Saracens is our secondary concern. Therefore, Mr Aitken will command the ship and Mr Southwick will go with him.

"Mr Rennick will, of course, command the detachment of Marines and Sergeant Ferris will be his second-in-command. Lieutenants Kenton, Martin and Hill will command detachments of seamen and the guns they will handle.

"My headquarters will be in the castle because that is the best place for seeing what's going on. And there's no doubt I will be able to see – the Saracens raid in daylight; or at least they have so far.

"One last thing for now," Ramage added harshly. "We are dealing with barbarians. I am not interested in prisoners. I warn you, if you are taken prisoner by the Saracens, then you'll spend the rest of your life chained to the oar of a galley. Any questions?"

"Are the local people here on our side, sir?" asked Martin.

"Completely. They regard it as a miracle that we arrived when we did. By the way," he asked Aitken, "do we have any musketoons on board?"

"About half a dozen, sir," Aitken said. "I'll tell the gunner to get them out." He knew Ramage's dislike of the gunner, which was why the man was not at the meeting. "Grapeshot for the carronades?"

Ramage thought a moment and then said: "No, I think case will be more lethal. The object is to kill as many Saracens as possible with every round. That's why I don't want to use grapeshot: they're too big; they're all right for damaging ships and sending up showers of splinters, but we are going to be shooting at men out in the open."

His officers were excited at the prospect: Ramage could feel the tension in the cabin – all except Southwick. The old man was sitting in the armchair like a sack of potatoes, his hair sticking out like a dry mop. The prospect of being out at sea while there was a good fight going on ashore was almost more than he could bear, but Ramage had warned him that street fighting was a young man's sport, and anyway Aitken needed a responsible second-in-command because they would be standing watch and watch about for several days and they would both be very short of sleep.

"Any more questions?" Ramage asked. "No? Well, let's make a start then: we have to get six carronades ashore and six boat guns, along with powder, shot and provisions. And rockets for signalling. That reminds me, we need provisions for all the men but not water; the mayor tells me they have a couple of good wells. Mr Aitken, I want you to stay behind: we have to work out what men you can spare."

As soon as the others had gone, Aitken sat at one side of the desk and Ramage the other. Together they worked out the minimum number of men Aitken needed to work the ship and both men were surprised at how few were needed. Aitken, saying that he would not be sailing under courses but would probably stay under topsails, decided that six topmen and twelve afterguard would be sufficient for sail handling while half a dozen idlers would be enough to do the rest of the jobs on board, ranging from providing meals – the normal mess system could not be used because it would waste men – to scrubbing the decks.

This left Ramage with nearly two hundred seamen and twenty-four Marines. Against how many Saracens? One thing he had failed to get from the mayors had been reliable estimates of the number of Saracens attacking them. The only thing he had been able to do was to find out the number of vessels attacking the first port, Marsala, and then guess how many men they were carrying.

The mathematics did not change the fact that the British would be outnumbered, and quite heavily too. Against that was their advantage of surprise and the carronades, and probably the musketry. The Saracens would certainly have muskets, but would they have the training in loading? He doubted it.

Later that afternoon Ramage was rowed ashore to meet the mayor of Licata on the quay and he took Rennick, Kenton and Martin with him. As they walked in the hot sun along the dusty quay, which glinted with fish scales and reeked of rotted fish, Ramage and Rennick discussed the siting of the carronades. Where possible they wanted a good crossfire. Not at the actual point of disembarkation – that would give the Saracens time to scramble back into their boats and escape. No, the crossfire should be at a point where they had left their vessels and were making their way along the quay to raid the town. Within range of the carronades and the muskets.

Ramage pointed out forty or fifty square yards on the jetty. "Here," he said. "This is where we kill them. If we haven't killed them by the time they are crossing this point, then there's a chance that they will get past us and into the town. Then they might think of taking hostages, and if they do much of that we're done for; we can't do anything that would lead to the killing of hostages."

He and Rennick agreed on the siting of the first carronade: there was a narrow alley between two houses, and a carronade placed there would cover what Ramage had called "the killing ground". There were seven houses along the edge of the harbour near the alley, and Rennick agreed they were a fine place for his Marines with their muskets. Each Marine would have two loaded muskets beside him, in addition to the one he was holding, so that providing every man stayed calm they would be firing three times twenty-four aimed shots into the killing ground before having to pause to reload.

The second carronade, they decided, would be placed in the donkey stable next to the third house in the row: built of stone, the stable had a wide doorway to allow a donkey laden with panniers to come in or out, and this would give more than enough traverse for the gun.

The mayor explained patiently to the owner of the house and stable, and the man, although fearful at the sound of the word "gun", agreed once he realized it would mean extra protection against the *Saraceni*.

There was another stable beside the sixth house in the row, and the owner agreed that his donkey should be tethered outside for a few nights so that the carronade and its crew could be housed. Ramage, inspecting the stable and checking the field of fire, decided he did not envy the gun crew who would have to live there: it was ankle deep in foul-smelling straw and had obviously not been cleaned out properly for years.

With the mayor very competently explaining to the owners the reason, Ramage and Rennick soon sited the other three carronades, and arranged for seamen to be billeted in the nineteen houses from whose windows it was possible to fire muskets to cover the killing ground. Then it was a question of distributing the remaining men among houses close to the quay, where the men would have to run only a short distance to open fire on the approaching Saracens.

"Now," Ramage announced, "I want to go up and look down from my headquarters." He pointed up to the Castel San Angelo. "That will also be our lookout tower. I see you have a flagpole," he said to the mayor. "Does it have a halyard so that you can hoist flags?"

"Why, of course," exclaimed the mayor, as though shocked at the idea that it might not. "We hoist flags on saints' days."

"Ah, once the frigate has sailed you must not hoist any more flags: she will return from time to time and look at the castle with a telescope. As soon as they see a flag flying they will know the Saracens have attacked, and they will come in and anchor."

"But it will be too late for her to help," the mayor protested.

Ramage patiently explained that the frigate's task was to stay out of sight and, because she could do nothing against a swarm of *Saraceni* vessels, be sure she did nothing to frighten them away.

"We want them to come here," Ramage told the mayor grimly. "Here we shall be well prepared to meet them."

"I hope so," the mayor said doubtfully. "There will be so many of them, and they move like snakes."

"But we have the guns," Ramage said, trying to reassure him.

But the mayor could not distinguish between a carronade and an ordinary gun; he did not know that another name for it was "the Smasher".

"The guns are so small," he said. "We want long guns!"

Ramage knew it was impossible to explain, and contented himself with saying to Kenton and Martin: "You fit the boat guns wherever you've got room. Try not to damage the houses too much. But don't forget they don't throw musket balls very far."

The ship's company of the *Calypso* were kept busy until well after nightfall hoisting out the carronades and lowering the barrels into the boats to be ferried ashore, and then when they had returned alongside, lowering down the carriages.

133

Once the guns were assembled on the quay the men fitted traces and hauled them into their prearranged positions. Then powder and shot had to be carried ashore and put in position. Finally at midnight a weary Aitken came into Ramage's cabin and reported that all the carronades and boat guns had been landed, and with them shot, powder, rammers and sponges. And Marines were now patrolling where the guns were sited.

He did not add that the men were worn out, but Ramage said: "Very well, let's call it a night. We'll ferry all the men ashore tomorrow after they've had a good night's sleep, and then you can hoist in the boats and disappear to the eastward."

"Don't forget to take that white ensign with you, sir," Aitken said. "We shall be watching out for that!"

"You'll be no more anxious than I will to hoist it!"

Ramage thought awhile and then said: "I must emphasize that you should not approach before the late afternoon, and then come in perpendicular to the coast, so that you are in sight for the shortest time possible."

"You're expecting the attack to be in the morning, sir?"

"Yes, probably soon after dawn. The Saracens won't have any difficulty identifying the place, thanks to Castel San Angelo and the church. They'll probably expect to catch the people while they're still in their beds."

"And you'll be up in the castle?"

"Yes, me, Orsini and half a dozen seamen who will act as messengers as soon as we sight anything."

"Supposing they come at night, sir?"

"Well, the carronades will be sited already and the messengers can raise the alarm. I'd prefer it in daylight, so that we can see who we're shooting at, but a night attack isn't impossible to deal with."

Jackson and his gun's crew shovelled and cursed as they cleaned out the stable. The carronade stood in the road outside the door because Lieutenant Kenton had agreed that apart from the dangers of the gun capsizing itself as it recoiled over so much straw, the stench was appalling, a dreadful mixture of donkey manure and urine which had collected over the years.

Ramage, thinking of the practical effect of keeping men shut up in houses and stables for days on end, had finally arranged with the mayor that the town should go about its ordinary business – which meant that the seamen and Marines were allowed out in the street – until the bells of the church, also called San Angelo, should start tolling. Because Ramage knew that ringing church bells was a skilled job, he sent two seamen – whom he would have with him in the castle as messengers – with the mayor to find one of the bellringers and to get instructions how to toll the bells of San Angelo. The mayor assured him that the tolling of San Angelo could be heard all over the port; they were loud enough to wake sleeping people, if the *Saraceni* should be sighted at night. The mayor agreed to warn all the people, and to tell the priest.

Jackson and his men were hot and tired and far from pleased at the sort of work. "I'm a sailor, not a farm labourer," grumbled Stafford. "These damned people have never cleaned this stable out since it was built."

"And it was built on a manure heap to start with," Gilbert said.

Finally Jackson agreed that the stable was clean enough to move in the carronade. The gun just fitted; they managed to haul it in through the doorway with only a few inches to spare, so that the muzzle protruded as though through a gunport.

As soon as the gun was in the stable Jackson set them to work hammering a hole in the wall on each side of the door into which would be fixed big eyebolts to fit the thick rope, the breeching, which would hold the carronade when it recoiled. The noise of the hammering and the dust soon upset Rossi.

"Staff is not a farm labourer, I am not a stone mason. And this noise; it is driving me mad."

"Don't worry, Rosey, no one will notice," Stafford said. "Dung spreading and stone work is all part of chasing Saracens. Very strange people, Saracens; they only hide in manure heaps and behind piles of rocks."

Finally the carronade was ready to be trained left or right. Jackson settled himself behind the gun and gave training and elevating instructions. When he was satisfied that it would sweep the killing ground the gun was loaded and laid and trained again. Now Stafford, as second captain, unwrapped the lock from the piece of cloth in which he kept it and checked the flint. As soon as he was satisfied that it was making a strong spark, he bolted the

135

lock on to the gun, threaded the lanyard through the trigger and then coiled it up and placed the line on top of the breech.

"It's going to make a bang when we fire it in here," he observed. "I'm not sure my sensitive little ears will stand it."

"I shouldn't worry," Jackson said. "I've noticed how deaf you get when you don't want to hear something."

Stafford looked through the door across at the quay. "Where we're going to shoot, the Saracens will be a hundred yards or more from their ships."

"Exactly," Jackson said. "That's why Mr Ramage chose it. We want to kill them in a surprise attack, so that they don't have time to get back to their vessels. Take 'em by surprise: Mr Ramage says surprise doubles the number of your men and guns."

"I 'ope he's right," Stafford said miserably. "I don't want an 'undred or so of these Saracens whooping round me and trying to cut my head off with those skimitars of theirs."

"Scimitars," Jackson corrected automatically.

"I don't care what you call 'em," Stafford said sulkily. "I saw one once and it was big and 'orrible."

"Just think of them as overgrown cutlasses," Jackson said.

"S'no good," Stafford said. "I shall never think of them with 'ffection: those Saracens are wild men."

"No wilder than a panicky Frenchman fighting for his life," Jackson said reassuringly.

"We'll see," Stafford said gloomily.

"Well, let's get the powder stowed properly; at the moment the cartridges look as though they've been abandoned by a retreating army. And the caseshot: we want that in a handy pile here, just where the muzzle will be when the gun recoils."

"How many rounds do you reckon we'll be able to fire?" Gilbert asked.

Jackson looked at him quizzically. "Depends how long the Saracens wait there, and how fast you load! From here, though, we shall also be able to fire into their vessels as they lie alongside the quay. Perhaps a dozen rounds. Maybe more, if we're quick: after all, it doesn't take long to load a carronade."

"If those Saracens have any sense they'll run towards the guns to slice up the infidels," Stafford said. "Yelling 'orrible things and

136

waving those skimitars. Is it true, Jacko, that if they get killed fighting they go straight to Paradise?"

"Where's Paradise?" Jackson said. "It's not Heaven because they're not Christians; they're just benighted heathens. They might think they're going to a special heathen Paradise, and good luck to 'em as long as they're dead. If they're in Paradise they're not bothering us," he added.

Up on the battlements of Castel San Angelo Ramage watched seaward as the *Calypso* sailed away south-eastward. In half an hour she would be out of sight. Ramage had to admit to himself that he felt nervous; never before had he been out of sight of the *Calypso* with someone else commanding her. It was not that he did not trust Aitken and Southwick; his feelings, he suspected, were more like those of a mother whose young son was away staying with an ancient and unreliable grandmother: there was a nervousness with no definable reason for it.

The castle was strongly built. The only thing it lacked, Ramage thought crossly, was guns. It had been built to protect the port, and it was well positioned. If only it had a few guns it would be able to rake the quay. He had considered landing some 12-pounders from the *Calypso* and hauling them up to the castle, but had finally decided that the carronades would be sufficient. The track up to the castle was so bad that it was hard climbing up it, let alone hauling up heavy guns with only manpower; Licata boasted only a few donkeys: it was too poor for horses.

But the view from the battlements was fine: it was a view he would like to share with Sarah. What was she doing at this moment? Either at the house at Aldington, enjoying the Kentish spring, or staying with her parents. He decided she would be at Aldington: they both loved the house they had inherited from his uncle, and it was reassuring to think that she would be well looked after by the staff there.

How he longed for her company. He tried to think of her only at night: there was usually enough work – especially these last few days – to keep his mind occupied in the daytime. But the night was different: he could fill it with fantasies, except that her absence was painful: it was not nostalgia, it was a painful longing.

Paolo Orsini was standing beside him, and the young Italian

137

said: "Excuse me, sir, but we don't know how long it takes a man to get from here to the church: it might be useful to know if they come in the dark. And perhaps the men ought to get used to it, in case they have to find their way at night."

Ramage smiled. "Good thinking, my lad. You take the men now and time yourselves. It took about ten minutes from the quay to the church, but it should be less from up here."

Once the young midshipman had gone off with two men of the six who would be acting as lookouts, messengers and bellringers, Ramage paced up and down the battlements. Supposing the Saracens had decided not to bother with Licata and instead went on to the next port, Gela, which was bigger?

But why should they? he argued with himself: Sciacca and Empedocle were hardly bigger than Licata, but they had been raided. And, perhaps relevant, Licata would be easier to identify from seaward because of the castle.

Very well, but supposing there are more than two hundred Saracens? Supposing he was underestimating their strength by a half? Since he had not been able to get estimates of their strength from any of the ports, his guess was entirely based on the number of boats he estimated they had. But they had been capturing more boats as they worked their way along the coast. Had they picked up more Saracens when they went back to their base to unload the prisoners? It was possible; indeed, it was more than possible, it was most likely.

So two hundred men could easily be three hundred, or even four hundred; the Saracens, as far as he knew, never lacked for men, and the one Saracen ship of any size that he had captured years ago had three or four times more men than she would have had under the Royal Navy.

Very well, he told himself, say they have five hundred men and they come into the port and put their boats alongside the quay. Would they then attack the port in an orderly fashion, or would they straggle ashore, a score here and a score there, confident that there would be no opposition and therefore no need to hurry? With luck they might congregate on the quay, talking and joking, taking their time – taking their time and lingering in the square area which Ramage and Rennick had marked down as the killing ground.

Then they would be blasted by the carronades, boat guns and

138

muskets. Then what? These Saracens were no cowards: would they try and attack the guns or would they make a bolt for their tartanes and galleys alongside the quay? Most of the carronades could be brought to bear on the boats, so if they bolted the Saracens would be suffering more casualties. If they bolted. If they did, it would only be because they had been taken completely by surprise. Which was of course Ramage's great ally; surprise was the ally that – he hoped – would make his two hundred men equal to whatever number of Saracens raided Licata. He was still working out all the permutations when Orsini came back with the seamen.

"Six minutes to the church because it is all downhill," he reported, "and eight minutes back. The route is obvious, and if you agree sir, the men only need to do the journey once more to be sure of it at night."

"All right, carry on Orsini," Ramage said.

With that he resumed pacing the battlements. There was plenty of room – twenty yards of flagstones, which were uneven enough that one had to watch one's step. Four signal rockets looked out, canted over the town, and beside them a slowmatch burned, the glowing end tucked into a crack in the wall. One of the rockets would be enough: the guns' crews and the seamen with their muskets would watch the Saracens landing, after being alerted by the church bells, and they would be waiting for the rocket to soar overhead, giving them the signal to open fire instantly. Ramage had impressed on them all the need to open fire the moment they saw or heard the rocket: every second they delayed would mean the loss of surprise: the Saracens would be warned that they were walking into a trap.

Ramage looked seaward. The *Calypso* was now out of sight. Wind shadows swept across a calm sea, which was only gently pewtered. Aitken had been lucky to find enough wind to get clear of Licata.

When would these damned Saracens arrive? Well, where were they taking their prisoners? Because it all depended on how long it took them to get there and return. If it was anywhere on the Cape Bon peninsula it would not take them long because it was less than two hundred miles to the west. There was no lack of ports – Bizerta, Tunis, Kelibia, Monastir. Or further west – Bône, Bougie and Algiers. Anywhere west of Algiers would be too far, although

Mostaganem, Oran and Mers-el-Kebir were notorious as slaving centres.

And of course he was assuming they were going west. In fact they might be going south along the coast of Tunis, to Sfax or Djerba. Ramage could not suppress a shudder: it was awful to think that slaves and galleys existed in this day and age; that vessels were propelled by men chained to the oars and kept rowing in time by the lash of a long-tailed whip and the tolling of a bell. He refused to think of the brothels: for the women it must be a worse fate than that of the menfolk in the galleys.

Ramage realized that for the first time in his life he was determined to kill every one of the enemy: this was no ordinary battle where men surrendered when they had had enough. It was, quite cold-bloodedly, a matter of revenge. There was no hope of rescuing the men and women who had been kidnapped from the ports; they were lost for good and all. But it would be possible to wreak revenge on the men who had kidnapped them, and a cold feeling told him that he would show no mercy: that was the least he owed to those who had been captured.

He forced himself to stop thinking about it. The empty horizon seemed to mock him: out there, out of sight, were the Saracens, planning their raid on Licata.

He heard footsteps and turned to find Rennick approaching. The Marine officer saluted and grinned cheerfully. "I came to report that the guns are loaded and laid, sir; I've just been round and inspected every one, and the guns' crews are eagerly awaiting that rocket!"

"None of them complaining about the smell in those stables?" Ramage asked jokingly.

"No, sir, they have cleaned them out," Rennick replied seriously. "Why, Jackson boasts that his stable smells just like home!"

"He didn't say where home was?"

"No sir, and I thought it better not to inquire."

"What about the men with muskets?"

"Both seamen and Marines have their muskets loaded, sir, and they have all selected their firing positions. The moment the church bell tolls they take up their firing positions, and then they wait for the rocket."

"You didn't find any sign of drink?"

"No, sir. It occurred to me that some of the men might have smuggled wine ashore, but I found no sign. And the mayor warned the householders yesterday, didn't he? I thought he was laying it on a bit thick, what with his angry gestures and rolling eyes, but it seems to have worked."

"Oh yes," Ramage said, "it will have worked all right. He simply told them that if they gave our people a single drop of wine they would get drunk and would be incapable of protecting them against the Saracens. That was quite enough."

"I hope they give our men enough water, though," Rennick said anxiously. "It's hot in those houses and stables."

"The women will look after them. You must have seen several of them walking to the well with big jugs balanced on their heads."

"I have, sir! I don't know how they do it. Each jug holds several gallons, and the women walk so gracefully."

"There's no reason why our men don't get their own water: they can borrow jugs."

"Unlimited water," Rennick said seriously. "I hope it won't get them into bad habits when they're back on board the *Calypso*."

"It doesn't matter if it does," Ramage said shortly. "There's the daily water ration and that's that!"

Rennick looked over the wall of the battlements and inspected the port spread out in front of him. "This place is well sited. I wonder who built it?"

"The Spaniards, I expect," Ramage said.

"You have a good view of the 'killing ground'," Rennick commented.

"That's why I chose it as my headquarters," Ramage said. "I can look down on everything. It is the only way of making sure the timing is exact."

Rennick nodded: he had already realized that it would be difficult to judge the timing from the level of the quay.

Ramage said: "I shall make an inspection this evening: every gun position and every house in which we have men. You will accompany me."

"Very well, sir," Rennick said enthusiastically. "The men will be glad to see you."

With that he saluted and departed, and Ramage resumed his pacing.

What was Sarah doing at this moment? Say she was at Aldington and it was late afternoon. She might be riding round the estate because she loved riding. She might have neighbours visiting for tea. It might be raining so that she would be sitting in an armchair sewing or embroidering, or reading. Whatever it was, he could picture her, and he felt a great longing to hold her in his arms. Naval service was a cruel one for married men; it took them away from their wives and never told them for how long, as though determined to tantalize both of them. Until he had married, Ramage realized, he had not given a damn where he was serving – the Mediterranean, the Channel or the West Indies. Now, married to Sarah, the parting would be more bearable if there was a term to it; if he knew he would be back in England, say, by the autumn.

The Aldington house would look beautiful now in the early spring, with the hitherto bare branches of the trees sprouting green leaves and blossom. Of course, Sarah might not be there: she could be staying with his parents in Cornwall or London, or with her own. It was the hell of not knowing that made separation so unpleasant. If he only knew for certain where she was he could fantasize; but being unsure added an element of unreality to the fantasies.

Paolo Orsini was standing at one end of the battlements, telescope under his arm, keeping a lookout with a seaman. The youth looked miserable and Ramage paused and beckoned him over.

"Your face is as long as a yard of cold pump water," he said.

"I was thinking of Volterra," Paolo admitted.

"Worrying about your aunt won't help much."

"I wasn't really worrying about her. I'm afraid I've given her up for dead."

And Ramage knew he could not blame the lad: the chances of Gianna surviving the attentions of Bonaparte's secret police after being caught in Paris by the resumption of the war were negligible: Bonaparte would be unlikely to let the Marchesa de Volterra, the ruler of the tiny state, return to Italy alive. And Paolo was her heir; by now he could be the legitimate ruler of Volterra – a role,

Ramage thought grimly, about as dangerous, if not more so, as serving in action as a midshipman in one of the King's ships in the Mediterranean.

But Paolo did not know for sure. Ramage knew that he loved his young aunt and that he had no pretensions as far as Volterra was concerned: the lad was happy serving in the Navy, and his happiest time had been when Gianna lived safely in London with Ramage's parents while the French occupied her kingdom. Then his aunt had been safe, and knowing Volterra was occupied meant there was no point in worrying about it.

But Gianna's decision to return to Volterra the moment the Treaty of Amiens was signed, despite warnings from Ramage and his father, had smashed Paolo's little world as effectively as dropping a china jug on to a stone floor.

"What was bothering you, then?"

"I was just thinking of the mess there will be in Volterra after the French have been driven out – especially if my aunt is dead."

"If you have inherited, you mean?"

"Yes, sir. I know nothing of politics or statecraft. All I know about is ships and the sea, and that isn't going to help me get Volterra back on its feet."

"No," agreed Ramage, "and I expect the French have set up a puppet government, and those fellows won't want to give up power when the French are chased out."

"The thing is, sir," Paolo blurted out, "I don't really care about Volterra. I am much more concerned about passing for lieutenant. Why, already I can't really remember much about the place, and I certainly don't want to go back there and play politics. It's such a dirty game."

"Well, it's all well into the future: the French aren't going to be chased out of Italy that quickly, and you'll probably have been made post by the time you have to go back to Volterra."

But Ramage's heavy attempt at joking did nothing to cheer up Orsini and he changed the subject.

Ramage said: "I want at least two lookouts on duty at night. Have you enough men up here?"

"Yes, sir: six. Two hours on and four off means they'll stay alert."

Ramage nodded. "I think the Saracens will come in daylight but there is no need to tell the sentries that. Now, moonrise is about midnight, so there'll only be three hours of real darkness."

"The wind has been dropping away at nightfall this last week," Orsini offered. "If they're not in sight on the horizon at nightfall, it'll be four or five hours before they could get here. Even then they wouldn't be sure of their position."

"You're assuming they'll be sailing," Ramage said. "Don't forget they have rowing galleys, and a flat calm is just the weather for them to slip along."

"What sort of speed can they make under oars, sir?"

"I've no idea. Say five knots, perhaps more. And don't forget they may have fresh slaves at the oars – some of the men they've just captured."

Orsini shivered even though the sun was still warm. "I still can't get used to the idea of these heathens using Christians as slaves," he said.

"Remember that while you're keeping a lookout," Ramage said. "When you start feeling sleepy, just think of those slaves chained to the oars."

At that moment Ramage realized he had nearly made a terrible mistake: he had visualized opening fire on the Saracens' vessels as soon as the killing ground was clear, but if he fired into the galleys he would be killing slaves.

Well, the choice was a truly dreadful one. If he fired into the galleys to prevent the Saracens escaping, he would kill innocent slaves. If he let any Saracens escape, they would soon be back at their pitiless work of capturing more slaves. Which should it be?

It was a decision which he had to make, Ramage knew; what was more he had to make it now; there was no delaying until the situation arose, when he would have only seconds in which to decide.

He turned away from Paolo and walked along the battlements, hands clasped behind his back, his mind a torment. Fire on the slaves or not? Let Saracens escape or not?

And then, without any further conscious effort on his part, his mind was made up: he would fire at the galleys: the slaves would have to take their chance. When the death of a few of them was put in the scales against the fate of many in raids on the couple of dozen ports still left in Sicily, there was no question.

That evening Ramage left Orsini in charge at the castle and went with Rennick on an inspection of the gun positions and the seamen in the houses with their muskets. The men were in high spirits; it was the first time they had been on shore for a very long time, and in most cases the Sicilian families were being very hospitable. Although neither could speak the other's language they made do with signs, and the men's rations of salt tack were leavened with helpings of pasta and vegetables.

Jackson's stable was by far the cleanest. Ramage peered along the barrel of the gun and saw that it was aimed at the centre of the killing ground. The next stable was not quite as clean but, as the gun captain commented, it was probably the first and almost certainly the last time that it had been "mucked out". The man's use of the phrase showed Ramage that he was a countryman; probably a farm labourer swept up by the pressgang. Or maybe, overwhelmed by debt, he had volunteered, knowing that the Navy protected him from the bailiffs for civil debts of twenty pounds or less.

As he checked the last gun, Ramage decided they were all sited in the best position: the long stretch of quay was wide enough to make a perfect area for the Saracens to straggle over as they made their way into the town, and thus offer perfect targets for the carronades.

Nearly two hundred seamen and the Marines in the houses took longer to inspect but Ramage found the men had selected the best firing positions. All were prepared to quit the houses and attack the Saracens with cutlasses and pikes as soon as they had fired their muskets.

Ramage went back up to the castle well satisfied with what he had seen. Rennick obviously knew his job and both Kenton and Martin were making sure that the men behaved themselves in the town and did not wheedle wine out of their hosts. "I've told 'em that any man with the smell of liquor on his breath will run up and down the quay for an hour carrying a hundredweight sack of rocks," Kenton said. "That's increased their appreciation of water."

Back at the castle, with darkness almost fallen, he found Orsini and two lookouts. "Just one fisherman in sight," Orsini reported. "It's the same boat that has been out all day."

145

"It'll give you good practice," Ramage said. "Watch him as he comes in and it will help you judge distances."

The *Calypso* came in sight in the late afternoon of the third day. She was within a mile of the castle when, obviously certain by then that there was no flag flying from the flagpole, she turned seaward again.

Ramage watched the ship with his telescope and felt a glow of pride: she had a beautiful sheer and the whole shape of the hull was perfectly balanced. The fact was, he admitted to himself, that the French could build better-looking ships than the British, and if the *Calypso* was anything to go by, faster ones too. It would be interesting to see what became of the Trafalgar prizes. Thanks to the storm which had blown up after the battle, not many of the prizes had survived, but he regretted he did not have the seniority to be given command of one of them. From what he had seen of some of the French 74s, even though they had been mostly hidden by the smoke of the guns, they seemed fine ships: fine sheers, gunports high so that the ships could be fought with a heavy sea running, and with masts that sat in the hulls as though they belonged there.

The truth of the matter was that the French shipwrights (and Spanish too, for that matter) had perfected that curious blend of science and art that was necessary to design and build a fine ship. It was something that eluded the British shipwrights. It was a fact admitted by honest men that the fastest and most seaworthy ships in the King's service were those captured from the French and Spanish. At least the Admiralty had the honesty to keep the original names – except where they were too similar to existing English names.

There was, he considered, something very British about the way the Admiralty had kept the French and Spanish names (and Dutch and Danish too), because he could not imagine the French, for instance, retaining the English name of a ship they captured. But just think of the ships at present in commission – the 68-gun *Admiral Devries* and the 56-gun *Alkmaar* were originally Dutch; *L'Ambuscade*, *L'Aurore* were former French frigates; then there were the *Bienfaisant*, *Babette*, *Bonne Citoyenne* and *Bonetta* which were French and the *Brakel* and *Braave* Dutch, and that only took him up to ships beginning with the letters A and B. Then came the huge *Commerce de Marseille*, *Caton*, *Concorde*, *Courageux*, *Constance* and *Cormorant*, all French, and the 74-gun *Camperdown*, Dutch. And so it went on, the *Delft*, *Généreux*, *Gelykheid*, *Haarlem*, *Helder*, *Heureux*, *Juste* (of 80 guns) and the *Impétueux* of 78 guns, *Impérieuse*, *Immortalité*, right through the alphabet to *Vryheid*, *Virginie*, *Volage*, *Voltigeur* and *Victorieuse* and the Spanish *El Vincelo*. The last three he could remember were Dutch – the *Wassender*, *Wilhelmina* and *Woorzamheid*.

And there was, of course, the 110-gun *Ville de Paris*, built in England. Would it be possible that the French would build a four-decker and name it *City of London*? The British, he decided, were either very special or very stupid, and he was not at all sure which it was.

Orsini came up and reported his sleeping quarters were ready. They had swept out a small room – presumably used as a magazine – on the top of the battlements and, after making sure there were no scorpions lurking around in the semi-darkness, they had put down a mattress. Its great advantage was that a cry from one of the sentries brought him on the spot within seconds.

And now it was dark. The single small fishing boat had come back in, to be welcomed by a group of women on the quay, a sure sign of their need for fish.

He was startled to hear one of the sentries challenging someone who had come up the track from the town, and pleased to find it was the mayor and a boy carrying pots of food.

"Supper for you and your men," the mayor explained. "We thought you would have difficulty in getting a fire going up here, so my wife cooked some extra *pasta*. And there is bread, and water. No wine, as you said."

Ramage ate his supper with Orsini and after an hour walking right round the battlements, he went to bed, more tired than he ever was at sea: the effect, he thought drowsily, of all the walking.

He woke up next morning when the mayor and boy – he was the mayor's youngest son – brought them breakfast, a simple meal of which the main course was a chunk of heavy bread. Then Ramage set off down the hill to find Rennick and inspect the men: it would do no harm for them to know that he was keeping an eye on them.

The rest of the fourth day passed without incident. The guns' crews exercised at the carronades and the seamen practised charging the quay, watched by wide-eyed children and curious adults. The mayor, who was looking on with Ramage, was most impressed, except that he thought that the *Saraceni* would probably outnumber the seamen and Marines.

Ramage explained about the carronades, pointing out that the seamen and Marines would not appear on the scene until after the guns had done their best to clear the quay.

The *Calypso* returned on the late afternoon of the fifth day and turned away when she did not see any flag hoisted. Ramage could imagine the disappointment felt by Aitken and Southwick. Impatience rather than disappointment: they would want to get the attack over with, so that they would have no more worry. Neither of them was contented with being left out of the fight; it was in the nature of both men that they could not admit that everything would go off all right without them being present. Ramage pictured Southwick bellowing his way down the quay, whirling his great two-handed sword like a scythe cutting down wheat.

Two more days: Ramage was sure that the attack would come then, which gave the Saracens enough time to get to their bases and then back again to Licata. There was no reason to expect the enemy to be punctual: Ramage was basing his calculations on the natural urge of the Saracens to finish their raids and settle down to some peaceful feasting.

Two more days: by then the Calypsos would have been on shore a week. They would have practised handling the carronades and charging the quay enough times that they would know exactly what to do, whether in daylight or darkness. They would have that advantage over the Saracens – they would know the ground while the Saracens would be strangers. Ramage knew it was not much of an advantage because Licata was such a small town. But in the coming fight the advantage would be with the side that could add up a series of small advantages.

By the sixth day in Licata, Ramage was beginning to feel the start of boredom: walking up and down the battlements and inspecting the men down in the town had its limitations. Up on the battlements he had counted the flagstones innumerable times; he had walked across them stepping on every join; he had walked their length careful to never step on a join. He had counted the lizards looking up at him with beady eyes and had in exasperation chased two or three of them, until one of them dropped his tail and Ramage tired of the sport.

When he was at sea he sometimes longed for a few days on shore, looking forward to the green leaves, the song of the birds, the lack of rolling and pitching. But Licata was not green, it was parched brown by the sun so that even the lizards were brown, not a lively green, and there were few birds: most had been shot to eat, especially the songbirds, which were so tame. And the damned dust; he forgot about the dust when he was at sea, but here in Licata there was plenty and every whiffle of wind sent up a funnel of it, so that it got in the eyes, the throat and the food. It was bad enough up in the castle: it must be far worse for the men down in the town. But they did not complain; for them the joy of being on shore for a change outweighed any drawbacks like dust.

Once again a fishing boat went out and tacked up and down in front of the port, and Ramage amused himself by trying to guess the range, but it was a game without a solution because he had no way of checking: his sextant and tables were still on board the *Calypso*. The fishing boat gave a curious air of normality to the port; as though the quay, houses, church and castle were not complete without a sail to seaward.

Ramage did not sleep well on the sixth night: he did not seem to be tired and it was hot and sultry. He twisted and turned on his mattress, and a dozen times got up and went outside to chat with the sentries and, several times, with Paolo Orsini. The moon was nearly full and the town seemed covered in menacing shadows. But the quay was lit up clearly; the stone gleamed white in the moonlight. Running figures, the Saracens, would show up well. If and when they arrived.

When the mayor and his boy brought up breakfast next morning Ramage felt jaded. They had been just a week in Licata and it seemed like a month; the guns' crews were now well trained at the carronades; the seamen and Marines were now used to practising with their muskets and then running down the quay screaming warlike whoops and threats.

"Well," said the mayor, as he had done for the past few mornings, "do you think they will come today?"

Ramage shrugged. "Who knows? Today, tomorrow, the day after . . . but, *Signor*, we are ready for them. The extra days have been useful. The donkeys have been shut out of their stables, but what we have in the stables in their place will be more useful!"

"That is very true, and the donkeys will come to no harm. Your guns will alarm them when they go off: the banging and the braying will make a noise such as we have never heard."

"How true," Ramage agreed, thinking too of the screams of the Saracens and the seamen, apart from the rattle of musketry. Licata would have a tale to tell that would be handed down for generations, growing in the telling.

When he had finished his breakfast Ramage went for yet another walk along the battlements, glad of the exercise. The lookouts, one at each end of the battlements, watched seaward. It was another pleasant day with a good breeze from the south blowing in through the port entrance and puffballs of cloud skimming inland towards the mountains.

Ramage was now definitely bored; he longed for his cabin on board the *Calypso* and the walk on the quarterdeck. He would settle, he decided, for a good horse and a vigorous ride inland to the foothills of the mountains, which were greyish blue and fresh looking.

He gestured to Orsini to join him as they walked. "Is this your first visit to Sicily?"

"Yes, sir, and I think I've had enough of Licata!"

"It doesn't buzz with activity," Ramage admitted. "Still, we have a castle to ourselves. In most of the other ports we'd be sharing stables with donkeys."

Orsini rubbed his wrists ruefully. "I think donkeys would be preferable to these damned mosquitoes. At dawn and dusk they just make straight for my wrists. Look at them!"

His wrists were badly swollen and covered with the weals of bites. "They seem to affect you more than me," Ramage said sympathetically. "In fact –"

At that moment one of the lookouts shouted and Ramage saw he was pointing seaward, to the west. And there, black specks on the horizon, were several vessels.

Were they the Saracens? They had only just lifted over the

horizon, and they could be the fishing fleet from one of the neighbouring ports. They could be – until Ramage remembered that the Saracens had taken most of the fishing boats.

"The church bells, sir?" asked Orsini, but Ramage shook his head.

"We've plenty of time so let's wait until we're sure who they are."

He collected his telescope from his little room in the magazine and pulled out the tube, adjusting it to the inscribed line. He started counting. Six . . . eight . . . eleven . . . and two more were just coming into sight.

"They're the Saracens all right," he said to Orsini, "but we'll wait with the bells. The town only needs half an hour's warning, and it is going to take those boats another fifteen minutes to get close enough for us to be sure of them."

"It's a relief seeing them at last," Orsini said. "It was worse just waiting."

"It always is," Ramage commented. "Anyway, they've come on time."

Ramage watched with his telescope and finally counted fifteen vessels, and by then the hulls were lifting over the horizon. Half the boats were tartanes, easily identifiable from their sails, three were larger galleys with sails and oars, and the rest were Italian fishing boats, obviously the craft stolen from the ports in the previous raids.

"Fifteen of them. Say thirty men in each boat. I don't think there will be more because they would leave plenty of room for prisoners. That makes four hundred and fifty men altogether. On paper they outnumber us more than two to one." Ramage was thinking aloud rather than talking to anyone and Orsini kept quiet, watching the approaching vessels with his telescope.

Finally, as the fishing boat obviously sighted the oncoming Saracens and hurriedly turned back to port, Ramage told Orsini: "Send off your men to ring the bells."

Two of the lookouts ran off down the hills and five minutes later the bells began to toll, a lugubrious sound that reminded Ramage of funerals and incense and weeping women and shuffling men in their best suits.

Finally the bells stopped and by then the fishing boat was nearly

151

back in the port, its crew ready to run for home and load fowling pieces, if they owned them.

By now Orsini was inspecting the rockets and blowing on the slowmatch. The long wait, Ramage thought, had cost them a lot of slowmatch – almost as much as there had been in the *Calypso* – but at least they were not now struggling with flint and steel and tinder box.

The sails of the Saracen boats had more patches than original cloth, but they were driving the boats well as they stretched along in a fine reaching wind.

Ramage swung his telescope down over the town. There was not a soul on the quay. Nor could he see anyone moving in the town. The people had taken the mayor's orders to heart: he had told them that as soon as they heard the church bells they were to go to their homes and, if possible, bar the doors. Many of the houses did not have proper doors: curtains of sacking hung down. This was a poor place and anyway there was little wood about, the only trees being shrubs which were burned for charcoal.

Chapter Eleven

Down in his stable, Jackson walked round the carronade like an anxious hen circling its chicks. "I hope we'll hear the rocket," he said. "Here, Rosey, you station yourself by the door. But make sure you jump back quick when you hear the rocket because I shall fire at once. Almost at once, anyway."

"You be patient," said the practical Rossi, moving to the door. "If I am to be sure of hearing the rocket I'll be standing only a foot from the muzzle."

"All right, all right," Jackson said and turned to Stafford. "To save our Italian friend from being blown to pieces accidentally, don't you cock the lock until the rocket's gone off. Does that satisfy you Rosey?"

The Italian nodded grudgingly.

Stafford was busy preparing the gun. First he took the long, thin, pricker and thrust it down the vent, jabbing it in and out until he was sure it had pierced the cartridge. Then he pushed a quill down the vent and then sprinkled some priming powder from the horn round his neck, so that it filled the pan and covered the top of the quill. The moment that Jackson pulled his firing lanyard and the lock was triggered to make a spark, the powder would fire the quill and a spurt of flame would flash down the vent and detonate the cartridge. But until the lock was cocked, there was no way that the flintlock could cause a spark.

His job as second captain completed, except for cocking the lock, Stafford stood back. Jackson crouched down and sighted along the barrel, although he knew the gun was already trained on the right section of the quay.

"I wonder how many there are," said Stafford.

"I heard Mr Ramage say he reckoned they'd have about twenty

153

boats," Jackson said. "Tell me how many men the boats carry and I'll tell you how many men they have."

"They'll be galleys and tartanes and maybe a few fishing boats. Thirty or forty men in each boat?"

"I doubt if they'd have as many as that," Jackson said. "They need room for prisoners."

"Even if they have only twenty in each boat, they'll outnumber us two to one."

"But they won't have six carronades, half a dozen boat guns and a couple of hundred muskets and pistols," Jackson pointed out. "Cheer up, Staff, you probably won't end up your days in a Saracen galley!"

Stafford shuddered. "I should hope not. I can feel that whip across my shoulders, and my hands are raw from holding the oar."

"It's your imagination that makes you tired," Jackson said unsympathetically. "You just keep this gun firing and we'll all be all right."

"We'll certainly surprise 'em," Stafford said, seeking some consolation in the fact. "There they come dancing ashore thinking they're attacking a helpless fishing port, and bang, bang, there are the Calypsos waiting for them."

"I suspect that's why we're here," Jackson said sarcastically. "I can't help thinking that that's what crossed Mr Ramage's mind when he first stepped ashore here."

"I 'spect so," Stafford said in the tone of voice that took it for granted that the captain worked miracles. "He's usually got a reason."

"I don't understand when we know to stop firing so that the seamen and Marines attack along the quay," Gilbert said.

"You weren't listening properly when Mr Ramage was giving us our orders," Jackson said. "There'll be a rocket – maybe more than one – telling us when to open fire, and three rockets when we're to cease fire and the seamen and Marines to go chasing up the quay."

"Supposing we don't hear the rockets?" Gilbert persisted.

"We'd better, otherwise we're going to kill a lot of our own men as they run out," Jackson said. "Anyway, we'll either see the rockets as they burst, or we'll hear the other guns stop firing. Or not hear them, rather."

"It's not a very good idea," Gilbert said. "Rockets don't make such a noise."

"As Mr Ramage said," Jackson growled, "there's no other way: men won't have time to run from gun to gun saying 'Please stop firing'. Anyway, rockets make a completely different noise from carronades or muskets. You listen hard, Gilbert – and the rest of you. Staff and Rosey and I will have enough to concentrate on."

"Rockets!" Gilbert said crossly. "Might as well have someone up at the castle blowing a whistle!"

Jackson stared at the Frenchman. "Say a prayer that we stay alive to hear the rockets. If those Saracens get near us with their scimitars, it will be all over!"

"They'll have to run fast to catch me," Gilbert said drily.

Up in the castle Ramage watched the oncoming Saracen boats. It was impossible to see how many men they carried but the telescope revealed one thing: the decks were not lined with men. The Saracens, Ramage concluded, were sure that all they were doing was attacking yet another undefended small fishing port; as far as they were concerned this was a repeat of Marsala, Mazara, Sciacca and Empedocle: a routine attack, nothing to get excited about.

"Light another slowmatch," he told Orsini. "I don't like having to rely on one. In fact light two more: let's have one each when we want to fire off three rockets. The men are more likely to hear three rockets fired almost simultaneously."

"We have about seven feet of slowmatch left, sir," Orsini reported.

"That's enough for another three Saracen raids," Ramage said impatiently.

The glare from the sea was strong now as the stiff breeze pewtered the water, throwing up small waves which reflected the sun like a million flashing diamonds. The Saracen craft were approaching like water beetles advancing across a pond. With this south wind, Ramage noted, the Saracens would be able to run into the port with a commanding wind, rounding up alongside the quay. It would be a head wind for them leaving – but, unless his plans went badly adrift, none of them would be doing that.

Five hundred yards? About that, then the first of the craft, a tartane, would be coming in through the entrance. Then a second and third tartane and then three galleys. They were gaudily painted. The tartanes were decked out in strakes of green and red, with blue and white triangles and stripes apparently painted on the hulls at random. The galleys were similarly painted but as Ramage swung his telescope further round he could see that the fishing boats were still painted in the Sicilian fashion, each with a big eye painted on either side of the bow.

Gaudy colours and patched sails, yet to give the devils their due the boats were fast: the tartanes were slipping along and the galleys, under sails and oars, were keeping up with them. The tartanes had pleasantly sweeping sheers while the galleys had almost flat sheers, with the banks of oars moving in unison as though the craft were breathing.

Now the first tartane had sailed through the entrance, followed by the second and then the third. The rest of the craft were beginning to turn like a gigantic tail. Very soon the first of the tartanes would be rounding up to come alongside the quay and the men at the guns, peering out of the stable doors, would be able to see them. If only all the Saracen craft had come alongside at the same time – then the guns could have opened fire on them before the men landed. A big if, Ramage thought.

The first tartane swung round head to wind and crashed alongside the quay. Ramage could not hear the noise but he saw the long yard quiver from the impact. The Saracens were more skilled at sailing their boats than handling them in confined spaces. Now the second and third large tartanes were alongside and the galleys were manoeuvring into position, an operation which took more care because each captain had to make sure the oars on the landward side did not hit the stonework of the quay.

"How do they boat those great oars?" Orsini asked.

Ramage shrugged his shoulders since he had no idea.

By now more tartanes and captured boats were streaming into the port but, Ramage noted, there was no mad rush to get on shore: the boats were giving themselves plenty of room, and they manoeuvred as though they had plenty of time, too. There was no hurry to attack the port. The Saracens knew that they had overwhelmed the other ports by sheer weight of numbers, and Licata was simply another like the others.

156

As he watched closely through his telescope Ramage could see men securing the first tartane alongside, throwing ropes over the stone bollards. The second tartane had come alongside the first and was securing to it, and while it was doing that, the third tartane came alongside her, so they were three deep. The first galley went alongside the quay and the second secured next to it, followed by the third. Then, like giant ants, the other boats came in and went alongside. The strange thing was, Ramage noted, that none of the Saracens had gone on shore, apart from the men throwing ropes over the bollards. It was a curiously leisurely invasion.

Soon all twenty or so craft were secured alongside the quay and then, as if someone had blown a whistle or bellowed an order that everyone could hear, the men started climbing over the bulwarks on to the quay. Ramage tried a rough count – twenty, forty, sixty, a hundred: that covered the first three tartanes and the galleys. Twenty, forty, sixty – that was two hundred. Quickly he reached a total of four hundred standing about on the quay, and that seemed the end of the exodus from the boats.

The four hundred stood in a crowd, as though undecided what to do next, but Ramage guessed that their leader – or leaders – were just getting their bearings.

If only the crowd would stay together and move into the area he had called the killing ground, but they would probably split up into groups as they made their way towards the town. Was there one leader or did each craft have its own leader – a man who became the chief of his own men as soon as they landed? It did not really matter except it might have some bearing on whether the men stayed together or split into smaller groups.

Then, watched by a startled Ramage, all the men turned to the east and flung themselves on to the ground. And from down on the quay Ramage could just hear a faint wailing: rhythmic and persistent but high-pitched.

"They're praying, by God!" exclaimed Orsini. "Those damned heathens are praying!"

"Praying for the souls of the infidels they are about to disembowel or drag off," Ramage said drily. "Don't forget we often have a prayer before battle – it's the same sort of thing."

"Yes," said Orsini, who did not agree with the prayers, "it gets everyone into the right attitude for murder and mayhem, knowing that God is on their side. These fellows call him Allah, but the idea is the same."

Then the Saracens stood up, gave a bloodcurdling shriek while waving their scimitars in the air, and turned towards the town. But they did not run: they did little more than amble, breaking up into small groups as they made their way along the quay.

Ramage could imagine six triggerlines belonging to six carronades being tightened as the gun captains took up the first strain. In the houses seamen and Marines would be cocking their muskets and pistols. The second captains of the carronades, too, would have cocked their locks and stood back clear of the recoil. Every one of the Calypsos would be listening for the crackling of the rocket as they watched the advancing Saracens.

The horde of men had covered about fifty yards so far: they must be very confident of themselves because they were not hurrying. And indeed, why should they not be confident? As far as they were concerned Licata was just another fishing port, so placed to provide Saracens with ablebodied men for their galleys and nubile women for the brothels.

The Saracens had covered seventy-five yards by now, a shambling group of men who were doing little more than shuffling their way towards the town. But more important, they were heading directly for the killing ground. They were not bunched up enough to make perfect targets for the carronades: in fact it was hard to believe that such a casual crowd of men were a menace to Licata. Except, Ramage realized, for the glint of the sun on the scimitar blades. The men were walking along swinging their scimitars just as men out for a peaceful walk might swing at flowers with walking sticks – in England it would be dandelions, but Ramage realized he was not sure that they grew in Sicily.

He almost laughed at himself when he found he was thinking about dandelions while at the same time he watched the Saracens through his telescope. No, there did not seem to be a particular leader, or at least no one man was heading the crowd. They were now thirty yards from the edge of the killing ground, and Ramage said to Orsini: "Stand by with the slowmatch."

Orsini picked it up and blew on it so that it glowed red, and he moved close to the rocket as it stood in its tube canted over the town.

158

Then the first of the Saracens had reached the edge of the killing ground itself. Ramage could see that all of the men were dressed in robes with scarves or cloths covering their heads. And they all had beards; black beards which made them look fierce.

Now half of them were in the area, the rest of them shuffling along as though they had all the time in the world – which, as far as they knew, they had. Most of them, Ramage thought grimly, have very little time left in this world, although they were blissfully ignorant of the fact.

Ramage felt the excitement gripping him now: so far his plan was working out and everything depended on the timing of that rocket. If it was too soon, it would raise the alarm for the Saracens; if it was too late then many of them would be outside the target area before the guns fired.

He watched and waited, looking sideways to make sure that Orsini was ready at the rocket with the slowmatch. Yes, the slowmatch was glowing. And he found he could judge the position of the Saracens better with his naked eye: the telescope distorted the view by foreshortening the foreground.

Damn, he had to watch that the leading men were not out of the area before the ones in the rear had entered it. There, now was the moment!

"Fire the rocket!" he snapped at Orsini and a moment later the rocket hissed up in the air over the town and exploded with a crackling noise as it sped over the quay.

Before the last of the rocket's noise was lost there was a series of deep coughs as the six carronades opened fire and the barrage was punctuated by the lighter banging of the boat guns and the popping of more than two hundred muskets and pistols.

The leading Saracens collapsed in piles, cut down by caseshot and musketballs as they walked, and the rest of the crowd froze, taken completely by surprise. Then the muskets crackled again as seamen and Marines fired the spare guns they had beside them. And Ramage could imagine the carronade crews desperately ramming home cartridges, wads and caseshot and then heaving away with handspikes to aim the guns again.

Again the carronades barked out, cutting down more Saracens, who were now beginning to crouch down, obviously puzzled where the noise and swathe of death was coming from. The boat guns joined in, like puppies barking, and many more Saracens collapsed: the bodies were beginning to pile up on the quay.

But to Ramage's surprise the Saracens did not run back to their craft alongside the quay: instead they seemed to bunch up together, shouting and waving their scimitars as though in defiance. As the third blast of fire from the carronades bit into the crowd, they started running towards the town and towards where most of the carronades were positioned. And Ramage realized he had made a mistake in keeping the guns and the seamen and Marines separate: there were no men to guard the guns; the carronade crews would be cut down by the Saracens, who did not fear death. In fact, he suddenly remembered, they regarded death in battle as a certain way to Paradise, so they were men without fear.

How many had been killed – or, more important, how many were left alive? Bodies were so piled up on the quay, sprawled in the ungainly poses of men unexpectedly hit by death, that it was hard to count, but Ramage guessed a hundred: that left three hundred getting ready to attack the guns and the town.

Again the carronades coughed and Ramage saw they were firing at ranges of only a few yards: the screaming Saracens were now running towards the wreaths of smoke spurting from the guns, which they obviously did not fear. There were fewer muskets and pistols crackling: the men had not had time to reload. The Saracens would be at the first of the houses in a couple of minutes. And the seamen would not be prepared for them: they had orders not to move until they heard the three rockets which would stop the carronades firing.

There was only one way out of this mess, Ramage decided.

"Fire the three rockets!" he shouted at Orsini and, looking round at the six lookouts, he added: "Bring cutlasses and follow me: we're going down to the town!"

The mad run downhill to the quay was a nightmare: the carronades had stopped firing the moment the rockets had crackled overhead, but as Ramage and the lookouts neared the quay in their wild dash through the town they could hear the screaming of the Saracens and the shouts of the Calypsos. Then, punctuating the shouting, they heard a single carronade fire.

It was the one of which Jackson was the captain. A couple of

160

minutes earlier, just before the rockets, the four Frenchmen and Rossi were hurriedly reloading the gun when Stafford, walking to the door, exclaimed: "Jacko! The Saracens are coming here! They're charging the guns!"

As the rockets crackled, Jackson said grimly: "This gun is our best protection: hurry up and load!"

Stafford stood by the door watching the approaching Saracens, until the last moment, when he ran with pricker, quills and powder horn. Although he could not see them he knew the first of the Saracens were only a few yards away when he clicked back the lock to cock it and then sprang back telling Jackson: "Ready!"

The American waited, listening as the shouting grew nearer and watching the doorway, the triggerline taut in his right hand. Suddenly half a dozen raggedly dressed Saracens appeared at the door, yelling and waving their scimitars, Jackson waited a moment and then, as the first three Saracens were bursting in through the doorway, pulled tight on the triggerline.

The three men vanished in the cloud of smoke spewing from the muzzle of the carronade and, as Stafford ran through the smoke to the doorway, he saw five or six bodies, with heads and limbs missing, scattered across the paving in front of the stable.

Ramage in the meantime had arrived at the quay to find the Calypsos in a desperate fight with the Saracens, cutlass against scimitar. As far as he could see the Calypsos were in three groups, led by Kenton, Martin and Hill, and the Marines making a fourth group with Rennick.

Ramage, with the six seamen and Orsini, flung themselves against the nearest group of Saracens, slashing with their cutlasses. Ramage heard Orsini cursing them in shrill Italian as he slashed with his cutlass. Ramage stabbed at the back of one Saracen who was about to chop at a seaman and then turned just in time to parry a scimitar slicing down at himself.

The shouting of the Saracens was so intimidating that Ramage realized it could affect his men, so he began shouting "Calypsos! Calypsos!" and the seamen and Marines began to take up the cry until they were making as much noise as the Arabs.

Followed by Orsini, Ramage slashed his way towards the party led by George Hill, which was the nearest, and was amused to hear the jaunty way that Hill was encouraging his men. Ramage lunged at an Arab who parried, shouting at the top of his voice. As his cutlass slid down the curved scimitar Ramage snatched it back and stabbed again and the Saracen collapsed. So much for the lessons learned as a boy from an Italian fencing master, Ramage thought grimly. But there was no question that the Saracens wielded their scimitars crudely; they were no match for the seamen, who had cutlass drill at least twice a week.

A screaming Saracen dashed at Ramage with his scimitar held high over his head and before he had time to slice down Ramage lunged with his cutlass, which penetrated the man's stomach so that he collapsed gurgling, almost disembowelled.

The Saracens were holding their ground: they were standing and fighting, instead of making a bolt for their boats, and Ramage saw that by now eight or ten seamen and a couple of Marines were lying among the Saracens dead or badly wounded. Then in the distance he heard the cough of a carronade and for a moment wondered if it was firing into the middle of the swirling mass of Saracens and Calypsos.

In fact it was Jackson's gun. The American had realized that the Saracens' boats, secured alongside the quay, made a perfect target, and he had guessed that the captain would want them destroyed or damaged. He had therefore ordered his men to train round the carronade so that it raked the craft. It took him only a moment to decide that the slaves in the galleys would have to take their chance, and he fired the first round. After each round Stafford ran to the smoke-filled doorway to see if any more Saracens were coming to attack them, but they all seemed to be occupied fighting the seamen.

After six rounds Jackson went to the doorway himself to inspect the boats and he was satisfied to note that the masts and yards of three tartanes were now slewed down over the deck.

"If only we had some roundshot!" he exclaimed to Stafford. "This caseshot is only pecking at 'em!"

"It's cutting the running rigging, and that's all that matters: we're trying to put 'em out of action for an hour or two, not sink 'em!" the Cockney replied, coughing from the gun smoke.

The Frenchmen and Rossi were also coughing and spluttering from the smoke that filled the stable, and they were loading and running out the gun more by feel and instinct rather than being able to see what they were doing. After another six rounds, when he was coughing so much his eyes were streaming and he was gasping for breath, Jackson went to the doorway again. This time he could see that the carronade was having a considerable effect on the boats: of the twenty or so craft, only four or five still had masts standing; the slanting yards of the *tartanes* had all fallen to the deck, probably because their halyards had been cut, and the squaresail yards of two of the galleys were slewed round drunkenly and no sail could be set on them.

"Let some of this smoke clear," he told his men, "we can't go on like this: the damned gun'll get doubleshotted or something stupid."

The smoke cleared quickly and after a quick glance at the confused fight going on across the quay, Jackson set his men back to work. In two minutes the stable was once more full of smoke as the carronade fired and Jackson again adjusted the aim, having to wipe streaming eyes as he gave new elevating and training instructions that set the men busy with handspikes and had them turning the wormscrew that took the place of a wedge-shaped quoin.

By now Ramage had the desperate feeling that his men were being overwhelmed by the Saracens, who fought like madmen. The Calypsos were too spread out to take advantage of their training: they needed to be concentrated so they could make an organized attack. But getting them into any sort of formation meant several minutes that they would be vulnerable while they reformed. Ramage quickly decided to take the risk; it was a lesser one than having his men overwhelmed.

He ran to one side and shouted at the top of his voice: "To me, Calypsos; to me!"

Many of the men heard him above the yelling and screaming and, led by Rennick, Kenton, Martin and Hill, the men ran to his side. As he waited for them he continued to hear the sporadic cough of a carronade and his eye caught sight of the twisted lateen yards of the tartanes. He realized that someone, probably Jackson, had seen how vulnerable were the Saracens' craft.

With the Calypsos collected round him, Ramage shouted at the lieutenants: "Form into sections; attack from different directions."

They were not orders that would be approved by the Marines but they were the best he could do shouting at the top of his voice in the middle of a battle. The men collected round their officers, choosing the lieutenant commanding their divisions of guns on board the *Calypso*. The sudden movement by the seamen and Marines had puzzled the Saracens, who stood nonplussed. Then Ramage, satisfied that his men were in some sort of order, bellowed: "Charge!"

Now the motley collection of Saracens were attacked by four separate columns and, lacking any discipline, were quickly broken into large and small groups. Ramage joined Hill's men, who were the nearest, and parried a scimitar as it sliced down on to the back of a seaman. The rasping of metal against metal made the seaman turn in time to slash the Saracen with his cutlass.

Orsini was shouting something at Ramage which he could not hear and pointing seaward. Ramage glanced up to see the *Calypso* sailing in through the harbour entrance: she must have spotted the smoke, since the flag had not been hoisted at the castle flagpole. But what could an undermanned frigate do? She could not open fire with her guns because she would kill more Calypsos than Saracens.

But Ramage had not realized the effect the great frigate – she seemed enormous in the tiny port compared with the Saracens' boats – would have on the Arabs: at that moment several of them spotted her and started a wild, demented howl which was quickly taken up by the rest of them. The moment they turned to look at the frigate the Calypsos redoubled their efforts, slashing at the Arabs in a desperate attempt to take advantage of their momentary preoccupation.

Suddenly the Saracens broke away and started running across the quay and back to their boats. At the same time they seemed to notice for the first time the twisted yards and this provoked more howling, as they realized that they were trapped.

At that moment Ramage heard a gigantic splash as the *Calypso* let go an anchor and then, as her sails were furled, began to swing round head to wind, to lie parallel with the quay and the Saracen craft, which were fifty yards away from her.

As the Calypsos ran after the Saracens, chasing them back to their boats, they hurled curses after them, slashing with their cutlasses at the unprotected backs of men who had at last panicked and were only concerned with getting aboard their boats.

Ramage paused a moment. Aitken had enough seamen to man a few of the 12-pounders; in fact Ramage was certain that as many guns as possible would at this very moment be in the act of being loaded and trained. And if and when the *Calypso*'s broadsides crashed into the boats, he did not want any of his men near.

He shouted to the lieutenants to halt the men. Hill and Rennick heard him and stopped their sections, and then the rest of the Calypsos, realizing that some of their comrades had stopped, halted and looked back. In the meantime the Arabs continued their headlong dash to the boats and started scrambling on board, despite the damage caused by Jackson's carronade.

At that moment the carronade barked out again and Ramage saw its caseshot cut a swathe through the running Saracens. By now there were few of them left on the quay: most had piled into the boats and were beginning frantically to cast them off.

Suddenly the *Calypso*'s side was a flicker of winking red eyes and a moment later plumes of smoke streamed out. Then the erratic crash of the broadside rattled across the quay as at least eight 12-pounders fired into the massed boats.

Ramage stood with his lieutenants and the seamen and Marines to watch as the *Calypso* fired a second broadside and then a third. Two tartanes began to sink, one of the galleys suddenly heeled over and filled, taking the slaves with it, and two of the captured fishing boats capsized.

"What a slaughter!" Hill commented. "What timing!"

Ramage suddenly felt rather weak; his knees no longer wanted to support him, and he wanted to giggle. Well, that was how relief took you because, he admitted, but for the *Calypso* he wondered if they would have been able to deal with all the Saracens.

"We'll wait and let Aitken finish them off," Ramage said. At that moment the carronade coughed again, and Ramage added: "And Jackson, too!"

Another two tartanes suddenly heeled over as water poured in through their shattered hulls and they slowly filled, and Ramage saw men floundering in the water. The Saracens could fight well enough, but they could not swim. The *Calypso*'s fourth broadside smashed into the remaining boats and Orsini commented: "There

165

go two more of them!" as two fishing boats suddenly sank, their masts vanishing as they disappeared into what Ramage guessed was five fathoms of water.

Yet again Jackson's carronade fired, and Ramage could imagine the American's glee at having caught the Saracens in such a crossfire. And the Arabs' own haste to escape had doomed them: they had cast off the craft alongside the quay, and all the rest of the vessels were secured to them. Slowly they drifted away from the quay so there was no chance for any of the Saracens to get back on to the land; instead they were doomed to drift closer under the *Calypso*'s guns.

Ramage noticed that the *Calypso* was not firing at the two galleys: obviously Aitken had thought about the galley slaves chained to the oars and decided to give them a chance. But Ramage wondered how they were going to get at the Saracens – fighting across the galleys' decks would be risky as far as the slaves were concerned.

Now the Saracens' vessels had stopped drifting: those left afloat were being held by the lines of those that had been secured to them and then sunk. Which meant that they were perfect for the *Calypso*'s guns, which had stationary targets at less than fifty yards' range.

In ten minutes the only craft left afloat were the two galleys, and the *Calypso* stopped firing, and so did Jackson's carronade. Ramage saw the frigate hoist out boats and through his telescope saw Aitken climbing down into one of the cutters, which then made for the quay. Ramage stood to one side and waved, and the cutter altered course towards him.

Aitken was jubilant. "I hope you approve of the timing, sir!"

Ramage smiled and said: "You were early – thank goodness."

"I saw all the masts and as soon as I could see the flag was not flying I guessed they were attacking. Then we saw the smoke of the carronade. Just one, sir."

"That was Jackson and his men firing on the boats. I had to stop the rest because the Saracens attacked them."

"I hope they didn't spike any," Aitken said anxiously.

"No – they didn't get near them, in fact. I had to let the seamen and Marines drive them off, which meant stopping the carronades firing. All except Jackson's gun: he took no notice and kept on firing at the boats."

"The galleys," Aitken said. "I didn't fire into them because of the slaves."

"Quite right, but now we have to hook out the Saracens."

"We can board them from the boats, sir."

"Ramage shook his head. "No, these fellows are madmen; our casualties would be enormous. I'm not prepared to lose that many men just to save slaves."

Damnation, it was a rotten dilemma. How was he to save the slaves without losing dozens of his men? The only way would be to swamp the Saracens; somehow attack them with a couple of hundred men.

It was easy. The idea came to him so quickly that at first he was suspicious of it, and tried to work out what could go wrong. But there seemed to be nothing wrong with it and he described it to Aitken.

"We want the two galleys back alongside the quay, so that we can board them from the land and completely outnumber them."

"I don't see any problem," Aitken said. "We just tow them back alongside."

"Yes, our boats with grapnels. Let them get close enough to heave grapnels on board and then tow them to the quay."

"Musketry," Aitken said doubtfully. "The men in the boats will be vulnerable for a long time."

Again Ramage shook his head. "The Saracens don't seem to have many muskets: they didn't use them when they attacked us, and I doubt if they'd have many in the galleys."

"Very well, sir, I'll go and give the boats their orders if you'll get your men ready."

"You'll be using just about all your men," Ramage commented.

"Yes, sir, but we've managed so far – thanks to Southwick!"

"What's he been doing?"

"Well, I had him dancing all over the quarterdeck, cursing and foaming when we guessed what was happening here. Then I suggested he went and helped at the guns, because we were so short of men, and he went off like a pistol shot. Enjoyed himself enormously. The last I saw of him just before I got into the cutter he no longer had white hair: it was grey from smoke and powder!"

With that Aitken jumped down into the cutter which was quickly rowed back to the frigate. It took fifteen minutes to get all the boats ready and surrounding the galleys, and by then Ramage had all his surviving seamen and Marines lining the quay two deep where the galleys would be towed alongside.

The grapnels were flung up from Aitken's boats and before the screaming Saracens realized what was happening all the *Calypso*'s boats were hauling the galleys back alongside the quay.

They had only ten yards to go, and while the Saracens lined the landward side of the nearest galley shouting what Ramage assumed were threats intended to curdle the blood, the seamen and Marines waited patiently to fight their way on board.

It was while watching the prancing Saracens that Ramage suddenly realized that these were the only survivors of the four hundred or so that had landed: the rest had either been killed in the fighting on shore or drowned as the boats had been sunk by the *Calypso*'s relentless fire. How many were there in the galleys? Thirty in each; not more. Sixty left out of more than four hundred. There were going to be many widows in whatever town they called home. More widows than one would at first suppose, Ramage thought, because most men probably had more than one wife . . .

Ramage saw that the galleys were sufficiently small for his men to line up four and five deep, and he shouted orders to Rennick, Kenton, Martin and Hill. Had Aitken brought over the blacksmith to free the slaves from their chains?

And then the galleys were alongside and the British seamen and Marines were pouring over the bulwarks, shouting and slashing with their cutlasses. It was such a violent and concerted attack, with Ramage and Orsini in the front row, that the Saracens quickly retreated into the second galley.

Ramage, noticing that Jackson, Rossi, Stafford and the Frenchmen had appeared from somewhere and were surrounding him like a bodyguard, was appalled by the stench: the galleys smelled like middens, and as he found his way from one galley to the next, Ramage just glimpsed the slaves hunched down, seated on benches.

As he slashed and parried, Ramage had to watch his footing: the galley, with its double row of oarsmen each side, had no deck in the

168

accepted sense; the ship seemed to comprise catwalks, a central one down which the men in charge of the slaves presumably walked with their whips.

He scrambled across to the second galley, noting in the red haze of fighting that they had taken the first, and then he saw that several of the Saracens – in fact many of them, those trapped against the bulwarks – were jumping into the sea, a flurry of long robes, turbans and long hair. And then suddenly the fighting was all over; the sudden silence was almost unnerving.

Ramage scrambled back on to the quay again, found Kenton and Martin and said: "Take a couple of dozen seamen and go back towards the guns and bring back our wounded here: the sooner we get them out to the ship so that Bowen can have a go at them, the better."

"What about the Saracens, sir?" Hill asked.

"Our men first," Ramage said abruptly.

As the first of the wounded were brought along the quay and made ready to be lowered into the *Calypso*'s boats, Kenton gave Ramage the butcher's bill: seventeen Calypsos had been killed and thirteen wounded. There were fifty-seven dead Saracens – many of them killed by the carronades, boat guns and musketry – and forty-four wounded, most of the men so seriously that they would not last out the night.

Just as Kenton finished his report – after adding that many of the men and women from the town were out helping the wounded – the mayor came up to Ramage, his face serious. He took Ramage's hand and said emotionally: "You saved us – but at what a cost to your men!"

"It was inevitable," Ramage said. "We were heavily outnumbered."

The mayor looked across at the galleys, startled by the banging of metal as the blacksmith got to work.

"Go on board and look," Ramage said. "We're freeing the men who had been taken as slaves. Once we find out where they come from we'll take them back home again."

The mayor clambered on board the first galley but was soon back, white-faced and clearly shaken by what he had seen.

"What our men have escaped!" he said apologetically. "It turns the stomach . . ." and before he could say any more he was violently sick. "The stench," he said apologetically. "But, *Commandante*," he added, "I was going to tell you that our people are doing what they can for your wounded over there. Unfortunately, we do not have medical supplies. But the dead, we will give them a great funeral – it is the least we can do," he said when he saw Ramage about to protest. "The *Saraceni* we put in a pit, all of them."

It took a moment for Ramage to realize the significance of what the mayor had said.

"Not all of them," he said. "Just the dead."

"They'll all be dead," the mayor said grimly. "They would have killed us – but for you. And if we let them escape alive, who knows, they might come back one day, looking for revenge. And you won't be here to protect us. No, *Commandante*, we do it our way; it is safer for us."

Ramage shrugged his shoulders. Much as the idea of slaughtering wounded men repulsed him, there was no arguing with the mayor's logic: there would not always be a British frigate to protect Licata; the little port would be defenceless in two or three days' time, once the *Calypso* left.

The mayor shook hands again and left just as Kenton and Hill led the second group of wounded. Hill said: "The Italians are taking away our dead, sir: carrying them up to the church."

"Yes, I know, the mayor has just told me. They want to arrange the funeral – a sort of thanks offering."

"But the Saracen wounded," Hill began lamely. "What I mean is, those that were wounded . . ."

Ramage guessed what Hill was trying to say. "You couldn't stop them?"

"No, sir, they were too quick. We didn't expect anything like that and we were busy attending to our own men first. When we turned round it was all over. Throats cut."

"It wasn't your fault," Ramage said. "These people are frightened that if any Saracens escape they'll be back seeking revenge as soon as we've gone."

"Can't say I blame 'em," Hill said. "A couple of dozen Saracens could cut everyone's throat in this town – judging from the way we saw them fight. No wonder the Italians dread the Saracens."

"It's a tradition," Ramage said. "The Saracens have been

170

raiding Italian coastal towns and villages for centuries. It's something that we who were brought up in England will never understand."

At that moment Aitken came up and reported: "All the slaves have been freed, sir. Some of them are in a bad shape: a few of them have gangrene where the chains chafed them."

"Once we've got the wounded taken out to the ship, take these Italians across and give them a good meal. As soon as Bowen has finished with our wounded, he can have a look at these fellows."

The funeral of the dead Calypsos was held next day, with all the people of Licata, right down to crippled old women and stumbling little children, there to pay their last respects. Ramage translated much of the service for the *Calypso*'s commission and warrant officers who attended the service, and then made a brief speech in Italian thanking the people of Licata.

Once he was back on board the frigate, Ramage settled down with his clerk to interview all the former slaves freed from the galleys. Bowen had treated the gangrene cases as best he could, and many of the men had bandages round ankles and shins.

Ramage had some trouble with the accents which, apart from being thick Sicilian, varied from village to village, a variation explained by the fact that very few of the men had ever visited other villages.

Slowly Ramage and the clerk progressed along the line of hammocks and benches, noting each man's name and the port he came from. All told the same story of being seized in daylight raids; some added the tragic postscript that their wives and daughters had been taken away too. They had first been taken to a town on the African mainland, and then transferred to the galleys and made to row back to Sicily. And as the clerk wrote down the names and home ports, Ramage realized that they came from every port from Empedocle to Marsala.

After saying goodbye to the mayor of Licata and the people, who lined the quay to cheer and wave, Ramage took the *Calypso* westward, to call in at all the ports and deliver the men who had long since given up hope of ever seeing their homes again. At Marsala – from where the majority of the slaves came – the mayor was so overcome that he wanted to give a banquet for all the

Calypso's officers, but knowing the town was almost starving Ramage got out of it by inviting the mayor and many of the senior citizens to dinner on board the *Calypso*, lucky to have Orsini help him as translator.

Chapter Twelve

Naples Bay looked as splendid as ever, guarded by Mount Vesuvius standing four-square to the eastward. The flagship, three 74s, a frigate and various sloops represented the King's ships, but there were dozens of local craft tacking, running and reaching as they went about their business of fishing, carrying vegetables, or taking passengers from one of the little ports to another round the perimeter of the Bay.

The weather was perfect: an almost clear sky, a fresh breeze from the west to raise a few small white caps, and the sun glaring down, warm and threatening to be hot by noon. A small white cloud lurked over the top of Vesuvius like a cap, making it seem that smoke was streaming out. Ramage saw it and thought momentarily of Pompeii and Herculaneum, still buried under the lava.

As the *Calypso* glided in there was no signal from the flagship telling him where to anchor, so he picked a spot half a mile to windward and Aitken patiently conned the ship while Southwick went forward to the fo'c'sle to prepare for anchoring. The frigate, under fore and maintopsails only, seemed in no hurry; she crossed the Bay with an elegance that Ramage found pleasing.

On the desk in his cabin was a report addressed to Rear-Admiral Rudd. Ramage had worked hard on it, careful not to omit anything without making it too verbose. And without giving Rudd any grounds for making trouble. After the head money episode, which had revealed the Admiral's preoccupation with money, Ramage had been careful to explain why none of the Saracen ships had been brought in as prizes; all had been sunk in action, except for the two galleys, which were very poor sailers but were due in Naples within the next day or two under the command of Lieutenant George Hill and Midshipman Paolo Orsini. Ramage had been careful to explain that without slaves at the oars and relying only on their sails, it was almost impossible to get the galleys to go to windward, but when last seen – off Licata – both of them were reaching along at three or four knots.

Would the Admiral buy them in? Ramage doubted it; galleys were no use to the Royal Navy, and it was unlikely that anyone in Naples would want to buy them, since without oars to assist them they sailed like floating haystacks. He had brought them in, Ramage admitted to himself, just to please the Admiral. No, that was not quite true. Not to please him exactly, but to show that the Licata operation had been completed successfully, right down to bringing in two prizes. Not to give the fellow any room for criticism, Ramage admitted to himself.

Aitken gave a brief order to the quartermaster and, picking up the speaking trumpet, sent the topmen aloft to the maintopsail. As soon as the men were up the rigging he gave the order to furl the sail and the men spread out along the yard like starlings on a bough. Within moments they were hauling in the heavy canvas in great folds, then they had it against the yard and were passing gaskets to hold it there. As soon as the sail was secured, Aitken barked out the order: "Down from aloft!"

Soon the *Calypso* was gliding the last few hundred yards before anchoring. The sheets and braces of the foretopsail were hauled so that slowly the sail was backed and the *Calypso* came to a stop as the wind blew on the forward side of the sail. Ramage signalled to Southwick to let go the anchor and, after a splash, Ramage noticed the familiar smell of rope scorching as it raced out through the hawse. There was something pleasantly final about the smell; as though it signalled the end of another successful voyage.

By now the backed foretopsail had thrust the *Calypso* enough to give her sternway, pulling out the cable and putting just enough weight on it to help the anchor dig in on the sea bed. Southwick was calling out the length of the cable that had been let out, and as soon as it reached five times the depth called out by the leadsman in the chains, he stopped and the cable was made up. Ramage left the topsail backed for a few minutes, just to make sure the anchor had dug in, and then told Aitken to carry on, which was another way of saying furl the sail and put over a boat for the master.

Southwick now had himself rowed round the ship "squaring the yards", making sure that the yards were hanging absolutely horizontally. Neatly furled sails and perfectly horizontal yards were the sign of a well run ship, and the phrase "I soon squared his yards" was part of the Navy's language, another way of saying "I soon put him in *his* place!"

With the ship anchored and the yards squared, it was time for Ramage to have himself rowed over to the flagship so that he could report to the Admiral. First he had to change into his second-best uniform, put on clean silk stockings and a fresh stock, and buckle on a sword. He decided to wear the sword recently presented to him by Lloyd's – not to show it off to the Admiral but because he had promised Sarah that he would use it on formal occasions. She had been very proud of it – so proud when it was presented to him at a dinner at Lloyd's that she was very near to tears. The memory of that moment stopped Ramage as he tied his stock: he could picture her so clearly, as though she was in the cabin with him. It was strange how a sudden memory could make you go weak. "I went weak at the knees" was a commonplace saying, but there were times when it was true, and now was one of them. He felt an overpowering desire to be holding her in his arms, with her tawny hair tickling his face so that he had to blow it away.

He shook his head to clear the memories and stood up, checking that his stockings were straight, feeling that his stock was square, and hitching at his sword. He picked up the leather case in which he was carrying his despatch to the Admiral, and his hat, and then made his way up on deck, where the cutter waited for him, manned by Jackson, as the captain's cox'n, and with Stafford, Rossi and the Frenchmen among the crew.

Admiral Rudd was formal: he did not smile, nor did he shake hands. He waved Ramage to a chair in front of his desk and, in an expressionless voice, said: "Well?"

The sparseness of the greeting startled Ramage, who said lamely: "I've just returned from Sicily, sir."

"I imagined so," Rudd said. "You carried out your orders?"

"Yes, sir: I have my despatch here."

Ramage took out the report and put in front of Rudd.

"There are no Saracens left along the coast?"

"None, sir. Of course, there's nothing to stop more coming, but I dealt with those attacking the ports."

"What do you mean 'dealt with'?"

Ramage tapped his despatch. "It's all in here, sir. They're all dead."

"How many were killed? Twenty, fifty?"

"About four hundred, sir," Ramage said soberly.

"Four hundred?" Rudd exclaimed incredulously. "But your whole ship's company isn't much more than a couple of hundred!"

"No, sir," Ramage agreed, "but we managed to turn our carronades on them."

"What! They attacked your ship?"

"No, sir," Ramage said patiently, "as I describe in my report, we landed men and guns at the port of Licata and waited for the Saracens to attack, using the carronades to make up for our lack of numbers."

Rudd stared at Ramage, as though disbelieving him, and reached out for the despatch. He opened it and smoothed out the first page. He skimmed the formal opening and then adjusted his spectacles and started reading closely. From time to time he grunted, a noncommittal noise that gave away nothing. Finally, after he had read the four pages, he put them down on the desk again. His attitude had changed.

"Very creditable, Ramage; very creditable indeed. The British Minister will be delighted. I am sure he will arrange for a translation of your despatch to be given to the King."

"I am honoured, sir," Ramage said, trying to keep the irony out of his voice.

"Tell me, what made you decide Licata was going to be the next place they attacked?"

"They seemed to be working their way along the coast, starting with Marsala. It was a question of getting ahead of them and waiting."

"What made you land carronades?"

"It was the only way I could make up for being so outnumbered, sir."

"But how did you know how many Saracens to expect?"

"The other ports that had been raided told me how many craft they had – tartanes, galleys and the like, and I guessed how many men they could carry."

"And how are you so certain there were four hundred?"

"I made a rough count when they landed on the quay at Licata."

"Very well," Rudd grunted. "And you say –" he tapped the report, '– that you brought in two prizes."

"They haven't arrived yet, sir. As I wrote, they are galleys and of course we have no one to man the oars. Each needs at least forty men, and I felt I could not spare eighty men – plus topmen to handle the sails – to bring them in."

Again Rudd gave a noncommittal grunt, obviously trying to put a price on the galleys and failing, since he had not seen them. "When do you think they'll get here?"

"Tomorrow or the day after at the latest, sir. They sail like haystacks but they've had a fair wind."

"Very well, that just about covers everything," Rudd said, picking up the despatch again and giving Ramage a dismissive nod.

As Ramage was rowed back to the *Calypso* he went over the interview again. Rudd had been cold and distant to begin with, thawing a little when he discovered that Ramage had rooted out the Saracens. When he learned, in other words, that he had something very positive to report to the British Minister, something that would put him in a good light and bring the King's thanks. Reflected glory, Ramage thought wryly. The Admiral must be very unsure of himself to get any satisfaction out of that . . .

The two galleys arrived late that night, with the last of the light, and both Hill and Orsini arrived on board the *Calypso* to report that their commands sailed like reluctant mules. "We needed a hundred *Saraceni* at the oars to get them moving," Orsini grumbled. "And they carry so much weather helm that it would have been easier to sail them in circles."

"Don't be so critical of a real command," Ramage said teasingly.

"It wasn't a real command, sir; I had to keep station on Mr Hill," Orsini said.

"Well, navigation wasn't very difficult: you kept the land on your larboard hand until you saw more appear to starboard, and then you followed that keeping it to starboard until you sighted Vesuvius!"

"It's true it was not much of a challenge. Still, a galley sails so badly I'm thankful I did not have to beat to windward all the way to Gibraltar!''

Hill took a more practical view. "They won't sail and no one has enough men to row them, so perhaps the Admiral can sell them to the Neapolitans as houseboats. Rig tarpaulins over the catwalks and you can sleep scores. Better than the hovels many of them live in now.''

"I'll suggest it to the Admiral," Ramage said jokingly. "I'm sure he will be grateful.''

The following afternoon the flagship hoisted the *Calypso*'s pendant numbers with the signal for captain, and once again Ramage dressed in his second-best uniform to go across to the flagship. He was puzzled by the signal. The Admiral had his despatch, and seemed satisfied with it: certainly he had not asked any questions indicating any doubts about it. He shrugged his shoulders: perhaps it was not trouble but new orders, some fresh task for the *Calypso*. There was one other frigate in the anchorage, but she was probably commanded by one of the Admiral's favourites; someone not to be burdened with run-of-the-mill commissions. Not that chasing Saracens was run-of-the-mill, but Ramage knew he had been given the job because it was assumed he would fail. And that was why Admiral Rudd had been distant and chilly yesterday: he had been anticipating the first of a string of excuses, and instead of that he had heard of complete success. What thoughts had gone through the Admiral's mind – anger, irritation, frustration?

This time, when Ramage entered the cabin after replying to the salute from the Marine sentry, the Admiral was affable, waving Ramage to the same chair with something approaching joviality.

"Your despatch," he began. "I had a copy made and I took it to the Minister myself. He was delighted: absolutely delighted. He took it along to the royal Court – after having it translated – and the King read it in his presence. You are probably going to receive some honour or other, as a token of the King's appreciation. You are collecting trophies – I see you have a sword from Lloyd's.

"The King's immediate reaction, Ramage, concerned the galleys: he was very affected by your release of the men in the galleys and wanted to know if they represented all the prisoners taken from the ports. The Minister was unable to reassure him on that point. Do they?''

178

"No, sir. There are five or six hundred more still at the Saracens' base, serving in other galleys. At least, so I understood from the men we freed. And all the women, of course. A hundred and fifty or more."

"Ah, yes, the women. His Majesty was equally concerned about them. They have suffered a dreadful fate."

Ramage nodded in agreement: it was sufficiently dreadful that he had shut his mind to it, being helpless to do anything about it. Some of the men released from the galleys had wept when they told him that their wives were among those women taken off; wives (and sweethearts) they would never see again.

"Do you know where the Saracen base is? I mean, the base of the particular Saracens concerned in these latest raids."

"Yes, sir. It's at Sidi Rezegh, south of Sfax. I discovered that from the men we freed from the galleys. It's a port of about ten thousand people. About six months ago the plague broke out there. It was a terrible attack – it wiped out all the slaves and the women kept in the brothel. They estimate a thousand or more Saracens died. It was because they lost all their slaves that the Saracens started raiding the Sicilian coast with *tartanes* – they wanted to get a large number as soon as possible to man the galleys.

"Sidi Rezegh itself is just an outpost in the sand, with a small fort. Just a harbour with a L-shaped breakwater made up of great rocks. Originally a Roman port, I understand. There are five or six other galleys left there. The men were taken off to a barracks; the women are kept in a big building which is the brothel."

"You seem to know a lot about the place," the Admiral commented.

"It was hard to stop the men we released from talking about it and the plague: they just wanted to share their experiences – and their woes about their women."

"Quite so, quite so," Rudd said sympathetically. "It's just as well they did."

There was a tone in the Admiral's voice that made Ramage look up quickly. "How so, sir?"

"The King wants those men, and the women in the brothels, rescued, and he has made the request to the British Minister, who has passed it on to me as an order. You are obviously the man for the job."

"It's a bit of a task for a single ship, sir," Ramage observed. "Unless you can let me have two or three hundred soldiers."

"I have in mind something better than that," Rudd said expansively. "I propose giving you a frigate and two sloops, and I have arranged for you to have three hundred soldiers, which you can split up among the ships in any way you choose."

"Thank you, sir," Ramage said, reflecting that a King and a Minister meant a lot of pressure applied to the Admiral (and to the general commanding the British troops). Obviously, the Admiral considered it an important part of his future to be able in time to report to the Minister that the King's wishes had been carried out. There would be honours for the Admiral, too, and Ramage could imagine the self-serving despatch the Admiral would send to their Lordships at the Admiralty. He would begin with clearing out the Saracens from the southern ports of Sicily, emphasize how pleased was the King of the Two Sicilies, and then go on to describe how all the prisoners, men and women, had then been released from Sidi Rezegh. And it would all seem to be the Admiral's idea, and their Lordships would be suitably impressed. The role of Captain Ramage would, of course, be mentioned but, Ramage guessed, the person who received most credit for the rescue would be the captain of the other frigate: the man who was obviously the Admiral's favourite but who was, equally obviously, junior to Ramage on the Post List, so he could not be given command of the little force.

Oh what a tangled story it all was; it angered Ramage that it was rare to be involved in any operation without favouritism entering the story. Favouritism? Why not call it nepotism?

This fellow Rudd was as guilty as any other admiral: he had sent off two favourite captains in their 74s to deal with the Frenchmen on Capraia, but it had fallen through. The favourite frigate captain had not been sent off to deal with the Saracens along the Sicilian coast because there was every likelihood of failure. No, the *Calypso* had been sent off, so that the scapegoat for any failure would be this newly arrived Captain Ramage, not the Admiral's favourite.

Now the Admiral's favourite was having to go on the Sidi Rezegh expedition because the Admiral dare not risk any failure, so he was sending all the ships he could spare, two frigates and two sloops. If the expedition failed, the fault was obviously Captain Ramage's, since he would be in command of the whole affair. If the expedition succeeded, well, much of the credit was due to the favourite, who conducted himself with great skill . . . Ramage could see the copperplate writing of the Admiral's despatch to the Admiralty.

Very well, that was the way things were done, and the only thing to do was to smile gracefully and do one's best – and, if one was honest, pray for the day when one became the favourite of a powerful admiral.

Suddenly Ramage felt almost ashamed of his thoughts: he had been something of the favourite of the late Lord Nelson; he must have aroused jealousy in other captains less favoured. Now he was out of luck but, if he was fair, that was no reason to get cross with this other wretched frigate captain. If you succeed, he told himself, no one can blame you, just as his recent success against the Saracens had made Admiral Rudd change his tune – to some extent, anyway.

"Yes," Rudd said judiciously, "another frigate and two sloops – and three hundred troops – should do the job. The troops will be a major's command, Major Henry Golightly, but of course he will be told that he takes his orders from you. The frigate will be the *Amalie*, Captain Herbert Roper, and the sloops the *Betty*, master and commander Jason King, and the *Rose*, master and commander William Payne. Your orders will be delivered by noon tomorrow, and by that time the others will have received theirs, and know that they are under your orders. The troops will embark tomorrow evening, by which time you should have let them know in which ships they are embarking. Now, is there anything else you want to know?"

Ramage thought for a few moments. "No, sir. I have to water and provision the *Calypso*, and it would be better if the other ships were watered and provisioned for three months."

Rudd nodded. "Very well, but do you expect to be away so long?"

"No, sir; but we shall be taking on five or six hundred men and women at Sidi Rezegh, all being well, as well as three hundred soldiers, so we shall need extra water and provisions."

"Quite so, quite so," Rudd said, revealing that he had not thought of it. "As many people as that?"

"They took around a hundred and fifty men and women from each port, sir. And I presume that if I find slaves taken from ships I should release them as well?"

"Yes, of course. But if any are French . . . ?" Obviously Rudd was doubtful about freeing any of the King's enemies, but Ramage was certain.

"If they are French they'll still be our prisoners. We can't leave them chained up for the rest of their lives in the hands of those heathens."

"No, of course not," Rudd said hastily. "But if there is any haste, the Italians have priority: you do understand that, don't you?"

"Of course, sir. There's just one other thing: I'd like to call at all the ports from which prisoners were taken – those places where we delivered men we freed from those two galleys – so that I can question the men more fully."

Rudd frowned. "Why do you want to do that?"

"Well, sir, I am going to attack a port I have never seen and for which I have no charts. Nor do I know where the slaves and the women are kept, except that they are in barracks somewhere there. These men know all the answers. After some questioning, I should be able to draw a serviceable chart to work with."

"Of course, of course," Rudd said impatiently, as though it was his idea originally and Ramage was questioning it. "It's most important that you have a good chart. And make sure it shows the barracks, or whatever it is, that the slaves are kept in. And the brothel."

"Yes, sir, I will," Ramage said, hard put to keep the sarcasm out of his voice. "I'll pay particular attention to that."

Chapter Thirteen

Back on board the *Calypso*, Ramage called Aitken and Southwick to his cabin, and as soon as they were in their accustomed places – Aitken on the settee, Southwick in the armchair – he told them of the Admiral's orders.

"So we get a frigate and a couple of sloops," Southwick chortled. "If we go on like this you'll get a commodore's pendant!"

Ramage grinned at the old man's enthusiasm. "More important are the three hundred soldiers," he said. "It was a damn' close-run thing at Licata because we had so few men, and we'd have been overwhelmed but for the carronades. Even now we'll be heavily outnumbered."

"Oh, it won't be so bad as that, sir," Southwick said.

"You're an optimist. It's really a job for those two 74s, with the two frigates, and a thousand troops. I'd have told the Admiral that but I realized that if the 74s are involved one of the two captains would be the senior officer."

"So you're not going to give up command, even if we are outnumbered three to one!"

Ramage laughed and said: "Very well, old chap, who would you prefer to serve under at Sidi Rezegh, me or the captain of one of the 74s?"

Southwick shrugged his shoulders and smiled. "The devil and the deep blue sea, sir. No, on balance, I suppose I'd choose you because you have more experience fighting these heathens."

"Thank you for that commendation," Ramage said lightly. "I'm surprised that you bargain away your skin so lightly."

"Habit," Southwick said succinctly. "One gets into the habit of serving under the same person. It'll probably be the death of me one day, but I live in hope."

"Right, now let's get down to details. Provisions and water for three months. That's so that we have enough food and water for the people we rescue. Arrange to berth a hundred and fifty troops – which means drawing more hammocks from the stores. That'll be a hundred and fifty men for us, and a hundred and fifty for the other frigate. We'll have to carry the major commanding the troops, so someone is going to have to give up his cabin."

"That'll be me, I suppose," Aitken said. "Oh well, everyone is going to have to move down one."

"And powder and shot," Ramage said. "Check with that fool of a gunner that we have a full outfit for the 12-pounders and the carronades. And muskets and pistols too: this might end up as a desperate business with a lot of fighting in the streets."

"I'll see to that, sir," Aitken said. "Will we have any chance of giving the soldiers some training in boat work before we arrive at Sidi Rezegh? Some of them can get seasick after a hundred yards in an open boat, and they're always so clumsy."

Ramage explained how they were going to call at Empedocle, Sciacca, Mazara and Marsala. "We'll practise landing from boats at all of them. We'll have Rennick's Marines going green with envy!"

Aitken laughed and then Ramage said: "The soldiers will need more training in embarking in the boats from the *Calypso* than landing on beaches. It'll be up to our boats' crews to get the boats in the right place for the soldiers."

"I agree," said Aitken. "Anyway, we don't know yet whether the men will be landing on the beach or on a quay, stepping ashore like gentlemen out for an afternoon's stroll."

"Whether it's on a beach or at a quay, one thing is certain," Ramage said grimly. "The reception committee will not be holding bunches of flowers."

"What are we going to do about a chart of this place, Sidi Rezegh?" Southwick asked.

"I just mentioned that we are going to call in at Empedocle, Sciacca, Mazara and Marsala. The whole point of that is to question the men we freed from the galleys. They rowed out of the place, and I presume they were housed in some sort of barracks, and they should know where the women are held. From the scraps they tell us, we should be able to draw some sort of chart. Enough to get into the place and know where we have to go."

Southwick sniffed disparagingly. "Men hauling at those great oars won't be paying too much attention to where the galley is going," he said.

"No, but if they have to make any turns they'll have had to back water or row faster to turn the galley, and they might remember that. And it's almost as important to know where the buildings are: we don't want to have to go round the town knocking on doors."

"Is the place going to be big enough to get in a couple of frigates and the sloops?"

"I've no idea," Ramage admitted. "Beyond the fact that it was once a Roman port, I know nothing about it."

"Who commands the other frigate – do you know him?" Southwick asked suspiciously.

"He's a man called Herbert Roper, the Admiral says. I've never met or heard of him. The commanders of the sloops are Jason King and William Payne. Never heard of them, either."

"It's not going to be easy," Southwick said gloomily. "All these ports along a sandy shore are shallow. Low land, shallow water; high land, deep water."

"Yes," Ramage agreed, "all these ports along the desert coast must be shallow, but we only need to get our bows in. We can put the men ashore in boats, if we can't get alongside a quay."

"There'll be hordes of screaming bashibazouks," Southwick said gloomily. "All shouting about Allah and waving scimitars. And popping away with muskets, too, I've no doubt."

"What's got into you?" demanded Ramage. "Grumble, grumble, grumble. Why were you so enthusiastic about Licata, then?"

"At least we knew where we were. We knew there were no sandbanks – and we got those carronades ashore in commanding positions."

"We still didn't know it was going to work," Ramage pointed out. "It's all very well looking back on it and saying how wonderfully we planned it, but at the time we weren't sure. In fact, it was touch and go; they outnumbered us two to one, and if you hadn't arrived with the *Calypso* it might have been a different story."

"Well, we got away with it," Southwick said, slightly mollified. "This time we should have enough men and guns. As long as we can bring the guns to bear and land the men!"

Aitken stood up. "If you'll excuse me, sir, I'd better see to the watering and provisioning. It's a pity we can't send out a wooding party: the cook's grumbling that he's getting short of firewood."

"How long will watering and provisioning take?"

"We should be completed by this time tomorrow, sir."

"Good. I'll get the other captains over this evening and plan to sail at noon tomorrow."

Captain Herbert Roper, commanding the frigate *Amalie*, was a tall and thin man with a narrow face and protruding teeth. His face was pale, as though he was never on deck exposed to wind and sun.

Roper settled down in the armchair and Ramage considered the older of the two sloop commanders, Jason King of the *Betty*. The captains of the two sloops were known as "masters and commanders", the rank that went with command of a sloop, and although they were in fact the captains of their ships, they were known as commanders.

King was a man of fifty; someone who had obviously failed to make the vital jump to the Post List, and who would end his days as a commander. He was stocky with a startlingly short neck; in fact his head seemed to fit directly on to his shoulders. He was red-faced, but that was due rather to a tendency towards apoplexy than exposure to the sun and wind. Ramage was not sure if he was not something of a drinker. Not a drunkard, but a man who liked his tipple. He was a north countryman with a broad accent of Yorkshire or Lancashire, and he seemed to be cheerful.

William Payne, commander of the *Rose*, was an open-faced young man who, Ramage guessed, had a chance of making the Post List on merit, assuming that merit ever got a man on to the List in preference to having "interest" with an admiral. Payne obviously had a clear brain and needed only a little luck to get command of a frigate in a few years' time, allowing him to call himself "captain", instead of "commander". And, incidentally, increasing his half-pay, should he end up on the beach between commands.

Payne was as much a southerner as King was a northerner and Ramage guessed that he came from Hampshire or Sussex. His voice was low and even, yet he spoke like a man who considered what he was saying, in contrast to the outspoken manner of King, who gave the impression of speaking freely without considering what he was saying.

"Well, gentlemen," Ramage said, "you have all received orders from the Admiral to put yourselves under my command. I don't know if the Admiral has told you anything about this operation. If he has not, you must be puzzled."

Both King and Payne nodded their heads, but Roper shook his, clearly the only one who had any inkling of what they had to do.

"So that you understand better what it's all about, I'd best describe the operation I have just completed."

Ramage went on to detail how the Saracens had raided Marsala and the other ports, and an appeal from the King of the Two Sicilies to the British Minister in Naples had resulted in the *Calypso* being sent out. He concluded with the fight at Licata and the rescue of many prisoners from the galleys.

"After hearing about this, the King has asked that we make an attempt to rescue the men and women taken to Sidi Rezegh, and that is what we are about to attempt. We are to get three hundred soldiers to help us – they will embark this evening, a hundred and fifty on board the *Calypso*, and a hundred and fifty for the *Amalie*.

"Now, you know what soldiers are like in boats: they are not used to them. I don't know if we'll be landing on a beach or at a quay, but we have to exercise the troops in the boats as frequently as we get an opportunity. It's probably more important to train them to embark from the ships."

"When shall we get the opportunity?" Roper asked.

"Ah," Ramage said. "You'll soon see. At present we have no chart or map of Sidi Rezegh. Being a port along a sandy coast, it may well be shallow. The only way we can get any information is to question the men we freed from the galleys, since they've been to Sidi Rezegh. So we'll call in at Empedocle, Sciacca, Mazara and Marsala to question them.

"All of these ports have both quays and beaches, so while I am on shore questioning the men, you will hoist out your boats and exercise the troops."

"When shall we get the charts, sir?" asked King.

"Empedocle is the last port. By then my master, Southwick, should have a decent chart drawn up, and something of a map of the town showing where the barracks are, and the brothel."

"Supposing some of the galleys are at sea?" asked Payne.

Ramage shrugged his shoulders. "Unless we can capture them, there's nothing we can do. Let's just hope that they're all in port and the slaves are in the barracks. Which reminds me, I hope you are well provisioned and watered – you'll be getting a number of freed prisoners, of course."

All three men assured him they were.

"The troops will be on full rations, of course. Make sure they don't use too much water: prisoners when they are released may need plenty. Fresh water is probably rare in Sidi Rezegh, and you can bet that the slaves will get only enough to keep them alive."

"You don't know yet how you will attack?" asked Roper.

"I've no idea, and until we have a chart drawn up, I'm not even thinking of it. But judging from what happened at Licata, I warn you, don't underestimate these people: they fight bravely and wildly. To them we are infidels, and their religion tells them that to die in battle means they go straight to Paradise. So they have no fear.

"But fortunately for us, they probably don't have many guns or small arms. With them it is spears and scimitars. Our tactics," Ramage said, "are to keep them at a distance and pound them with our guns. And, of course, the Marines and seamen will have muskets and pistols, and the soldiers will add another three hundred muskets."

Roper, thinking aloud, said: "Three hundred soldiers, plus say one hundred and fifty seamen and Marines from each frigate, make six hundred, and fifty from each sloop means seven hundred altogether. That should be enough."

"I very much doubt it," Ramage said. "They had four hundred men at Licata. Now we're attacking the nest; the home of these Saracens. And don't forget that men will fight desperately in defence of their homes. Not only that, they'll know every street and alley. I'm thinking more of fighting a thousand of them."

"That makes formidable odds," observed Roper.

"Indeed it does. But we mustn't fight a pitched battle with them – if we have to do that, I don't think we'll stand a chance. No, we make two concentrated attacks – on the barracks and on the brothel. We are not interested in capturing the town – though we might be able to set fire to it, if it will burn. No, we have limited objectives, which is a big help. And I hope we can get in close with the ships; as many broadsides as possible will mean fewer Saracens for our men to fight. If need be, we can pound 'em for hours before making our attacks on the barracks and the brothel. No one is going to come to the help of the Saracens, thank goodness, so we needn't hurry."

Ramage looked round at the three men. "Are there any more questions?"

All three of them shook their heads.

"Very well, written orders will be in your hands by this evening. They will be brief; final orders will come at Empedocle, when we have the chart. So off you go and get ready to receive the troops."

Chapter Fourteen

Ramage's little flotilla got under way at noon next day, the *Calypso* leading the way out of Naples Bay, followed by the *Amalie* and with the two sloops astern of her.

Southwick, standing next to Ramage at the quarterdeck rail, was in bubbling good humour. "Congratulations, sir; this is the biggest flotilla you've ever commanded. It'll be a fleet before long, mark my words."

The remarkable thing about Southwick, Ramage thought, is that the man does not understand the word "flattery". His comment about a fleet was a genuine expression of his feelings, and given that when he had first met him Ramage had been a very junior lieutenant (and since then they had been in action together dozens of times, and Southwick had become quite a wealthy man from prize money) it meant the remark came from the heart.

"I'm glad I made charts of Licata and the rest of those ports," Southwick said. "Admittedly, I never thought I'd be using them again so soon."

"If only we'd made notes from what the prisoners said after we freed them from the galleys," Ramage said. "Still, I must admit I never thought we'd need a chart of Sidi Rezegh."

"Let's hope this decent weather lasts: I don't fancy trying to get in there with a *scirocco* blowing."

"We can wait for good weather," Ramage said. "For once we're not in a hurry. We can wait for the weather, and we can stand off and pound them for a couple of days, if necessary."

Southwick gave one of his doubting sniffs. "We'll probably find that the town lies a couple of miles back from the beach, out of range of our guns."

Ramage shook his head. "Perhaps, but I doubt it: that wasn't the way the Romans built ports. Very practical people, the Romans; they'd decide there's no point in carrying supplies a couple of miles from ships . . . they'd build warehouses right next to the quays."

"That was then," growled Southwick. "The Saracens could have spread out since then."

"I doubt if they have any more wish to carry supplies unnecessarily."

"We'll soon know, once we start questioning our former galley slaves," Southwick said. "That's one thing they'll know about, even if they aren't sure about depths in the harbour."

For the rest of the day it continued to blow a good breeze from the north-west as the little flotilla stretched its way south-west towards the western tip of Sicily, leaving Ischia and Procida to the north and Capri to the south. And it was a simple course: the first land they would sight would be the tooth-shaped volcanic island of Ustica, forty miles north of Sicily and directly on the line to Cape San Vito, where they started turning to larboard to pass Trapani and then Marsala, Mazara, Sciacca and Empedocle.

Would it be necessary to visit every one of the ports, or would they get enough information from the first two? Ramage knew that although there was no great hurry, he did not want to waste too much time sailing up and down the Sicilian coast. Way to the south was the challenge of Sidi Rezegh, at present an unknown quantity. Unknown but not necessarily unwelcome. Not having the faintest idea of what was ahead, the operation had a tinge of mystery.

Supposing, Ramage thought to himself, the Saracens so outnumber us that they capture the two frigates and two sloops: would all the ships' companies and the troops be sent to galleys? The Saracens would probably have too many slaves for the number of galleys they now possessed. Well, Ramage thought harshly, they would have a spare set.

He had thought a lot about the slaves in the galleys. Theirs was a terrible fate. Kept on shore in what were no doubt terrible conditions, they were (according to the prisoners they had released) taken to the galleys as needed and then held in position at the oars by chains round the ankle, so their bodies were free to work at the oars but they could not leave their seats.

They were kept in time as they rowed by one of the Saracens beating a gong (some of the galleys had bells), and to make sure

191

that they rowed with all their strength one or two Saracens walked along the catwalk on the centreline of the galley lashing them with long-tailed leather whips.

They were fed in the morning and at night; there was no midday meal. Water was issued three times a day, half a gourd for each man, and it was handed out so clumsily that often half of the water spilled.

If a man collapsed over his oar – from exhaustion or sickness – the master of the galley, who lived in a small open-sided cabin aft, came and inspected the man. If it was exhaustion he was left an hour to recover and then roused with a flogging, but if the man was ill (fevers were very common) the man was freed from the manacle round his ankle, and then he was thrown over the side. There was no fuss or ceremony; the manacle was unlocked, the man lifted out of his seat, and then he was pushed out through the oar port.

This meant, of course, that there was one man less at the oar: there were usually two, but in the bigger galleys three. If there were only two, the other man was put on another oar as an extra; if there were three, then the remaining two had to carry on rowing alone.

The most common cause of a man collapsing was gangrene: two manacles round the ankles caused hideous sores which turned gangrenous. There was no attempt to treat any of the sick men; they were worked until they collapsed and if there was no chance of them recovering, they were hove over the side. It was brutal, but it was in line with the Arab attitude towards death, with the difference that infidels did not go to Paradise.

So a man captured and sent to the galleys was, in effect, sentenced to row until he was no longer fit to pull on the oar, then he drowned. How long did a man last? Was it weeks, months or years? Obviously not long; the Saracens were always looking for slaves; presumably they were the replacements.

They reached Marsala the following afternoon and the *Calypso* anchored. A cutter was hoisted out and Ramage and Southwick were rowed ashore, the master equipped with pencil and paper. The mayor was delighted at seeing Ramage again but at first was nervous, afraid that Ramage's sudden arrival off the port meant that another Saracen raid was expected.

As soon as Ramage explained the reason for his visit the mayor sent several small boys off through the town to collect up the former prisoners and bring them in for Ramage to question.

When the men arrived they too were excited at seeing Ramage again, anxious to shake his hand and assure him that they had recovered from their ordeal in the galleys. When he explained the reason for his visit he met with an excited chorus. He then divided his questions into sections, starting off with the general shape of the harbour and town of Sidi Rezegh. All the men agreed on that and they drew a large diagram in the dust outside the mayor's house, each of them adding to it as he remembered something.

Finally Southwick said to Ramage: "Ask them about the channel in and see if they know any depths."

To Ramage's surprise, several of the men not only remembered how the channel ran, but could give reasonably accurate estimates of depths. These men were the fishermen among the former prisoners, and although they did not remember all the facts immediately, they soon scratched in details in the dust as Ramage questioned them and they recalled details which they did not realize they knew.

The greatest difficulty was in agreeing to a scale: the men had varying ideas about distance. Finally it was agreed when they worked out how many paces they walked from their barracks to the galleys. They all agreed on the size of the barracks and the brothel and were able to describe where the doors were. They also agreed that the population of Sidi Rezegh was about six thousand, a figure they could visualize because they compared it with Marsala.

There was a small fort on the seaward end of the quay and the men argued whether there were three or four guns on the top. Certainly no more: they were all agreed on that.

Muskets? Their guards at the barracks had a couple of muskets. Very old and elaborate, and engraved with complex designs. They estimated that there might be half a dozen muskets in the town. And no, they had never heard the cannon on the little fort fire. Nor, for that matter, had they ever noticed any men up there; they could not remember seeing any lookouts.

The one thing that they all remembered vividly was the frequency with which the men prayed. Several times a day – one man said five – they flung themselves to the ground and prayed, the signal being given by a horn blown from the mosque at the back of the town.

Finally, with no more details to be added to the diagram drawn in the dust, Southwick made a copy of it, carefully scaling it off. After he had completed the drawings, they were shown round for the men to inspect. Southwick had done two, one of a chart of the harbour, with as many depths as the men could remember, and a map of the town, showing the important buildings. Most of the men had never seen a chart or a map before, and none could add any more details.

Ramage thanked them for their help and said goodbye to the mayor who, Ramage realized, was so proud of the diagram drawn in the dust outside his front door that he would have liked to have it framed.

Back on board the *Calypso* the two men went down to Ramage's cabin and examined the chart and map more carefully, and Southwick drew in a compass rose. "I wonder how much more detail we're going to get from the other places," he said.

"Not much, I fear," Ramage said. "These men remembered the obvious things, and I don't think anyone else will be able to add much."

"Well, at a pinch we have enough already. We know what the place looks like now, and we know how to get in. And we know where our objectives are. We're lucky that both the barracks and the brothel are near the quay."

"We're lucky that there is a quay," Ramage commented. "I was afraid we might have to land on a beach some distance from the town and storm the place."

"I wouldn't give much for our chances if we did: we couldn't do it without raising the alarm, and a couple of thousand of those Saracens ready to drive us off doesn't sound like the recipe for victory."

The *Calypso* weighed and they sailed along to Mazara, at the mouth of the *torrente* Mazara. The frigate anchored off the silted up harbour and once again Ramage and Southwick went ashore in the cutter, Southwick holding his chart and map. The master gestured up at the clear sky and commented: "I don't think we shall be bothered by Il Marrobbio. They say it only occurs when it's hot and humid."

Ramage, who had no wish to experience the small tidal wave for which the port was famous, nodded his head. "Certainly, it doesn't seem the weather for it."

Once they had landed on the quay, Ramage led the way up towards the domed cathedral and the bishop's palace, sending a man on ahead to warn the mayor that they were coming. The man, recognizing Ramage, was only too anxious to carry the message after being reassured that Ramage's arrival was not a warning that the *Saraceni* were coming.

The mayor, like his counterpart at Marsala, was pleased to see Ramage after being reassured that the *Saraceni* were not coming, and once Ramage explained the reason for his call, he sent off a crowd of small boys to collect up the former prisoners.

"We still miss our four tartanes that those *Saraceni* stole," he said. "And as for the men who did not return – well, we say a Mass for them every Sunday, but losing so many men – not to mention the women – is a grievous loss. Not," he added hastily, "that we aren't grateful for the return of those of our men the *Commandante* rescued at Licata."

The first of the former prisoners soon arrived and greeted Ramage like a long-lost father, their attitude being a mixture of awe and respect.

As they gathered round him outside the mayor's house, Ramage explained what he wanted. He had given a lot of thought to his approach and knowing that the majority of the men would not be able to read a chart or map, decided to repeat the method he had used at Marsala – scratching a diagram in the dust.

But at first he asked the men how many people they thought lived at Sidi Rezegh, and they were unanimous in saying about the same number as lived in Mazara.

Ramage looked at the mayor for help. "More than five thousand live here," he said. "I don't know the exact number – I can only give you the number on the tax roll and guess how many women and children there are. But not less than five thousand, I assure you of that."

Then the men started giving details of the harbour. Three men – again fishermen – remembered more depths, judged from the draught of the galleys and the courses they steered to get out of the harbour. But two of the men could give accurate figures concerning the depths in other parts of the harbour – they had noticed how much rope had been paid out when they had anchored. There was a section of the harbour near the entrance where there were depths of twenty-five to thirty feet – more than enough for the frigates. Two more of the men knew the whereabouts of a shoal in the centre of the harbour, and this was drawn in the dust.

They were all agreed that there were four cannon on top of the fort and that they never saw lookouts or guards up there. Several of them commented on the number of times that the *Saraceni* prayed during the day.

"They would keep our bishop busy," one of the men commented. "He would not have time to grow that great paunch of his."

Ramage noticed that one of the men was silently weeping, and he quietly asked the mayor the reason. "The poor man's wife was one of the women taken away," the mayor said. "He knows he will never see her again."

"There's a hope," Ramage said, "but perhaps no more than that, so it is better not to mention it."

The Mazara men were better at gauging distances than those at Marsala and their estimates were added to the diagram. When they all agreed they could remember no more, Southwick added the extra details to his diagrams and explained them to the men, who looked at them closely without being able to give any more information.

"Now," Ramage said, "I want you to remember how many galleys there were, including the two you were in."

They thought a few moments and then one of them said definitely: "Eight. Five of them were big ones and we were in the three smaller ones."

"Were all the Mazara men put in the same galleys?"

"No," the man said. "We were split up. It was a matter of chance which galley you went to: we were all mixed up in the barracks. This last time I was chained up in the galley next to a man from Sciacca: it was just the way we were marched out of the barracks. That's why so many men from Mazara are still at Sidi Rezegh: they were not marched out to man the other galleys. Ah, *mamma mia*, how were we to know which of us was to be lucky?"

"How many men do you think there are left in the barracks

now?" Ramage asked the man, who seemed to be of above average intelligence.

The man shrugged his shoulders helplessly. "I don't know. Perhaps five hundred. Only a very few of us were marched out to the three galleys: we left behind a lot of men. Oh, the poor fellows: they thought they were lucky, avoiding a few days' rowing."

"And what about the women – how many do you think?"

The man thought for some time. "Not two hundred – probably about a hundred and fifty. Most of them were young girls: the *Saraceni* did not take many adult women. They think the young girls last longer," he added bitterly.

Ramage looked at Southwick. "Have you any questions?"

The old man waved his sketches and said cheerfully: "No, sir, we've added a bit more with those depths, and that's my main concern now."

Ramage thanked the mayor and the men, shook hands with all of them and returned to the cutter. It was always surprising how the ground seemed to sway underfoot after a long time at sea, especially if going to windward.

"Now for Sciacca," Ramage said. "We'll see if we can find some more soundings for you."

At Sciacca the routine was the same: the *Calypso* and the rest of the small flotilla anchored off while Ramage and Southwick went on shore in a cutter of which Jackson was the coxswain. They found the mayor who rounded up the former slaves, several of whom had seen the ships anchoring and watched Ramage come on shore, congregating on the quay to greet him. Ramage gave his usual explanation for the questions that would follow, and this time Southwick started by drawing a sketch in the dust outside the mayor's house, explaining what he was doing for the men unused to charts and maps.

The answers to the first questions hardly varied from those given by the men at Mazara: they thought there were four or five hundred men left behind and about one hundred and fifty women. They agreed there had been eight galleys, including the three they were in, and that the other five were bigger, needing many more men to row them.

Ramage then used the diagram in the dust to question them about distances. They all agreed on the distance from the quay to the barracks, and from the quay to the brothel. There were four cannon and no guard on top of the fort. The big difference came in judging the population of Sidi Rezegh: the men were all agreed it was at least a thousand more than Sciacca which, the mayor said, meant that the *Saraceni* numbered more than eight thousand.

The men were able to add more depths: several of them had been out in two of the big galleys and had noted how much cable had been let go when they anchored. More important, they confirmed the position of the shoal in the middle of the harbour and one of them was able to give rough bearings from the fort and the barracks.

From what the mayor said, it was obvious to Ramage that there were more men from Sciacca still in Sidi Rezegh than from either Marsala or Mazara and that by chance there had been fewer Sciacca men in the two galleys.

The worst part of the visit came when Ramage and Southwick took their farewells. The men and the mayor sought reassurances that their brothers, friends, wives, daughters and nieces would be rescued: reassurances that Ramage was reluctant to give, knowing the small size of his force.

Back on board the *Calypso*, with Aitken and Southwick, Ramage spread Southwick's two drawings out on his desk and asked the master: "Do you think we have enough detail to sail into the harbour?"

"I can never have too much," Southwick answered, "but I doubt if we'll get much more that matters from Empedocle. I'll make fair copies of these for the rest of the flotilla and a copy of the map for our gallant major."

Ramage looked up at Aitken. "How are the troops getting on with embarking and disembarking from the boats?"

"Very well, sir. Far better than I expected. We have a lot to thank Hill for: he suggested putting a Marine in charge of every five soldiers, to show them how to do things, and it was so successful that I took the liberty of suggesting it to the first lieutenant of the *Amalie*. Then Kenton started the boats competing against each other, and that spread to the *Amalie*.

"In fact," Aitken said, "the only question mark now seems to be whether the gunnery in the *Amalie* and the two sloops is up to the standard we like."

Ramage nodded. Gunnery training was very much up to individual captains. Some made an obsession of it; others scarcely bothered because guns firing scorched paintwork and scored decks. Well, the flotilla could sail south under easy sail for a couple of days and give the guns' crews plenty of exercise.

In the meantime, Ramage thought, he would have to put a lot of thought into how they were going to attack Sidi Rezegh. And that, he realized, was the wrong way of thinking about it: they were not going to attack Sidi Rezegh as such; they were just going to raid the place and free the slaves from the barracks and the women from the brothels: if that could be done without disturbing the Saracens at prayer in the mosque, so be it.

It had been interesting making the charts and the map: it had given shape to somewhere that had hitherto been only a name. Now, if he closed his eyes, he felt he could imagine the look of the place. In fact, once Southwick had completed his first fair copies, he would try and draw an elevation of the place: that would help the flotilla find their way about. Not every sailor, Marine and soldier could read a chart or a map.

Chapter Fifteen

By now Jackson had become an authority among most of the ship's company: he had been on shore with the captain and master at all three ports and he had heard them discussing their findings.

"I tell you what bothers *me*," Stafford said as he sat at the mess table, "and that's how many of these A-rabs we'll find at this place."

"Arabs," Jackson corrected. "You worry too much. Everything will be all right."

"It was a damned close-run affair at Licata," Stafford maintained stubbornly. "I still don't know what would have happened if the *Calypso* hadn't turned up like that."

"We'd have scraped through but we'd have lost a lot more men," Jackson said.

"Well, we lost enough as it was. I ask you, this time we've got to capture a whole A-rab town."

"No, we haven't," Jackson said mildly. "We're just going in to rescue the slaves and the women. That's all."

"That's all, eh?" jeered Stafford. "You don't really think these A-rabs are going to let us walk off with their slaves just like that, do you?"

"They might not be able to stop us. If we're quick."

"Quick? Well, you said yourself there's a fort at the entrance to the harbour."

"Steady, Staff. If you'd known the odds would you have been happy at Licata? Yet it worked out all right."

"Sheer luck," Stafford declared. "We was lucky."

"But luck always comes into it," Jackson persisted. "It's good luck if it happens to you, and bad luck if to the enemy. And admit it, Staff, with Mr Ramage we get more than our share of luck."

"Is it luck?" Gilbert asked quizzically. "Most of the time I think luck is good planning, and the reason for what you call Mr Ramage's luck is that he plans carefully."

"Is right," Albert said unexpectedly. "Luck no, planning yes. Bad plans that fail are blamed on bad luck. Is an excuse."

"Well, the *Calypso* turning up at Licata was luck," Stafford said stubbornly. "There was no planning about that."

"No, but there's no saying we'd have lost either," Jackson said.

"Come on, Jacko, you never thought we'd get out of there alive. What with all those skimitars."

"Scimitars," Jackson corrected automatically. "Anyway, I don't agree we'd have been beaten. Yes, we'd have lost a lot more men, but I think we'd have pulled through. The minute they realized all their boats were being sunk and they couldn't escape – that's when they'd have broke."

"You're saying that because your gun was firing on the boats," Stafford said. "You'd have thought different if you'd been out on the jetty playing cut and thrust with that screaming 'orde."

"Staff, I don't know when we haven't been fighting screaming hordes: it doesn't make any difference whether they are French or Saracen. You're as dead whether you get your head cut off by a Saracen scimitar or a French cutlass."

"Very comforting," Stafford said. "I'll sleep better tonight knowing that!"

"All those women," Gilbert said, as if talking to himself. "Just imagine, if those Arabs were raiding a town in France and carrying off all the young women. It is too horrible to think about."

"I know what you're going to say," Stafford said. "We have to take any risk to rescue the women. But 'ow are the Italian husbands left behind going to treat those women after we've rescued them? After they've been in an A-rab brothel for a few weeks? I'll tell you: they won't want anything to do with them. It's the women I feel sorry for. They're doomed if they stay in the brothels, and they're doomed if we rescue them. All these Italian men have a rotten streak in them: the streak of pride. They're quick to see an insult, but they won't be big enough to forgive those women something they couldn't avoid. If anyone's to blame it is the men, for not fighting off the Saracens."

"You're probably right, Staff," Jackson said, "but there's

nothing we can do about it. Just rescue them and hope for the best."

"Kill as many Saracens as you can, that's the only revenge," Rossi said. "You're right about the Italian men; it's one thing I'm not proud about. Not that Sicilians are real Italians," he added.

"But it would be the same if the women were Genoese," Stafford persisted. "You chaps from Genoa would still treat them wrongly."

"We would and it would be unfair," Rossi agreed. "But that's the way life is, and you can't change it."

"Give the bread barge a fair wind," Stafford told Rossi, who was sitting at the outboard end of the table. "I'm hungry." He took out one of the hard biscuits that passed for bread and automatically rapped it on the table before starting to eat it. "These have gone soft already," he grumbled, inspecting it carefully for weevils. "I dunno, salt beef is too hard and the bread is too soft. This commission's lasted too long."

"You're getting soft; I don't know about the bread," Jackson said. "Must be old age. The years are beginning to show, Staff."

"Beginning to show!" Stafford exclaimed. "What about you? Is that baldness I see – or are you growing up through your hair?"

"We're all growing old," Gilbert said lugubriously. "Seeing each other every day, we don't notice it."

"Be that as it may," Stafford said, "Jacko's still losing his hair."

"He might be, but he's still the handsomest American on board the *Calypso*!" Rossi said unexpectedly.

"That's not difficult, since he's the only one," Stafford growled. "Why, his head will soon take a shine."

Ramage sat squarely at his desk and put Southwick's two sketches in front of him. He looked at them for a few moments and then commented: "We're lucky: Sidi Rezegh could have been a lot more difficult."

"We'll need the right wind," Southwick said. "It's got to have a lot of north or south in it, if we are to get in and out."

"With the soldiers, we have enough men so that we can tow out if necessary," Ramage said grimly. "We can tow out taking our time."

"We'll have to watch out for the fort. The fact that none of the men saw sentries up there doesn't mean that the guns are out of action."

"No, it doesn't," Ramage agreed. "But what are the chances of them being usable? When was Sidi Rezegh last attacked? Not once in the last hundred years, I expect. So the gun carriages will probably be rotten or worm-eaten, and so all the ropework will be, too. The powder may not be damp because it is a dry climate, but I wouldn't like to be the man that fired those guns. The recoil will probably send them flying over the ramparts."

"It had better, because that fort's built so the guns can rake all of us as we lie at the quay."

"Yes, but the Saracens would have to pass us to get to the fort – don't forget that."

"We can hope," Southwick said, giving one of his famous sniffs, one which Ramage interpreted as expressing doubt.

"Well, what have we got?" Ramage said, picking up the diagram which Southwick was going to redraw as a chart. It showed Sidi Rezegh as a rectangular-shaped port lying north and south along an east coast which was backed by sand dunes and palm trees. It had a northern and an eastern breakwater to form the harbour, with the town on the west side opposite the harbour entrance which was at the bottom right-hand corner – at the north-east end, in other words. The northern stone breakwater – a relic of its Roman origins, Ramage thought – had a small, round fort, with the four guns on the top at the seaward end.

The quay, lying east and west, ran from the fort to the town. A third of the way along the harbour side of the town stood the barracks, in which the slaves were locked when they were not in the galleys. Fifty yards further along stood a white stone building which was the brothel. The mosque stood further inland from the barracks. And that was it, apart from a shoal lying north and south right in the middle of the harbour. The galleys were usually anchored between the shoal and the eastern breakwater.

There was enough room for the *Calypso*, *Amalie* and the two sloops to lie one beyond the other along the northern breakwater, the nearest sloops being only fifty yards from the barracks. And if there was north in the wind all four ships would be able to get away by drifting off the quay under foretopsails and then, with a bit of smart sail handling, wearing round to avoid drifting on to the shoal and then luffing up to get through the entrance. With a south wind they would need to approach the quay at a sharper angle, dropping an anchor so they would be able to pull themselves off.

"It could be worse," Ramage said, putting down the chart. "And, more to the point, at least we know what it looks like."

"I'll draw it up then," Southwick said. "Six copies each of the chart and the map."

"Combine the two," Ramage said. "The less paperwork the better. The major should be able to follow a chart as well as a map!"

"Very well," said Southwick, relieved at not having to draw maps. "I think we'll end up with some very adequate charts."

That evening the three captains, the major, Aitken and Southwick were crowded into Ramage's cabin. Roper of the *Amalie* sat in the armchair, the major shared the settee with King of the *Betty* sloop and Payne of the *Rose* sloop.

Southwick and Aitken sat on chairs brought from the coach and all except Aitken held copies of the chart of Sidi Rezegh. Ramage tapped the chart on the desk in front of him, looked round at the men and said: "I trust you have all studied this."

They all murmured that they had. Ramage then decided they should all hear what the major suggested. "Well, Major, what has the Army to say? How do you see the attack?"

The major, Henry Golightly of the 65th Foot, was a tall, sandy-haired man who was regarded as taciturn by his regiment but who enjoyed the company of naval officers because they encouraged him to talk. He coughed, as if it was expected of him, and then said: "I know nothing about what your ships can do, but as far as I'm concerned we need surprise. If the figures I have heard prove correct, we're going to be heavily outnumbered. So we have to use surprise.

"That's the first thing. Then I'd like my troops put ashore on the quay and then with as many of your sailors and Marines as you can spare, I propose we rush the barracks, free the men, and then go on to the brothel to free the women. I would keep the force together to concentrate them: all the men to attack the barracks before going on to free the women.

"If there's any chance of trouble from that fort, then we need to detach thirty men to silence it. If it isn't manned, then our men should be able to stop the Saracens getting along the quay to it – they would have to pass our ships first."

Ramage nodded, pleased with what the major said. "Thank you, Major: your ideas seem to coincide with mine. Captain Roper, what do you think?"

"I agree surprise is about the only ally we have. It seems to me we have to wait for a wind with some north or south in it – waiting out of sight if necessary. And then I think that quay is long enough for all four ships to get alongside. After that – well, Major Golightly has said all that need be said."

Ramage gestured towards King, who cleared his throat vigorously. "The only trouble I see so far is that we haven't used our guns to clear the streets. If all four ships go alongside the quay, none of them can bring any guns to bear – except bowchasers – on the barracks area. I'm wondering if there isn't enough water for me and the *Rose* to get alongside the wall next to the barracks, at right angles to the quay. From there we should be able to cover the whole area and keep up a brisk fire until Major Golightly's force arrives.

"Then, once the barracks are cleared and if the Saracens are in any numbers, we can warp along the wall and keep up a hot fire on this brothel, so that the women can be rescued. It might be better if they were brought to the sloops, rather than led all the way round to the frigates. It's just an idea which occurred to me."

"And a very good idea it is," Ramage said. "Southwick, do you think there's enough water along that wall for the sloops to get in there?"

The master consulted his original diagram. "I have only two soundings along there – well, not soundings, of course, but guesses by the former prisoners. One is fifteen feet and the other twenty. That's enough for the sloops. Providing there aren't any rocks along there," he added cautiously. "I'm fairly sure there aren't any shoals."

"Very well," said Ramage. "Now, how about you, Mr Payne?"

"I agree with King, sir. I think we should risk it. We should be able to lay down an effective covering fire for the troops, Marines and sailors coming round from the frigates. And, as King says, we can warp along to cover the building with the women in it."

Ramage looked at Golightly. "Well, Major, how does that idea strike you?"

"I like it," Golightly said emphatically. "I didn't think the sloops could get alongside there, but if they can give us covering fire it means the Saracens can't reinforce the guards at the barracks. And putting the women on board the sloops is a good idea: I didn't like the idea of them having to run all that way back to the frigates: some of them might be in a very distressed state. So, yes, I think it a splendid idea, absolutely splendid!"

Ramage smiled at King. "Well, Commander, thank you very much: everyone seems in agreement with your idea. I must confess myself slightly jealous of your shallow draught: I dare not risk trying to get the frigates alongside over there, but it seems you are going to see all the action."

King grinned in reply and said: "From what I've heard and read about you, sir, in the West Indies as well as the Mediterranean, it won't hurt you to have something of a back seat for once!"

Ramage nodded and laughed. "We'll see. You might find my fellows at the barracks before you have had time to open fire."

He thought for a few moments and then looked round at the men, who were waiting expectantly. "Very well," he said, "we will wait just over the horizon for a wind with some south or north in it. Then we will sail in. And this is how we'll attack." He then outlined his ideas, modified by Jason King's suggestion about the sloops.

When he had finished he said: "Tomorrow morning we have one last exercise, embarking the troops, Marines and sailors, and landing them on the beach. I'm not concerned with the beach part of it, but we might change our plans at the last moment and need to use the boats."

It was easy to spot where Sidi Rezegh was yet still stay beyond the horizon and out of sight of the Saracens: Sidi Rezegh was midway between four humpbacked hills, two to the north and two to the south, and quite unmistakable.

The wind was light, from the west, and when he had worked out the noon sight Southwick commented to Ramage: "There's half a knot of current, and it's probably due to the wind."

Judging the strength of the current along the coast of Sicily and in the channel over to the Tunisian coast was always difficult: the usual eastgoing current sometimes turned into a counter-current as it swept into the great gulf along the east coast of Tunisia, and became a hostage to the wind: a prolonged westerly wind could set up a two-knot eastgoing current; an easterly wind could set up a current going west at a couple of knots or more. And a light wind or a period of calms could mean no current at all. It was an area not favoured by navigators: a few days' *scirocco* hiding the sun with dust haze or cloud could prevent sights and bring a lot of guesswork into navigation.

"We're about eleven miles due north of Sidi Rezegh. As close as we need to go until we get the wind we want," Southwick added.

Ramage agreed. "We don't want to be spotted by any Saracen vessel going into Sidi Rezegh, but even if we're sighted by one of them this far out they'd never guess our destination."

He turned to Kenton, who was the officer of the deck. "Make a signal to the flotilla to heave-to, and stand by to heave-to this ship when I give the word."

After Kenton passed the instructions to Orsini, who was in charge of signals, he picked up the speaking trumpet and started giving orders preparing to heave-to.

The seamen running to the rigging had to pick their way over the bodies of soldiers who, finding it too hot below, were allowed to lie down on the deck. Many of them had stripped down to trousers; already some were red from sunburn, although Ramage had given instructions through Major Golightly that no man should be bare for more than an hour.

Now it was a question of waiting: being patient and waiting for the wind to swing north or south. It rarely stayed west for any length of time, according to Southwick, although these were waters that Ramage did not know. It was annoying to have to wait; yet again Ramage cursed that he had not been born with more patience.

Within ten minutes the *Calypso* was hove-to with the *Amalie*, *Rose* and *Betty* lying to leeward, pitching slightly in the barely perceptible swell. There was just enough movement and little enough wind for Ramage to detect the smell of the bilges. There was always a few inches of water that the pumps could not suck out, and which stank. Normally, with a good breeze blowing through the ship, the smell was not too offensive. But now, with just enough movement to stir up the bilges but not enough breeze to clear the ship of the smell, Ramage found it unpleasant, and cursed the shipbuilders who could not build a pump that cleared those last few inches. It was very unfair on the worthy French shipbuilders who had constructed the *Calypso* in the first place, because no ship that Ramage knew of had such a pump. The smell of bilges was something that one lived with.

As Ramage stood at the quarterdeck rail, he tried to think of what was expected of him as the senior officer of a little flotilla, but he could think of nothing except that perhaps, while they were held up, hove-to and waiting for a fair wind, he ought to invite the captains over for dinner. He thought about it and then decided he had not the patience to go through the ritual of being polite to strangers. He would have to invite Major Golightly, but he quite enjoyed the soldier's company. The man had travelled, and he had kept his eyes open. He had spent five years in India, and had a fund of stories about life out there. He had also served in the East Indies and the West, and it seemed that he had only just missed meeting Ramage in the West Indies on a dozen occasions.

One thing for which Ramage liked him was that he shared Ramage's loathing for Antigua. He had many unhappy memories of guard duty on Shirley Heights, the high cliffs overlooking English Harbour, and at Fort St James, guarding the capital, St John. He had been intrigued to find that the *Calypso* had been captured from the French off Martinique, to the south, and then taken to English Harbour to be fitted out as a British ship of war. When Ramage had told him of the inefficiency and corruption he had found among the dockyard workers at English Harbour Golightly had been sympathetic: it seemed the Army was in no better state, there being constant complaints about the quality and quantity of rations, with the men once threatening to mutiny.

Ramage supposed there was the same corruption in the dock-yards and barracks in England and then found himself doubting it. He had never come across it so obviously in England. There was probably corruption in the dockyards but it was confined to the workmen (and probably the port admirals): it did not affect the ships and their captains as it did in the West Indies. It was as though the tropical sun made morals fester; that once removed from England men decided they were going to get rich, no matter who suffered or was cheated. A British ship of war cheated by some dockyard official was suffering as though harmed by the enemy. English Harbour was the worst offender in the West Indies, but how did it compare with Gibraltar, or Malta?

The real fault, he realized, lay with the Admiralty and the Navy Board and, for that matter, with the government. He had been browsing through the *Royal Kalendar* recently when he came across a particularly glaring case of nepotism. Coming under the Pay Office was the Pay Branch for Paying Seamen's Wages. The Deputy Paymaster in London was John Swaffield, paid £660 a year. The Deputy Paymaster at Portsmouth was John Swaffield junior, paid £440 a year, while the Deputy Paymaster at Plymouth was Joseph Swaffield, also paid £440. What was more significant was that they each had a deputy, paid £330 a year. In other words, they left their deputy to do the work. But the Swaffields did not confine their activities (or lack of) to the Pay Branch: in the next column, under Victualling Branch, was another one of them: the Cashier of the Victualling for Paying Bills, was G. Swaffield, paid £660 a year.

Nor was this sort of thing confined to the Admiralty: he remembered the pages headed "British Governments in America and the West Indies", where Jamaica seemed a favourite spot for absentees. The Receiver in Chancery was the Hon. P. C. Wyndham; the Secretary was the Hon. Charles Wyndham and, most surprisingly of all, the Clerk of the Court was Evan Nepean – who was earning £4,000 a year as Secretary to the Board of Admiralty in London.

It was very doubtful if the Wyndhams or Nepean had ever been to Jamaica; it was even doubtful if they could find it on a map without a careful search. But they – and dozens more like them – were paid for the job they never did. If there was any work to be done they hired a substitute: there was a good profit in paying a man £50 a year for doing a job for which you were paid £660. And, of course, in the islands it was possible to keep things in the family – as in Bermuda, for instance. The President of the Council was the Hon. H. Tucker; the Secretary and Treasurer was H. Tucker junior (presumably the President's son); while the Speaker was the Hon. James Tucker, and the Surveyor was John H. Tucker. There were dozens of other examples, though the names concerned he could not remember. In the West Indies, he knew very well, it was not unusual for someone comfortably resident in England to have two or three jobs in islands a thousand miles apart – jobs which he obviously could never carry out.

If you were paid for a job you never did, or paid very well to do a job for which you hired a deputy at a sixth of the salary, that was, as far as Ramage was concerned, corruption; it was legally stealing from the nation. Well, in the Royal Navy you could not be paid for commanding two ships at once!

He remembered a cynical comment his father had made some years ago, when Ramage had commented at the time on what he had found in the then current *Royal Kalendar*. "Corruption, my boy, makes the world go round. Great men have tried to put an end to it, but they all failed because always there are greedy men."

Aitken was pointing up at the clouds. "The highest ones are coming from the north, sir," he commented.

"There's no sign of a veer down here."

"Perhaps during the night, sir."

"Perhaps," Ramage said. "Try and time it so that we can get under way at dawn!"

Chapter Sixteen

Ramage was wakened next morning before daylight by the urgent voice of Orsini repeating: "Captain, sir; Captain, sir!" When Ramage sat up in his swinging cot, Orsini said: "Mr Southwick's compliments, sir, but the wind seems to have set in from the north."

"Tell Mr Southwick I'll be on deck in a few minutes."

With that a drowsy Ramage swung himself out of the cot and hurriedly dressed in the dark, cursing as he stubbed his toe against a chair. Why the devil did things always happen at night? Up on deck he found it a starlit night and the breeze was steady; it was obviously set in for several hours.

"What's the course for Sidi Rezegh?" Ramage asked Southwick.

"South by west, sir."

"Very well, hoist lights telling the flotilla to get under way, and then hoist the signal for the course."

Southwick shouted for the watch to prepare lanterns and the wooden frame which would hoist them in a set pattern. As soon as the lanterns were lit and hoisted, Ramage gave another order: "Stand by to get under way, Mr Southwick."

It was a warm night and Ramage noticed Aitken joining him at the quarterdeck rail. "A very good time for the wind to change, sir," the first lieutenant commented.

"What time is it?"

"Just before four o'clock, sir. It should take us down to be off the port just after dawn."

"Couldn't be better. I wonder if Saracens are early risers."

"I suspect they are; they probably go to bed when it gets dark and rise with the sun."

211

"But do they keep lookouts in that fort, I wonder?"

"I doubt it," Aitken said. "Why should they? They probably haven't been attacked for a hundred years so they won't be expecting anything."

At that moment, as the frame was lowered again and the lanterns extinguished, Ramage told Southwick: "We'll get under way, course south by west, you said."

The watch on deck scurried round as Southwick shouted orders. Topmen hurried aloft to cast off gaskets and let fall the topgallants and topsails; the afterguard braced up the yards and tended the sheets. Soon the *Calypso* stirred to life: instead of being an inert mass wallowing in the sea, she began to pitch gently as the sails filled. The hull creaked as the planking worked against the frames; the yards creaked as they pulled against the pressure of the wind. And Ramage gave a shiver as the down draught from the mainsail chilled him.

Then he remembered the rest of the flotilla. "Mr Southwick – we've no stern lantern!"

"Bless my soul!" exclaimed the startled master. "I completely forgot," he admitted. "I'll see to it at once."

The flotilla leader, in this case the *Calypso*, had to burn a lantern for the rest of the flotilla to follow, particularly at a time like this when all the ships were forming up again after lying to. For a few moments Ramage thought of the responsibility of getting a fleet under way; twenty or thirty ships of the line, not to mention attendant frigates. He thought of Lord Nelson manoeuvring his fleet the night before Trafalgar. Not only did his Lordship have the problem of manoeuvring the fleet, but he was having to work out what the enemy was doing, and make moves to counter them. And the enemy that night had made some strange moves. Suddenly he felt very humble; he had another frigate and two sloops under his command, and he had forgotten the elementary thing of a stern-light. Well, he thought, let's hope the lamp trimmer has done his job properly and the light is bright enough for the rest of the flotilla to follow.

Sidi Rezegh – at last they were really on their way to attack it. He wondered what Rear-Admiral Rudd's thoughts had been when he gave him the orders. It was strange that the Admiral had not committed any of his 74s. Admittedly it was unlikely that any of them would have been able to enter the port because of their draft, but they had enough guns to pound the place before landing a considerable number of troops, Marines and seamen. A 74 could easily land three times as many men as a frigate, and she carried more than twice the number of guns, of vastly superior calibre.

But Admiral Rudd had not seen fit to send even one 74. Why? Ramage thought the answer to that was simple and twofold: he did not think a 74 would be able to do the job, and he did not want either of his two captains saddled with failure. So he had been reduced to sending a couple of frigates and a couple of sloops, to show the British Minister (and the King of the Two Sicilies) that at least he was doing something. Ministers would know nothing of the tactical problems of attacking an enemy port, especially a strange one with the natural problems of Sidi Rezegh.

There was even a touch of irony: one of the frigate captains was his favourite, and he would suffer if the venture failed. Indeed, Ramage thought wryly, he might spend the rest of his life chained to an oar in one of the galleys if the failure was complete. He shivered: the price of failure would be very high.

That was the worst of these early starts: one's spirits were at a very low ebb at this time of the morning: prey to fears which would never enter one's mind in daylight, or when one's stomach was decently full of food and a hot drink. He guessed that most men were cowards at four o'clock in the morning – he was, and he freely admitted it. Now, Southwick was a man who never suffered from it; Southwick exuded four o'clock in the morning courage.

A cast of the log every hour showed that the flotilla was making just under six knots with a fair wind, and dawn brought a cloudless day, the early dawn shadowing the four hummocks of hills surrounding Sidi Rezegh. There was an air of excitement in the *Calypso*, whether it was among the men holystoning the deck, the watchkeepers occasionally hauling on braces and sheets to trim the sails to a slight change in wind direction, or the successive officers of the deck as the watches changed.

Major Golightly had his troops formed up on deck as soon as there was light enough to see and Ramage watched them performing arms drill amid clouds of pipeclay. Their boots thumped as they marched and countermarched, and Aitken, who was on watch, shuddered with each stamp.

"I hope they're not tearing up my deck with their damned boots," he muttered to Ramage. "If I'd known Golightly was going to march them up and down, I'd have waited before having the deck holystoned."

"The gallant major means well," Ramage said consolingly. "Just think of those soldiers thundering down the quay and chasing those Saracens. Why, the sound of their boots pounding alone should frighten them!"

By now the hummocks were getting close and with the glass Ramage could distinguish the town of Sidi Rezegh. It comprised a clump of white buildings, still pinkish in the early light, and the round fort at the end of the quay showed up dark. It was easy to make out the dome-shaped roof of the mosque, which seemed to be built on a slight hill in the middle of the town.

How many miles off? Ramage guessed at three and Southwick agreed. Half an hour's sailing. Well, the flotilla had its orders and knew what to do. "Stand by to hoist out the boats, Mr Aitken," Ramage said and then turned to Orsini. "Make the first signal!"

In less than five minutes the two frigates and two sloops were hove-to and hoisting out their boats, leading the painters aft so that they would tow astern. As soon as he saw all the boats in the water, Ramage told Orsini to hoist the second signal, to get under way.

It was the first time in his life that Ramage had issued a list of signals to ships under his command, but having special signals got rid of some shortcomings of the signal book. For instance, he would want to signal "Sloops to go alongside the wall", a signal which could not be made with the standard signal book. He only needed – or might need – a dozen signals, but they were important, and he had numbered them in the order in which they were likely to be used. Thus signal number one had been to heave-to and hoist out boats; number two had been to get under way again towing boats. From number three onwards the signals would be concerned with the actual attack.

Two miles to go. He turned to Aitken. "Beat to quarters, if you please, Mr Aitken."

Aitken picked up his speaking trumpet and shouted the order and a few moments later the Marine drummer was at work sending the staccato order through the ship. Ramage had heard it dozens of times (no, hundreds) but it always excited him: to an actor it would be like the moments before the curtain rose on the first act. Of course, one could look at it another way: to the man about to be hanged, it was like having the noose adjusted round his neck.

"Orsini," he said, "my compliments to Major Golightly: in fifteen minutes' time I would like his detachment drawn up ready for landing."

By now the washdeck pump had been rigged and was spluttering water across the deck, and men were following behind it flinging sand on the planking as though sowing seeds.

Down below the gunner would have unlocked the magazine and let fall the thick felt "fearnought" curtains intended to prevent an accidental flash from reaching the powder. While men wetted the curtains he would be preparing to issue flintlocks and prickers to the second captains as soon as they arrived at the halfdoor. They would be followed by powder monkeys, boys whose job it was to take cartridges up to the guns, using wooden cylinders to carry them.

It was all a drill which had long since become a ritual the men could perform with their eyes shut. On the quarterdeck men prepared the carronades, and Lieutenant Rennick inspected his Marines, all of whom were standing stiffly at attention, eyes fixed firmly to the front.

Ramage reflected that he had to do no more than give a few orders: thanks to training – years of training by now – he did not have to go round making sure that his orders had been obeyed properly. The young lieutenants, Kenton, Martin and Hill, would all be standing by their division of guns.

Up here on the quarterdeck an extra two men had gone to the wheel, so that there were now four, and Jackson had taken over as quartermaster. That meant a change on Jackson's gun, Ramage knew; Stafford would now be the gun captain and Rossi the second captain. Aitken and Southwick stood close to him by the quarterdeck rail. The *Calypso*, in other words, was ready for action.

The same drill would be carried out on board the other frigate and the two sloops. Altogether, counting the troops, more than nine hundred men would be prepared for battle. How many would answer a roll call in two or three hours' time?

Ramage cursed himself; this was always the time when he started having black thoughts like that. He would be all right by the time the first shot was fired; it was just the waiting that left him prey to doubts and fears for success or failure. This time failure meant the galleys – or worse.

Over on the starboard bow he could make out Sidi Rezegh with the naked eye: he could distinguish buildings and clumps of palm trees, and on either side the dun-coloured desert, sand scattered with rocks throwing shadows, and scrub: bushes which fought hard for life amid drought and broiling sun.

Had the approaching flotilla been spotted and the alarm raised? Even now were the Saracens preparing what weapons they had? Were the cannon on the fort being made ready? There were plenty of questions and no answers.

He turned and looked astern. First there were the *Calypso*'s four boats towing quietly in her wake; then a cable astern of them came the *Amalie* frigate, looking fine under all plain sail. Roper had already run out her guns, and Ramage could imagine the soldiers and Marines paraded on deck.

Then came the *Betty*, and Ramage could picture the stocky figure of King watching the coast through his telescope. Much depended on the *Betty* and the *Rose*, and Ramage was confident of both King and Payne. In fact he was lucky with all three of them: Roper was a level-headed young man, even though he was the Admiral's favourite. In fact, for a favourite, Ramage thought wryly, he was a sound type of person.

Ramage took another look at the port through his telescope. The entrance, lying at right angles to the *Calypso*'s present course, was clearly defined. With this north wind it would be easy enough to turn and reach in to get alongside the quay. He thanked the former slaves: they had good memories and they had built up an accurate picture for Southwick to turn into a chart. His own elevation drawing had been fairly accurate but, thanks to Southwick's chart and the humpbacked hills, not really necessary. And there were the galleys, five of them, masts sticking up behind the breakwater.

A mile to go? Perhaps a little more. The ship was cleared for action and it only remained for the guns to be loaded and run out. Ramage gave the order to Aitken, who repeated it through his speaking trumpet.

Behind him the carronades grumbled as they were run out. They were easier to load and run out than the 12-pounders. All the guns were being loaded with caseshot – forty-two four-ounce shot packed into tin cans which fitted the bore of the guns and which burst after being fired, spreading out a deadly hail and best suited to cutting a swathe through a crowd of men. Caseshot had been very effective at Licata against the hordes of Saracens, and they should be equally effective here. He had given orders for the other three ships to use case, and particularly the sloops at the wall.

By now they were closing fast with the entrance: if anything the wind seemed to be freshening and he guessed the *Calypso* was making a good six knots. The *Calypso* was to be the first through the entrance, and as soon as she turned the *Amalie* would follow. The *Betty* and the *Rose* would come round in turn and while the frigates made for the quay, the sloops would pass outside them and head for the wall, turning at the last moment to come alongside opposite the barracks.

Ramage was thankful that each captain knew what he had to do. King's suggestion had been so simple, and like the rest of the plan for the attack on Sidi Rezegh, depended on only one factor – the depth of water inside the port. Depths had been the only thing that the former prisoners had had to guess at; depths were the only question marks on Southwick's chart. Depths could ruin the attack.

Ramage looked at the land on either side of Sidi Rezegh. It was low, flat and sandy, with grazing suitable only for camels and goats. Low shore, shallow water: it was an old rule of thumb, whether one was in the cold North Sea, the temperate Mediterranean or the heat of the Tropics. Cliffs meant deep water close in, and if there was anything that Sidi Rezegh lacked it was anything approaching a cliff.

Now the entrance was coming up fine on the starboard bow and Ramage glanced across at Aitken and Southwick. Both men were ready. "Stand by, Jackson," he called.

There were no defiant shots from the fort, which was almost abeam. Perhaps they had caught the Saracens unawares: there was nothing like a hundred years of security for making you careless. Nor were the Saracens great fishermen: he had half expected to find several fishing boats clustered off the entrance – boats which would spot the flotilla as it approached and raise the alarm. But he

217

had been lucky: Sidi Rezegh's fishermen had stayed in their beds.

And then it all happened in a rush: a shout to Jackson to put the wheel over, an order to Aitken to brace up the yards and trim the sheets, and an instruction to Southwick to watch the following ships.

The *Calypso* turned to starboard amid the flapping of sails and the creaking of yards as they were braced up. Now she was heading for the centre of the entrance, perfectly positioned, with the wind on the starboard beam and the sails soon drawing well.

Two hundred yards to go before she was abeam of the fort at the entrance, and still not a shot fired.

"The *Amalie*'s just beginning to turn," Southwick reported.

Aitken put down his speaking trumpet: the yards were braced and the sails trimmed.

Ramage picked up the speaking trumpet and called down: "Major Golightly, are your men ready?"

"Ready and willing!" shouted back the major.

Ramage aimed the speaking trumpet at the Marines.

"Mr Rennick, how about you?"

"Ready, sir," he replied.

The fort was fifty yards ahead, now thirty, and then the *Calypso* was surging through the entrance, followed by the *Amalie* and the two sloops. Then she was abreast the fort, then on the quarter, and the *Calypso* slowed to a stop.

It was gentle but there was no mistaking what had happened. The fort and the beginning of the quay, which had been speeding past, came to a stop. The *Calypso* was aground, forty yards short of the quay. And astern the *Amalie*, further out, came to a stop on the same sandbank.

Just as Ramage swung round to watch her and the sloops, he saw the *Betty* and the *Rose* turn slightly to larboard: Jason King was taking a chance that deeper water lay on the side away from the quay.

Chapter Seventeen

There was no time to watch the sloops: Ramage snatched up the speaking trumpet and called forward: "Major Golightly! Have your men stand by to embark in the boats!"

Then he shouted louder: "Boats' crews, to your boats. Afterguard – smartly there, haul the boats round to the entryports."

There was going to be a mad rush of soldiers, Marines and seamen for the quay: the boats were ready to ferry them, but it would take minutes to row them across: minutes in which the Saracens could prepare for the attack.

Now the *Betty* had passed safely and was heading for the wall. The *Rose* was swinging out to follow in her wake. Was there another sandbank between the sloops and the wall? Jason King was taking a chance that there was not; the *Betty* was still under full sail, though Ramage could see men aloft preparing to furl the canvas.

By now the cutters were alongside, one to larboard and the other to starboard with the jolly-boat and gig waiting, and the soldiers were scrambling down after the boats' crews. They were making good time: all the exercising was paying off. They knew how to sling their muskets; they knew how to kick their swords out of the way so that they did not catch between their legs.

As the last of the soldiers disappeared over the side, the Marines split in two sections, one going to starboard and the other to larboard, one led by Rennick and the other by Sergeant Ferris.

Apart from the soldiers, the quay was still empty: obviously the flotilla had not been spotted approaching. Ramage picked up the speaking trumpet and shouted to the seamen below at the guns: "Boarding parties fall in."

Nearly two hundred seamen armed with cutlasses, pikes and

219

tomahawks stood by at the entryports. Ramage intended that only twenty-five seamen would be left behind on board. Would they be enough to work under Aitken to get the *Calypso* off the sandbank?

"Will you have enough men to refloat the ship?" he asked the first lieutenant.

"I'll make do," Aitken replied. "You need all the men that can be spared."

"Very well, it's time I went on shore. I'll tell the jolly-boat to come back as soon as possible so you can use it to take soundings. I think you'll find deeper water a few yards further out – where the sloops went. We were just a bit too close to the quay."

"Leave it to us," said Southwick, who had got over his disappointment at not being in the landing parties. The argument with the master had been brief: Ramage had pointed out that Major Golightly had two ensigns with him to command the troops, there were Kenton, Martin and Hill to command the seamen, and Rennick and Sergeant Ferris could look after the Marines. Meanwhile, unless Southwick stayed behind, Aitken would be left alone in the *Calypso*, having to face any emergency alone. And, as it happened, there was now a real emergency: the frigate was stranded on a sandbank right at the beginning of the attack.

Ramage scrambled down into a boat and found himself among a party of Marines and a few seamen. The boat cast off and the crew struck out for the quay. It was not high; it took only a few moments for all the men to scramble out of the boat and up on top.

Suddenly Ramage realized that he had come on shore in the jolly-boat and he shouted to its coxswain to return to the *Calypso* and report to the first lieutenant, who would use it to sound round the ship.

The sudden roar of the *Betty*'s first broadside showed that not only had she arrived alongside the wall but there were Saracens there. Were they the normal guards at the barracks or were they men from the town? Ramage had not heard any alarm.

He saw that Major Golightly was already leading his soldiers, including those from the *Amalie*, at the double down the quay, running round towards the barracks. Now Rennick's Marines were following and the three lieutenants were hurriedly forming up their seamen, the last to get on shore.

Ramage drew his cutlass and waited for the seamen. Then, as

soon as they were ready he waved his cutlass in the air. "Come on lads, follow me!"

As he began running he heard the *Rose*'s first broadside, followed a few moments later by the *Betty*'s second, and he thought of the balls of the caseshot cutting into the Saracens. And the popping of distant musketry showed that the Marines on board the sloops were adding their share.

The quay was uneven and twice he almost stumbled as he ran. The quay seemed longer than he expected. He saw Major Golightly's troops reach the end and turn left for the final dash to the barracks, and saw that Rennick was not far behind with his Marines. Then he saw the first of the Saracens beginning to pour out of the side streets, and pour was the right word: they were running out, screaming and waving scimitars, as though they had been lying in wait.

Golightly's soldiers stopped, knelt, raised their muskets and fired a volley. Immediately they resumed their dash, loading their muskets as they ran. The *Rose* fired her second broadside as Ramage reached the end of the quay and turned to lead the rush of seamen towards the barracks. By now he saw dozens of turbans and beards in front of the soldiers while more came running out of the side streets. They seemed to be gathering in front of the barracks and just as he was registering the fact the *Betty* fired another broadside of caseshot into the middle of the Saracens.

Ramage guessed that thirty Saracens had been cut down, perhaps more, because he could not see very clearly. And Major Golightly was going to be facing a difficult decision in a few moments: should he halt and wait for the guns of the *Betty* and *Rose* to clear the front of the barracks of Saracens, or should he continue advancing, forcing the sloops to stop firing.

Ramage wanted to shout at him to stop and leave it to the sloops for the time being, and just as he was cursing that the major would never hear him he realized that Paolo Orsini was running beside him. "Here, quick! Tell the major to halt and leave it to the sloops!"

The Italian youth ran through the Marines, dodging them like a jinking hare, and Ramage, deliberately slowing down, saw him reach the troops.

King's plan had been a good one; it was working perfectly. For some reason the Saracens, as soon as they appeared, were making for the barracks instead of forming up at the end of the quay. Did they regard the barracks, with its contents of scores of slaves for the galleys, as their most valuable possession? It would make sense: without the galleys they were powerless; without the slaves the galleys could not move.

Finally, as soon as he saw the troops halt, showing that Orsini had got through to Golightly with the order, Ramage halted the seamen and was glad to see that Rennick had halted his Marines behind the soldiers. On their right a series of narrow streets led away into the town and Ramage saw that Saracens were now beginning to come out of them, instead of making for the barracks.

He shouted to his men to face right and in moments they were firing muskets and pistols, followed almost immediately by the Marines as Rennick saw what was happening.

At the same time broadsides continued thundering out from the *Betty* and the *Rose*, the detonations being almost simultaneous. The soldiers must also be reloading quickly and calmly because between the thunder of broadsides Ramage heard the popping of muskets.

By now many more Saracens were pouring out of the side streets wielding scimitars and spears and screaming at the top of their voices as they grouped in front of the Marines and seamen.

Any moment now, Ramage thought, and it's going to be hand-to-hand fighting. The *Rose* and the *Betty* could keep the courtyard in front of the barracks clear – indeed, they were doing so, most effectively – but the Marines and seamen were going to bear the brunt of the rest of them.

The crowd opposite, Ramage saw, were working themselves into a frenzy: they were waving scimitars and spears and screaming even louder, and behaved as if they were awaiting an order to charge. The Marines and seamen formed a column three or four deep facing them. Should he form them into a square, or anyway form them into a line six or seven deep? Ramage finally decided against it; the Saracens would probably charge while the Britons were in the middle of the movement.

Suddenly, yelling demented cries, the Saracens charged just as the Marines fired one more volley. Ramage saw several Saracens collapse under the hail of musket shots. Then Marines and seamen dropped their muskets and stood by with cutlasses, pikes and tomahawks. The approaching Saracens looked fearsome, heads swathed in turbans, bearded and wearing what looked to Ramage like white nightshirts.

Within moments cutlass was clashing with scimitar, pike was warding off spear. Ramage, at the head of the column, found himself almost alone as he slashed and parried attacks from two Saracens. He managed to parry one attack and slashed back to send the Arab reeling when the Arab beside him collapsed, gurgling horribly, twisting to his knees with Orsini's cutlass in his side.

Ramage just had time to see Jackson and Stafford fighting their way towards him when a screaming Saracen ran at him with a spear. He managed to deflect it with his cutlass but the man cannoned into him and, as Ramage struggled to stab at him with his cutlass, fell gurgling as once again Orsini attacked from the side.

In the brief moment after the attack Ramage realized that the Marines and seamen were being overwhelmed: they were outnumbered two to one by men who fought with a terrible ferocity. The only place where the British attack was succeeding was in front of the barracks, which was being kept clear by the broadsides of the *Betty* and the *Rose*.

Ramage turned to slash at the next Saracen, conscious that the Arabs were among the seamen and Marines, many of whom were now lying on the ground dead or wounded. This made the fighting at Licata look like a tea party; as he parried a scimitar and thrust with his cutlass he realized that the Marines and seamen were doomed by the sheer weight of numbers. Every man was fighting two or three Arabs. There was no chance of retreat: for a start there was nowhere to go because the boats could never take them off to the *Calypso* or *Amalie*. And anyway the Saracens were too mixed up with the British. It was as he had feared: they were outnumbered and they would end their days – if they survived – in the galleys.

With Jackson on one side and Orsini and Stafford on the other, with Rossi and Gilbert close enough for Ramage to hear cursing in French and Italian, he fought on. A wild-eyed and black-bearded Arab hurled himself at Ramage, scimitar whirling like a scythe. Ramage deflected the sword with his cutlass but the Arab's impetus sent him spinning towards Stafford, who jabbed at the man's throat with his cutlass, and Ramage saw him fall, blood spurting through his beard.

Just as Ramage was deciding it was only a matter of time before they were all slaughtered there was a wild yelling from his left and almost before he had time to register what was happening, Major Golightly's soldiers were in the mêlée, swords flashing and yelling at the tops of their voices.

The surprise attack by three hundred soldiers drove off the Saracens, who broke and ran back into the streets behind them. It all happened so quickly that Ramage was left holding his blood-stained cutlass and staring at the backs of the Saracens.

Suddenly Major Golightly appeared in front of him, grinning happily. "Just in time, eh?"

"Only just!" Ramage exclaimed. "Thanks!"

"We weren't doing any good where we were – thanks to the guns of those two sloops – so I thought I'd lend you a hand."

Ramage looked towards the barracks. The quay was clear. "Come on," he said to Golightly, "let's get those slaves out!"

With that he shouted to his men and Golightly barked out an order to the troops, and nearly five hundred men started running up the street along the quay towards the barracks.

"What about the sloops' guns?" Golightly gasped as he ran beside Ramage.

"They'll stop firing when they see us coming. Then they'll guard our rear."

Ramage heard another couple of broadsides as he ran and, seeing that the road and courtyard in front of the barracks was clear of Saracens, guessed that King and Payne were now firing up the streets.

The barracks was a plain rectangular building with a big double door on one narrow side, which was the nearest. The only windows were slits, too narrow for a man to crawl through. They looked at first like gun loops but Ramage saw they were too high for that. They were narrow, he decided, because they were intended to let in a little air and not much sun.

He saw that the right-hand door had a small wicket gate and it was open: the guards must have fled when the sloops began their broadsides, which must have made a terrifying noise.

Later Ramage had no memory of that last frantic dash up to the barracks, but he remembered vividly the stench that hit him as he ran through the door with Golightly: it was like diving into a midden.

In the half darkness of the building he saw a long corridor with cell doors opening off it. Perhaps twenty cells, each door padlocked.

"Blacksmiths!" he yelled, thankful that he had detailed half a dozen men to bring sledge-hammers and chisels. Several men thrust their way past him and without further orders began attacking the padlocks.

As soon as the first one fell to the ground, the door was swung open and half-naked men began pouring out. Realizing that there would soon be chaos, Ramage bellowed in Italian, telling the men to go back in the cell until told to come out.

He ran to the door and called: "How many in there?"

"Forty-seven," came back the answer in an excited chorus.

Forty-seven? And twenty cells? More than nine hundred men? Perhaps not all the cells were full; the Saracens might crowd the slaves into the first few.

As the men designated as blacksmiths smashed away at the padlocks, Ramage ran back to the wicket gate and peered out, momentarily dazzled by the bright sunlight. No, the Saracens had not come back: they were being held off by the sloops' broadsides. From this position, less than forty yards from the muzzles of the guns, the noise was deafening; the noise alone seemed powerful enough to knock a man down.

The padlocks were crude affairs and each one took the blacksmiths only two or three minutes to smash open. At each cell Ramage had to explain to the inmates that they had to wait; that it was impossible for them to escape from the building at the moment.

When would the moment arrive? Getting back to the frigates meant running the gauntlet of the men in the side-streets where the seamen and Marines had their desperate fight before Major Golightly arrived with his soldiers. And there were the women held in the brothel a hundred yards further along the quay. They would be no problem because it had already been arranged that they would escape to the sloops.

Finally the blacksmiths reported that the last padlock was opened but there were no men in the last eight cells. Ramage decided to keep the freed slaves in the building until the women were rescued and put on board the sloops; then the men could all be convoyed back to the frigates using everyone he had – soldiers, Marines and seamen. He looked round for Major Golightly, found him by the wicket door, peering out into the courtyard, and gave him his orders: with the seamen they would make a rush for the brothel and the Marines would be left behind to keep an eye on the freed slaves and to protect them from any marauding Saracens. He called to Rennick and gave him his orders.

He decided that the seamen should lead the charge and shouted to his men as he led the way to the door. He stood at the wicket gate for a few moments, watching the two sloops continue blasting the ends of the streets with caseshot, then led the rush along the road beside the port that led to the brothel. He had expected to have to fight every inch of the way but there were no Saracens: clearly they had regarded the barracks as the only target that the infidels would attack.

Chapter Eighteen

There were no guards on the building, which was much smaller than the barracks but was also rectangular, with narrow slits for windows. It took the blacksmiths two or three minutes to smash open the door, which was small and held shut by an enormous padlock, the largest Ramage had ever seen. It was as crudely made as the others in the barracks, but effective.

As soon as the door was swung open the same stench came out that they had met at the barracks but it seemed every woman in the building was screaming in hysterical terror, frightened first by the gunfire and then by the pounding on the door as the blacksmiths went to work.

Ramage went into the building and started shouting in Italian to the women to be quiet. His sudden arrival and obviously peaceful intentions – even though he was holding a bloodstained cutlass and more of his men were coming through the door – had a calming effect on the women. One large woman with long black hair, whose unkempt appearance made Ramage think of a witch, seemed to be the leader, and as soon as she understood what Ramage was saying she screamed at the rest of the women to be silent. Ramage's shouts had been loud, but the woman's shrill command had much more effect.

She turned to Ramage. "What do you want us to do?"

"There are two British ships waiting at the quay. I want you all to run to them and get on board. They are British and no one will speak Italian but we are going to take you home again."

"Our men!" the woman exclaimed. "They are shut up in the barracks."

"They have just been freed. They will go in the other two ships. You will all be home again soon."

"But the guns!"

"It has been necessary to kill the Saracens," Ramage said drily. "Come on now, let's not waste time. Don't forget, no one in the two ships will speak Italian, but don't worry: they are English."

He beckoned to the big woman. "Follow me, and tell the rest of them to come along."

She followed at once, shouting at the other women, who hurried to join her. They were a haggard-looking crowd who, even though they had not been prisoners very long, showed signs of under-nourishment. All of them had their hair hanging in greasy ringlets; most had dark smudges like bruises under their eyes. Almost all of them were now crying almost hysterically, overcome with relief, and, Ramage was sure, hardly aware of what they were doing.

Once out in the open air Ramage called to his men to form up round the women and led the march to the sloops, which were still firing desultory broadsides.

King and Payne obviously saw the motley crowd approaching, and the guns fell silent while men appeared at the bulwarks to help the women on board. Ramage saw Payne first and explained that the women had been told no one would speak Italian. "They know they are going home, so all they need is feeding – and let them wash, if you have enough water."

With that he hurried along to repeat it to Jason King. He then remembered he had forgotten to tell Payne about resuming fire. "I am going to march the slaves out of the barracks now – we'll make a dash for the frigates, but if the Saracens come back open fire on them as you cast off. Get out of the harbour as best you can – but don't waste a moment."

With that he was leading his men back to the barracks, followed by the soldiers. He found Rennick and his men outside the big double doors.

"Just guarding against a surprise attack," the Marine explained, "but the sloops' guns seems to have frightened the Saracens off."

"Right, now we'll escort the Italians round to the boats: the Saracens might try to rush us as we embark them. It's going to take time – these men are dazed, and they'll be clumsy. And as we go, pick up any of our wounded that you see; these damned Saracens will otherwise torture them to death."

Ramage went back into the barracks and shouted down the

corridor in Italian: "Come out everyone, we are going to the ships."

The men who streamed out were long-haired, wild-eyed men almost hysterical with a mixture of fear and excitement. "Where are we going, *Commandante*?" one of them shouted.

"Out to ships that will carry you home," Ramage said. "Now, calm yourselves and obey orders, we may have to fight our way through."

Major Golightly's soldiers led the way to the boats, followed by the Italians, then came the Marines and the seamen followed up behind.

Then Ramage had a moment to look at the *Calypso* and the *Amalie* and saw that they were in the same position, aground on the sandbank. He caught sight of boats rowing round them, and just as he was despairing of the time they were taking he realized that only about twenty minutes had passed since they had landed from the boats. Taking soundings round the ships would be a tedious job for Aitken and Roper. Roper! For the first time he realized that the frigate captain was not leading his men. He had not noticed who was leading the *Amalie* seamen, but it certainly was not Roper. Why? Was the man frightened of the smell of powder? He thought of the attitude of Aitken and Southwick, both angry at being left behind, and compared it with Roper's. Staying behind in his ship had not helped much; she was still aground . . .

Well, they were past the first lot of streets: the Saracens seemed reluctant to attack, contenting themselves with waving their scimitars and screaming threats from a distance. There were many bloodstains in the dust and fifty or so bodies, all Saracens. Golightly's soldiers had obviously collected the bodies of the dead Britons, as well as the wounded. A considerate act, Ramage thought; Golightly knew the bodies would be defiled if they were left.

Now they were at the quay and they followed the soldiers round. Ramage glanced over his shoulder yet again. The Saracens were leaving the side streets now but they were not following. The *Rose* had her sails set and was drawing away from the wall; the *Betty* was casting off. Well, the women were safe.

They were halfway down the quay when the Saracens charged: they ran, shouting and waving scimitars and spears, their robes flying. Ramage looked across at the *Calypso* and was thankful to see that Aitken had anticipated him and the four boats were waiting at the quay, while the four from the *Amalie* were rowing the last few strokes before they too were ready to embark men.

The Saracens still had nearly a hundred yards to go before they caught up with the seamen from the *Calypso* and the *Amalie* and Ramage was just going to send Orsini ahead with the order when Golightly anticipated him and broke into a trot with his troops and the Italians.

Clumsy soldiers helping panicky Italians into the boats would quickly reduce the quay to chaos, so Ramage shouted: "Kenton and Martin: get your divisions ahead and help those Italians into the boats. Pack them in, we don't have much time!"

Soldiers, Italians, Marines and seamen had all reached the boats by the time the Saracens arrived. Golightly and his soldiers covered half the quay while the seamen and Marines from the two frigates spread out over the other half. All had time to reload their muskets and pistols and, at orders from Golightly and Ramage, they held their fire until the leading Saracens were only ten yards away.

Golightly, who had a stentorian and unmistakable voice, bellowed "Fire!" and the crackling of the muskets rippled the width of the quay. The first row of Saracens collapsed but the men behind them leapt over the bodies and charged the British.

Ramage guessed there were perhaps three hundred of them: the sloops' caseshot must have taken a dreadful toll, and the first fight with them near the side streets had also killed dozens. For once the Saracens were outnumbered: there was a good chance of embarking everyone in the boats – if they could hold this crowd off long enough.

And then Ramage and the rest of the men were parrying and slashing. Ramage realized that the Saracens had attacked to one side, throwing all their men against the seamen and Marines and leaving the soldiers alone. And they were driving the seamen and Marines back by the fierceness of their rush; they fought like men who had gone berserk, rarely bothering to parry: they kept on slashing wildly with their scimitars or jabbing with their spears.

Ramage was just beginning to despair of holding the Saracens away from the boats when Major Golightly and his troops swept in from the rear, whooping and yelling. The Saracens paused for a moment, caught between the seamen and Marines in front and the soldiers behind. Then, as if suddenly realizing they were outnumbered, they ran out to the side and then bolted back along the quay, still shouting what Ramage took to be defiance.

Seeing Golightly in the mêlée he shouted his thanks and pointed back towards the boats. Golightly understood at once and hurriedly the soldiers and the men from the frigates formed in a half-circle round the point where Kenton and Martin were hurrying the Italians into the boats, which were being rowed off at top speed to the frigates.

Ramage elbowed his way through the men to talk to the two lieutenants. "How many have you got off so far?"

"That's the sixth boat, sir," Kenton reported breathlessly. "The Italians are stepping lively, thanks to Orsini!"

Only then did Ramage realize that the young Italian was with the two lieutenants, shouting orders at the Italians, who were now formed up into orderly groups.

Ramage glanced at the boats. Well, the oarsmen were bending their backs. The danger would come when there were only a hundred seamen and Marines left: that was when the Saracens were likely to make a last desperate attack.

But the *Calypso*'s carronades could hold them off. Ramage acted quickly. "Martin! Go out in the next boat and warn Mr Aitken to stand by to open fire on the quay with the carronades using case: the Saracens might well try and rush us when there are only a few of us left."

The first of the boats were returning and Orsini was giving sharp orders to get the rest of the Italians embarked. Now that the Italians were being given clear and concise orders they were much calmer, and they scrambled down into the boats without any delay.

Ramage realized that Golightly was standing beside him and the major said: "We'll form the rearguard while your seamen and Marines get off."

Ramage shook his head. "Very kind of you, but my men will stay on the quay until all your men are embarked. You've saved us twice, now it's our turn!"

Golightly shrugged his shoulders. "Please yourself, Ramage."

Ramage quickly explained that the *Calypso*'s carronades should

231

be able to cover them for the last few minutes, and Golightly nodded approvingly. "Very good," he said. "I hadn't thought of that."

Finally the last of the Italians dropped down into a boat which shoved off at once, making for the *Amalie*. When the next boat arrived alongside the quay Ramage signalled Golightly to start embarking his troops. At once thirty soldiers dropped down into the boat, which set off for the *Calypso*.

Ramage then noticed that the *Rose* was now outside the harbour and lying hove-to while the *Betty* was passing outside of the *Calypso*, using her as a mark to keep clear of the shoal. King and Payne had done their jobs perfectly; at least the women had been rescued, even if the men were for the moment marooned on board two grounded frigates.

If only the frigates had more boats; four each seemed enough for most occasions, but now they needed eight to embark men from the quay while two more continued taking soundings – or even laid out an anchor if it proved impossible to sail off the shoal.

What was Roper going to do during the next fifteen minutes? Ramage had to admit that his opinion of the young man had gone down considerably when he realized that he had stayed on board, instead of leading his landing party. Staying on board had not done any good – the *Amalie* was still as hard aground as the *Calypso*, so Roper's presence had contributed nothing.

Ramage glanced up the quay. The Saracens were still waiting at the far end. Had they been genuinely scared off by Golightly's attack on their rear or were they waiting until the last of the frigates' men were waiting to be embarked? It was impossible to guess. Had they got over the shock of being attacked from the sea so that they could work out the tactics for counter-attacking? As far as Ramage could see, they were men who fought bravely and desperately up to a certain point: after that their nerve failed them and they quit. Yet was that reading too much into what they did at Licata? Was it reading too much into Golightly's two attacks on them? Well, when they outnumbered their enemy they fought well; perhaps when they equalled him they would fight well. But when they were outnumbered – there was the question mark.

But outnumbered or not, the important thing for the moment was that they were staying at the other end of the quay and

Golightly's soldiers were being embarked in the boats of the *Amalie* and the *Calypso*.

There were heads looking over the bulwarks on the quarterdeck of the *Calypso* and Ramage could see that the carronades had been run out and trained as far forward as possible, covering the quay between the Saracens and the landing place. Ramage could imagine Southwick watching the Saracens through a telescope while Aitken was at the entryport, hurrying soldiers below as soon as they climbed on board. Aitken, he guessed, was anxious to get the ship afloat again; being aground induced a strange feeling of physical helplessness, like having one's arms tied behind the back.

Did Aitken and Southwick already know the direction of the deep water? Had they just completed the soundings when the time came to send the boats over to the quay? Or did that interrupt them in the tedious job of rowing, a cast of the lead, note the depth on the slate and row on farther? Had they already decided that a backed topsail (perhaps topgallant as well) would swing the bow round enough, or would it need an anchor carried out in the boats and laid in the right place to let them warp the ship off, using the brute strength of the men at the capstan?

Ramage realized that there was nothing to compare with the helpless feeling of a captain standing on shore while his ship was lying aground: Aitken and Southwick might feel helpless, but at least they were on board and not standing here on a dusty quay looking after four hundred seamen and fifty Marines from two frigates, and embarking three hundred soldiers.

Well, look on the bright side, if there is one. At least the women are safe in the sloops and the Italian men are in the *Amalie* and the *Calypso*. Apart from the two frigates being aground, the orders (request, rather) of the King of the Two Sicilies had been carried out (probably much to the surprise of Rear-Admiral Rudd).

Carried out except that the two frigates were aground. And you might as well face the fact that if you sailed a frigate on to a sandbank with all plain sail set, you were making enough knots to drive on hard; hard enough for it to be very difficult to get off.

At least it had not felt as though there had been rock under the sand – rock that would wedge the ship. It had been a gentle business, like sliding off a mattress filled with goose down. It was sand (of that he was fairly certain) and not mud, which sucked at the hull and would not give a decent bite to an anchor. If you are going to go aground, for preference always choose a sandy shoal.

And three more boats left the quay loaded with soldiers while two more came alongside. Sixty soldiers scrambled on board them and they cast off, and Major Golightly walked across and said: "Your fellows are making quick work of it: they must be exhausted with all that rowing."

"They're used to it," Ramage said. "You should see them when they have to tow the ship for eight or ten hours in a flat calm."

Golightly shuddered at the thought. "That must be equal to a fifty-mile route march under a tropical sun."

Now it was Ramage's turn to shudder. "Perish the thought! Think of those blisters on the feet!"

"Think of the blisters your men are getting on their hands!"

"My men's hands are probably as tough as your men's feet," Ramage said. "In other words, they are well trained for their individual jobs."

Golightly gestured along the quay towards the Saracens. "Those fellows seem to be getting more excited."

And Ramage realized that the major was right: the Saracens were shouting more excitedly, and seemed to be jumping up and down more vigorously. He looked round and saw that fewer than fifty soldiers remained, with the seamen and Marines from the two frigates.

He then saw more Saracens streaming along the road to join the rest at the end of the quay. He estimated there must be a couple of hundred of them hurrying to join the three hundred already waiting. Obviously they were concentrating for another attack. Would there be more reinforcements? Five hundred raving Saracens . . .

Finally Golightly said: "That's the last of my men."

Ramage turned and saw two boats leaving the quay. "Why didn't you go with them?"

"I thought it would be more interesting to stay with you."

"You should be with your men."

"They know their way round the *Calypso* now, and the rest are safely on board the *Amalie*."

Ramage shrugged his shoulders. "There's nothing for you to do here now."

234

Golightly grinned cheerfully and said: "I enjoy stretching my legs on shore: very confining, being on board a ship. Besides, I enjoy killing a few Saracens."

There was little left to do but prepare for an attack by the Saracens, and Ramage gave orders to Rennick, Kenton and Hill to assemble their men round the embarkation point. The lieutenants from the *Amalie* quickly obeyed Ramage's order and grouped their men next to the Calypsos.

More than a hundred of the *Amalie*'s and *Calypso*'s seamen had been taken off in the boats when Hill suddenly called: "Here they come!" And at last the Saracens, scimitars waving and robes flying, came running along the quay, screaming at the tops of their voices.

They were, Ramage decided, the most frightening sight he had ever seen on land. He knew that not one of those men cared whether he lived or died: that the only thing that made him retreat was knowledge that he was outnumbered, and the mathematical certainty that he would be driven off.

Now, though, they knew they were not outnumbered; they were charging to cut off the hundred or so British seamen and Marines left waiting on the quay.

Ramage hoped that Southwick was watching with his telescope – not that one needed a bring-'em-near to see what was going on. Nor, for that matter, an ear trumpet to hear.

The Arabs had covered thirty yards. Now fifty and they were another fifty yards away. Ramage imagined the carronades trained round to cover a small area of the quay into which the Saracens were now running. The guns would be loaded with case; forty-two four-ounce balls to a case. The locks would be cocked; the gun captains would be taking the strain on the triggerlines.

Then, suddenly, they fired: there was a shattering concussion and spurts of smoke, and Ramage felt the muzzle blast. And the oncoming horde reeled as the barrage of caseshot bit into them. At first glance it seemed to Ramage that fifty or more of the turbaned figures now lay sprawled in the dust, and while the rest stood paralysed by the shock of the attack, Rennick's Marines and the seamen opened fire with their muskets.

The gunners on board the *Calypso* would be reloading the carronades knowing their shipmates' lives depended on their

235

speed, and for the moment the Saracens were stopped in their tracks, obviously uncertain what to do next.

"What a sight!" Golightly said conversationally. "Close-range caseshot . . . Most effective."

He might, Ramage thought, be commenting on the progress of some game. How impressed he would have been had the 12-pounders been able to fire, but they could not be trained as far as the carronades, and with the *Calypso* firmly aground there was no way of turning the ship.

Even before the Saracens had collected themselves, the carronades thundered out again, cutting another swathe through them. Just at that moment four boats came alongside the quay but none of the seamen made a move to climb down into them. Ramage turned and shouted at the men nearest the boats to embark, but they did not move.

"We want to stay with you, sir," one of the men shouted.

There was no point in arguing – or giving overriding orders – with men showing that spirit, so Ramage threw up his hands. "Keep up a hot fire, then!"

Looking back at the Saracens, Ramage saw that the second blast from the carronades had been more effective than the first because they had bunched up with the shock. The second round had swept into the heart of the crowd of men and bodies were beginning to pile up, one on top of another.

A couple of crazed men began a desperate dash towards the seamen and were picked off by Rennick's Marines, sprawling into untidy heaps, looking as though someone had dropped two piles of old clothes.

"The third should do it," Golightly said judicially.

"There are plenty more," Ramage said grimly. "I want to kill 'em, not drive 'em off. We've got to refloat the frigates yet."

At that moment Orsini came up. "The men in the boats want to know if they can join in, sir: they've muskets with them."

"No they can't," Ramage growled. "This isn't a party!"

Golightly said: "Your sailors seem to be in fine spirit."

Ramage realized that he had become so used to the men's attitude that he was in danger of taking it for granted, and it took the comments of someone like Golightly to draw attention to it.

The third round of fire from the carronades crashed out and once again the caseshot cut a swathe through the Saracens, who were by now grouped helplessly and obviously did not know what to do next.

Ramage guessed that there were a hundred and fifty bodies now lying on the quay: the carronades had killed a good third of the men who had been gathered at the end of the quay. Now, he calculated, the seamen and Marines were not outnumbered – not that the Saracens looked as if they were going to resume their charge.

In fact even as he tried to gauge how many of them were left, the first of them began to run back along the quay towards the town, and they were quickly followed by the rest, who left the dead and wounded where they were lying.

Had they lost their nerve? Ramage decided not. They had simply realized that they were outnumbered and that they could do nothing against the guns that were firing at them, and very sensibly they were withdrawing.

Ramage waited until he was absolutely sure that all the Arabs had withdrawn and then he shouted an order for the men to start embarking. Three more boats had arrived alongside the quay and they were soon on their way back to the frigates with the majority of seamen and Marines.

Chapter
Nineteen

Southwick handed him the slate on which was drawn the plan of the frigate and, scattered with soundings, the rough outline of the sandbank on which the *Calypso* had grounded. Ramage saw that the sandbank was halfmoon-shaped and stuck out from the quay so that both the *Calypso* and the *Amalie* had just caught the eastern edge of it, and there was deeper water to larboard.

"Very conveniently placed to stop us getting alongside," Ramage said bitterly. He looked at the soundings and took into consideration the *Calypso*'s draft. "Another foot and we'd have gone over it."

"At least we're not hard on," Southwick said. "We must just be perched on it, like a starling on a fence."

Ramage nodded. "Backed forecourse, topsail and topgallant should swing the bow off. Main and mizentopsails set and shivering should keep us under control and see us heading for the entrance as soon as we're clear and can wear round."

He thought for a few moments. "Has Roper seen these soundings?"

"Yes, sir, a couple of the *Amalie*'s boats helped with the soundings and made a copy."

"Well, if he's at all worried, he'll see what we're doing," Ramage said, trying not to show his doubts of Roper.

Ramage glanced along the quay and saw that the Saracens were still grouped at the end, obviously concerned that the guns would open fire on them again. Well, there was no point in wasting time.

"Are all the Italians below now?"

"Yes, sir," Aitken replied. "Orsini soon got them sorted out. They were excited at being on board a British frigate, apparently, and grateful that their womenfolk are in the sloops."

Aitken added: "They were anxious about how they were going to get home again, but Orsini reassured them. Told them how we had saved the men and women at Licata. I don't know what else he told them, but *il Commandante* is already their hero, sir!"

"I'm glad to hear it," Ramage said briskly. "Now, let's see about getting this ship afloat again."

He gave Southwick and Aitken detailed instructions. The risk was, he said, that the *Calypso*'s bow would swing off all right under the thrust of the backed forecourse, topsail and topgallant, but unless the after sails – kept shivering and with no weight on them – were quickly brought into action there was nothing to stop the frigate blowing on to the big shoal in the middle of the harbour.

"We haven't much room to play around in," he said. "The moment we are off the sandbank, we must wear and then head for the entrance. Missing that shoal in the middle is going to be a close-run thing. If we go aground there, it'll be to leeward of us, and that'll mean laying out anchors to haul ourselves off."

Aitken grinned confidently and said: "It's like one of those imaginary situations that the Board set you when you're taking your examination for lieutenant!"

"The only difference," Ramage replied, "is that if you failed then you just carried on as a midshipman or master's mate. If you fail here, you might end your days in the galleys!"

Aitken turned and looked at the five galleys, riding at anchor between the outer breakwater and the shoal in the middle of the harbour. "They're bigger than I thought. The two we captured at Licata were smaller."

"These row another twenty or thirty oars," Southwick said. "But they look clumsier than the ones we captured. Much beamier, too."

"Let's get on with it," Ramage said impatiently. The manoeuvre was going to be difficult, and the consequence of failure did not bear thinking about.

Were the decks clear for the seamen? "What about the soldiers – are they below as well?"

"They're all below, sir: I wanted the ship clear when we start to get off the shoal."

"Very well. We'll start off with a backed topsail: that may be enough, with the topgallant. I'd just as soon not set the course."

He estimated that the wind, still from the north, was not blowing at more than ten knots. A backed topsail in a ten-knot wind was not going to apply much sideways thrust, but he wanted to get off with as little as possible: the other shoal in the middle was lurking like a trap.

Aitken picked up the speaking trumpet and shouted the order for topmen. Soon the men were running up the ratlines like spiders, and then out along the yards. Quickly they let go the gaskets and the sail flopped down like a tired curtain.

A quick order to the afterguard and men hauled down on the halyard and lifted the yard into position. Another order braced the yard and yet another saw the sheets trimmed. Now the sail was flat, pressing against the mast and trying to thrust the ship sideways, away from the quay and off the sandbank.

Ramage watched the bowsprit and jibboom outlined against the town but they did not move. The topsail was not enough.

"Topgallant, if you please Mr Aitken."

The first lieutenant gave a sequence of similar orders and the topgallant was let fall and sheeted a'back.

Ramage watched the jibboom against the houses beyond. There was a slight movement.

"Mr Aitken – let fall the main and mizentopsails: I want them shivering!"

More topmen raced up the other two masts and cast off the gaskets. Halyards were hauled and then the yards were carefully braced and the sails trimmed so that the wind blew down both sides of the canvas, without exerting any thrust. The sails flapped and shivered, like drying laundry.

As Ramage watched the bow moved agonizingly slowly away from the quay with the two backed sails pressed hard against the mast. The pressure was just enough to lever the *Calypso*'s bow off the sandbank. Ramage walked over to the starboard side of the quarterdeck and looked over the side. Yes, the sea forward was turning muddy as the keel slid across the sand and stirred up the water.

He looked across at Southwick and grinned. "Slow but sure!"

"Aye," said the old master, running his hand through his hair after carefully removing his hat, "at least we know where the shoal is if we have to come here again!"

240

"Once is enough," Ramage said. "Almost too much!"

Foot by foot the *Calypso*'s bow swung clear, carrying the ship into deeper water; any minute now, Ramage realized, she would come clear of the shoal so that there would have to be fast work to get her under control again and heading for the entrance. He looked longingly at the galleys: a pity he could not give them a broadside, but the angle was wrong and anyway the frigate would be swinging too fast for the gunners to do any good.

Yet without slaves to row them, the galleys were no use to the Saracens. What did they use them for anyway – to raid to get more slaves? Or did they prey on passing ships? If so they must confine themselves to coastal traffic: Ramage could not remember any complaints that they were capturing passing British ships.

Now the bow was swinging faster and he had time to look astern at the *Amalie*. She was just letting fall a topsail; obviously Roper was waiting for the *Calypso* to get clear so that he could manoeuvre without risk of collision. How carefully Roper must be watching the *Calypso*, and how relieved he must have been when he saw her starting to swing – an indication that the *Amalie* would be able to get off without too much trouble, since she had hit the shoal astern of the *Calypso* and had driven that much less on to the sand.

Aitken was standing at the fore end of the quarterdeck with the speaking trumpet in his hand, and Ramage looked across at Jackson, who was the quartermaster for what was going to be a very difficult operation. For the moment there was nothing for Jackson to do, since without headway on the frigate the rudder was not acting. And it was a good thing that the frigate was sliding off the shoal by the bow, otherwise there would have been a risk that the sand could tear the rudder off.

The wind was fluking: it was blowing generally at ten knots or so but occasionally there were stronger puffs, and each puff put more pressure on the backed sails. Gradually the bow came round so that the frigate was lying at an angle of forty-five degrees to the quay and a glance at the slate showed that she must be almost off the shoal.

"Stand by," he said quietly to Aitken and then called to Jackson: "Ready at the wheel there – we'll be off in a few moments!"

And then suddenly the *Calypso* was free: she swung even more

241

to larboard and the foretopsail and topgallant gave a bang as the ship turned and the sails filled with the wind on the after side. Ramage felt the frigate come alive as she refloated, the deck moving under his feet, and he shouted to Aitken: "Sheet home those after sails!"

It was a strange order but as the sails were set and had been shivering it saved time. Yards were braced and sheets trimmed and as Ramage snapped a helm order at Jackson the frigate luffed up slightly until she was heading for the entrance, well clear of the *Amalie* and under complete control. The feared swing out to the shoal in the middle of the harbour had not happened; the *Calypso* had come off the shoal smoothly enough for Ramage to keep control.

The ship started pitching slightly as she passed through the entrance into the open sea and Ramage looked back to see the Saracens running along the quay, waving their scimitars, angry but helpless now that their erstwhile victims were sailing out. Ramage said a silent prayer of thanks that the Arabs had not used their cannons: if the fort had been equipped with four effective 18-pounders they could have pounded the two frigates all the time that they were stuck on the shoal. Not only that, the frigates would not have been able to bring a gun to bear to fire back.

Ramage looked astern and saw that the *Amalie* now had her foretopgallant set in addition to the topsail, and she was already half off the shoal.

The *Betty* and the *Rose* were lying hove-to a mile from the entrance and Ramage told Aitken to steer for them. "We need a course for Marsala, Mr Southwick," he said to the master, who bustled below to consult his charts.

"We've never had so many men on board, sir," Aitken commented. "I don't know how many Italians there are, but it must be getting on for three hundred and then we have a hundred and fifty soldiers. With more than two hundred of our ship's company, we are carrying upwards of six hundred and fifty men."

"Well, Admiral Rudd will be pleased. We've carried out his orders, and now all we have to do is deliver these Italians back to their homes – and reunite them with their families. Many of their wives will be in the sloops. It'll be a series of tearful reunions. Brace yourself for an emotional time!"

"I shall burst into tears on every occasion," Aitken said laconically. 'I can never resist an excuse for a good cry."

A few minutes later Ramage looked over the taffrail to see the *Ama ie* sailing out through the entrance under all plain sail. He pointed at Orsini. "Make the signal for captains to come on board," he said. It was necessary to make some plans, otherwise their arrival at Marsala and the other ports would be chaos.

As soon as Orsini had attended to hoisting the signal and seeing it answered, Ramage said to him: "I have a tedious job for you. I want you to board the *Amalie* and then the *Betty* and *Rose* to sort out where the Italians come from. I don't want to go to Marsala, for instance, and then find out we have no one on board from there."

"I understand, sir," Orsini said. "I only wish these Sicilians didn't have such thick accents: I find it hard to understand them."

"What about me?" Ramage protested. "Italian is not even my native language."

"Sicily is a long way from Tuscany, sir," Orsini said apologetically. "Still, it could be worse; they could be from Bergamo, and then no one would understand them."

Ramage laughed: the accent of Bergamo, in northern Italy, was reckoned to be the hardest to understand. "We'll keep away from there."

He gave orders for the *Calypso* to heave-to near the sloops and wait for the *Amalie*. Half an hour later the other three captains were coming on board, all cheerful and, as King said, glad to be out of Sidi Rezegh.

Ramage sat them down in his cabin and then said: "I hope you have totals of the number of Italians you have on board? I am sending one of my officers who speaks Italian round to each ship so that he can see where they all come from and draw up lists. Otherwise we shall have problems sending them to their homes."

Roper said: "I have two hundred and twenty-eight Italians on board: all very excited, but we can control them."

"Good," Ramage said. "We have three hundred and three, so that is five hundred and thirty-one men altogether."

"I have ninety-seven women," King said. "All hysterical but they are settling down now we have given them some food."

"I have seventy-seven women," Payne reported. "Much the

same condition but giving them food and water quietened them down."

"Ah, five hundred and thirty-one men and one hundred and seventy-four women – more than I expected. No wonder the people were so upset in the ports – they must have lost just about every ablebodied man and nubile woman. The Saracens were very thorough."

"What sort of conditions were they keeping them in?" King asked.

Ramage shook his head. "Unbelievable. The stench in the barracks and the brothel was incredible: there were no sanitary arrangements at all. I should think the Saracens lose a lot of men and women from disease."

Ramage unrolled a chart in front of him at his desk. "Now we have to take all these people home, so we'll go to Marsala first, and then work our way along the coast. It's going to take time, because I do not imagine you have any Italian-speaking officers."

The three captains agreed they had not.

"Well, I have one, so he is going to have to do all the translating. Once we anchor off a port the men should recognize where they are, but the women probably won't. So my officer will have to sort them out.

"They'll all be very excited, so make sure the boats you use to send them on shore are not crowded. And give strict orders to your boats' crews – there will be plenty of wine flowing. If the Italians invite you to any reception or anything like that, they'll have to do it through my officer – a young midshipman called Orsini – and you can accept, sending men whom you can trust not to desert or get beastly drunk. Any man misbehaving himself will be punished severely; I don't want all we have been through for these people spoiled by a few drunken scenes."

Roper asked: "Would it be better if we sent just a token number of men to any festivities?"

The *Amalie* and the two sloops probably faced the risk that men would desert at the first opportunity and end up having "R", for "Run", put against their names in the muster book. Ramage was thankful that he could even send the *Calypso*'s men away on leave and have them all return on time, but they had served with him a long time and earned a lot of prize money. He knew that he was lucky: not many ships could trust all their men, either not to desert or to stay sober. Not that he could trust all the Calypsos to stay sober; that would be asking too much.

"Each captain must make up his own mind," he told Roper. "I shall hold each one of you responsible for the behaviour of your men, so it will be up to you. But if the mayors give out invitations I want at least some men at any festivities, if only out of politeness. I am sure all of you have enough men you trust to make some sort of showing."

Looking round at the three captains, Ramage had his doubts. It was probably not desertion but drunkenness they were worried about: there were few seamen that could safely be left to drink a reasonable amount: for too many of them wine or spirits represented oblivion, to them a blessed state even if it resulted in a flogging.

"Right," Ramage said, "Marsala will be our first port. Are there any questions?"

There was none and the captains left the cabin and returned to their boats, and fifteen minutes later the *Calypso* hoisted the signal to get under way. The wind had backed a little, to north-west, and as the ships began to roll slightly the wailing started as the rescued men and women in the flotilla began being seasick.

Major Golightly joined Ramage on the quarterdeck. "I am a lucky man," he commented.

Ramage raised his eyebrows questioningly.

"Seasickness. I am one of the lucky ones who seem to be immune."

"How about your men?"

Golightly shrugged his shoulders. "About a third of them suffer from it. And having all these Italians retching and wailing isn't helping much."

Ramage grimaced sympathetically. "It won't be for long," he said. "Only a few hours, and we shall be anchored off Marsala."

"I have three men who are so seasick at anchor that they cannot function. They could not even take part in the landing at Sidi Rezegh."

"The poor devils: they're going to suffer until we get back to Naples."

"Yes, they didn't bargain for sea passages when they took the King's shilling."

Golightly was silent for a while, and then asked: "Tell me, Ramage, are you satisfied with the way we carried out the attack?"

Ramage was not quite sure what Golightly meant. "I was more than satisfied with your soldiers," he said. "I am angry with myself that this ship went aground, although there was always such a risk since we did not have proper charts."

"I think you did brilliantly," Golightly said, suddenly and spontaneously. "Particularly the way you used the ship's guns to drive off the last attack. I thought at first the damned Saracens had us trapped. I hadn't realized you could train your guns round so far."

"We were lucky," Ramage admitted. "That was one of the reasons why I was angry with myself for going aground – we could not haul the ship round to bring all the guns to bear where we wanted them."

"You didn't do too badly!" Golightly said.

"I know, but if we'd been able to bring our broadside to bear on the square in front of the barracks we wouldn't have lost so many men."

"How many did you lose in the end?"

"Eighteen dead and twenty-six wounded," Ramage said. "About the same for the *Amalie*. A high price."

"Yes, add them to my seventeen dead and twenty-three wounded and it gets less of a bargain."

"About fifty-three dead – I am not sure about the *Amalie*'s figures – and some seventy-five wounded. More than 125 dead and wounded."

"When you look at it like that it doesn't seem such a great victory," Golightly said soberly.

"I don't know about your general, but my admiral will be satisfied: we rescued the Italians, and that is what we were sent to do. Admirals tend not to worry about the price as long as their orders are carried out."

"Generals are the same: I shan't be blamed. In fact it often works the other way – the bigger the butcher's bill, the higher the praise."

"It's the same in the Navy. Any captain fighting a ship-to-ship action in which he loses half his ship's company is regarded as a hero. No one asks if he fought the ship properly and could have avoided such casualties."

"Well, we've killed enough of our men to be secure from blame," Golightly said bitterly.

Chapter Twenty

When the flotilla arrived off Marsala, Ramage signalled to the two sloops to anchor as close in as possible, wanting to avoid a long trip in open boats for the women.

The Marsala men on board the *Calypso* had been separated and now waited on deck. As soon as a boat could be hoisted out, Orsini was sent off to the *Amalie*, and after he had separated the Marsala men there, he went on to the *Betty* and the *Rose*, to check up on the women. In the meantime Ramage ordered the cutter prepared, with Jackson as coxswain, and had himself rowed ashore.

He was met on the quay by an anxious mayor and many other leading citizens of Marsala, all agitated and puzzled at the sudden reappearance of the flotilla. The only explanation they could think of was that they came to warn of another attack by the Saracens.

Ramage heard the mayor's excited questions and then smiled. "Yes, I have returned," he said, speaking very clearly so that the whole crowd could hear him, "but not to warn you that the Saracens are coming. No, the Saracens will not be back for a long time. No, I bring you your men and women back again. They are thin and frightened, but they are alive and unharmed."

For several moments the mayor stood transfixed, unable to believe his ears. "You have . . . brought back . . . our men and women?"

Ramage patted him on the shoulder, hoping that physical contact would reassure the old man. "Yes, our boats will be bringing them to this quay in the next half an hour. You have time to warn your people to be down here to welcome them."

The old man suddenly burst into tears, and then he embraced Ramage, enveloping him in the smell of garlic. "Do you hear that?" he cried to the crowd. "He brings back our people! *Mamma mia*, what a man! Did you kill many *Saraceni*?"

"Enough," Ramage said shortly. "We taught them a lesson. And now you can have a big celebration."

"Oh, we will, we will. Will your honour attend and bring your sailors?"

Before Ramage could reply a woman weeping hysterically had flung herself round Ramage's neck. "My man, have you brought back my man?" she cried.

Ramage, suddenly fearful that some of the men might have died before he arrived at Sidi Rezegh, said placatingly: "I am sure he is all right: wait here and you will see."

The mayor insisted on taking Ramage to his house for a glass of wine, asking to be told all the details of the rescue. Ramage tried to describe it in terms the old man would understand, but found difficulty in describing the lethal effect of a round of caseshot from the *Calypso*'s carronades. But the old mayor was content with what he heard. He then declared: "Today will be a *festa*! And tomorrow. And the next day. Oh, what a holiday! As soon as the priest hears, you will hear the church bell ringing out. Oh, what a day!"

It was a good half an hour before Ramage could get back to the quay and by that time the *Calypso*'s red cutter, with Orsini on board, was bringing the first of the men on shore.

Ramage was startled when several women started shrieking as they recognized their men sitting in the boat, and by the time the boat was alongside the quay more women, all of them laughing and crying with excitement, were jostling each other and too excited to talk sensibly.

Ramage found himself strangely moved by the touching reunions: each of the men had a dozen or more men, women and children round him, many of them patting him or holding on, as if to reassure themselves of his presence. Every five minutes or so the mayor ran up to Ramage and shook his hand again, babbling his thanks, and calling to whoever was nearest: "This is the man! You owe it all to him!"

Orsini, who had come on shore, said: "You ought to stand as mayor, sir; you are sure of being elected!"

Eventually Ramage left to go back to the *Calypso*, by which time the boats of the *Betty* and the *Rose* had started bringing in the women and the *Amalie*'s boats were carrying in more men. On board the frigate Ramage told Aitken: "Send twenty-five men on shore with Orsini. They can join in the celebrations at the invitation of the mayor. But warn them what will happen if they get drunk. Tell the other men that they will get their chance at the other ports."

He thought a moment and then said: "You go as well, and take Southwick with you: you deserve a little celebration. Orsini will introduce you to the mayor."

"Why don't you come, sir? You haven't had a chance to relax for years."

And suddenly the prospect seemed too good to miss. "I believe I will," Ramage said. "It will do Kenton good to be responsible for a whole flotilla!"

The calls on the other ports were as touching as the one at Marsala: in each case the mayor thought their arrival heralded bad news; in every case the town then went wild when the men and women were landed, and seamen and Marines from the ships went on shore to join in the celebrations.

Ramage suggested to Golightly that some soldiers should go too, but the major refused. He knew the result, he said: the men would get beastly drunk, start fighting among themselves, and some of them would desert.

"They've no personal loyalty to me," he explained. "I only took command of them five weeks ago. Your men are loyal to you personally; they know that getting drunk or misbehaving will upset you, and they care about that," he told Ramage. "With your permission, we'll give my fellows an extra tot: that'll satisfy them."

Ramage agreed and the soldiers seemed satisfied. It seemed that – for those who were not seasick – just being afloat was a good enough change from drilling on a hot and dusty square in Naples. Those who had been seasick were still feeling shaky enough to be thankful to be left alone in their hammocks.

After the final port, Empedocle, the boats were hoisted in and the four ships prepared for the voyage back to Naples. Southwick, standing at the forward end of the quarterdeck, said to Ramage: "I wonder what the Admiral will have in store for us this time."

"Nothing as complicated as last time," Ramage said. "At least, I don't expect so. Probably escorting some convoy. How would you like a beat to windward all the way to Gibraltar, escorting half a dozen stubborn merchantmen? No excitement, except chasing the mules back into position after they've reduced sail for the night."

Southwick groaned and said with a grin: "There must be something between charging into Sidi Rezegh and escorting merchantmen!"

"I'm sure there is, but I don't think we stand high enough in Admiral Rudd's estimation to get it. No, my old friend, resign yourself to a convoy."

Southwick seemed to have lost his sense of humour temporarily and gave a prodigious sniff. "There are times when I long for the West Indies. When I look back it always seems something was happening there."

"Don't forget we once escorted a convoy from Barbados all the way back to England, and thanks to that madman it ended up with me being court-martialled for something I didn't do."

Southwick chuckled at the memory. "Yes, that was quite a trial. One of few courts martial where the accused ends up a hero!"

"Don't remind me of it: it still gives me cold shivers."

Southwick laughed heartily. "Very exciting it was; I can remember it almost word for word."

"So can I," Ramage said. "That's why I wish I could forget it."

The voyage back to Naples was uneventful. The wind gradually backed to the south-west, giving them a beat as they sailed round the western end of Sicily, but after that they had a soldier's wind to give them a straight run into the Bay of Naples, where the flotilla anchored in the shadow of Mount Vesuvius.

Ramage noticed that there were no new ships in the port; at the moment there were just the flagship and the two 74s, apart from a host of merchantmen and smaller craft.

After the usual salutes were fired, Ramage had himself rowed over to the flagship. Jackson and the boat's crew had smartened themselves up for the occasion, their hair neatly tied in fresh queues, newly shaven and with clean shirts and trousers. Ramage wore his second-best uniform and his Lloyd's presentation sword. He carried his own despatch on the operation and a copy of Major Golightly's report to his senior officer.

251

When Ramage entered the great cabin, he found Rear-Admiral Rudd in a good mood. Not jovial, but not cold and abrupt. It was a mood, Ramage suspected, which the Admiral used while he waited to see what his subordinate had to report: it would require little effort to change one way or the other. Congratulations or recriminations could flow without much effort.

"Well, Ramage, how did you get on?"

Ramage said offhandedly: "Well enough, sir. All the Sicilians the Saracens kidnapped are now safely back home. We lost about 125 soldiers, Marines and seamen dead and wounded."

"As much as that?"

"The Saracens are brave fighters and we were outnumbered, sir. I have my despatch here, and a copy of Major Golightly's report." He got up and put them on Rudd's desk.

"I'll read that later. Tell me in your own words what happened. Leave nothing out."

Ramage began with them leaving Naples, including the call at the various ports in Sicily so that Southwick could draw up a chart, and then their arrival off Sidi Rezegh. When Ramage described how the two frigates had gone aground on the shoal, the Admiral sniffed but made no comment. Finally, when Ramage had described how the women had been taken on board the *Rose* and *Betty*, and the men embarked in the *Calypso* and *Amalie*, Rudd nodded, the first indication he had made so far apart from the noncommittal sniff. Then Ramage described the Saracens' last charge and the toll taken by the *Calypso*'s carronades.

After he had described how he had taken the men and women back to their respective towns, Rudd allowed himself a comment. "It was careless of you to go aground," he said, "but at least you carried out the rescue. The Minister will want to see a copy of your despatch, of course, and he will tell the King that his people have been restored."

"Very well, sir," Ramage said, relieved that the Admiral had not added a stronger condemnation about him going aground, a factor which had seemed to absorb him, at least temporarily.

"Now, Ramage, your ship is still provisioned for three months, less the time you took for this expedition?"

"Yes, sir," answered a puzzled Ramage.

"I may want you to go to Gibraltar. It will be a special operation and the final decision does not rest with me. I want you back here on board at noon tomorrow, is that clear?"

"Yes, sir, perfectly," said Ramage, standing up ready to leave.

Chapter Twenty-one

Southwick was sure it meant a convoy, but Ramage pointed out that the Admiral had said the final decision did not rest with him, which seemed to rule it out.

"It's going to be a convoy of troopships, and the Admiral has to get the General to agree to a small escort," the master persisted. "You wait and see. The Admiral wasn't expecting us back yet, and now he has a frigate to spare he's going to use us as escort. Perhaps with the sloops."

"Perhaps," Ramage agreed, because he could think of no other reason for the Admiral's enigmatic remark, "The final decision does not rest with me."

Next day he dressed in his second-best uniform again, carefully pressed by his steward, pulled on his high polished boots, straightened his silk stock and put on his Lloyd's sword. He felt no excitement: whatever Rudd had in mind would possibly be unpleasant and certainly boring, perhaps both. Rudd's attitude over the Sidi Rezegh operation had been at best grudging; whatever he had in mind was not a reward for a good job done; it was simply the next operation on the list, too unimportant for a 74, but perhaps too important for a mere sloop – so what the devil was it? Ramage gave an impatient shrug as he climbed down into the cutter and told Jackson to cast off.

Once again it was a bright sunny day with a ten-knot breeze from the west: just enough to stop the sun getting viciously hot. That was the difference between the Mediterranean and the West Indies. Out in the islands the sun was a lot hotter but there was nearly always a Trade wind blowing to keep a man cool. Here in the Mediterranean, during the long summer, the sun was often blazing hot with no cooling wind, so that one just sweltered, particularly at night when there was no breeze to blow through the cabin.

Apart from the hurricanes during the season and the particularly vile diseases for which the area was notorious, the West Indies were perfect. Almost every day of the year brought a wind between north-east and south-east, so one could plan passages with more confidence.

The cutter was rowed past a couple of tartanes which were working their way through the anchorage. The *Amalie*, he noticed, had not squared her yards properly: the foretopsail yard was not horizontal. At least, he thought inconsequentially, the yards are not a'cockbill, each alternate one hanging at a different angle, as a sign of mourning – the death of the captain, or the admiral. (Did admirals ever die? They seemed to have a grim hold on life. The only admiral he knew who had died was Lord Nelson, a man who deserved to live into ripe old age.)

Ramage felt he was in no hurry to get to the flagship: he was tired of the Admiral Rudds of this world, devious men who never said what they really thought, and who never thought fairly in any case. Come at noon: yes, sir, I shall be prompt, with my hat under my arm and my sword clasped in the other hand. Look sir, my boots are highly polished in your honour; my steward spent an hour on them this morning.

And then the cutter was alongside the flagship and Jackson had hooked on. Ramage climbed through the entryport and was greeted by the first lieutenant, who led him to the Admiral's cabin.

Rudd was alone in the cabin and he waved Ramage to the settee, not to the chair opposite his desk.

"Sit down, we have to wait for a visitor. I may as well tell you now who he will be: I am expecting Mr Arthur Paget, his Majesty's Envoy Extraordinary and Minister Plenipotentiary to the Court of the King of the Two Sicilies."

The Admiral said it with such a flourish that Ramage guessed he was supposed to look impressed. "Indeed, sir."

"Yes. And by now he will have read your despatch on the Sidi Rezegh affair – not that this is what he is coming to see me about. No, he is coming to look you over."

"I'm flattered, sir," Ramage said, knowing that the sarcasm would be lost on Rudd.

With that the Admiral picked up some papers from his desk and began reading them. Ten minutes later there was a knock at the door and the first lieutenant called: "Mr Paget is coming alongside, sir."

"Very well. I'll come down to meet him."

The Admiral got up from his desk and jammed on his hat, saying to Ramage: "Wait here."

When he came into the cabin with the Admiral, Ramage saw that Arthur Paget was a red-faced man of medium height, too fat and puffing after his exertions. He flopped down in the chair opposite the Admiral's desk and said: "I must say it is easier to call on the Army, Rudd; none of this damned messing about with boats. I just climb into my carriage!"

"Quite so, sir," Rudd said ingratiatingly, "but at least it is pleasantly cool afloat; you'll grant me that."

Paget grunted and said suddenly: "Is this the young fellow?"

"Ah yes, may I present Captain Ramage?"

As Ramage stood up, Paget said sharply: "Ramage? Not *Lord* Ramage, the son of the Earl of Blazey?"

"Yes, sir," Ramage said bowing slightly.

Paget turned to Rudd, "Well, that settles that – no question about it. By the way, that was a splendid effort of yours at Sidi Rezegh: I read your despatch this morning. The King will be very pleased. The war between the Sicilians and the Saracens has been going on for centuries: not often that the Sicilians come off on top."

Paget stood up and shook hands with Ramage, and then sat down again, motioning Ramage to be seated.

"What have you told him, Rudd?"

"Nothing, sir. I thought it best if I left it to you."

"Very well. Now, Ramage, the King is also involved in this. It is of the utmost importance that a passenger is carried safely to Gibraltar, where a passage onwards to England can be arranged."

Ramage nodded without saying anything.

"This passenger's life is very valuable, I must impress that upon you."

"Yes, sir."

"And it is very important that you are a good host. You will of course give up your cabin."

"Of course," Ramage said, feeling resentful.

"Very well. Then we had better introduce them," Paget said.

"My flag captain is acting as host," Rudd said. "I will send for them."

He called to the Marine sentry outside the door to pass the word for his flag lieutenant, and as soon as the man appeared he was sent off to fetch the flag captain and "our guest".

"I don't need to tell you, Ramage, that this is a very delicate situation. You must be very tactful, apart from being a good host. This person has great influence in London: one word of criticism could blight your career."

"Indeed. I will take care, sir," Ramage said, beginning to be resentful of the fact that he was being inspected like a prize bull.

The door was flung open and a woman came in, took one look at Ramage and, saying an unbelieving "Nicholas!" ran across the cabin and flung herself into his arms, kissing him on both cheeks and laughing with surprise and pleasure.

Paget, who had sprung to his feet, exclaimed: "You know each other?"

"The Marchesa di Volterra and I have met before, sir," Ramage said.

"Met before!" Gianna exclaimed. "Why, he rescued me from Bonaparte's cavalry many years ago, when I first escaped!"

Suddenly she was serious. "Nicholas, now you are married, will I still be able to stay with your parents in London? I mean, will it be proper? Will your wife mind?"

"On the contrary," Ramage said. "I hope you will go and stay with Sarah as well; we have a pleasant place in the country."

"And what ship do you have?"

"The same – the *Calypso*."

Gianna laughed and clapped her hands. "And tell me – you still have my nephew Paolo, and Southwick, and Jackson, and Stafford, and Rossi – all my old friends?"

"Yes," said Ramage, "Paolo will be excited and relieved to see you – he thought you were dead. There are a few new faces, but you'll feel at home."

Suddenly Gianna was serious. "You and your father were right," she said. "You told me not to go to Paris because the Peace

257

would not last, and you were absolutely right. I was seized by Bonaparte's men, and thrown into prison."

"But how did you get here?" asked a puzzled Ramage.

"Eventually they took me to Volterra. The people kept on revolting and they wanted me to set up a government – a puppet government obedient to Bonaparte. But I would not. I kept on refusing – and waiting. There are still people loyal to me, and one day they helped me to escape. I knew the way from the last time I escaped, when Bonaparte first invaded Italy. I got to Florence and then to Rome, where more friends helped me to get to Naples. So here I am. And going to be your guest all the way to Gibraltar. I long to see your parents again. Tell me, your father, he won't be cross with me, will he?"

Richard Sharpe

bold, professional and ruthless
is the creation of

Bernard Cornwell

A series of high adventure stories told in the grand tradition of
Hornblower and set in the time of the Napoleonic wars, Bernard
Cornwell's stories are firmly based on the actual events.

Sharpe's Eagle
Richard Sharpe and the Talavera Campaign, July 1809

Sharpe's Gold
Richard Sharpe and the Destruction of Almeida, August 1810

Sharpe's Company
Richard Sharpe and the Siege of Badajoz, January to April 1812

Sharpe's Sword
Richard Sharpe and the Salamanca Campaign, June and July 1812

Sharpe's Enemy
Richard Sharpe and the Defence of Portugal, Christmas 1812

Sharpe's Honour
Richard Sharpe and the Battle of Vitoria, February to June 1813

Sharpe's Regiment
Richard Sharpe and the invasion of France, June to November 1813

Sharpe's Siege
Richard Sharpe and the Winter Campaign, 1814

'Consistently exciting . . . these are wonderful novels.'
Stephen King

FONTANA PAPERBACKS

The Flashman Papers
George MacDonald Fraser

'If ever there was a time when I felt that watcher-of-the-skies-when-a-new-planet stuff, it was when I read the first Flashman' P. G. WODEHOUSE

Flashman
Royal Flash
Flash for Freedom!
Flashman at the Charge
Flashman in the Great Game
Flashman's Lady
Flashman and the Redskins
Flashman and the Dragon

'. . . remains in a class of his own' *Observer*

FONTANA PAPERBACKS

Fontana Paperbacks: Fiction

Fontana is a leading paperback publisher of fiction.
Below are some recent titles.

- ☐ ULTIMATE PRIZES Susan Howarth £3.99
- ☐ THE CLONING OF JOANNA MAY Fay Weldon £3.50
- ☐ HOME RUN Gerald Seymour £3.99
- ☐ HOT TYPE Kristy Daniels £3.99
- ☐ BLACK RAIN Masuji Ibuse £3.99
- ☐ HOSTAGE TOWER John Denis £2.99
- ☐ PHOTO FINISH Ngaio Marsh £2.99

You can buy Fontana paperbacks at your local bookshop or
newsagent. Or you can order them from Fontana Paperbacks,
Cash Sales Department, Box 29, Douglas, Isle of Man. Please
send a cheque, postal or money order (not currency) worth the
purchase price plus 22p per book for postage (maximum postage
required is £3.00 for orders within the UK).

NAME (Block letters)_____

ADDRESS_____

_____